PRAISE FOR

Watching from the Dark

"Gripping." —*Publishers Weekly*

"Readers will enjoy the fast pace, red herrings, and intriguing characters in this British police procedural–slash–psychological thriller."
—*Booklist*

"Lodge alternates between chapters following the investigation into Zoe's death and chapters that recount the final twenty months of her life, allowing the reader to understand Zoe as a fully rounded and complicated character, not just a victim. This choice, trendy in thrillers but almost always effective when the characters are strong, consistently reminds us to look beyond simplistic binaries of victim and perpetrator, innocent and guilty, and recognize that all humans make problematic choices, sometimes for good reasons and sometimes for bad. Lodge's choices celebrate the complexity of humanity and elevate this police procedural." —*Kirkus Reviews*

"Gytha Lodge's sophomore thriller delivers an opening worthy of Hitchcock. . . . The beauty of Lodge's writing is her ability to juxtapose the careful sleuthing of a police procedural against an emotional deep dive into the lives of her characters. . . . Eminently satisfying." —*BookPage*

BY GYTHA LODGE

Watching from the Dark
She Lies in Wait

WATCHING FROM THE DARK

WATCHING FROM THE DARK

A NOVEL

GYTHA LODGE

RANDOM HOUSE

NEW YORK

2021 Random House Trade Paperback Edition

Copyright © 2020 by Gytha Lodge
"Murder on Zoom" by Gytha Lodge copyright © 2021 by Gytha Lodge

Published in the United States by Random House, an imprint and division of Penguin Random House LLC, New York.

RANDOM HOUSE and the HOUSE colophon are registered trademarks of Penguin Random House LLC.

Originally published in hardcover in the United States by Random House, an imprint and division of Penguin Random House LLC, and in the United Kingdom by Michael Joseph, an imprint of Penguin Random House UK, London, in 2020.

LIBRARY OF CONGRESS CATALOGING-IN-PUBLICATION DATA
Names: Lodge, Gytha, author.
Title: Watching from the dark : a novel / Gytha Lodge.
Description: New York : Random House, 2020.
Identifiers: LCCN 2019035947 (print) | LCCN 2019035948 (ebook) |
ISBN 9781984818096 (trade paper) | ISBN 97819848089 (ebook)
Classification: LCC PR6112.O275 w38 2019 (print) | LCC PR6112.o275 (ebook) |
DDC 823/.92—dc23
LC record available at https://lccn.loc.gov/2019035947
LC ebook record available at https://lccn.loc.gov/2019035948

Printed in the United States of America on acid-free paper

randomhousebooks.com

2 4 6 8 9 7 5 3 1

Book design by Victoria Wong

This book is dedicated to two Pauls.
To Mr. Paul Brooke, passionate, inspirational teacher
of English. You helped so many of your students
to love books, and in so doing turned many
of those into writers. Grazie.
And to Dr. Paul Worth, aka the Sexy Neurologist.
I feel hugely thankful to have such a tirelessly
supportive, smart, kind, and epically silly human
being on my team. All my love and thanks.

WATCHING FROM THE DARK

Prologue

Something clicked in the house and he froze, looking toward the closed door, his heart racing. Had it been the front door? Had someone come in?

Aidan turned his head, straining to hear more. A footstep. Rustling sounds of movement.

But there was nothing. It was just the sound of something contracting somewhere, the normal ticking of the house.

He tried to breathe out some of the tension. He'd been looking forward to this evening all week. He was, for once, free and unhampered, and had imagined a whole evening with Zoe. But of course, that wasn't how it had panned out. He might be free, but Zoe still had her own schedule. He was back to waiting for eleven o'clock. A standard, frustrating Thursday.

Instead of settling in to watch a film on the sofa, he'd ended up hunkered over the desktop PC, checking Zoe's Skype icon for the moment she turned her machine on. But it had stayed resolutely red, and he'd wasted hours scrolling through newsfeeds and reading articles.

He'd spent so many nights like this, waiting for Zoe to come online. Half the time she was late. He'd been sulky about it at first, until he'd learned that sulking made her rebellious. She needed to feel free.

He'd had to learn to accept that he would see her when he saw her. That he wasn't the only one who had a busy life to work around.

At 10:52 Zoe's icon turned green. It took him no more than a second to click on it and connect.

The pickup was instant, and he was already smiling in anticipation before the image appeared. But then he saw that Zoe's chair was empty. She was off camera, with only a moving shadow thrown on the wall as evidence that she was there at all. What was she doing?

He turned up the volume on his speaker and realized he could hear running water. Was she about to take a bath? Now?

He felt instinctively that this must be some sort of game. Like the times when she undressed for him, her gaze distant and her lips very slightly apart. It drove him wild.

But what was the point if he couldn't see her? Frustrated, he adjusted his own screen. But of course it did nothing to the angle of the camera in her room. He could still see only the empty chair and beyond it the wall, with a slice of curtain on one side and the hinges of her front door on the other.

The sound of the running water tapered and then ceased, and there were other sounds of movement and the squeak of wet skin against the acrylic of the bath.

Aidan sighed. She really was going to have a bath while he sat there and waited.

He thought about hanging up in protest. But if she was only going to be quick, he might miss seeing her body dripping with water. Or her breasts barely held in by a towel as she leaned toward the camera and clicked with the mouse.

There was another sound within his own house, and although it came from somewhere upstairs he still paused to listen, his eyes fixed on the wall. He knew it was nothing and after a moment he relaxed again. He was strangely jittery.

And then there was a clicking sound. He saw motion and realized that it was the door to Zoe's flat. It was moving, the hinged edge that was within his view pivoting inward.

Pure fear hit him then. Had she asked another man over? Was she letting someone in to watch her bathe, perhaps to touch her, while he was forced to watch?

He expected to hear the newcomer call out, but the door closed almost silently and there was no greeting. No other sound. He reached out and turned the speaker up still further, almost in spite of himself. There was a slight buzzing, and over the top of it the sound of water as Zoe moved in the bath. It was only by straining to hear that he caught soft footsteps. Whoever had come in was moving across the room.

A moment later, there was the sound of sudden movement from the bath, and Zoe's voice raised in surprise.

"What— Jesus. What are you doing in here?" And then what almost sounded like a laugh, but the kind of laugh that comes out of fear. "Look, I'm . . . I'm really sorry . . ."

The water sounds dropped away with a pair of clicks in quick succession. Whoever had come in had closed the bathroom door. Locked it.

His heart rate was back up again. Who had gone in there? Who the hell was shutting themselves into the bathroom with her?

And then there were other sounds. Sounds that were, unmistakably, of a struggle. Zoe's muffled voice sounded hoarse and desperate.

Then, abruptly, there was silence. Absolute silence.

The fear was different now. Something was very, very wrong.

He had to do something. He had to help her. Oh God, what if he was too late?

He scrabbled around on the desk until he found his phone. He'd started to dial three nines when the realization of what this meant hit him. He stalled. He could see it all: the phone call, the follow-up, being asked in to see the police. Everything finally coming out, and his life collapsing.

And then he heard the bathroom door click twice again as it opened. There were those same quiet, even steps, and then a pause. Scuffling sounds, which he couldn't make sense of. He willed whoever it was to come into the frame. To show their face. But the steps continued after a while, and the door to the flat moved again. The figure he had never seen left, and the door clicked shut.

1

Jonah had almost let it go. The call. The report. He'd almost let it go.

He asked himself, later, what difference it would have made if he had. This was what you did when you were tying up a case. You looked for mistakes and for their opposite. For the good things you'd done. You asked yourself how they had affected the investigation, and in this case, the biggest question mark was over the report of a murder that he almost let slide. Whether things would have gone differently if he'd acted earlier, and how different they would have been if he had never acted at all.

It was possible that neither scenario would have changed anything. That events would have gone on implacably to their conclusion. But it was also possible that everything would have changed.

The report made itself known during the tail end of a tortuous Friday-morning caseload meeting, made decidedly worse by Detective Chief Superintendent Wilkinson being away. Without him to push everything through, the meeting had descended into rambling discussions on every detail. It was soul-destroyingly boring.

But then they had finally limped through to new case allocation, and Jonah had watched his intense counterpart in the uniformed police, Yvonne Heerden, take on three thefts and a traffic accident.

"We've had an unauthenticated murder claim passed on by the

crime desk," Heerden said next. "I've given you a transcript," she added to Jonah, "but I think it's unlikely to come to anything so we're happy to take it. The caller claims that his girlfriend was murdered while he was talking to her on Skype, but that he didn't see the killer. He hung up when asked for his name and details. Crime desk tried to look her up and found no trace of a woman with that name anywhere online."

Jonah skimmed over the transcript, noting that the girl's name was Zoe Swardedeen.

I need to— My girlfriend's been murdered . . . he read.

Heerden was probably right. This would, in all likelihood, involve admin of a simple kind. Cross-checking with missing persons. Trying a few variations of the spelling.

"OK?" Heerden asked as he read on.

There was something in the phrasing used in the call that made Jonah hesitate. Something that unsettled him.

He was aware that Heerden was waiting for an answer, however, and he trusted her and her team to do this right. His own team was neck-deep in a complex blackmail case and had little time for unnecessary extras.

"Sure," he said. "Keep me posted if it comes to anything."

The meeting moved on to cover another multi-casualty traffic accident that had probably been caused by a truck driver using his phone. Jonah was glad he didn't have to be involved. Those were the kinds of cases that scarred you. The kind that made you impulsively check up on all your loved ones. The kind that made life seem flimsy and the world a random, uncaring place.

With those thoughts foremost in his mind, his uneasiness about a strange, anonymous murder report was pushed aside.

THERE WAS SO much Aidan should have been doing. Three of his students had sent essays over, and he had a whole raft of faculty admin, but he hadn't managed to read a line. He'd opened email after email but failed to understand them through the pounding of his heart and the ringing in his ears. He wasn't seeing words; he was seeing the slow opening and closing of a door, played over and over.

The not knowing was the worst. He would loop through a conviction that it had all been some strange misunderstanding, or a dream, and then he would remember that Zoe had never reappeared from the bathroom. Not while he'd been watching. He knew in his soul that she had been in desperate need of help, and that she might never have received it.

He'd searched news and social-media sites the moment he was up, looking for any mention of an incident. He'd rechecked at regular intervals since, too, but there was no mention of any murder or violence in Southampton. Nothing about a young woman being attacked. A total void of anything relevant.

There was a way to find out, if he felt he could take it, of course. He could call the police again. This time, when they asked him for his name and address, he could give it to them.

He'd come close last night. The police call handler he'd been put through to had been female. He'd heard her typing everything he'd said, turning it into data. She'd typed away when he'd admitted he didn't know the number of the pay-as-you-go phone he was calling from, because it was a spare he'd dug out from his desk. And then she'd typed up his attempt to tell her that he thought his girlfriend had been murdered.

Right at the end of the call, she'd asked for his name. There had been a long, tense silence as he'd teetered on the edge of telling her. And then he'd heard a car door slam outside.

He'd ended the call and listened, tense and sick, for more sounds. He tried telling himself that there was nothing to be afraid of, but he knew it wasn't true. There was a lot to be afraid of. There was Zoe being killed in front of him. There was the truth all pouring out.

He couldn't let it happen. He had everything to lose. Everything.

He'd thought about closing the Skype window, to shut out the scene. But it was the only way he had of checking on Zoe. Of waiting to see if the police arrived at her flat.

Midnight had come and gone, punctuated only by his eyes flicking over to the clock at the bottom right of the screen. Where were the bloody police?

There had still been nothing by two-forty, when he had finally closed the program in a rush of despair and gone to bed.

It was now eleven hours since he'd seen the door to Zoe's flat swing open. Eleven hours, and no sign, no message, no news report.

He could still call the police back. He could still go through it all again, and tell them who he was.

But every time he thought about that, chilled sweat would bloom on his skin. Knowing that he couldn't risk it created a frustration that was visceral. He could feel it in his stomach and in his loins, and it made sitting still unbearable.

Zoe, he thought, willing her to call him. *Zoe, please. Fucking call.*

JONAH APPROACHED DOMNALL O'Malley, the only visible member of his team, on his way through the bright, modern expanse of CID.

"Are you genuinely the first one in?" he asked, disbelieving.

"Ah Jesus, no," O'Malley answered, leaning his heavy frame back in his chair. "I rolled up about five minutes ago. Juliette's been here since seven-something. Ben's a little late, though, he says."

"Ben said he was *late?*"

"I know," O'Malley said. "That threw me, too. Maybe he's finally gone and got himself a girlfriend and didn't sleep well."

"But it's Ben," Jonah countered. "He doesn't need sleep."

"Ah, you're right, so. Well, whatever it was, I plan to take the piss mercilessly."

Jonah grinned and went on to his office, leaving the door open. He took his phone out of his pocket briefly, wondering whether he'd have a message today, or whether Jojo was once again in some desolate place with no signal.

Their communications were an unquestionable bright spot to his days. Her irreverent banter and humor had the power to make him grin for a good while afterward. It was such a refreshing feeling. He'd spent so many months pining for Michelle, his most recent ex-girlfriend. He'd thought he might spend the rest of his life missing her.

The sudden reappearance in his life of Jojo, his teenage crush, had changed all of that. They'd agreed that an investigation she'd been involved in would need to be tied up before they could see each other. And Jojo had then made the decision to take herself traveling until repairs to her house were done. Given that her social circle had also been devastated by a murder inquiry, it was only natural for her to need space. But he'd still felt a pang when she'd told him she was going.

She was in Namibia now, gradually touring a series of spectacular climbing sites that were miles from anywhere. Jonah should have been nervous at her being out there alone in the wilderness, but for some reason he wasn't. Perhaps it had something to do with how fiercely capable she had always been, and the fact that she'd survived a serious attempt on her life.

Well, there was nothing from Jojo. He put the phone down and logged on to his desktop. A few more blackmail files had been added to the database but he took it all in only vaguely. For some reason, looping through his mind were the words *Please help her. She could still be alive.*

HANSON HAD MADE coffee on autopilot. She didn't really need it this morning. She knew in her bones that she was a whisker away from a breakthrough, and she'd been awake before six, her mind whirring with a series of payments to different accounts that she was positive were connected to her case. She was enjoying herself profoundly.

It was strange to think she'd very nearly sidestepped the financial side of it. It was more Ben's kind of work. Lightman was the most painstaking, meticulous member of the team and easily had the best memory of the three of them. But he'd been in the middle of something else, and she'd felt it was her turn to step up.

She was surprised to find Lightman's desk empty. In her five months with the team she'd never known him to arrive late, and it was difficult to imagine him having some kind of unplanned disaster. But just as she was thinking of asking O'Malley about it, she saw Lightman emerge through the door to CID, looking as unruffled as ever.

"Ben, my man," O'Malley said, grinning hugely. "What happened? Did you oversleep?"

Lightman gave a small smile and dumped his car keys on his desk. "A few things to do, that's all."

"Ahhh," O'Malley replied with a knowing nod. "A woman, then? One who didn't let you sleep or leave the house?"

Lightman laughed and shook his head, but said nothing as he removed his coat and settled himself into his chair.

AIDAN FOUND HIMSELF searching for the Southampton police on Google when he should have been preparing for his tutor groups. Southampton, he read, was part of Hampshire Constabulary, which had its own website. He clicked through to it, though what he was looking for was anyone's guess. He doubted they published details of cases or summaries of houses broken into to save injured women.

Of course there was nothing like that. Instead a series of big headlined boxes offered various options to the visitor, and he decided to click on the "Help and Advice" section. But there was nothing relevant there.

Back on the homepage his eye was caught by an option to report a crime online. If the Southampton police hadn't taken his call seriously, perhaps he could try again this way.

The first thing it asked for was the postcode where the crime had taken place, which made him want to bang his head on the desk. There was no box to write "I don't know the fucking postcode!" But it let him put "Southampton" and click onward.

Once he'd given the details of the crime, it asked for an email address or telephone number. Feeling that it couldn't be a betrayal right now, he put in Zoe's email address and hoped they wouldn't lose time trying to check with her before they did anything about it.

And then he submitted the form, but felt no sense of relief. He couldn't feel anything at all while Zoe might be dying. Might already be dead.

He couldn't let himself think about that, and the denial made him feel worse. But at least he'd done something. He'd done *something*, and not just left her there.

By MIDAFTERNOON JONAH had finished his report on the blackmail case and found his mind wandering back to that morning briefing. He was curious to know whether Heerden's team had uncovered the truth about the singular murder report.

He found the case on the database and read that a constable from Heerden's team had made some efforts to identify the possible victim. They'd found no Zoe Swardedeen anywhere in the UK, however, and there had been no reports of a missing person that day. The constable had suggested closing the case.

Jonah gave a small, dissatisfied sigh, wondering why the constable hadn't tried other spellings, but also wondering why he cared so much.

Please help her. She could still be alive . . .

He found himself imagining the desperate tone of voice, and decided he'd like to listen to the original recording. It was only a minute long.

It was easy enough to open up the file and play it. The call handler's voice boomed out, and he hastily turned the volume down.

And equally hastily turned it up again when the caller began to speak. He was all but whispering.

Jonah felt goosebumps gradually rising along his neck and arms as he listened. He'd heard calls like this before, usually as evidence in courtrooms. The attempt to be quiet and the electric fear through the voice felt like a domestic-abuse victim hiding from a partner.

It jarred, hearing it from someone who had apparently only seen something online.

"I was online with her. I couldn't see what happened, but I heard it. And someone entered her flat. . . ."

The call ended shortly after the caller was asked for his name. Jonah listened to the muffled noises that came before the line was cut off and then sat, staring unseeing at his computer screen.

He was still in that position when a new file appeared on the database with a cheerful chirrup. A crime report filed that morning through the online system, which the crime desk had decided might belong to the same case.

Jonah opened it quickly and read what was a very similar report. This time the girl's name was written as Zoe Swardadine.

He typed the new spelling into Google, and this time found image after image of a young woman with deep-brown skin and dark curly hair; when he clicked on one of them it took him to what seemed to be her website. It was a simple WordPress page about a Southampton-based artist who painted stylized figures on ominous backgrounds. There was a phone number low down on the page, which seemed a little trusting to him. But perhaps not many people stumbled across Zoe's site.

He used the landline to call her. It rang eight times, and then a standard voicemail told him that the caller was busy, and asked him to leave a message.

He left numbers for the station and for his mobile in a light tone, asked her to call back, and then hung up, feeling an increasing sense of urgency.

It didn't take him long to find Zoe's father. Martin Swardadine was an investment banker at a firm called Knight and Maynooth. There was an intimidating black-and-white headshot at the top of the page, taken from one side in a way that exaggerated Martin's strong jawline. Underneath there was a bio of the man himself. The last paragraph informed Jonah that Martin was married to an exceptional GP and had a daughter who was a budding artist.

Martin took Jonah's call with the kind of strong, breezy greeting that implied he was taking time out of some very important things. Cheerfully important things; things that were making lots of rich people even more money.

"This is DCI Jonah Sheens. I'm calling from Hampshire Constabulary. We just wanted to check up on your daughter. A friend of hers was worried."

"Check up on . . . on Zoe?" The honed manner slipped a little.

"Yes," Jonah said. "I just wondered whether you'd been in touch today."

"I— Not today, no," her father said. "But I had lunch with her on . . . earlier this week. She's probably messaged since. Hang on."

There were a few friction noises down the line as, presumably, Martin checked his message history.

"She messaged yesterday evening."

"Thank you," Jonah said. "What time was that?"

"Eight-twelve, it says." There was a very slight pause, and something in his voice was different when he spoke again. "Is there some reason to worry?"

"A friend of hers was trying to contact her and couldn't," Jonah said. "It could well be nothing. It often is. But would you be able to check with her friends, perhaps? Or with Zoe's mother?"

"OK. I'll . . . I'll ask around."

Jonah gave him the switchboard number and hung up. He read through the second report more carefully. There was no contact for whoever had sent it. The email address said zswardadine@soton.ac

.uk, which was disquieting. No phone number, and the address of the crime said only Southampton.

Martin Swardadine called back seven minutes later to tell him that nobody had heard from her, and within ten more minutes, Jonah was out of the building and driving swiftly toward Zoe's flat.

ANGELINE COULDN'T STOP shaking. The police car had started it. Until then she hadn't really felt afraid. It had all seemed like a hassle, getting on her bike and heading over there, into a cold headwind, when she was tired and behind with her deadlines. She'd also failed to find any bike lights with charge in them, and it was a murky sort of two-thirty that threatened an early twilight. She'd felt angry for most of the ride over.

But the police car changed it somehow. She'd imagined the detective she'd spoken to as an ordinary person, not someone in uniform. He'd sounded so calm. He'd explained that he needed her to let a couple of officers into Zoe's flat. That they just needed to check on her. That he'd be along shortly afterward and make sure everything was OK.

He'd been so calm, in fact, that she hadn't been worried. But now, confronted with a police car and a male and female officer, both in uniform, she felt sick with fear.

She nodded to them, pushed her bike over to the wall, and tried to lock it. Her hands had a jerky shake to them, and it took her three goes before she managed it.

"Are you Angeline?" the tall, bulky male officer asked her. His black uniform didn't suit him, she thought. The padded vest with its protruding pockets made him look even bigger around the middle than he really was.

"Yes," she said. And then, in sudden fear: "You haven't been in yet, have you?"

"No, we tried buzzing but didn't get an answer. We're just waiting for you and the key," he said with a small smile. "If you can let us in, we'll go and check on Zoe."

Angeline nodded, a shudder running through her, and fished in her satchel for her big heavy key ring. She managed to separate out the little hoop that Zoe had given her, complete with its chunky security key and its smaller one for Zoe's door.

She let them into the entrance hall, which still, a good two years since it had been built, smelled like new carpets. She inadvertently let the door swing half shut on the police officer and apologized, but he didn't seem bothered.

"A bit nicer than your standard student accommodation," he said to her in a light voice. He was trying to put her at ease, she could tell.

It made her feel worse. She felt utterly cold as she walked up the stairs ahead of them both.

On the second floor, she let them through the varnished fire door and onto the landing. She'd always found the door heavy, but today it didn't seem to weigh anything at all. She remembered to hold it open behind her this time.

The corridor was empty. Zoe's flat was marked 16 in big silver numbers. She paused in front of it, looking at her reflection in the numeral 6.

"Should I . . . ?" she asked, gesturing at the door. At the female officer's nod she knocked, her knuckles making almost no sound on the wood of the door. Then the bulky officer leaned past her and banged more loudly.

"Zoe?" he called, his head down as if he could hear better that way. "Are you able to come and let us in?"

There was silence, except for a very distant bass beat that must have been coming from another floor.

"OK," the officer said. "If you can unlock it . . ."

Angeline somehow managed to get the key into the lock and turn it. She stepped back once the door had opened a crack.

"Can you . . . ?" She couldn't voice the awful dread of going in there. But they clearly understood anyway.

"We'll just be a minute," the officer said, glancing at his female colleague. They filed in through the wide door.

She folded her arms over herself and tried to stop the shaking and the squeezing thumps of her heart as she waited. She'd never known fear so acute. It felt like it might kill her, and the more she thought about that, the more she felt light-headed. Like her heart might be damaged already.

There was a very long silence inside. Then the click of a door opening somewhere in the flat, and, after a moment, a low voice that was answered by another.

And then there were quiet footsteps, and the female officer appeared.

"Is she OK?" Angeline asked, before she had a chance to say anything.

"It looks like she's had some kind of accident," the officer said gently. Through her speech, Angeline could hear the bulky male officer in the background. He must have been talking into a phone or radio.

". . . ambulance and Scene of Crime."

Angeline felt an awful coldness. She said nothing, but darted forward. She slid past the female officer, who told her sharply to stop. Angeline almost cannonballed into the bulky guy, who was listening to a crackling response on his walkie-talkie, his big form blocking the gap between the desk and the door. She went to move past him, too, but the woman suddenly had hold of her upper arm.

"I'm sorry, but it's not a good idea," she said.

Angeline twisted in her grip and was rushing onward, toward the bedroom and the open bathroom doorway immediately inside it.

Then there were two sets of hands on her, and she was being pulled firmly away.

"Come on, Angeline," the bulky man said. "You can't go in there. I'm sorry."

"I need to see! Please let me see."

But all the strength to fight them was leaving her, and she found herself being held up by them instead. They moved her out into the hallway, and she found herself sitting on the deep, low window ledge at the end of the corridor.

"We'll find you some water," the bulky officer said gently. "Or a tea. How about a cup of tea?"

She nodded, even though she wanted to shout at him and tell him that tea wasn't going to make anything better.

"Zoe's dead, isn't she?" she asked, but neither of them answered.

2

I t was six minutes past twelve by the time Zoe had finished with her eye makeup. Fourteen minutes to get out the door and into a cab so they were on time for the wedding. Plenty of time.

She slotted the brushes away, rolled up the nylon carry case, and pulled open one of the drawers of the jewelry chest. The new spiraling silver earrings gleamed as she picked them up, a match for her silver-dusted eyes.

The bathroom door opened on the floor below, and she called out, "How are you doing, Maeve?" as she fastened the earrings on.

"Ah, I'm getting there!" Maeve's Northern Irish accent had the slightly harried fake cheer of the serially late.

"Are your clothes actually on you . . . ?"

"Mostly!" came the reply. And then there were rapid footsteps heading toward Maeve's bedroom.

Zoe couldn't help laughing. Maeve's problem was perpetually trying to cram too many things into any given day. To Zoe, a 12:20 taxi had meant a single hour of work after breakfast and then two hours of getting ready. For Maeve it had meant a long coffee date with a friend, followed by a run, and then a frantic twenty minutes of tearing her room apart to find her dress before hurling herself into the shower.

"Do you have tights, Zo?" Maeve shouted after a minute.

"Yes," she called back. She looked herself over in the vanity mirror for a moment before opening up the top-left drawer in the big oak chest. "What kind?"

"Like . . . flesh color?" Maeve's voice grew louder as she came to the bottom of the stairs. "Or maybe black?"

"Going to have to be black," Zoe told her, deciding that it wasn't the best time to have a conversation about how useless "flesh-colored" tights were when you were half-Kenyan. She pulled three pairs out of the unit, picked up her shoulder bag, and headed carefully down the stairs. The Christian Louboutin shoes may have been the most beautiful things she'd ever owned, but they sure as hell weren't easy on stairs. Or uneven ground. Or over long distances. Zoe wasn't sure she'd manage the whole day without putting on the ballet flats she'd packed in her shoulder bag, but she was determined to try.

Maeve was at least dressed by the time Zoe made it down the stairs. The tight little long-sleeve top and high-waisted, flared skirt made her look like a 1950s belle, though the wet hair dripping onto her shoulders wasn't a great addition. Neither was a glob of mascara she'd just managed to get on her cheek while leaning into the mirror.

Zoe recognized the jerky, rushed hand movements that were only going to cause more mess. Eye makeup never, ever went right if you rushed it.

Zoe threw the tights onto the bed. "I can do that," she said, holding out a hand for the mascara brush. "You can blow-dry your hair while I do. Multitasking."

"Thank you," Maeve said with feeling. "I need eyeliner as well."

Zoe waited while she switched the hair dryer on and fired it up, and then set to work on the smeared mascara with a cotton pad and cleanser. The mascara went on easily enough, despite Maeve blinking whenever the wand approached her eyes.

Zoe glanced at Maeve's illuminated bedside clock before starting in with the eyeliner. Seven minutes. Time enough for a proper job. Maeve could get her tights on while Zoe went down to the cab.

She spent a moment looking thoughtfully at Maeve's pale-blue eyes, trying to decide how to shape them to get the most out of them. *Not an underline,* she thought.

"Will you stop doing that?" Maeve said loudly over the hair dryer. "Makes me feel like you're about to drop to one knee and ask me to marry you."

"What if I am?" Zoe asked, grinning. "Right, you need to stay still for this bit." She worked quickly, and then grabbed a jeweled hairnet to tame Maeve's still-damp mouse-brown curls.

Maeve looked herself over in the mirror and gave Zoe a small, slightly grudging smile.

"All right. That looks a lot better than the pre-Raphaelite mess I was planning."

Zoe's phone buzzed, and she said, "Taxi," before checking it.

"Fuck, I've still got to find my shoes," Maeve said.

"Does your mammy know you swear?" Zoe asked with a grin.

"She taught me all the words," Maeve replied, leaning almost entirely into her wardrobe and pulling out a series of odd shoes. "And I'll be no time at all, seriously. You go ahead."

Approximately eleven minutes later, Maeve came charging out to the taxi, looking no less gorgeous, Zoe thought, for the flush in her cheeks and the way the belt of her jacket had come loose on one side and was dragging on the path.

IT WASN'T THE most relaxed entrance to a wedding. The cabbie had chosen the wrong route to the venue, deciding for some inexplicable reason to go through the city center. They'd lost another fifteen minutes crawling along the Mall with all the Saturday shoppers. Maeve had apologized continually until Zoe had told her firmly that it wasn't her fault, and made a decisive conversational change by asking Maeve to give her the full story on her date of the previous night.

"Oh, fine, you know." Maeve looked away from her, her pale eyes scanning pedestrians as the cab moved torturously slowly past them. "I mean, kind. A little old-fashioned. Nice to talk to."

Zoe gave a wicked laugh. "What else is going to happen with church dating? You're basically guaranteed an old-fashioned nice guy."

Maeve made a dismissive noise. "A good half of them are *nothing like,* you know. The place breeds as many sexist feckwits as it does nice guys."

Zoe smiled at her. "Sounds like the non-Christian dating scene."

"Exactly," Maeve agreed. And then she sighed. "I don't know. I don't think I'll see him again. He just wasn't . . . interesting enough."

By which, Zoe knew, she meant that he wasn't Isaac. And she wished, all over again, that Maeve would get the crush out of her system and find someone who really wanted her. Someone who valued her for herself instead of just liking it when she stroked his ego.

"You can't force it" was all Zoe said lightly.

"Ah, I'm fine on my own," Maeve said with a flap of her hand. "I'm happy in my own company, and it's nice to remember that."

"Yep," Zoe agreed. "At least you're sort of interesting. Sometimes."

"Sod off," Maeve said with a smile.

They didn't manage to keep much conversation going the rest of the way, as it became obvious that they were getting later and later and the two of them descended into a taut silence. The cab eventually arrived at the Vinery at 12:58, two minutes before the official start of the ceremony. They had to pull up a little way back, behind the silver Rolls-Royce that had already arrived and disgorged a cluster of white-lace-and-lavender figures onto the steps.

In spite of the height of her heels, Zoe managed an awkward jog over the pavement.

"Sorry," she said with a grin at Gina, who looked transformed from her usual practical self in a figure-hugging bridal gown with a high collar and a train.

"Zoe!" she gasped, and then gave a raucous laugh. "We were about to go in!"

"It was Maeve's fault," Zoe said, just as Maeve, behind her, chimed in with, "It was me! I'm so sorry!"

They ran ahead over the marble tiles inside and into the large conservatory full of peony-decked pews. At least half the audience looked around at them, expecting the bride in spite of the lack of entrance music. Zoe tried not to laugh as she saw Angeline's wide-eyed look. She and Victor were sitting halfway down the room with space next to them. Which was a relief.

Angeline shuffled along to let her and Maeve in, and she shook her head.

"We thought you must have been in an accident!" she said in a whisper that carried. "We've been here *ages*."

Zoe grinned at her and then turned as some recorded string music started for the bride's entrance. It was hard not to get a little emotional as Gina came in.

Gina, who was technically Zoe's boss, was the most hardworking person Zoe knew. The success of her fantastic little coffee shop, where Zoe worked on Thursdays and Sundays, was based as much on universal love of the owner as it was on the food and drink. And if the guy she was marrying, Michael, was slightly dull, he was also the kind of man who would be there for her, and who loved to spoil her. It seemed to Zoe like exactly what Gina deserved.

3

The call came through on Jonah's Bluetooth when they were ten minutes from Zoe's flat, and Jonah knew all he needed to from the way the sergeant said "Sir." This was a death they were investigating now, and he was glad O'Malley had been on hand to come along. Of the three members of the team, he was the most hardened to violence, and it was a scene of violence that Jonah was now expecting.

By the time he brought Lightman and Hanson on-site, it would be easier. Scene of Crime would be there, with their Post-it notes and arrows and labels: paraphernalia that had the effect of sterilizing it all. It would look like myriad pieces of evidence, not quite as much like a person who had suffered and died.

HE PARKED THE Mondeo along Latterworth Road, a suburban-looking residential street that ultimately terminated at the A35 to the north. He and O'Malley had driven past dozens of identikit 1930s houses, all of them white-painted on the top half, with shallow bay windows and a rectangular front garden. Zoe's block of flats was the only aberrant structure. It looked to Jonah as though it had been built over two sets of semidetached homes, and had been designed with no apparent nod to its respectable surroundings. It was entirely modern, with an angular stepped front that bordered on aggressive.

They were waved past by a PC standing at the door. An incredibly slender woman who must be Angeline Judd was sitting on a window ledge with a female police community support officer, a cup of tea clutched in front of her, and a series of crumpled tissues alongside. There were signs of tears in her eyes, too, and the area underneath them looked raw.

The PCSO nodded to him, and Angeline looked up at him as if he were a predator.

"I'm DCI Sheens," he said, coming to a stop in front of Angeline. "I'm in charge of investigating what happened to Zoe. I have a few questions for you, if that's all right?"

"Yes," Angeline said after a short pause while she stared at him. "Yes, that's fine."

Looking at her, bundled into an oversized gray cardigan and leggings, it was hard not to notice how thin she was. Her arms and legs appeared almost skeletal, and the effect of her incredibly thin frame was to make her face look too large, her eyes huge within it like a doll's. The short, fluffy hair had no more substance to it.

He wondered whether she might be ill, and it created a complex reaction in him. The effect of her appearance was childlike. It brought out a protective instinct.

He spoke gently to her, thanking her for helping them and offering sympathy, until she agreed that she was ready to answer a few questions. Though when she did, it was largely to shake her head at everything he suggested while her eyes oozed tears.

Zoe had no enemies that she knew of. No money troubles. No recent arguments. No strange behavior.

"She was—so kind," Angeline said thickly, in the end.

He had to wait for her to swallow a few times before she could carry on, and tell him that she'd known Zoe from uni.

"Do you do art, too?" he asked, smiling.

"Oh. No. I'm . . . on the dance and teaching program."

The responses to everything were much the same, until Jonah

told her they needed to talk to Zoe's boyfriend. And then Angeline's eyes focused on him sharply.

"She— You mean Aidan?"

"You might need to tell us," Jonah said, treading carefully as he wrote the name down. "Her boyfriend told us we needed to check on her, but we don't have contact details."

"I've got them," Angeline said, and pulled her phone out. She read off the number, and Jonah scrawled it in his notebook. "I thought they might be back together," she added, and the way she said it made it sound like it had been a personal injury to her.

"They broke up?"

"Yes, a couple of times."

"They didn't live together?"

Angeline shook her head. "Just her. She used to share—with a friend. But she came out here."

"When was that?"

"I think . . . June."

Jonah nodded slowly. "It'd be great if you could come to the station later," he said. "But in the meantime, you should probably head home and look after yourself. Is there anyone you can call . . . ?"

Angeline nodded, and then suddenly dissolved into tears again. "It'll have to be my mum. I usually—I usually call Zoe."

ZOE'S FLAT WAS as modern and as unforgiving as the exterior of the building. It was sparsely furnished, with packing boxes in two corners of the living area. A sleek black kitchen showed signs of use: Smeared marks on the oven. Crumbs on the worktop. A couple of glasses on the side with the remains of red wine at the bottom.

"Maybe she had a visitor last night," Jonah murmured to O'Malley.

In the corner of the kitchen, a bowl of cat food and one of water, but no sign of the cat itself. Scared into hiding by the police, perhaps.

A desk sat to the right of the door and was dominated by a desktop computer. In the bottom corner of the screen, an orange light slowly brightened and faded, brightened and faded. Hibernating but not switched off. Below it sat a phone that he itched to touch but left for the cyber team.

On the other side of the room, a single sofa looked at empty space. No TV. No paintings. Just two packing boxes beyond it, one of them with the word *Sculptures* scrawled on it with a Sharpie.

It all struck him as soulless. Stark. Totally unlike what he would have expected from an artist. She'd lived here since June, Angeline had said. But she hadn't unpacked or decorated during those five months.

He moved over to the far door, which opened into a bedroom. She was in the bathroom, the first responders had said. The door on the left.

He edged through the open door without touching it, and saw Zoe at last, her body leaning back in the bath. The water was flat and absolutely opaque with her blood. Only her shoulders, head, and upper arms showed above the waterline at one end. Farther down the tub, her knees formed two tiny islands. Whatever wounds had done this to her were hidden below the profound red of the water.

A needle-thin trail of dark blood ran down the far side of the bath, following a path from a red-handled knife to the water. *A Stanley knife,* he thought. *An artist's knife.*

His gaze traveled briefly over the curling hair that had been pulled up into a bun on top of her head, and over the face, which was a purplish bronze and slack. The eyes were closed, but there was no suggestion of sleep. Her face had the unmistakable vacancy of death.

He could sense O'Malley over his shoulder, hovering until it was his turn to stand where Jonah was standing.

He backed up, wanting to hear O'Malley voice his thoughts. To tell him that it looked like suicide. Absolutely and perfectly so. That the two crime reports were the only reason he might have had for thinking otherwise, and he wasn't entirely sure that he trusted them.

His phone rang and he gave a sigh as he read the screen. "It's Zoe's father," he said to O'Malley. "I'll talk to him while you take a look."

IT NEVER GOT any easier, that first call with the family. Zoe's father had barely been able to talk through choking tears, and when he'd handed the phone over to Zoe's mother, she had asked Jonah over and over why it had happened. He had no answers, of course. He rarely had any on that first call.

He'd done everything he could to soothe them. He'd told them that death would have been quick and painless. He thought about explaining that the warm bathwater would have helped her bleed to death quickly, but those were details he wasn't yet ready to lay on them. They had enough to deal with.

"Please tell me the truth," Zoe's mother had said at one point. "It's not . . . She didn't do it to herself, did she?"

Jonah let out a breath. "I'm afraid we won't know until we look closely at the scene and try to build a picture of the last few days."

He'd asked them then if they wanted to come to Southampton. He was thinking of formal identification, and of all the things he would need to tell them in person.

"There's no requirement to be here now," he added. "Identification is often done through a video link." He didn't add *because it's less distressing*.

"No," Zoe's mother had said. "We want to come. Now. As soon as possible."

AS HE WAITED for Scene of Crime, Jonah made an effort to think about the practicalities he now faced. It was likely to be a very long day. He mentally opened his calendar, grateful that he rarely booked anything much on a Friday evening. He generally tried to see his mother on Saturdays, but she was, for the first time in eight years, away.

It had taken him entirely by surprise when his lapsed-Catholic mother had been adopted by the local Anglican church community. The worshippers had decided that she needed help, which Jonah couldn't really argue with, and had created a rota of activities and company that had drastically reduced the time she had been spending alone with alcohol. It had all been a huge relief to Jonah, despite the slightly accusatory looks the church ladies tended to give him if they crossed paths. He was still waiting for his mother to decide she hated them all, though. Or to swear at them all to the point where they couldn't forgive. She had a habit of eviscerating any efforts to help her.

So Saturday could easily be spent working. The Saturday-evening stag do for his cycling friend Roy might need to be bumped, though. That particular event he would happily forgo in the name of justice, and even if he finished up the day's work in time, it was unlikely he'd want to go. Murder investigations and boozy nights out didn't generally mix well.

His team probably had their own plans, he thought. Plans they would be less enthusiastic about ditching. It was probably time to let Ben and Juliette know what was happening.

HANSON WAS THOROUGHLY immersed in her financial hunt when the chief called. She held off answering it for a good four rings, while she scribbled down the point she'd got to, and then tried not to sound irritated as she answered.

"Chief?"

"Have you got Lightman there? It'd be easier to update you both at once."

Hanson could hear in his tone what had come of the trip.

"Yeah, he's here," Hanson said, catching Lightman's eye. "I'll transfer the call to a meeting room."

Once they'd picked the call up again, the two of them listened in silence as Sheens told them how Zoe had been found.

"It was a classic suicide setup," the chief said. "Only, we were told she was attacked. Which means the first thing on my list is tracking down the boyfriend. I'll need one of you on the scene, too, and I'm afraid it's going to be a late evening for whichever of you that is. Scene of Crime are only just here, the family are on their way, and I'll be requesting a postmortem."

"Sorry, sir. Can't be me," Lightman said, and Hanson looked at him in surprise. "I have to head off at four."

Hanson almost protested that he couldn't have plans. It was Friday. Pub night. They always did pub night. At least, they had for the last four months. Whenever they weren't madly immersed in something, they headed down the road to the Anchor, and stayed till eight or nine. Lightman never drank more than two beers, and rarely talked much, but he always came.

"No problem," the chief said. "Juliette?"

"I can do it," she said.

He read off the address of Zoe Swardadine's flat, and Hanson scribbled it down.

She found herself watching Lightman carefully as she ended the call. He finished making himself a note and rose. He was as hard to read as ever, but she was fiercely curious about what was going on.

"Typical," she said, standing, too. "It's taken me three weeks to get into the blackmail stuff, and now I'm finally making headway and I'm being called off on to something else."

"Ah, sorry," Lightman said with a grin. "My fault. I owe you one."

And then he left the meeting room without further explanation. Hanson looked after him, feeling unaccountably bad-tempered. It wouldn't have hurt, she thought, to explain.

Though maybe she didn't need an explanation. It was a Friday night, and Lightman didn't seem to have any trouble attracting female attention. Someone trying to chat him up had become a regular feature of their pub nights. And she knew he'd dated in the past.

Fine, she thought. *Let him go on some date while I do the hard work.*

4

March—twenty months before

The wedding after-party had bloomed into two distinct gatherings: one a warm and noisy crush within the hotel's long, thin bar and the other a delicately lit conversation piece in the larger dining room across the hall, where there were still seven or eight occupied tables.

Zoe had extracted herself to head to the bar, but had eventually given up on trying to order drinks. The trouble with a free bar was that people over-ordered, and the situation only perpetuated itself as the long wait caused people to stock up further once they finally got there. She returned empty-handed to the dining room, where Angeline was involved in an earnest conversation with Maeve.

Predictably, Maeve was giving Angeline an impassioned speech on positive thinking.

"Look, I mean, I know I go on about this a lot, but it's not just about telling yourself to cheer up. It's about *choosing* to be happy. Telling yourself inwardly and out loud that you're worth a lot." Maeve held her hand up in front of her face, her palm toward her. "I will literally say it to myself in the mirror. I will say, 'I am strong, and I am beautiful, and I am worth loving.' And it helps."

Zoe couldn't help smiling. Maeve believed in positivity as decidedly as she believed in God, and her mantras to herself included determined repetitions of how much she loved herself and all those who scorned her. The trouble was that Maeve was not instinctively a patient and positive person, and no matter how many times she told herself all this stuff, there were times when a truer version of herself shone through: one that was fed up with everything and found other people both needy and irritating.

Victor, to Maeve's right, was fiddling with the message stones that had been left out on the table. They were designed to be written on and put into a jar, but Victor was ignoring the pens and gathering a few stones into a pile. He looked as though he had a bad mood brewing. Which wasn't really surprising. He'd apparently been gaming until past 4 A.M., and he was never great at social situations even when well rested.

Zoe dropped into the chair beside him, wondering what to say to snap him out of it. She couldn't get him dancing, even if the band at the head of the room turned out to be half-decent. Victor never danced.

She felt weary. There had been a series of tense moments during the dinner. Gina's cousin, a loud, self-important man of fifty, had watched Angeline pushing her plate of smoked salmon away, with a murmured "Too pink," and said to her, "Come on! Eat up! Nobody likes a skinny girl!"

The effect on Angeline had been immediate and devastating. All the color had left her, and she'd risen and bolted from the room. Maeve had shaken her head at Zoe, a look of helplessness on her face, and Zoe had hurried out after Angeline. She'd found her in the toilets, crying in one of the cubicles, and it had taken twenty minutes to talk her into rejoining the party. By that time, the starters had been cleared and the beef Wellington that had replaced them was almost cold.

There had been a quiet ten minutes while they ate, and then Maeve had gone to talk to the bride and tripped on her heels, spraying red wine over a slim fortysomething woman in an ivory silk skirt and jacket. It had obviously made a mess, but the victim had, even after Maeve's profuse apology, been spiteful and critical, refusing offers of help mopping up and declaring that it was ruined and needed paying for.

Maeve had finally snapped back, loudly, "So you've got wine on your dress. You don't have to be a dick about it. Grow up and accept that things don't always go the way you want, all right?"

Zoe had wanted so badly to high-five her friend as she'd stalked off, but given that the bride and groom's table were staring, she'd had to suppress her glee. She'd caught Gina's eye, though, and winked at her.

Victor had behaved himself throughout the dinner, and had even managed to engage Gina's other cousin in a political discussion that remained friendly. He'd sat politely through the speeches and Zoe had been full of gratitude that he was keeping his temper in check.

Now, however, as she sat beside him, she felt a dropping sensation in her stomach. She knew the signs. He was sinking into a foul mood, and it was usually Zoe who dragged him back out of it. But even she wasn't always successful, and trying to find ways of managing him could be exhausting.

Seizing on an obvious point of interest, she said, "Look at the bloody cake!" and stood.

Victor didn't stand with her, so she went closer to the wonderful pink-and-white creation and took her phone out to photograph it. Gina had made it, she knew. God, she was good.

She kept expecting Victor to come over and join in, but he stayed put, and it was Felix who eventually appeared next to her. The silver fox, as the other waitresses liked to call him. He was one of their coffee-shop regulars, perpetually dapper and the most handsome man over fifty Zoe could think of. Zoe, like the other female baristas, had a habit of exchanging slightly flirty compliments with him, and the gallant way he responded always made it a high point of her day.

Seeing him here, even more suave than usual in a pale-gray suit and azure tie, she couldn't help grinning at him. "Look at you, all handsome."

"I was about to say the same," he said, leaning in to hug her lightly. There was a smile on his face as he said, "You should consider wearing this stuff to work."

"Ha, it'd be ruined within minutes," she countered. "You have no idea how many spillages those black T-shirts hide." She put a hand on his arm. "I'm glad you're here. I didn't see you at the service."

"I was late," he said with the slightest hint of a sigh. "Tenant at the flat I own locked herself out, and then it turned out she hasn't actually seen her keys in weeks and she'd just been keeping the door on the latch. Which meant I had to go and get a new lock and install it." He shook his head. "I'm thinking of adding interview questions that cover levels of organization. And maybe a procrastination test."

"Ooh, I'll help!" Zoe volunteered. "I saw a documentary on how to spot when people are lying."

"You're hired," he said. "If you do it, you can have ten percent of my wedding cake."

"Hey! I want at least half."

"I tell you what, how about I stand you a gin and you get to keep all the cake?"

"If you're sure you can brave the bar," Zoe said, raising an eyebrow.

Felix put an arm round her shoulders. "That's why you have to come and protect me."

And then Victor was suddenly there, saying in a low, unfriendly tone, "Excuse me. Did you ask permission to go touching her?"

Felix's arm dropped, and he gave Victor a slightly startled look.

"Victor, it's fine," Zoe said, trying to sound lighthearted. "I was just going to help him fight through to the bar."

Victor took half a step closer to Felix. "She's not at work. You can go and get your own drink and leave her to have fun."

"Victor," Zoe said, feeling heat blaze in her face.

"It's all right," Felix said calmly. He nodded at Victor. "I understand you looking out for your friends. It's places where there's drink flowing that people can be vulnerable. It's good to keep an eye on each other."

There was a long, tense silence while Victor simply stared at Felix. And Victor could really stare. She'd seen him make younger and stronger men flinch. But Felix didn't seem cowed.

The stare-off was broken by the band testing their microphones at the far end of the room. Felix smiled. "I'll head to the bar. You young things go and dance."

Zoe took Victor's arm, feeling the tension in the muscles of his forearm as he watched Felix leave. She tried to laugh. "We're young things. That means we *have* to dance."

"Not going to happen," Victor said. He was still looking at Felix's retreating form.

"Honestly," Zoe said, "don't worry about him. He's a flirty old queen and he'd be mortified if he thought he'd stepped out of line."

"He's gay?" Victor asked.

"Yes, all the girls think so," Zoe said with a little more certainty than she really felt. In reality, she had no idea what Felix's sexuality was, but it was completely irrelevant either way. He was her father's age, for God's sake.

A stream of guests began reentering the dining room, called by the music. Zoe wondered whether Gina and Michael would do a first dance, but the current music was lively. It was clearly intended to get the guests dancing.

"The bar's emptying out," Zoe said. "Go and rescue Angeline from the life lecture, and I'll get us Jäger Bombs."

Victor gave her a doubtful look, but moved when she gave him a shove.

She smiled as she left him, but she felt even wearier as she made her way against the moving crowd. Worrying about him and his anger was like carrying an extra weight.

She made her way to the bar a little more easily this time, her eyes scanning for Felix. She felt half-inclined to talk to him further about Victor. To apologize. She thought he might understand. But she also liked the fact that, right now, she could stand unobserved amid the guests and not have to make conversation.

The bar grew emptier as she queued, until there was nobody left waiting behind her. Just her, a couple to her right, and a solitary drinker to her left, who was occupying a high stool.

"What can I get you?" the girl behind the bar asked.

For some reason, ordering shots always went the same way. Zoe started with a low number, and then quickly talked herself up as she mentally added more and more people to her list of recipients. "Four Jäger Bombs" became "Actually, no, eight."

The waistcoated barmaid gave her a beaming smile as if she'd never had such a great order to make. The guy on the barstool turned to look at her. "I'll admit I'll be impressed if those are all for you."

Zoe glanced over at him, sizing up the leather jacket, the dark hair, the sharp cheekbones, and the full, slightly sulky-looking lips. He was giving her a smile that was somehow different from all the smiles she'd been given all day. This one was more . . . irreverent. And in a strange way more intimate.

"Don't tempt me," she said, and grinned. It wasn't really a conscious decision. It was just hard not to smile back. She could feel the dimpling in her cheeks before she'd made any kind of decision.

"Oh, bad day?"

She shook her head. "It's a wedding. Of course it's been a bad day."

He gave a deep chuckle. "Not close to the bride or groom, then?"

"Ah, I am really," Zoe said, watching the barmaid pouring out shots of Jägermeister for a moment. "It's not them I mind."

"Which one?"

"Which . . . ? Oh. I know Gina." She glanced at him. "You?"

He leaned forward, glancing past her for a moment with a gleaming wickedness in his expression. "Neither. I came in for a drink and realized I'd crashed an event with a free bar."

She couldn't help a note of shock in her laugh. "That's terrible!"

"I know," he said. "Do you think they can afford it?"

"Probably," Zoe said. "But I wouldn't go assuming. Some of us have morals, you know."

"Not those of us sitting on my side of the bar," he replied, and lifted up what looked like a gin and tonic and poured the rest of it into his mouth.

Zoe watched his throat as he swallowed, her gaze traveling over his neck, shoulders, and abdomen while he couldn't see her do it. He was older, she thought. Not by any means as old as Felix, but definitely somewhere in his thirties. Probably the sort of age she would have hesitated before including on a dating app, in fact.

But he was fit, too. That was obvious. She would have laid money on him having a really defined set of muscles under that shirt.

And then she made herself look away, because it was definitely not a good idea to start looking at him that way less than five minutes after they'd met.

"All done," the barmaid said brightly. She'd lined the shots up along the bar, Zoe realized, with the shot glasses expertly balanced between the tumblers of Red Bull. Which made Zoe feel bad, as she needed to transport them through to the other room.

"Could you make another four?" her barstool neighbor said. "Sorry. I want to join in."

The waitress took it well. Zoe shook her head at him slightly. "Do you need four?"

"I figured that was two each," he said. "Nobody—*nobody*—says no to a Jäger Bomb."

He said it so mock-seriously that Zoe couldn't help laughing. It was one of those fits of laughter that was actually quite hard to stop. It was still there as she downed both the shots ahead of him, and he promised to beat her on the next round.

"Who says there'll be a next round?" Zoe asked, but she was smiling as she said it.

"The little voice of your conscience," he countered. "It says, 'Don't leave Aidan to drink alone. Look at the poor man. He doesn't know anyone else.'"

"That's because you crashed the party!" Zoe said, half-outraged and half caught by his name. She'd had a crush called Aidan in secondary school. A floppy-haired boy who had played drums.

"And I'm very glad I did," he said, in another moment of almost-seriousness that caught her off guard. "So, tell me," he went on. "Why has the wedding been hard? A long-standing feud?" he pressed. "An argument with a boyfriend? Ex-boyfriend?" And then, after a pause: "Girlfriend?"

"No," she said, trying very hard for some reason to disguise her pleasure. He was trying to find out if she was single, and the idea made her feel jittery with excitement. "Just friends, and a couple of them have been having a hard time. They're the ones who've been struggling, really. I'm fine."

He gave her a thoughtful look, and then said, "That's a shame. Not that you're fine. The rest of it." He looked over at the row of glasses. "You're never going to be able to carry all those, you know. . . ."

Zoe looked at them, and found herself overflowing with laughter again. "No, I know. I always do this."

"I could be a gentleman and offer to carry some of them for you," he said.

The idea filled Zoe with a strange sort of anxiety. If he came over and talked to her friends, then he would potentially be part of things for the rest of the night. But the thought of Victor's reaction if she returned with another older man was not appealing in the slightest.

Before she could protest, however, Aidan had continued, "But I'm not very good at the gentlemanly thing. So I'm actually going to suggest we drink them to make your life easier."

"How am I supposed to explain that to the others?" she asked. "Taking twenty minutes to come back with nothing?"

"Just don't go back," he said with a shrug and another one of those wicked smiles.

Zoe found herself saying, "I think Victor might hit the roof . . ." And then stopped, fiercely regretting having said it.

"So Victor, who can't be a boyfriend or an ex . . ." Aidan said slowly, lifting the glass. "He must be . . ."

"Just a friend," she said quickly, feeling the blush creeping up her face. "He's just . . . stupidly protective." She gave a forced laugh. "He squared off against one of our regular, very gay customers earlier because he put his arm round me."

"I see," Aidan said, and when Zoe looked at him, he was smiling. "This could be fun."

5

Linda McCullough had arrived at the flat just behind the Scene of Crime team, and Jonah felt better about everything the moment she crossed the threshold. Hampshire was immensely lucky to have a forensic scientist who not only wanted to attend every crime scene but was qualified independently in biology and chemistry as well as forensic science.

McCullough was also good to work with. Her perpetual dry humor and her deadpan manner were just as invaluable, and Jonah had come to rely on her judgment and eye for detail. He knew only too well how many of his cases would never have been brought to trial without her.

"Try not to get in the way, Sheens," McCullough said with a little smile, indicating a small square of plastic for them to stand on just inside the doorway.

"I'll do my best," Jonah replied in the same tone. "Any news on the pathologist?"

"He said twenty minutes." McCullough glanced at her watch. "So he should be here in five. We'll start out here. I'll wait for him before I look at the body."

"There are a couple of glasses on the counter that I'd be interested in getting prints or DNA from," he said, tilting his head in the direction of the kitchen.

"I'm sure you would." McCullough pulled up her mask and walked past him toward the kitchen.

Jonah's phone rang again, the intrusive alarm-like ringtone telling him it was the detective chief superintendent calling back.

"Is that seriously your ringtone?" McCullough asked, turning to fix him with a disbelieving stare.

"Only for Wilkinson," he said with a smile, and took the call. "Sir," he said, stepping out into the hallway.

"I hear you've picked up a new murder inquiry?" the DCS said, sounding politely interested.

"You heard correctly. Though I'm suspending judgment on whether it was murder. It looks a lot like suicide, but her boyfriend reportedly witnessed it on a Skype call. I'm at the crime scene and the pathologist should be here any minute." He paused. "Was Yvonne OK with me taking it on?"

"She was fine. Not her sort of case. I'm happy for you to take it, too," the DCS said. "But I'm coming under a lot of pressure to get the blackmail case tied up."

"Understood," Jonah said. "I'll keep half my team on it."

"Right," Wilkinson said wryly. "So that's precisely one and a half people?"

"Exactly, sir," Jonah said, grinning though there was nobody to see it.

"OK. Keep me posted."

And that, Jonah thought as he hung up, was what was so good about Wilkinson. He was quite happy to trust Jonah's decisions.

The door to the stairs opened as he was putting his phone away and a thirtysomething man in a suit and tie emerged. The pathologist, he assumed, though not one he'd met before. All Jonah's cases so far had been handled by the much older and less keen-looking Dr. Stephen Russell. Jonah wondered whether this was a junior colleague of his, and whether he'd been waiting for his chance to shine.

This probably wasn't an issue, but Jonah felt a twinge of worry. They had a possible murder scene that on the face of it looked very much like suicide. If they ended up pursuing a murder case, they needed rigor. Not to mention a pathologist who would sound convincing in court.

Just don't miss anything, Jonah thought as he nodded to him.

JONAH'S WORRIES APPEARED to be unfounded. Dr. Shaw's steady, methodical examination was as thorough as Jonah could have asked for, and his commentary was quietly authoritative.

One particular observation interested Jonah, and that was the lack of any visible blood around the bath. If she had been held down and attacked, you might, the pathologist commented, expect some blood spray. Bloody fingerprints. And probably watered-down blood from the bathwater sprayed around the room.

"So that's looking more like suicide," Jonah said, not quite sure how he felt about that.

"Yes, though there may be other reasons for it," the pathologist said.

At the point where the pathologist leaned in and seemed to sniff close to Zoe's mouth, Jonah felt momentarily quite nauseous.

"Interesting. There's a chemical smell around the face." He reached for the small kit he had placed next to the bath and pulled out a plastic tube with a bright-blue lid. "I'm going to take a swab."

"Can you define what you mean by 'chemical'?" Jonah asked as the pathologist unscrewed the lid and pulled it out, complete with a small cotton-padded stick.

"Well, it's hard to define the substance just yet, but there's a distinctive aroma. Slightly sweet but astringent."

"Not something she's eaten?"

"I don't think so," he said, moving the cotton-padded stick over Zoe's skin. He took another and did the same gently to the inside of

her nose. "I'd guess something in the chloroform family." He straightened up and glanced around. "Which may well explain the lack of
any struggle, and if true, would rule out suicide."

"How long until we know?"

"The swab would normally be back next week, but perhaps your
forensic science officer . . ."

"I'm sure she'll be able to help," Jonah said with a grin. McCullough might not be particularly enthusiastic about spending her Friday evening in the lab, but he knew she'd do it anyway.

HANSON COULDN'T HELP feeling relieved that the pathologist had
completed his examination by the time she arrived at the scene. The
Scene of Crime team was already getting Zoe ready to be moved.

Not Zoe, she thought. *The body. Just the body.*

But relief or not, she wanted to have the same insight that the
DCI and O'Malley would have, and so while Sheens was being shown
around the various fingerprints and footprints by McCullough, Hanson borrowed the forensic photographer's camera and scrolled
through the pictures.

It was disturbing to look at, even on the small screen. The blood-
drained arms. The stark red against the white of the bath. She saw
what the DCI had meant about the lack of splashing. The only blood
was in the darkly stained water, which was so red that it looked solid,
and in a small, long-dried trickle from the knife down the edge of the
bath.

She clicked onward to different views of the bathroom. The
fourth one showed the sink. It had what was clearly a box of medication on the edge of it.

She couldn't read the label, but clicking some more she found a
close-up. The prescription was printed in the name of Zoe Swardadine, 7.5mg of zopiclone to be taken once daily.

"Have you seen this?" she asked Sheens, and brought the camera
over to him. "It's Zoe's, for zopiclone."

The DCI peered at the camera. "Yes," he said. "I was going to look it up."

She couldn't help blushing as she said, "It's a sleeping medication. I used to take it at university sometimes. I was a useless sleeper back then."

The DCI gave her a nod. "Is this a recent prescription?"

"A week ago," Hanson said, checking the date. "And she's unlikely to have been on it for long before that. It stops working if you keep taking it. They told me no more than four weeks."

Sheens nodded again. "Interesting."

There wasn't much else to see in the bathroom photographs. She could see Post-its and arrows where the forensics team had marked a series of fingerprints on the door handle, the edge of the bath, and the wall.

She drifted over to where McCullough and the DCI were crouched by the front door, looking at further prints. The fingerprints were scattered around the lock and the doorjamb, the tiny Post-its like colorful bunting.

Sheens stood upright and turned to Hanson. "It's a Yale lock."

"So either it was on the latch," Hanson replied, "or the killer had a key."

VICTOR DUMPED HIS bike in the small yard at the back of the coffeehouse, fed up with the grinding noise the pedals were making. It had been going on for weeks and was getting steadily worse. But it only ever occurred to him that he should get it fixed when he set out somewhere on it. And it was a piece of crap anyway. He was always on the verge of ditching it and getting a new one.

He let himself in by the staff door at the back, and nodded to tiny Mieke, who was shifting boxes in the cramped store cupboard.

"Hey, Victor. Could you hold this second?" she asked, and heaved a plastic-wrapped pallet of coffee beans into his arms. "I just need to . . ."

He stood and waited while she shifted several things.

"It's chaos in here," she said tetchily. "I didn't have time for chaos this morning."

"Was it crazy busy?" Victor asked her, shifting his grip on the coffee beans. The slippery surface made them hard to hold.

"It wasn't so much busy as me being on my own," Mieke said. "Didn't you hear from Luca? Zoe didn't show."

Victor felt suddenly very uncomfortable. His voice was hoarse as he asked, "Is she ill?"

"Not that she told us," his colleague answered, finally taking the packets of coffee from him and dumping them back onto a pile of boxes. "Just didn't come, and didn't answer her phone. I thought Luca was going to ask you to come in early."

"He didn't say anything," Victor said, and then cleared his throat. "I'll try and message Zoe. It's not like her."

"You think? I seem to remember her doing this quite a lot last year when she was with her new man and not really sleeping."

Mieke locked up the cupboard grumpily. Victor wanted to defend Zoe, but he'd hated that time, too. The whole idea of her being with someone made him . . . what? Angry? Hurt? Heartbroken?

All of those things, he thought as he swung his bag around in front of him and started pulling his phone out. *All of those things.*

It was a painfully bad class. Aidan knew that, but he couldn't make himself focus on it. Three or four times he found himself flicking through textbooks with no idea of what he was looking for or what he had meant to say. He'd looked up to find his students gazing at him with a range of expressions. Some looked worried about him. Others were clearly trying not to laugh.

"Sorry," he said in the end. "I've got a cracking headache. I'm open to anyone pushing the debate in a better direction."

The laughter broke out at that, and then Leena, who was one of his favorites, said sympathetically, "Do you want some Nurofen?"

"I'm OK . . ." he said, and then realized he sounded like those people he hated. The ones who complained that they had a headache but "didn't take painkillers." Which Aidan was happy for them to do, as long as they admitted it forfeited their right to complain. "Actually, that would be great," he corrected himself, not sure why he cared about how he came across. He waited while she rooted in her bag for them, and leaned over to pop two of them noisily out of their blister pack into his hand.

She gave him a small smile, and he nodded his thanks.

"OK," he said, once she'd sat down again. "Thoughts, then. Let's see who's doing better than I am today."

And then his phone was buzzing and he felt almost disembodied with anxiety as he pulled it out of his jacket pocket, trying not to drop the red capsules that he hadn't yet swallowed. The display had lit up with a mobile number he didn't recognize.

"Sorry, I need to take this," he told the class, who were watching him uncertainly. He answered and stood up all in one motion. "Hello?"

He was walking to the door as a male voice on the other end of the line said, "Is that Aidan Poole?"

"Yes," he said, walking through the door and closing it behind him, still feeling as though his legs and arms were floating in thick liquid.

"I'm DCI Jonah Sheens. I believe you reported witnessing violence toward your girlfriend, Zoe Swardadine."

He didn't know what to say for a moment. He didn't know whether he ought to deny it. But they'd called him. They knew who he was.

"Yes," he said. "I did. Is she . . . ?"

"I'm sorry to have to tell you that Zoe has died in suspicious circumstances," the voice told him levelly. "I know that must be distressing news."

"Yes," he said again, sounding like some sort of stupid echo, even to himself. "Yes, I . . ."

He couldn't think of anything else to say, but the police officer was talking. He was asking him to come to the station to talk to them.

"OK," he said. "I'm teaching until . . . I suppose I can be there for six, if . . ."

And he meant: *If I can face it.*

"Six will be fine," the officer said. "Thank you, Mr. Poole."

He was left listening to nothing except a wash of blood back and forth inside him. His gaze had fallen on the candy-red Nurofen, and he shoved them into his mouth and swallowed with a strange surge of belief that they might help him.

Then he moved slowly back into the room and sat in his chair in front of his students. It was hard to look at them. Hard to focus on anything, really.

"Right. I'm going to do what I should have done before and re-schedule for when I'm not such a useless git." There was laughter again, and he said, "I'll be in touch. Enjoy forty minutes of unex-pected freedom. Use it wisely."

Hal and a couple of the other more work-shy students in the group were gone within seconds and most of the rest of them fol-lowed. Leena packed her essay and notebook away more slowly, and said, "I hope you feel better."

"Thank you," Aidan replied, nodding at her. He couldn't bring himself to smile as he normally did at Leena. She usually went slightly pink when he did it, and he'd always found it heartening to know that he could have that effect on a pretty nineteen-year-old.

She left, and there was almost total silence for a minute in the seminar room. He listened to the retreating conversation of his stu-dents for a moment.

After that, he leaned over in his chair until his head almost touched his knees. And then he collapsed farther, his whole body tipping side-ways and sliding, sliding as he cried.

. . .

"So what's our game plan?" Hanson asked after Jonah had ended his call with Aidan Poole. They were all standing out there while the forensics team continued their work.

O'Malley put his own phone away, and Jonah wondered whether his sergeant had been looking something up or browsing the Internet out of boredom.

"I'd like you to call Zoe's friend Angeline, who has a key and let us into the flat. She may know of others who have keys, too, and I'd like a list of all Zoe's close friends from her. She's a little fragile, so . . ."

Hanson nodded. "I'll go carefully."

"And after that, CCTV cameras, if you wouldn't mind."

"Sure."

"Domnall, can you start doing background checks on the family and the boyfriend? Juliette, if you could pass on any contact details for Zoe's other friends that Angeline gives you, Domnall can go and see them, too."

"So we think the boyfriend who reported it might actually have done it?" O'Malley asked.

"Eighty percent of women," Hanson said meaningfully, pulling out her mobile to take down Angeline's number, which made Jonah smile. They'd talked about that particular finding the week before. The fact that four out of five murdered women were killed by a partner had hit the headlines, and the research had been a kind of validation of how they already approached murder inquiries. You always looked at the partner. Always.

"Statistically less likely if it turns out he was actually Skyping her from home at the time," O'Malley pointed out with a grin.

Jonah realized that they were all now thinking of this as a murder. Between Aidan Poole's report and the chemical smell, it seemed pretty much a given. But it still made Jonah feel uneasy. He had a hardwired hatred of jumping to any conclusions.

McCullough called over from the entrance to the flat. Jonah made his way back inside to her. "Nothing drastic, but I've got the case the knife came from. We've printed it, so I've taken a look inside and it's definitely the right one."

He followed her over to one of the boxes in the corner of the flat, which had the flap pushed back. Beneath it was the tin box of the Stanley knife. It lay open, the high-density foam showing the empty shape where the knife would have sat.

"Was it open when you found it?"

"No. It was all closed up and put back in the cardboard box," McCullough said.

"Pretty tidy," Jonah said.

"For a killer?" McCullough asked. "You mean if you wanted people to be positive she'd done it to herself, you'd want to leave the box out so it was clear it was hers?"

"Possibly," Jonah said, refusing to be drawn into any assumptions. It was McCullough's greatest joy to shoot down the brilliant theories of overconfident officers. "But it would be pretty tidy for a suicide, too. So it doesn't tell us much. It's just odd."

"People are, I find," McCullough answered. "Even the non-criminals."

ANGELINE PROVED TO be hard going. Hanson called her from the ground floor of the building, sitting on a window ledge with her notebook balanced on her lap. It was obvious that Angeline was already crying when she answered the phone.

"I only have a few things to ask," Hanson said soothingly. "My DCI tells me you have a key to Zoe's flat. Was that for a particular reason?"

"So I could feed her cat." And then Angeline had given a sobbing wail. "Oh God. What's happened to him? I didn't— The police might have let him out, and he could have . . . could have been run over, or . . ."

"I'll check on him," Hanson replied quickly. "It's OK. What's his name?"

"Monkfish," she said in a voice that shook. "He's a Persian."

"Is that . . . white?" queried Hanson, whose knowledge of cats was limited to stroking any that her friends happened to own.

"Yes," Angeline said. "Like . . . like Blofeld's cat, Zoe said."

"Thank you," Hanson said, and wrote that down, too, for no good reason. "Did anyone else have a key?"

"No," Angeline said. "I don't . . . Oh, well, maybe Felix."

"Felix?" Hanson thought for a moment of another cat.

"He's the landlord."

"Ah, right. Do you have his address?"

"He lives downstairs."

"The floor below Zoe's?" Hanson asked, thinking that that was a pretty unusual setup.

"Yes," Angeline said. "I don't know what number but . . . if you turn right onto the first-floor landing, it's the first one on the left."

"That's really useful, thank you," Hanson said in the kind of voice she would have used to talk to a child. "Did she have any other close friends?"

"Yes. Maeve. She used to live with her. And Victor. From the coffee shop."

"The coffee shop. Did she work there?"

"Yeah," Angeline said, and her voice broke again. "She should have been there this morning."

"I'm sorry" was all Hanson could say before asking for their contact numbers, which Angeline gave over readily enough, though Hanson could hear that she was still barely holding it together.

"Oh," Angeline said suddenly. "I'm not sure that's Victor's newest number. He changed it and . . . I always forget to save them."

"I'll try it," Hanson told her. "Don't worry. One last question, and then you can be left in peace for a while. When did you last see Zoe, and how did she seem?" Which was obviously two questions, but Angeline seemed not to notice.

"Yesterday morning," she said. "I keep thinking . . . I got upset with her. I was only there to model, and she . . . she hurt my feelings, and the more I think back over it, the more I think it was just me . . . being stupid."

"How so?" Hanson asked. For once the words were coming out quite quickly, and she wondered if Angeline had been waiting to make this small confession.

"She said it was my . . . my brokenness that she liked about me. When I sat for her drawings and paintings. And it hurt. I thought she was going to tell me I was beautiful."

"Was that . . . unusual behavior for Zoe? To say something a little harsh?"

There was a pause, and Angeline said, "Yes. Well . . . I don't know. Maybe not recently."

"You think she'd changed recently?" Another pause. "Become angrier? Less kind?"

"I suppose so. I don't know. She just retreated into herself a bit, you know?"

"Was there any obvious reason?"

There was another pause, and then Angeline said shakily, "That relationship really damaged her. I mean, he did nice things, but he also made her feel bad about herself."

"Was he . . . abusive in any way?"

"No, no," Angeline said hastily. "I'm not saying it was that. Just . . . sometimes people aren't good for each other."

O'MALLEY LET THE chief dwell on things in the car. He'd learned long ago not to interrupt the DCI when he was thinking things through. It suited O'Malley, too, who liked to let impressions settle in silence.

Sheens headed straight to his office once they were back at CID. Lightman had left, presumably to do whatever it was he'd had planned for the evening, and there weren't a lot of other detectives there at almost five on a Friday. It was the sort of quiet environment conducive either to good concentration or to a soporific wind-down.

O'Malley woke his desktop and logged in to the database. He started looking for previous convictions for all the names they had so far, beginning with Zoe's parents. There was nothing related to them, or to any other spellings of the name that O'Malley could think of, so he moved on to Aidan Poole, who also had a clean slate.

To O'Malley's momentary excitement, Angeline Judd actually did appear in the system. But on checking, it turned out to be a caution for cannabis possession at the age of fifteen. She'd been picked up with a group of friends, and nothing much had come of it. He made a note, but overall wasn't inclined to link that episode with their current case.

With no further results, he decided to try Google. Angeline had a minimal online presence outside social media, where she seemed to be moderately active on Twitter. Most of her posts, however, were about feeling sad and betrayed. The rest generally featured kittens. Not particularly promising when it came to guessing whether she had murderous intent. Though when he clicked on a few of the more morbid ones from a few months ago, he saw that Zoe Swardadine had been one of the few people to reply to her. The essential message was always the same: *Hang on in there. Be strong. You are loved. It's all going to be OK.*

But as the months wore on, Zoe's replies had become sporadic. O'Malley could hardly blame her. He was pretty sure he'd be fed up with the very public emoting in no time.

Aidan Poole had a much more extensive online presence. The top entry was a Southampton University staff web page. O'Malley opened it, and was confronted with a somewhat moody image of a dark-haired man taken from above and to the side. It was an arty shot, and made Poole look sulkily handsome, to the point where O'Malley couldn't help laughing to himself. What the photo didn't do so well was convey an air of professionalism, but perhaps it hadn't been his choice of shot.

O'Malley read the brief bio, realizing that Aidan Poole's undergraduate degree had come from Warwick, which was where Hanson had gone. They were a good fifteen years apart, though, so that was unlikely to be a useful link.

There wasn't much else of interest on the page, so he clicked back and tried the Royal Economic Society listing. Aidan's photograph was that same sulky one. So Aidan probably had chosen it. There was a certain vanity to it that he found both interesting and amusing.

Having found little else beyond a series of publications, O'Malley rang the numbers he had for Victor Varos and Maeve Silver. There was no reply from either of them, but Hanson had sent an email including details of Victor's work at Gina's coffee shop, which was back toward Zoe's flat. Victor should, it seemed, be on his shift now.

With a sigh, O'Malley rose again to gather his coat and keys. He tapped on the DCI's door on the way out.

"Off to see if I can track down one of the friends," he said. "Do you want me to call the university on the way to break the news?"

"I tried a few minutes ago," Sheens answered, shaking his head. "I got a secretary who wouldn't budge on the chancellor being busy all day."

"I wonder what it would take to make him not busy," O'Malley said, considering. "If you like, I could call and say someone's broken into his house."

Sheens laughed. "If I don't get a call back, you're on."

CAFÉ GINA LOOKED expensive from the outside. It was well lit, with a series of stylish bare-bulb lamps hanging down from a ceiling that was crisscrossed by obvious pipework. It hung so low that he was positive it must have been added in for effect. There was a large handwritten blackboard out at the front that read *Coffee, like life, is for savor-*

ing in artistic writing. He had a funny thought that Zoe might have been the one to write it, if she worked here.

O'Malley let himself into the warm, bright interior. It looked expensive from inside, too. They had what he thought of as deliberately uneven tables, the kind that looked like they'd been individually carved out of pieces of oak by someone determined for you to know that they'd done it by hand. There was a wide blackboard behind the counter with decorated lists of food and drink, and he could see a coffee for almost a fiver.

At the moment there was only one person behind the counter: a short, stocky young man with an air of slight amusement.

O'Malley approached him and gave him a small smile. "I'm looking for Victor."

"Oh, he's . . ." The barista waved toward the rear of the counter, but at that point a tall, lean man with very dark hair and intensely blue eyes emerged from a door to the rear of the coffeehouse.

"Victor," O'Malley said. "I wondered if I could have a quick word. I'm from the police."

Victor froze in place, and then there was movement behind him, and suddenly a young woman's Northern Irish voice cut through the moment of silence.

"Is it about Zoe? What's happened?"

He had to turn to see her. She'd come to a stop a short distance from him. Her face was absolutely white except for two smudges of red color on the cheeks.

"Are you a friend?"

"Yes. I'm . . . I used to be her housemate. I'm Maeve."

O'Malley gave a nod. "Ah. I tried to call you earlier."

"My phone was . . ." She indicated a table by the wall, where an iPhone was connected to the power by a tangled white cable. "What's happened? There were police cars."

O'Malley gave her a smile that he only ever used when breaking bad news, and then turned toward Victor. "Is there a back room we can all talk in?"

If Maeve had looked frightened, Victor looked worse. His face wore the expression, in fact, of a man whose world has just crumbled in front of him.

6

April—nineteen months before

Zoe had felt periodic rushes of excitement every day since Gina's wedding. They had hit her at random intervals, while painting, while cycling, while at lectures, while talking to friends. She'd found it almost impossible not to smile every time she remembered something Aidan had messaged her, or his expression at the bar when he had finally said goodbye, in the long seconds before he had leaned in and kissed her.

God, that kiss. It had been electrifying. Muscle-weakening. It had been everything that kisses should be.

It was such a long time since she'd felt like this. Every other relationship she could remember had started with intense conversations about the saddest times in their lives. None of them had begun with this constant urge to laugh.

With infuriating timing, Aidan had been away for the last week and a half. She'd had to make do with messages and occasional Skype chats until this week. But now it was Thursday at last, and they were meeting tonight, and she was so keyed up it felt like she was about to win some kind of award.

Aidan already had a hotel booked so he wouldn't have to commute home to "the wilds of Alton." The idea of that hotel room had crept into her thoughts a few times. Which wasn't the way things usually ran with her. It generally took her time to get to know some-one. To feel like spending the night together was a natural next step. But Aidan . . . Aidan made her feel like someone else entirely. Like someone impulsive, who was willing to risk everything on a whim.

She was thinking vividly of that kiss again as she let herself into the house. She felt wrong-footed as she walked through into the living area and found Maeve there, moving up and down the kitchen with jerky steps, whiter than Zoe had ever seen her and with clear marks of tears down her face.

"Hey," Zoe said, dumping her bag down on one of the armchairs. "Are you all right? What's going on?"

"I'm . . . The bastards at church have . . . they've been spreading lies about me," she said before her face contorted and she turned away to hide the fact that she was crying.

"What?" Zoe went over to her and hovered, wondering whether to try to hug her. She knew Maeve hated it under normal circum-stances, and that she might hate it even more when she was genu-inely upset. Zoe settled for a brief rub of her shoulder. "Hey, if they're lying, then we can do something. They can't just do that."

"They've already spread it everywhere!" Maeve said, turning around and looking upward in an effort to control the tears. "There was this . . . this horrible atmosphere, and I knew something . . . was up. And then Alison . . . Alison told me that Isaac's wife had said something . . ."

Zoe was too shocked to answer for a moment. "What . . . But you've never met her! How can she complain about you?"

Maeve shook her head and wiped her eyes on her sleeve. "I don't know."

"Did she see some messages?" Zoe asked. Her stomach squeezed. Maeve had poured her heart out in her messages. She'd shown Zoe a few of them. If Isaac's wife had found out . . . Well, they'd both look bad, but somehow the cheat never ended up in trouble. It was always the other woman who was condemned, in Zoe's experience.

Not that it had been full-on cheating. Maeve didn't believe in sex before marriage, and the two of them had never done more than kiss. Which had only been twice, and which Isaac had then said he felt wretched about.

Zoe wasn't sure she believed him, however profoundly Maeve did. He was not only a married man but also the pastor of their church. Faith Leader Isaac. He should never have involved himself with a student. And he definitely shouldn't have strung her along, telling her he was going to leave his wife and children to be with her, but never quite doing it.

Zoe had been overwhelmed with frustration about the whole thing. She had come to the conclusion, after listening to hours of Maeve's defenses of him, that Isaac was an asshole. And even if he was marginally better than Zoe thought and he meant what he said about leaving his wife, she wished Maeve could have more willpower. This was a family she was thinking of wrecking. There were kids. It was all so wrong.

And then it had all gotten better. Maeve had reached breaking point, and told him she'd had enough. She'd promised Zoe that it was over. She'd gone on dates and talked about other things. She'd seemed better. Why was this happening now? Was it just unfair timing?

"What has she been saying?" Zoe asked.

Maeve shook her head again, and then reached out and grabbed two pieces of paper towel from the dispenser and blew her nose into it. "I'm sorry. I'm so . . . so pathetic . . ."

"Don't be silly!" Zoe said. "You have to cry sometimes. You can't be positive when life throws shit at you."

"But I always am," Maeve said with what was almost a small child's wail. "Even after he invited me for a stupid coffee, and then told me he couldn't stop thinking about me. I was strong about it. And then . . . and then she starts telling everyone I'm some kind of seductress."

"Oh, Maeve," she said. "Didn't he admit that it was his fault?" She didn't really need to ask the question.

"I don't know," Maeve said. "He won't answer my calls."

Zoe winced. Maeve ringing him repeatedly was only going to make her seem obsessed. "Look," she said, "if he . . . if he told her it was just you, and protected himself at your expense, then that's shit of him. It's understandable, but it's still shit. Please don't blame everyone else at church and not him."

"I'm not," Maeve said. "I'm not. But he didn't tell them. It was her. . . ."

And Zoe had the familiar sinking of her heart when, once again, Maeve slid into blaming Isaac's wife for everything. A woman who had only ever been wronged.

She looked past Maeve and realized that it was a lot later than she'd thought. She had only half an hour to get ready before she needed to be out the door if she was going to meet Aidan on time. Given that she needed to shower and then dry her hair, that would be pushing it even if she hadn't stopped to talk to Maeve. But she couldn't just walk away from her now.

"Let me make tea," she said firmly, "and we'll talk about what we can do to stop the gossip."

And then, as she went to put the kettle on, she messaged Aidan.

Slight crisis here with Maeve. Would you mind if we made it half an hour later? I'm really sorry. Not a normal situation. Will explain. xx

She was tipping milk into the tea by the time Aidan replied.

I'm positive this is just a ruse to make me wait, but I'll do it. You're worth it. xx PS don't talk yourself dry. I want to hear everything about everything to do with you.

Zoe smiled, more out of relief than anything else, and went to force-feed Maeve tea.

. . .

SHE WAS STILL a few minutes late, even for the later meet time. She'd wanted to look spectacular, but not the same kind of spectacular as at the wedding, so she'd got a black dress and a slouchy sweater that had turned out to have a mark on it that needed scrubbing. The eye makeup she'd decided on was a blend of ice white and hot pink, and wasn't the easiest to apply.

She'd eventually rushed out of the house five minutes before she was supposed to be at Brown's, with a twelve-minute cycle ahead of her. On her way out the door, she'd waved to Maeve, who was curled on the sofa watching *Breakfast at Tiffany's* and looking considerably less distraught. Zoe hauled her bike out from the side passage and pedaled like the wind, turning her lights on as she went.

Aidan was seated at a table near the bar, his eyes on the menu, when she rushed in. He was easy to spot in profile, with his dark curls falling onto his forehead and his sculptured lips set into what looked like slight amusement. God, he was beautiful. Just beautiful. She felt a squeeze of nerves.

He glanced up at her and smiled warmly. Dangerously. "Definitely worth it," he said, and rose to kiss her, a brief touch of his lips on hers that cut through the nerves and seemed to hit a point right in the middle of her abdomen.

"I ordered us gin," he said as he drew away. "Unfortunately I've picked somewhere that doesn't seem to do Jäger Bombs."

Zoe grinned and unhooked her bag from her shoulder so she could sit down. "You fail. But I'm sure we can move on somewhere else later."

"This sounds like one of those evenings where I'm mysteriously ill the next day, and miss classes," he said.

"Classes?" she asked, leaning forward to rest her elbows on her knees. "Are you a mature student?"

Aidan shook his head. "Worse. I'm an immature lecturer."

Zoe gave a little laugh of shock. "Oh no! That's, like . . . worse than being a politician. You're one of *them*."

"Right," he said, snatching up her gin and tonic with one of those wicked grins, "I'm having that back."

"No, don't! I need it!" She held out her hand, laughing, but he moved the glass away.

"I'm not buying drinks for people who compare me to politicians," he said.

"All right, all right," Zoe said. "You're not as bad as a politician. Unless you're a lecturer in politics, in which case . . ."

"Not quite," he said, shaking his head. "Economics. Am I allowed?"

"Ooh, proper clever, like," she said, and then grinned. "Yeah, you're allowed."

With her drink returned to her, she asked him a little more seriously, "But you don't mind? You know, dating a student?"

"I'm not teaching you, am I?" he asked with a shrug. "And it's not like you're some fresh-faced eighteen-year-old. You're . . . twenty-six, you said, right? You're practically elderly."

"Right. I'm not talking to you," she said.

"Yes, you are," he replied. "At length. You promised."

By the time they were seated at their table, he'd already got the full story of Maeve out of Zoe, and an expanded version of Victor's strange attitude. And she couldn't help liking the way he listened thoughtfully and asked further questions, then made gentle suggestions. He made her feel like all of this was his problem now, too.

After that, she ended up telling him about her dad, and the alcoholism he was hiding from her mother, and all the times she'd ended up having to go to his rescue.

"Isn't it unfair that he leans on you?" Aidan asked gently in the end. "You're supposed to be the daughter. I can't help feeling he should be looking after you."

Zoe shrugged, giving him a small, embarrassed smile. "I don't need looking after."

There was something delicious in the way Aidan nodded slowly, and said, "We'll see about that."

She eventually grilled him on his own life, and the mother for whom nothing had ever been quite good enough; the girlfriends he'd chosen because they reminded him of her; his mother's death and his complex grief over it.

"Do you think I'm like her?" Zoe asked.

"No," Aidan said with a bright-eyed grin. "You're nothing like her. And I think I might finally have got past all the trauma and chosen someone who is actually good for me."

It should have been embarrassing, but it wasn't. It made her feel warm and a little dizzy.

It seemed inevitable that they should go from the restaurant to Aidan's hotel room. That they should unwrap each other slowly, and then move into each other.

In the moments afterward, he murmured, "God, you're wonderful," and for some reason there were tears standing in his eyes and hers.

7

"I'm assuming you're from the police?"

Felix was poised in the doorway. Hanson took in the pale-gray suit and open shirt. The immaculately groomed hair and trimmed beard. He looked as though he'd either just got back from work or got dressed for an upmarket evening out.

Hanson gave him a smile. "How did you know?"

"It's just your manner," Felix said, and then grinned. "And maybe the squad cars and vans outside. My kitchen window looks out onto the road."

As Hanson opened her mouth to suggest that they talk inside, he said, "You look like you have something sensitive to ask. You're welcome to come in. If I'm going to shop my neighbors, I'd rather do it in private."

He stood back to let her into the flat. The layout was the inverse of Zoe's, Hanson saw. It was probably the exact same size, but thanks to being fully furnished, it seemed smaller. A big sofa sat in the middle of the room and a huge square bookshelf dominated one wall, full of neatly marshaled paperbacks, with hardbacks below. There were a few pictures, too. Some seascapes and a few certificates in frames on two walls, plus a couple of smaller pictures standing on a high bookshelf. And Felix had a huge plasma screen on a unit with DVDs lined up neatly beneath it.

Where Zoe's flat had had surface mess, however, Felix's had none.

The place was spotless, and the cloths that hung over the sink and on the oven-door handle were utterly straight. They looked as if they might have been ironed.

"Here," he said, pulling a kitchen chair over toward the sofa. "You take the sofa."

"Thank you." Hanson sat herself down carefully. "I believe you're Zoe Swardadine's landlord. Is that right?"

There was a pause, while Felix stalled in the act of sitting. And then he continued to sit smoothly, as if nothing had happened.

"Yes," Felix said. "Is this . . . is she all right?"

"I'm afraid Zoe has been found dead," Hanson said. "I'm so sorry to have to give you the news."

"Are you . . . are you serious?" There was a look in the man's eyes that was almost hunted. "I only spoke to her yesterday."

"We were called in by a friend who was worried about her," Hanson said, choosing her words with care. "And on entering her flat, we found her dead."

"Jesus," Felix said, and then, again, "Jesus." He stood and put a hand on the counter. "Did she . . . did she do it to herself?"

Which Hanson thought was a strange question. "I'm afraid it's too early to tell," she said. "Did you have any reason to think that she was suicidal?"

"No, of course not," Felix said, and then added, "I would have . . . I would have done something . . ."

There was a silence, and Hanson got the impression he was deeply immersed in some kind of memory.

"I think you have a key for her flat?" she said eventually.

"Yes, of course. I need to be able to get in and fix things. Or let workmen in." Hanson wondered at the defensive tone. Felix was looking toward the door now, where a row of hooks had been installed on the wall. "Do you need it . . . ? I could dig it out. But I do only have the one . . ."

"I'll check with the chief," Hanson replied. "It'd probably be worth having it to hand. You said you spoke to her yesterday. Could you tell us when?"

"In the afternoon," he said quickly. "Just a quick phone call."

Hanson smiled. "Do you talk to your tenants often?"

"Oh, no. I only have one flat that I let out, and Zoe was a friend rather than just a tenant. I knew her from the coffee shop before she moved in. God." He seemed to lose strength suddenly. His arms sagged down by his sides.

"How was she when you spoke?" Hanson asked.

Felix shrugged. "It's hard to say. Busy, I suppose. She didn't seem to have as much time as usual."

"And you didn't see her after that conversation?" Hanson pressed.

"Well . . . I suppose I saw her. I saw her coming back home."

"Saw her . . . ?"

"Down there," he said, nodding through the kitchen window, which gave a view over the road. Hanson rose to check, wondering whether the door itself would be visible. Standing to the far right, she could only see the pavement that must have been outside the door, but it would be easy to keep track of anyone coming and going.

"What time was that?" she asked him.

"I'd say eightish, maybe eight-thirty." He gave another shrug. "It was dark. I don't think I checked the time, but it had been dark awhile."

Hanson pulled her pen out of her notebook and wrote that down, and then slid them both back into her jacket pocket.

"Thank you," she said. "That's really helpful. The chief would like you to come into the station to give a full statement. Probably this evening, but we'll let you know. Will that be OK? Do you have . . . work?"

There was a brief pause, and then Felix said, "No. No, that's fine. I can free myself up."

He showed Hanson to the door, and she left thoughtfully. Halfway down the stairs, she stopped and sent a quick summary of the chat to the chief in a text message, and then headed out to start looking for CCTV cameras.

O'MALLEY RETURNED TO the station before Aidan Poole or Zoe's parents had made it, and gave Jonah a rundown of his brief chat with Victor Varos and Maeve Silver at the coffeehouse.

"There's a lot of emotion there," he said in summary. "Particularly Victor. I'd say he held a candle for Zoe. We're going to want to talk to both of them properly."

Jonah had agreed, and asked him to sort it. And then he'd started rereading the transcript of Aidan's first call, comparing it to the crime report that had been logged earlier. The blindingly obvious question was why Aidan had called the police instead of going to check on Zoe himself. More than twelve hours had passed between the two calls, and Aidan Poole had apparently known no more about his girlfriend's well-being at the end of that time than he had at the start.

Several possible explanations had occurred to Jonah. The first was that Aidan and Zoe had argued about something, and she was deliberately not answering his calls or visits. Such an argument would have been another reason for him to worry about her, of course. This theory presupposed that the apparent witnessing of a murder had been pure fabrication to force the police to check on her.

His second thought was that Aidan knew full well that Zoe was dead, because he'd killed her. Thinking he would look suspicious if he were the one to find her, and wanting to cast suspicion in another direction, he had reported it in the hope that the police would charge in there, and had then tried again when nothing seemed to have happened.

The third thing that occurred to him was a lot simpler, and chimed in with the way Aidan had written "Southampton" under the location of the crime. This third theory was that Aidan hadn't gone round there because he didn't actually know Zoe's address. And although it was the simplest option, it might raise just as many questions as the other two. If Zoe had been there for five or six months, how had he not known where she lived?

AIDAN EVENTUALLY ARRIVED before Zoe's parents, which was a relief. There were a lot of questions Jonah wanted answers to before he started talking to Mr. and Mrs. Swardadine.

Dr. Aidan Poole was, in person, a great deal less suave than he'd been in his photo, though Jonah was prepared to accept that a large portion of that might be circumstantial. The jacket and jeans were tidy enough, but his skin looked sheeny, and what should have been a reasonably healthy tan seemed sickly. The glassy, bloodshot eyes did him no favors, either. Touches of grief, all of them, that had scuffed and smudged the perfect portrait until it looked tatty and unappealing.

"I should have given my name when I called," the lecturer said, the moment the tape was running. "I'm so sorry. Did it . . . did the delay make a difference?"

Jonah glanced up from the pages of the transcript that he'd taken in with him. "It's hard to say," he said neutrally. "It might have made some difference."

Aidan's jaw twisted, and he looked away as he nodded.

"So Zoe was your girlfriend?" Jonah said when Aidan failed to say anything more. When the lecturer nodded, he went on, "I need you to take me through what you saw. As clearly as you can."

"Yes," Aidan said. His jaw muscles stood out, and Jonah could almost feel his teeth grinding together. The tension.

Aidan went through what he'd already reported, his voice shifting pitch frequently with apparent stress. The Skype call. The sudden intruder he'd never seen. The sounds of a struggle.

From Jonah's perspective, it didn't sound rehearsed. There were frequent pauses while Aidan considered his words. And, in fact, those were what interested him the most.

"So you called the police?"

"Yes." He gave Jonah a slightly desperate look. "I didn't do a very good job of telling them what to do and I . . . I really regret that."

He tailed off and Jonah watched him carefully, assessing. And then he said, "You know this is a murder investigation now. So other things are less important than they would be."

Aidan sat back, instinctively moving away from him.

"I need you to tell me what you're hiding," Jonah continued.

Aidan shook his head. "She's . . . a student." He grimaced. "I'm a lecturer. We kept the relationship secret because it shouldn't have been happening. There's no question that the university would take a poor view, and if something's happened to her, and I'm implicated . . ."

Jonah gave him a long, steady look. Aidan returned it for a moment, and then looked away again.

"Do you have any reason to think that anyone wanted to harm Zoe?" Jonah asked quietly.

"I don't," he said. "But I keep wondering if she had met someone, you know? If there was someone else, and that's why she wasn't available earlier . . . Maybe she was going to tell me that night. Could they have killed her? If there was someone else? Someone she'd given a key to?"

"She never said anything that implied that?"

Aidan shook his head. But then he added hesitantly, "But there were people who were, you know . . . interested. One in particular. Her friend Victor, who worked at the coffee shop with her."

"What makes you think he liked her?"

"It was pretty obvious," Aidan said with a touch more strength. "The day he realized we were dating, he tried to square off against me, and then he wrecked my laptop. He should have been bloody fired. He wouldn't socialize with the two of us for months after he knew, and he clearly hated me."

Jonah looked at Aidan thoughtfully, and asked, "Do you happen to know Zoe's address?"

He saw a slight heat appear in Aidan's cheeks.

"Not her new one, no," he said.

"When did she move in there?"

"I . . . A few months ago?"

Jonah simply looked back at him, and Aidan's gaze slid away.

"I know it's a bit weird. When we had a break a while ago, she moved away, wanting a new start. But then when we started things off again, we did what we'd done right at the start. We had dates, and they always ended up back in my hotel . . ." He closed his eyes briefly. "Which makes it sound . . . it makes it sound awful. But it wasn't. It was . . . wonderful."

The glowing glimmer in his eyes started to spill over, and Aidan rubbed at them with an embarrassed anger. Jonah decided to call it a day. He had the strong sense that Aidan Poole was holding back a great deal, but he was also aware of how attacking a witness who was clearly grieving would sound on the tapes. How everything Aidan said might be needed if this came to trial.

"That's all I want to ask for now," he said. "I'll need you to have prints taken, though. Let me see if someone's available."

"Why?" he asked, and Jonah could see instant tension running through him. "You know it wasn't me."

"We need to rule yours out," Jonah said. "Even if you hadn't been to the flat, you will have touched possessions belonging to Zoe."

"Oh," Aidan said. "Of course. Sorry."

Jonah rose. "I'll take you downstairs."

HANSON'S HUNT FOR security cameras had produced two potential results. The flat block had a camera in the rear car park that pointed toward the gates. It showed the road through the archway under the building. The door to most of the flats was next to the archway, so there was a good chance of snapping anyone coming and going from the direction of town.

Down at the bottom of Latterworth Road, toward town, there was also a CCTV camera positioned on a lamppost. It should catch anyone walking up the road from the city center. Unfortunately the other end of the road had no coverage at all, so with both of the cameras, they were only going to catch people who had come from the south side.

It had, naturally, rained throughout her reconnaissance. With only a jacket and scarf, she was soaked through by the time she made it back to her car. She climbed in and cranked up the heat, so she was at least halfway to dry by the time she got back to the station.

DI Walker, one of the detectives who covered East Hampshire, grinned at her sympathetically as she walked in. "Did you get sent door-knocking?"

"Close," she said. "CCTV hunt."

"It's worth keeping a coat and waterproof trousers in your car," he said quietly. "They look shit, but . . ." He shrugged. "It's better than spending the whole day freezing your arse off."

"That's a good tip," Hanson said. She didn't go on to say that she'd had waterproofs in the car for weeks, packed into the overnight bag she used to drive around with. It had been there because she'd needed to know she could escape from the abusive boyfriend she'd been living with. Finally being free of him and feeling she could take it out of the car had been a very good step psychologically. It was unfortunate that it had also been a bad move practically speaking.

She booted her desktop and went through the crime-scene photos once again. At one of the kitchen photographs, which showed two bowls on the floor, she paused. She'd forgotten about the cat.

She was readying herself to tell the DCI about it when she saw him emerge from an interview room with a dark-haired, slightly pouty-looking man who was probably somewhere in his late thirties. Underneath a haggard expression, he was a good-looking guy, she thought. Sulky and artistic, as she'd always imagined Byron must have looked.

She realized that this must be the boyfriend. The one who had apparently witnessed his girlfriend's death online. She watched him intently from behind her screen as he drifted toward the door, trying to tell whether the grief was real, whether he'd been telling the truth. It was a pretty hard one to call.

JONAH LET AIDAN into the lift instead of walking him down the stairs, an instinctive note of care for him. The lecturer seemed to be drifting apart while Jonah watched, his eyes off somewhere in the distance and a hopeless sag to his shoulders.

Aidan's expression remained unfocused until the lift doors opened, and then a sudden jolt ran through his whole body.

"Oh God," he said very quietly.

He had just as much of an impact on the couple standing outside. It took Jonah no time at all to recognize Martin Swardadine and to guess that the attractive, beautifully groomed black woman beside him was his wife. The look they were giving Aidan was nothing short of horrified.

Jonah gave a small sigh. He wouldn't have chosen to have Aidan Poole meet Zoe's parents at this point. Though he couldn't deny that the strength of each reaction was interesting.

Jonah walked ahead of Aidan and held his hand out to each of the Swardadines in turn.

"I'm DCI Sheens. I'm so sorry. I just need to show Mr. Poole out."

Zoe's mother gave a rapid nod, her eyes sliding immediately to Aidan. It wasn't a friendly look.

Jonah decided, as he walked Aidan to the door, that he would find a tactful way of asking what that look meant in the privacy of the relatives' room, but he didn't have to wait that long. The moment he'd returned to the couple, Zoe's mother said in a low, urgent voice, "What's he doing here?"

Deciding that the reception area wasn't the right place for this, he said carefully, "Mr. Poole was the one who reported that she'd been attacked."

Zoe's mother gave her husband a strange look. It was full of anger and hurt.

"Let's talk upstairs," Jonah said in as soothing a tone as he could.

8

April—nineteen months before

Zoe was full of a sense of well-being, and it only increased during lunch with Aidan at the Mercure. They'd agreed to eat at the hotel, and it had been a move that would unquestionably end in sex. Aidan didn't have any seminars until four, and Zoe was already thinking about heading upstairs with him as they started eating tagliatelle. She'd been daydreaming about their night together the week before. She had blazed with frustration for the six days he'd been away again, and the feeling had mounted into an uncharacteristic impatience to get him back to the room.

The wine didn't help. She wasn't sure why she'd asked for a second glass of rosé, except perhaps that being around him made her feel like doing all the wrong things, over and over.

They were close to finishing when Zoe's phone rang.

"Angeline," she said briefly, and tried to keep her smile in place.

"You're not thinking of answering, are you?" he asked with slightly narrowed eyes.

"I—I don't . . ." She made a frustrated noise. "She's not very well and I don't think she's getting the help she needs. She does stupid things. Well . . ." Zoe sighed. "She drinks, and sometimes she cuts herself. Not stupid, I guess, if you're desperate."

The phone was still buzzing. Angeline wasn't giving up.

"Is it always you she calls?" he asked, giving her a very steady gaze.

"I—I think so," she said.

"Do you think that's quite fair on you?"

Aidan put the question so mildly that it didn't make her feel under attack. It did something else. It made her wonder fleetingly whether it actually was fair. But then the memory of Angeline's limp body, looking like a heap of debris on her bedroom floor, struck her. That had been the result last time Zoe hadn't been there. There had been nobody else to help.

The phone stopped finally, and Zoe looked at it wretchedly. When she didn't reply, Aidan reached out and squeezed her hand. "Sorry. I'm not saying you shouldn't help her. Of course you should. I just want to make sure you don't drain yourself dry. Maybe you need looking after, too, sometimes."

He rubbed his thumb along hers, and then, turning her wrist, he slid it along the underneath, where her skin was at its palest and most sensitive. She felt a response deep within herself, and checking up on Angeline seemed less urgent.

"Let's ask for the bill," Aidan said intently, and when Zoe nodded, he gave a wry smile. "And I'd better go for a pee, because there's only so much wine I can take."

"Such an old man," Zoe muttered.

He laughed and stood.

Zoe took her card over to the waiter, full of thoughts of the hotel room and that kiss.

"Can I pay?"

The waiter looked flustered as he went to find a card machine. He'd clearly expected them to stay longer. But then she was handing him her card without checking the amount, and keying in her PIN.

Aidan returned as she was putting her card back in her purse.

"Wait, you're not allowed to pay for all of that," he said.

"Why not?" Zoe asked with a lift of her chin.

"Because it was extravagant. And I had more wine than you did," he said. "And you paid for your share last time. Look, let me transfer you half." He pulled out his phone. "If you decide you like me enough to want to see me again, you can treat me to your heart's content, but I'd feel bad about you doing it now."

Zoe gave an exaggerated sigh. "All right. Just half. Which is . . . about forty-two." She took her card out again and let him read her account details off it.

"Check I've done it right," he said as she put it away. Zoe rolled her eyes, but logged in to her banking anyway.

"Yup, done," she said. And then her eyes moved across the line and stopped on the name of the account holder. *Mr. & Mrs. A. Poole.*

It took her a second to get her head around it, and when she did, a horrible, cold feeling spread across her chest.

"You're married," she said in a flat, hard voice. And then she looked up at him and saw his expression. It was like an animal in headlights, and she knew it was true. "Mr. and Mrs. A. Poole."

He looked down at his phone, and said, "Oh . . . the joint account thing . . ." And for a moment, he seemed lost. Glib, charming, fascinating Aidan, struck dumb.

After a moment, he sighed, and looked up at her. "I am," he said firmly, holding her gaze. "But not like you think. I'm married on a technicality, because I'm not going to screw her over by divorcing her a few months before my mum's inheritance comes." He stood up straighter, his posture open. Honest. "It's not a marriage; it's a bloody farce. We live in the same house, and we don't have a clue who the other person is anymore. I think she would have left me by now if she hadn't felt a little sorry for me, underneath it all."

"For fuck's sake," Zoe said. She looked away from him because she wanted to push him over. And also for it not to be true.

"Zoe," he said, reaching for her hand, but she snatched it back and shook her head again, so he said it again more urgently. "Zoe. I'm not trying to trick you. I've been trying to get up the guts to tell

you since I met you. I felt like you'd run away, all because of a marriage that hasn't meant anything for a very long time."

"Yeah, I'd have run away," she said, and moved past him. "I'm running away now."

"Please don't," he said, and then, in a low, earnest voice, "We'd
both regret it."

Zoe shook her head, that awful coldness spreading further and
further through her. She kept walking.

"You wouldn't go if you knew how unhappy Greta and I both
were," he said behind her. "I know I should have ended it before looking elsewhere, but sometimes that's not how people are. And she's
not . . . She doesn't deserve to be swindled out of half of that money,"
he said. "She cared for my mum for the whole of her illness, like I
did."

Zoe hesitated at the door to the restaurant. She could feel her
heart thumping in her chest. God, she wanted that to be true. But
what if he was no better than Isaac, who'd lied to Maeve for months?
She said, without turning, "Don't try to call me."

She managed to keep from crying until after she'd left the hotel,
and then it was the kind of crying that feels like your insides are being
wrenched out through your mouth. She needed to leave, but the
world suddenly seemed empty of places that meant anything.

9

In spite of her unfinished work with the blackmail case, Hanson was half hoping that she'd be brought in to talk to Zoe's parents. Having sent off the CCTV requests, she found herself thinking about the flat; the girl; the blood. The money trail she'd been following suddenly seemed trivial.

Talking to two grieving parents was unlikely to be fun, but at the same time Hanson felt that she wanted to be part of it. She'd seen Zoe's body, and felt some small echo of the loss her parents must be feeling. She wanted to be there, showing them that they would all do everything they could to find out what had happened.

On top of that, she wanted to see how the DCI handled it. There was always something to learn. Despite an inward certainty that she was good at interviews, she could see the difference. Sheens was in a league of his own.

She'd been asked more than once by other Hampshire officers why Sheens did so much grunt work, and made excuses to miss so many meetings and events where there were opportunities for promotion. Most coppers were understandably looking to rise through the ranks. There were very few who clung to a DS or DI title, because the pay went up so steeply with promotion. And a superintendent's role, the next big step up, came with a serious salary.

It had been hard to explain exactly why Sheens was so hands-on, particularly with interviews. She'd always said that he was good at it, which he was. But that didn't go nearly far enough. It was as if a hugely important part of him only existed when he had a subject to dissect and manipulate.

Sheens left Zoe's parents in the relatives' room and came to ask Hanson to come along, nodding at O'Malley but not extending the invitation to him.

"Great," Hanson said with a smile. "I'm ready when you are. I've sent off the CCTV requests already, and the only other thing I was thinking was that I should head to Zoe's flat tomorrow morning and see if I can find her cat."

Sheens looked at her properly, a small smile on his lips. "What are you going to do with it?"

"Feed it?" she suggested. "You never know. Might be a witness."

JONAH WAS MORE relieved that Hanson was in the relatives' room with him than he would ever have admitted. It wasn't just that she was good at giving sympathy without going overboard. It was also that having a colleague sitting next to him somehow kept Jonah from being dragged too far into the family's grief. She could have been Lightman or O'Malley or a PCSO, it didn't really matter. Just by being there, she acted as an anchor. Someone to keep his cool in front of.

"What happened to her?" Zoe's mother asked. Suki. No. Siku.

Siku, he thought. *Get it right.*

It was slightly problematic that his mother's cat was called Suki. Names were easy enough to get wrong when he was under pressure without that added source of confusion.

"It looks as though she was attacked while in the bath," Jonah replied. "She seems to have been incapacitated, perhaps by something like chloroform, which allowed the perpetrator to injure her wrists. It was the blood loss that caused death."

Siku nodded and asked, "Arteries?" and he suddenly remembered that she was a GP. That made things a little harder. He wasn't going to be able to gloss over as many of the details.

"Yes, the pathologist thinks so," he said. "The radial artery on each side. The postmortem should confirm that."

He could see her thinking it through. She probably didn't have to ask how long it would have taken. She would have known that there had been only a ten- or fifteen-minute window in which Zoe could have regained consciousness before the lack of blood to the brain would have taken its toll. And that the bathwater would have kept the blood flowing continuously.

Siku's piercing gaze came to rest on him again, and she asked, "What did they use?"

"Siku," Martin said in a choked voice. Jonah realized that he was a sick-looking white. He didn't want to hear any of this.

"I'm sorry," his wife said quietly. She slid her hand over his and then squeezed it. "I need to know."

She looked back at Jonah, and while Martin turned away, he said as lightly as he could, "A Stanley knife from her art kit."

There was a brief pause in which he was aware of Martin's unsteady breathing, and then Siku said, "So they knew her." There was a resonant certainty in her voice. "They knew there would be a weapon there."

"They also had access to the flat," Jonah said. "We'll check further, but we know that her landlord had a key and that Angeline had one. Are there any others you know of?"

Siku glanced at Martin, and then shook her head. "We never had one. I don't think she would have given them out at random."

"She was quite careful," Martin said. "Particularly with all the goings-on with her and Aidan."

"How so?" Jonah asked neutrally.

Martin gave his wife a long, questioning look. She lifted her chin, and Martin said, "You had him in here. Are you investigating him?"

"We're certainly keen to find out what was going on," Jonah said carefully.

"He shouldn't have been anywhere near her," Siku said in a low, angry voice. "She broke up with him."

Jonah raised his eyebrows. "You weren't under the impression that they'd got back together?"

"No," Siku said firmly. "She'd made up her mind, and finally stopped being talked round. She blocked him and she moved to get away from him. It was terrible, her having to move. Terrible. She had a gorgeous place in St. Denys with Maeve, with a view of the estuary and all that *character* instead of some featureless box. Moving away broke her heart, and it was clearly all for nothing." She shook her head. "He must have found her."

"Actually, it seems that Aidan Poole might not have known where she lived," Jonah said, deciding that this was a point he should reveal. "However, it seems that the two of them may have picked up their relationship."

"Who told you that?" Siku asked, her voice steely. "Did he?"

"It's partly circumstantial," Jonah said gently. "It was Aidan Poole who reported the crime. By his account, she was attacked while they were Skyping, and he tried to get help. Now, we are checking that, but it seems unlikely at this point that he would or could have lied about it, particularly if he was in any way implicated in her murder."

There was a pause, and then Siku said, "God, why would she give him the time of day?"

"Because she was too warmhearted," Martin said, his eyes glimmering under the overhead lights. He put a hand out to Siku's shoulder. "And maybe she did want to be with him. You used to like him."

"Before I realized what he was like," Siku said harshly.

"So you didn't approve of the relationship," Hanson said quietly, as Jonah watched the mother's expression.

"How could we?" Siku asked. "Who would want their daughter seeing a bloody married man who wouldn't leave his wife for her?"

Jonah looked over at Hanson, whose expression mirrored his own shock. "I'm sorry?"

Siku recoiled. "He hid that little gem, did he?"

"We weren't aware, certainly," Jonah said.

"He's a liar," she said harshly. "It's what he does. He hid his wife from her, and when she found out, he claimed they were getting divorced. Then when that didn't happen, he said there were delays. He lied and he lied and he kept her hanging, and it made her miserable. And now he's killed her."

THEY'LL TELL THEM *I'm married*, Aidan thought. He had made it to the train station, but then had come to a total stop by the ticket barriers. Even habit only carried him so far. In his mind, he was hundreds of miles away from the ticket machines and the barriers. At times, he was a year away, remembering how he had met Zoe. And then, with the next breath, he would be in an interview room again, knowing that she was dead.

It would have happened by now, he realized. Siku and Martin would have told the police all about it. They knew.

But of course they bloody knew. Aidan had been kidding himself. He could never have kept Greta's existence quiet. Maeve, Angeline, Victor . . . they'd all known he was married.

It was a royal mess, and it was entirely self-caused. He'd let all this happen, though when he looked back on it, he felt that someone else must have made all those stupid decisions. It couldn't have been him.

Even that very first night, he'd felt like there was someone else inhabiting him. Someone wittier and more charming. Someone who was free to flirt and make promises. He'd regretted the exchange of phone numbers almost the moment he'd left the building, and then he'd felt compelled to call Greta straightaway.

He often wondered whether things would have gone differently if Greta hadn't been away that weekend. For starters, he probably wouldn't have gone from a film with colleagues to a bar. He'd have gone home to Greta and actually had dinner, and not sunk eight drinks in a row on an empty stomach.

And even if, for some reason, he'd done all those things anyway, he would have gone home to her later and had to face her. He would have remembered at that key moment all the wonderful things they had. And, as a consequence, he would have deleted Zoe's number and blocked her from his phone. He knew he would.

Instead of which, he'd called his wife from the taxi and heard her irritation at being interrupted when she was busy networking.

"Is everything OK?" Greta had asked, and he understood the subtext: that if everything *was* OK, he shouldn't be calling.

"Oh, fine. I was just . . . checking in."

"Right. Well, I'm just at the bar with some of the editors. Can we talk later?"

"Sure," he'd said breezily. And then he'd felt compelled to add, a little petulantly, "Though I might be asleep by the time you're done."

"OK, well, we'll catch up in the morning if I miss you."

And that had cemented everything he'd been feeling. That final sentence that told him she really wasn't bothered whether they talked or not. That she had far more important things to think about.

He'd rung off and gone straight to his messages. It had taken three comments from his wife to erase all the regret. He typed quickly, though he had to go back and correct a few typos. He was rolling drunk and the movements of the cab weren't helping.

It was so good to meet you. I'm glad I was a freeloading bastard tonight. Hope to see you soon. A xx

And he'd been glad in that bubbling, can't-stop-smiling way that characterized the start of a relationship when, a mere two minutes later, he'd had a reply.

Totally agree. Sometimes it's obviously good to be a bastard. Let
me know when you're free for a drink. Xx

The battle had basically been lost right then.

That said, Greta's arrival home from her Berlin trip had triggered
the worst recriminations. When she'd dropped her bags in the hall
and come to give him a long, lingering kiss and a smile, he'd wondered if he'd been misremembering what she was really like. She was
so much warmer than he'd been thinking, and so much more tender.
He'd kissed her furiously in return, and they'd ended up moving upstairs and having one of the most satisfying lovemaking sessions he
could remember.

He'd lain next to her afterward, telling himself he was an idiot but
that he was lucky to have realized his mistake. That he had been
about to risk a wonderful marriage for no reason at all.

And then Greta had gone for a shower, and his phone had buzzed
with a message from Zoe. He'd already set his phone so that messages didn't show up on the home screen, but he'd still felt a jolt of
fear.

It had been a simple message, but for some reason it had cut
straight through all the guilt and hit the reward centers of his brain.
It had brought surging back all the excitement he'd felt since meeting
her.

Hey Aidan. How's your day going? I just served Judi Dench in the
coffee shop. I kid you not. Judi fricking Dench. AMAZING xx

He'd grinned to himself as he'd written back saying he didn't believe her, and demanded photographic proof.

And that, for some reason, had been his last chance of escape
gone. Even during the breaks that were to come, their relationship
had never really released either of them.

All of it had brought him here, and he felt as though he were poised on the edge of a chasm. The loss of one person he cared about was going to drag every other good thing with it, one by one.

HANSON WAS NOT looking forward to the next few hours, however readily she'd volunteered to accompany the DCI. She'd yet to witness a postmortem and knew she had a high chance of being very ill at some point. But even that might be better than taking Siku and Martin Swardadine to identify the body of their daughter.

While she and Jonah climbed into the Mondeo, the Swardadines left to find a hotel somewhere nearby, a waiting room where they would kill time until Zoe's body was ready. Later, they would have to be fingerprinted. They would in all likelihood be questioned further, too. But for the time being, they were only grieving parents.

Hanson watched the back of Martin's sleek BMW leave the station car park and then said, "He seems like a pretty manipulative guy, this Aidan Poole. Do you think there's any truth in what they think?"

"He's clearly a liar," the DCI replied thoughtfully, starting the engine and pulling out onto the main road. "I'll want to check that he really was Skyping her from home, and look at fingerprints. But I don't think he's lying about the murder. That phone call he made . . . He sounded genuinely terrified. And I can't see why he'd lie. If he killed her and then went to the effort of making it look like a suicide, why would he then call us and tell us it was murder? It would have been a lot bloody safer to leave everything alone."

"I suppose so," Hanson said, wondering if it was ridiculous to suggest that it was all some kind of a bluff. Did people really do that? And would Aidan Poole be the type? "What about the wife?"

"We need to talk to him about that," Sheens answered. "I'm going to ask him to attend voluntarily after we're back from the mortuary." He glanced over at Hanson. "It's OK. You don't need to be there."

"I'd quite like to be, actually," she said a little awkwardly. "If you don't mind."

"If you genuinely don't mind wrecking your Friday evening, I'm always happy to have company," he said.

"Nothing to wreck," Hanson replied with a crooked grin. "Friday pub's off and I'm a sad case with no other plans."

"Snap," Jonah said, and shook his head. "We both seriously need to get a life, Juliette."

THE MORTUARY WAS not what Hanson had been expecting at all. She wondered whether a diet of American cop shows had given her a slightly warped expectation that it would be all gloom, flickering strip lights, and metal sliding drawers.

The reality was a softly lit, comforting entrance hall that let onto a room that looked like it belonged in a private hospital. There was little visible through the gap except a few seascapes on one wall, but it seemed neither gloomy nor full of horrors.

There were two people waiting for them on arrival. The first was the pathologist, who it turned out was called Dr. Peter Shaw. Alongside him was a fortysomething woman, who introduced herself as Pauline and explained that she worked there. Hanson felt clueless. Was she a funeral director of some kind, or just staff there? What would you call that? A mortician? She needed to ask the chief about that.

"I'm ready to start," Shaw said. He had a soft voice with a hint of a Scots accent and a habit of ducking his head so that he had to look over his glasses at them. It made him look older than he really was, which Hanson guessed was in his early thirties. He wasn't much older than she was. How had he become tough enough to cut people up on a regular basis?

He led them into the rear of the mortuary, which gradually became a little more like what she'd been expecting. The carpeted areas gave onto marbled gray linoleum, and behind one of the doors was a clinical-looking room with a table in the center of it.

Zoe's partly covered form lay on it, and Hanson felt a flicker of fear that she wasn't going to be able to do this. The victim was too real to her, even though she didn't know her.

But there was something calming in Shaw's soft voice as he started to describe what he had done so far.

"I took several swabs of a substance around the victim's mouth," he said. "Those are with your forensic scientist, but I've kept one and compared the odor to several other chemicals in similarly small quantities. I'm fairly confident that our traces are of desflurane, which would have rendered her unconscious within seconds if administered effectively."

"This would be by a cloth to the face?" the chief asked.

"Yes," Shaw agreed.

"And its effects would have lasted awhile?"

"Between five and ten minutes," Shaw said. "It would have taken only around ten minutes for the victim to become unconscious from blood loss, so if she woke up at some point, she would have been disoriented and uncoordinated, and therefore unable to save herself."

Which Hanson tried very, very hard not to imagine.

"On to first observations. Cuts to each forearm have, as first observed, severed the radial artery." He lifted the right arm gently and rotated it slightly. "The right arm has two cuts, one of which looks like a false start."

"Is that common in attacks?"

"It's more common in suicides," Shaw said. "But in a situation where an attacker has planned it and isn't enraged, it also happens." He paused over her hands and eventually lifted them to examine them more carefully. "There's swelling and signs of scabbing on the left knuckle," he said, and the DCI moved closer to look. "There's bruising there, too, I think."

"Sign that she struggled with her attacker?" Sheens asked.

Shaw paused, and then said slowly, "Possibly. But given that the cuts on her arms are so clean, it looks unlikely. And there's grazing with some scabbing. I'd say it's more likely to have happened earlier in the day."

Hanson met the DCI's eye. "She fought someone earlier?" she asked.

"Or she fell," Shaw said, "and caught herself on a balled fist." He nodded. "But I'll take swabs anyway. If she did struggle with someone, there's a chance some of the killer's DNA made it onto her knuckles or under her nails."

"Let's hope so," Sheens said.

HANSON WAS SHAKING by the time Shaw called for one of the mortuary assistants to close Zoe's torso back up again, but she'd made it. She hadn't been sick while he'd opened the body up to reveal that Zoe's stomach was empty, and she hadn't felt like passing out or crying.

Shaw had finished up his observations by giving them a time of death with an unfortunately wide range. This was thanks to the immersion of the body in water and the lack of food in the stomach to judge amount of digestion from. Zoe had died at some point between late afternoon and the early hours of the morning—a range of hours that did, however, encompass the time that Aidan Poole claimed to have witnessed her attack and also allowed for Felix's alleged sighting at 8:30 P.M.

She found herself stuck on those bruises to Zoe's hand, and on the emptiness of her stomach. She'd died late in the day, having most likely eaten nothing since the day before. Hanson had looked again at Zoe's angular face and slender limbs and trunk, as dispassionately as she could. And then, outside the room with her gloves peeled off, she had pulled out her phone to look at the web page her DCI had found earlier that day.

The Zoe pictured there had been round-faced. Curvy. Her smile dimpling. And Hanson wondered quite how she had died with an empty stomach at probably only a little more than half the weight she'd once been.

SIKU AND MARTIN weren't really taking much in, as far as Hanson could see. Pauline, the mortuary attendant, explained the process, and the DCI added reassurances that they could take their time and back out at any point. But their eyes kept straying to the doorway into the other room, and their expressions were such a complex mixture of dread, longing, resolve, and sadness that it was hard to look at either of them.

It was Pauline who took them through, and Hanson was glad she wasn't going back in there with them. She and Sheens sat in the soft chairs of reception instead. Hanson listened while the DCI rang Aidan Poole and asked him, in a flat voice, to attend the station once again, and then sat picking at bits of fluff on her trousers in the silence.

"You did well in there," Sheens suddenly said. "I should have said. I had to go and puke during my first postmortem. And then I tried to avoid the next one until the pathologist basically dragged me in."

"I hope not puking is a good thing," Hanson said, pulling a face.

"Well, either you're good at keeping it together under tough circumstances," Sheens said, "or it means you're a psychopath. But I'm sure there's a place for you on the team either way."

Hanson snorted with laughter, and then suppressed it. It wasn't appropriate when Zoe's parents were seeing their daughter's body. She tried to sit still after that and be somber, even while the adrenaline still running through her made her want to get up and pace.

Siku emerged first, and although there were tears standing in her eyes, there was also fire in her expression.

"What's being done to find out who did this?" Siku asked.

Sheens stood, and Hanson rose with him. "Everything that needs to be done," he said with a small nod. "Looking for potential witnesses, searching for CCTV, questioning her acquaintances, and looking for any reason for anyone to do her harm. I'll do a press conference tomorrow and ask for anyone who thinks they might know anything to come forward."

Hanson felt, not for the first time, that it was a relief to have the DCI around. She wasn't sure how she would have handled that question. Defensively, probably.

Siku gave a slow nod and then took her husband's arm. Where she seemed to be all fire, Zoe's father looked simply shattered. His wife drew him along, away from their only daughter's body and out into the November evening.

10

Zoe had spent an hour walking without aim or direction. There were furious, hurt conversations playing on repeat in her head. In every one she imagined screaming at Aidan, asking him how he could do this to her. In the better versions of these he would then admit that he was a horrible piece of work and she would walk out. In the worse, weaker ones, he explained that he had already left his wife, and that he'd done it for her. That she was all he'd ever wanted.

She'd found herself, in that tumultuous hour, standing on a station platform. She knew that she needed to do something with this feeling. Needed to turn it into something. And so she climbed on the train to Winchester and paced the small square of carpet by the doors until it pulled in. She climbed off, and then she was suddenly at the School of Art without being aware of anything except the anger. God knew how she'd crossed any of the roads safely.

It was quiet in the studio. This early in the summer term, most of the students were still treading water. Drinking. Relaxing. Procrastinating.

Zoe dropped her bag down in her section, which showed the clutter of a great deal of work. She had filled so many empty hours between messages with painting, and she tried not to think about how she'd wanted to show her current piece to Aidan. She didn't need him to validate her.

She'd been so happy with this piece. Something about it put it above anything she'd ever painted. She thought it might be the way she had asked Angeline to pose, with her back arched and one arm over her head, her mouth slightly open. It looked so much like someone in the throes of passion. But it also looked like someone who was tortured by pain.

She'd only chosen that pose in the exhilarated aftermath of meeting Aidan. Out of hundreds of photographs, it was the one that had spoken to her. And the painting had come together so quickly that she was now all but finished. She'd been adding a background of boiling clouds above and crashing waves against a shore below.

But looking at it now, she could see that it wasn't nearly finished. There were hugely important elements missing.

Well, she could fix that. She would make it the painting it should be, a real piece instead of one based on fantasy. And even as the sight of Angeline's form made her feel a throb of guilt about that missed call, she started to unpack her paints.

She squeezed tans, browns, blacks, and vivid reds onto a palette and, with a feeling of strange abandon, began to paint two entirely new figures onto the canvas. The first was shadowy, and it twined itself around the figure of Angeline. It shadowed her where it wrapped around her, but it didn't blot her out. It lacked form. Realness. But its fingers still twisted through Angeline's where her arm was stretched out over her head. It was the cause of Angeline's pose, the other half of a grotesque act of lovemaking.

It was challenging to add the figure in, but with all the hurt rushing through her she felt no fear of going wrong. It was almost as if nothing mattered, and she might as well listen to the pull within her to do something.

Once the shadowy figure was finished, she began immediately on a third figure, standing so close to the lovers that she could have reached down to touch them. Another woman as naked as Angeline and as angular, but standing upright, proudly. Smiling. She didn't seem to notice that the two outstretched hands had opened up a wound in her stomach.

With a sense of strange delight, Zoe made the cut bloody and horrific. She painted in a layer of fat in the torn flesh, and a glimpse of pale, tangled innards. She used crimson and scarlet with abandon after that, to trace the blood down onto the ground under the woman's feet.

It was hours after she had arrived that she stood back to look at it, her breath coming quickly and her heart thundering. Something in her felt immeasurably better now that it was done, even though what she had painted was an image of her own guilt. An image of her and Aidan and the harm they had done to his wife.

She let her eyes drift over it all, wanting to feel what she had done. She was glad that there were a few other students in the studio with her now, and that they must be able to see this, too. There was a strange satisfaction in feeling the guilt of what she had done unknowingly. But a sense of creeping doubt came over her. It wasn't quite right yet.

She angled her head to look at the second woman. At the figure of an imaginary Mrs. Poole. And then she leaned in and smudged and scratched at the half-dry eyes. She had made them a piercing blue, but she realized that that was wrong. She shouldn't have eyes at all.

Once she was finished, there was nothing but a flesh-colored smear over the eyes, as if she had been deliberately blinded.

ZOE PACKED UP her paints long after the lights had flickered on outside the building. It was a twilit seven o'clock on a beautiful April evening, and the grounds outside looked a strange, seductive deep blue from the window. She looked out at it and wondered why she didn't seem to feel anything. She was someone who always noticed beauty.

Perhaps, she thought, she had wrung herself dry. Or perhaps it was simply that the world didn't help anyone by being beautiful.

And then feeling returned to her, but it wasn't any kind of soothing balm. It was the heavy weight of responsibility she felt toward Angeline, who so badly needed looking after. It was in Angeline's nature to seek to destroy herself, and Zoe was the only one who could really step in.

She pulled her phone out and breathed out a long sigh.

There was music in the background when the call went through. Then Angeline's voice saying her name, stringing out the second syllable so that it sounded like a celebration.

"I'm so sorry I missed your call," Zoe said, wanting to explain but unable to. "Are you out somewhere? Do you need help?"

"Why didn't you . . . come?" Angeline asked.

There was a squeeze of familiar guilt, and then Zoe felt a strange longing for Angeline to be the one looking after her. For Angeline to cuddle her while she cried her heart out over Aidan.

"I'm coming now," she said as lightly as possible. "Tell me where you are, sweetheart. I can come and see if you're all right."

"I'm not telling you where I am," Angeline sang down the phone at her. And then she was suddenly crying instead, telling Zoe that she was all alone and frightened.

It took Zoe fifteen minutes to get her to admit that she was in a dockside wine bar called the Zoo, because she'd been kicked out of the lunch place she'd gone to.

"What lunch place?" Zoe asked.

"I was supposed to be . . . to be having lunch with a guy . . . but he stood me up."

Zoe felt doubtful. Who would Angeline have been meeting? Some guy off Tinder? During the day? It seemed a lot more likely that she'd gone somewhere alone, hoping to latch onto someone who might buy her a few drinks.

Zoe called a cab. Angeline was clearly far gone, and if Zoe messed around with trains and her bike, there was every chance that her friend would end up in trouble. She'd just have to walk to Southampton Station in the morning to pick up her bike.

The cabdriver wasn't quite sure where the Zoo was, but they found it in the end. Or at least a board advertising it. It seemed to be accessible only on foot.

"Will you wait?" Zoe asked, handing him a tenner. "I just need to grab my friend and take her home."

"I'm not sure I should be waiting here," the driver said doubtfully. And then, "I guess I can do a circuit if I have to move."

"Thank you," Zoe said with a warm smile. "I'll be as quick as I can. Keep the meter running."

The Zoo turned out to be a wine bar on the waterfront side of the harborside Ocean Village, a modern creation of flat blocks with a series of bars and restaurants set into the ground floor. All of them had views over the moorings for smaller vessels, and this one had fairy lights and low jazz music spilling out. It was definitely not the kind of place to get seriously drunk before dinnertime.

She made her way in and saw Angeline immediately. She was slumped against the bar on a high wooden stool and was not, in fact, alone. Sitting right up close next to her was a stranger.

Zoe felt immediately uneasy, a feeling strong enough to cut through the tight little ball of pain she was carrying. It wasn't just that she didn't know this guy. It was the way he was sitting with his arm slung possessively around Angeline, his fingers grazing her upper thigh. He was probably a few years older than Zoe, but it was hard to tell with the half beard he was sporting. And he was a pretty big guy, which made Angeline seem all the smaller and more fragile.

He picked up a full cocktail glass and whispered in Angeline's ear. She giggled, and sat up for a moment to tip the bright-pink liquid into her mouth.

"Angeline," Zoe said loudly.

Her friend faltered and spilled part of the drink down herself. She tried to wipe her mouth, with what looked to Zoe like a guilty expression.

"Zoe, what . . . are you doing here?" Her whole body waved as she said it, and her eyes were clearly failing to focus properly on Zoe's face.

"You asked me to come," Zoe said with a pretend smile. She moved forward, ignoring the guy draped around her. "It's time to go home, remember?"

"Why?" Angeline asked with a frown.

"Because we have a few things to do," Zoe said.

"Hey, I don't think she wants to go," the guy said, and gave her a self-satisfied smirk. "She has her own things to do."

"Oh, really?" Zoe asked, raising her eyebrows. "And do you think she's sober enough to make up her mind about that? Because I sure as hell don't."

She glanced at the barman, who was emptying drip trays a few feet away. She wondered if she could count on him if things got aggressive.

"Well, it's interesting how you're suddenly all concerned," he said, withdrawing his arm from Angeline a little. "Were you that worried hours ago when she tried to call you?"

Zoe could feel heat flooding her face. So Angeline had been telling him about her. Angeline dipped her head, her hand going out to her half-empty glass.

"I've already apologized for missing the call," Zoe said quietly. "I'm here for her now. As I am most of the time."

"Just not when she was being thrown out of a pub," the guy said quietly. He lifted a half-full glass of red and held her gaze for a moment before he drank it. There was a sense of threat to it, but Zoe wasn't in the mood to be threatened.

"Oh, and I suppose you know all about it," Zoe said loudly. "Having just met her. Jesus. What actually is your name? Because I don't think either of us knows you."

"I'm Richie," he said. "And Angeline knows me pretty well."

He gave a small smile, and to Zoe's revulsion Angeline leaned in toward him and put her head on his shoulder.

Zoe took Angeline's hand. "Let's head home. I'll make you some tea and we can snuggle on the sofa."

This clearly didn't seem like fun to Richie, but Angeline, who loved to feel looked after above everything else, gave her a small smile. "That sounds nice," she said. She sat up straight and jumped down from the stool, still holding Zoe's hand.

"Aren't you going to finish your drink?" Richie asked her with clear displeasure.

"I think she's had enough," Zoe said. Her smile was cold.

"All right," Richie said with a shrug. "I'll see you soon, Angeline."

"Come on," Zoe said, and slid her arm around Angeline below her armpits. It was a good thing she was light.

"Bye, Richie," Angeline called.

"I'll come and see you," he called back, and Zoe's insides felt cold as she looked back at him. She really hoped Angeline hadn't been stupid enough to give him her address.

11

The end of everything started here.

Aidan was standing alongside the train he'd meant to get onto, readying himself to tell Greta that he was going to be late tonight. He'd rehearsed a dozen different fabricated stories, but in the end he'd realized that this might drag on. That he would have to tell some version of the truth.

As the call rang, he imagined Greta sitting at the kitchen table and answering brusquely, listening to him in cold silence while he tried to explain everything. And then she was suddenly speaking clearly and warmly in his ear.

"Hey!" she said, elongating the word, a slight laugh to her voice. "How's it going?"

He felt all his rehearsed speeches crumble. He'd been expecting coldness and immediate suspicion. That light laughter caught him off balance. He felt, as he'd felt before at times, that he'd gotten his wife wrong somehow. That he was misremembering her each time he left her presence.

And when it came to it, he just couldn't bear to burst that happy mood of hers. He'd done enough harm to Greta already in the last year and a half.

"It's going irritatingly," he said as lightly as possible, after what was probably too long a gap. "I'm going to be late back. Unfortunately I have to head to the police station. I saw an attack yesterday while I was in town, and the police want me to come and give a statement. It's a total ball-ache."

JONAH CALLED MCCULLOUGH through the Mondeo's Bluetooth as they drove toward the station, hoping that they might have some fingerprint results back. But McCullough gave him a snort of derision as she turned down the loud Rachmaninoff that was playing in the background.

"Print comparisons being run on a Friday evening? You'll be lucky," she said. "They all buggered off to the pub at four. They did Zoe's before they went but everything else will be Monday. Though you can have my summary of the prints we found, if you like."

Jonah sighed. "That would be better than nothing."

He heard a riffling of paper, and then she spoke again. "We have four distinct, probably male sets around the house. I'm not going to say absolutely that they're all male. There are women whose finger sizes fall within the range for two of them. Outliers, but there."

"OK. Where are those?"

"Male one, the most distinct, is on the main door, inside and out, plus on one of the two glasses we collected and a light switch. Nothing on the bathroom door." She paused, and then went on, "Male two is vaguer, and quite spread around the flat, including the bathroom door and various other spots. Overlaid in some cases. So a frequent visitor but unlikely to have been there on the night."

"Thanks," Jonah said. "The other two?"

"Male three is interesting," McCullough said. "He appears only on the lock to the bathroom door. We've not found him anywhere else. And those are quite definite and don't look to be overlaid."

"That's very interesting," Jonah said. "If that door was locked by the killer, then unlocked, that would produce that result, yes?"

"Yes, although I would note that if people have tended not to lock the door, they may not be quite as recent as they look," McCullough added. "There aren't a lot of Zoe's prints on there, for example."

"Fair point," Jonah agreed. "And male four?"

"Largely just on the front door and a lightbulb," McCullough confirmed. "Could be a workman."

"OK. What about the girls?"

"We have three," McCullough said. He could hear her turning a page. "One is Zoe. The other two are spread around fairly extensively, particularly in the kitchen."

Jonah pondered for a minute. "No prints from others in the bedroom?"

"No complete ones," McCullough said. "Some much overlaid partials but I'm going to suggest those are most likely to have been a previous tenant."

"That's great, thanks," he said.

"I did look at the stuff swabbed from around her mouth," McCullough went on, grudgingly. Jonah smiled. He'd been sure she'd get it done today.

"And?"

"Desflurane. Shaw was on the money."

Jonah nodded to himself. It was satisfying to hear, in part because the odor Shaw had noticed would only have been present for a short while. If Jonah hadn't followed up the report and searched for Zoe, it might have been several days before she had been found. There would have been no scent of any chemical left. And on top of that, if nobody had ever linked that errant crime report with the body's discovery, the whole scene would have been treated as a suicide.

"That's really great," he said to McCullough warmly. "So no question of suicide."

"It would seem so."

"Thanks, Linda. Are you off home now?"

"Is that a subtly coded request for me to hang around in case I'm needed?" McCullough asked dryly.

Jonah laughed at that. "No, for once, that was just an attempt at social conversation. I've got one more interview, but it doesn't look like there's anything more for you until prints and bloods are back."

"Well, that's a turn-up," McCullough said. "I'm going to get out of here before something happens. Enjoy."

Hanson turned to him once they were done. "That third male is still interesting, I think," she said. "I'd like to know whose prints those were."

"As would I," Jonah said. "But it looks like we'll be waiting until Monday for that little mystery to be solved, assuming we manage to get whoever it is printed before then. But being able to pin it down as murder is a good first step."

There was a brief silence, and then Hanson asked, "I wonder about her dad. He hardly says anything, and his expression is so haunted. Part of me wonders if it's guilt."

"Yes, I've wondered that, too," Jonah agreed. "It wouldn't have been right to ask about alibis today, but I will tomorrow." He let out a sigh. "I did work on a case a few years ago where a father did his daughter in during a fit of rage. He looked . . . destroyed."

"People can be so screwed up," Hanson muttered. "Guess I lucked out with a crappy cheat for a dad instead."

Jonah thought of his own abusive father and gave a small smile. "I guess you did."

"So," SHEENS SAID, once he had greeted Aidan Poole with excessive and deliberate formality. "You failed to mention, in your last interview, that your relationship with Zoe Swardadine was not simple girlfriend and boyfriend."

"Yes," Aidan said in a low voice. He seemed, if anything, a little more together than he had been when he left the station earlier. Less zoned out, Hanson thought. Despite the worse situation he now found himself in.

"Why exactly did you feel the need to conceal that you have a wife who lives with you in Alton?"

"I'm sorry," he said. He gave the DCI a slightly beseeching look. "I know I should have mentioned it. I was just so afraid of it getting back to Greta. It wasn't even . . . Look, if I'd been thinking more rationally, I would have realized that it made no difference. But I suppose I imagined you asking to see her, and it all coming out. And . . . now that Zoe's gone, the idea of losing her as well is just . . ."

"If you cared about Zoe, then surely you want us to find out who did this," Jonah replied.

"Yes," Aidan said, sitting up a little. "Yes, of course I do. I just thought . . . I suppose if I thought at all, I was assuming that my marriage had nothing to do with it."

"You don't think it's relevant?" Sheens asked. He glanced down at the handwritten notes he'd made after their earlier interview, not yet typed up and on the system. "When you mentioned her friend Victor, who was angry about it. You don't think the fact that you were married might have increased his feelings of resentment?"

Aidan looked uncomfortable. "I didn't think about it like that, no."

"What was your wife doing last night?"

Aidan was clearly caught off guard by the change in tack. "What? Greta?"

"You'll have to tell me if she's called Greta," the DCI said. "Having heard very little about her before now, I'm not on first-name terms." The comment was dripping with sarcasm, and Hanson felt slightly sorry for Aidan Poole. It didn't look like he was in for an easy time of it.

"She's called Greta," Aidan said after a breath, "and she's forty years old. We've been married for seventeen years."

"And last night?" Sheens repeated. "I assume she wasn't in the house while you were engaged in a covert chat with your girlfriend, or did you wait till she'd gone to bed?"

Aidan shook his head. Hanson could see his jaw tightening in an attempt at self-control. The DCI could get to most people when he wanted.

"She was out at an awards dinner," he eventually said. "She's a science writer for a lot of the big newspapers. She was presenting an award."

"And where was this?" The DCI was now looking at his notebook, where he had begun making notes. Somehow he managed to make the mere action of writing intimidating.

"London. It was . . . some hotel."

"If you can't be more specific, the name of the organization running the event would be useful," Sheens said.

"Oh. Yes . . . the Press Association, I think?"

"What time did she get home?"

"Two . . . two-thirty."

"And you're sure she was there at the time of Zoe's murder?" Sheens asked.

"Yes. For fuck's sake," Aidan said. "Why in the hell would Greta have anything to do with it? She'd never even heard of Zoe."

"So she had no knowledge of the affair?" Sheens insisted.

"No," Aidan said. "Do you really think she'd still want to be with me if she knew I'd been shagging a twenty-seven-year-old student?" Aidan's voice caught, and he looked away suddenly, swallowing repeatedly.

"So you were careful about it," Hanson interjected, leaning forward and striving to appear like the more understanding of the two.

"Yes," he said. And then he lifted a hand in a gesture of resignation. "I was a total devious shit about it. I set my phone so that Zoe's messages never gave a notification. I had all her emails auto-filtered into a work folder. And I deleted everything, without fail. That's how it is when you're having a bloody affair. You learn to be a constant liar."

"What about since last night?" Hanson asked, considering. "Did you delete your Skype call history?"

Aidan blinked at her. "Oh. No, I didn't. It was the only time I haven't. I needed it."

"Because it's your alibi?" the DCI asked with irony.

"No!" Aidan answered, his frustration evident. "To prove to myself that . . . that it had actually happened."

"We would like you to show us that conversation," Sheens said.

"Do you have the app on your phone?" Hanson asked, glancing at the chief and then back to Aidan Poole.

"Yes." Aidan sat up a little straighter. "Yes, I do. It'll show up on there." He pulled out his phone, spent a moment or two fiddling, and then brought up a conversation with a Zoe Swardadine, whose photo was clearly that of the girl they'd seen in the bathtub and on the mortuary slab.

Hanson glanced at the DCI for permission, then took the phone and clicked on the profile for Zoe Swardadine. The Skype ID was just Zoe's first and second names run together. Hanson wrote it down as Jonah described what was going on for the benefit of the tape. She then checked the call time, which had begun at 10:52 the previous night, and had then run for three hours and forty-nine minutes.

"So you hung up at two forty-one in the end?" she asked as she handed the phone back.

"Yes," he said. "When Greta rolled in."

"She was drunk?" Hanson queried.

"Very, as she usually is after a journalism event," Aidan said. "And I was hugely relieved that she was, because she passed out within a minute of getting into bed and didn't notice me getting up repeatedly." He shook his head. "I couldn't sleep. I kept trying to believe that I'd got it wrong, but I knew."

The DCI nodded and then sat forward. "I think we can leave it there for this evening. We may well need to see you again this weekend, depending on what else emerges."

"All right," Aidan said, rising and putting his phone back into his pocket. "Just let me know. I do want to help, even if I was being an idiot about the affair."

They showed him out through CID, which was now empty. O'Malley had been gone before the two of them returned from the morgue.

Hanson turned to the DCI once the door shut behind Aidan Poole. "I'll check whether that's really Zoe's Skype account."

"Sure," Sheens said. "I'm pretty sure it will turn out to be."

"You don't think he's guilty?"

"Oh, I think he's guilty as hell of a lot of things," Sheens said with a grin, "all of which are about to come tumbling out. I just don't think any of them are the murder of a young woman."

"So we're working on the assumption that he genuinely witnessed her murder," Hanson asked, a little pointedly.

The DCI shook his head with a smile. "We won't work on any assumptions, as you well know. We'll investigate him as thoroughly as the next person. But if I had to make a prediction, I'd say that as soon as he stops scrabbling around trying to protect himself, Aidan Poole is going to help us solve this thing. Because it's ninety-nine percent certain that Zoe knew her killer, and I'd wager that Aidan Poole knew them, too."

HANSON SHUT HER desktop down and stretched. It was nearly nine, and she wondered whether she ought to be finding something else to do or just call it a night. Without a scheduled pub trip, she had a free evening to do other, nonwork things. She ought to feel grateful instead of slightly lost.

Well, if she had free time, she ought to do something with it. She pulled out her phone and was mulling over which of the many friends she hadn't seen in too long she should call, when a message arrived from Ben Lightman.

I'm free now. Could we still do pub?

Hanson felt momentarily irritated. Had his date gone badly? Were she and O'Malley a backup option, or maybe expected to sit and listen to how awful it had turned out to be?

Somehow, though, she couldn't imagine him drowning his sorrows, and with a sigh, she messaged back to say that she was around, but O'Malley had already left.

OK. See you in twenty?

HANSON HAD INSTALLED herself at a window table in the Marriott bar. The venue had been her choice. O'Malley's nonattendance meant they could go somewhere with a wine list instead of what she would generally term an "old-man pub." And sometimes a wine list was what you wanted on a Friday night.

She was still wearing her work clothes, of course. She wondered whether Lightman would be in something more casual. Or something geared toward going out.

She had her iPad out now, and was scrolling through the interview transcripts from their questioning of Aidan Poole, comparing his two accounts with each other and with what Zoe's parents had told them. She made handwritten notes as she went, but was struggling to concentrate fully.

She wasn't quite sure how drinking with just Lightman was going to go, and it was making her nervous. She found herself, as a result, looking frequently toward the door.

He appeared in the end, and she saw, with relief, that he was also still in his suit from earlier on. She lifted a hand. He was grinning as he came over.

"Surely you've done enough for one Friday?"

She gave him a wry smile. "It's how they get to you, isn't it? Make you feel like you have free time, but make you so curious about the case that you can't help working on it."

"Could I make you curious about a drink instead?" He glanced toward the bar.

"I guess so," Hanson said. "Gin for me."

"Anything in that . . . ?"

"Well, tonic if I have to."

The barman moved slowly, so Hanson finished reading O'Malley's interview with Victor and Maeve while Ben loitered, and then turned the iPad off and shoved it in her backpack along with the notebook.

"Here you go," Lightman said eventually, putting two highball glasses on the table.

"Thanks." She took two good swallows of gin, and then she said breezily, "I was surprised you made it. You sounded . . . busy."

"Yes," Lightman said, and then his expression became very slightly uncomfortable. "I've got a lot going on, but . . ."

Hanson suddenly felt like she was interviewing an unwilling suspect, and looked away. "Sorry. I'm not meaning to pry."

"You're not," Lightman said, and then, "I had to see my dad. He's not well."

Hanson hadn't been prepared for news of that kind. It was so far removed from a rant about a date gone wrong that she felt an awkward pause arising.

"I'm sorry," she said in the end, and briefly put a hand out to touch his arm before withdrawing it to her side of the table. "Is it . . . a sudden thing?"

Lightman shook his head. "No, not exactly. We thought he was all better and now it's come back."

"Right. That's . . . shit," she said quietly. "Your poor dad."

"Yeah," he said. "Anyway, what are you thinking about Zoe Swardadine's killer? Any wagers?"

She couldn't help feeling disappointed. She'd thought he was going to open up to her about it all. But she supposed that wasn't really how Ben Lightman worked.

She started talking about the case anyway, quietly enough that none of the distant occupants of the bar could hear. It only took her a minute to get well and truly into the conversation. She updated him on Aidan Poole's affair, and how he'd neatly hidden that he was married in their original interview, despite the fact that it would clearly come out.

"Which makes me think hiding things is an ingrained habit," she said. "My experience of people like that is that they're pretty used to living a lie. They instinctively conceal everything."

He looked at her, a very slight smile on his face. "Was that the terrible ex's style? Covering up everything?"

Hanson gave him a wry nod. She'd never given him the full story on Damian, but she'd outlined some of the harassment, and Lightman was smart enough to know that what she had described was an abusive relationship. "Sure was. He hid messages to girls, attempts to get in touch with old flames, any meet-ups . . . receipts for crazily expensive purchases . . ." She gave a short laugh. "Damian loved to pretend that he'd had all this stuff he was buying 'for ages.' Or that his mum had given it to him for his birthday, when he owed me thousands and should have been paying me back." She shook her head. "Anyway, Aidan Poole may or may not have been a huge narcissist, but I can potentially see some parallels."

"Agreed," Lightman replied. "Did you read O'Malley's summary of his chat with Victor Varos? It made me think of that Brontë novel *Villette.* The one where she's clearly in love with the handsome young man and he's totally unaware he's hurting her when he falls for someone else."

"Wait. You read a *book*?" Hanson asked.

"Shut up," Lightman said amicably.

"I haven't read it anyway," Hanson admitted with a grin. "So does she kill him? In the book?"

Lightman laughed as he picked up his gin. "No, she falls for someone else instead."

"Questionable relevance, then," Hanson replied.

"Hey," Lightman argued. "This is the early stages of a new case. And as the chief says . . ."

" 'Never discount any lateral thinking,' " Hanson said, and then shook her head. "Not sure that's quite what he meant, Ben."

Lightman drained the rest of the glass. "I need another one. Maybe another three or four."

"I'm in," Hanson answered. "But the next couple are on me. And after that, I'm going to need a really dirty pizza. Just to warn you."

"I'm pretty sure we can schedule it in."

From then on, they descended quite rapidly into drunkenness. Drunk Lightman was surprisingly silly. Hanson's joking comment about him being OCD produced a loud "Right!" and then a deliberate messing up of all the contents of their table.

Hanson started laughing at him.

"What?"

"That's not exactly a mess, is it? Two glasses near the edge and a menu on its side."

"You want to see a mess?" he asked. He got up and went to a recently vacated table of six. There were still a dozen or so glasses sitting on it, and he began stacking them up. The eight other people still drinking in other parts of the bar started looking over in confusion.

"What are you doing?" Hanson's laughter had grown to the level where she was trying to stop but failing.

"I'm being messy," Lightman said, and carried two unstable piles of assorted glasses back over to their table. "Look." He started placing the glasses down. "A mess. See?" A few more glasses. "And it doesn't bother me at all."

Once she'd managed to get the laughter under control, Hanson said to him, "All right, all right. You're not OCD. You're just . . . an idiot. OK?"

Lightman gave her a triumphant smile and sat down in front of the nest of dirty glasses. "Much better."

Hanson shook her head at him, and he looked back at her with a strange expression. And then he let out a breath. "We'll probably have to work tomorrow," he said.

Hanson tried to keep smiling. "Yes. But we've got ages to sober up."

He looked down at the glasses and then said, "I shouldn't . . . make you stay up drinking. But thank you for the cheering-up session."

"Anytime," she said as he rose. She felt like everything had been turned around on her suddenly. She was left looking after him in confusion and wondering why.

12

Zoe had taken Angeline home, away from Richie and whatever Angeline had been planning with him in the bar. She fed her tea and stroked her hair until she'd fallen asleep in front of a showing of *The Fugitive*. Zoe hadn't mentioned Aidan. She'd told herself it was because it wouldn't be fair when Angeline was struggling, but the truth was that the idea hurt too much. Telling Angeline that he'd lied meant that things really were over, and it made her ache to think that.

She spent the next four hours trying to work out whether Aidan had been telling the truth. She looked on his Facebook page and university pages for mention of a wife who was still a life partner, and she saw nothing. There were no recent photos, only some from a couple of years before. The lack of trace gave her a ray of hope, until it occurred to her that he might be a serial adulterer and good at hiding his tracks.

Some of his words had floated back to her in the darkness before midnight. She remembered how he'd defended his wife, who he said didn't deserve to be robbed of money. He hadn't blamed her. He hadn't done what Isaac had done to Maeve, and made his wife out to be some horrible, controlling bitch.

Remembering it again, something about it chimed with her. It had sounded real, she realized. It had sounded true. And the expression in his eyes had been real, too.

With the anger gone, all she had was a yearning to hear that it was all right, and she didn't have to let him go. She pulled a sweater on and walked slowly downstairs. At the door, she heard Maeve moving in the kitchen, and in a sudden nervous rush at being discovered and made to talk, she grabbed her coat and fled the house.

Even then, she wasn't quite sure. She found herself walking back to his hotel, so slowly that it took her forty minutes. Her hands were numb with cold by the time she arrived.

She came and stood in the deep-red-and-cream entrance, and eventually pulled out her phone. She'd had so many things to say to him, but she didn't have it in her anymore.

He picked up after a single ring, and she heard fear in his voice as he answered with her name.

"I'm in the lobby," she said, and then she sat heavily on one of the chairs.

Within a minute, he was stepping out of one of the lifts and over to her. As she stood, he put his hand out to her face and stroked her cheek. It was profoundly reassuring. Not just the touch, the fact that he was happy to be seen with her. He wasn't trying to hide her away. It was like this was all legitimate. OK. Moral.

"I'm sorry," he said, his voice a broken thing. "I'm so sorry."

"It's OK," she said. And she followed him to the lift with her hand tucked into his.

"Economics?" Maeve asked with a slightly disapproving note. "Come on. If you're going to date a lecturer, you should at least choose one who marks your work."

"Yeah, I know. It's unfortunate," Zoe said, and gave a short laugh.

"Maybe he could switch," Maeve said. She was sitting cross-legged on the scuffed, sagging red sofa they shared with the rest of the house.

Zoe was in the kitchenette, pulling shopping out of Tesco bags to pack it into the fridge and her two cupboards. She wasn't really doing it efficiently. Too much of her attention was on the conversation. She was torn between wanting to talk about Aidan, and not wanting to have to answer any questions at all.

In truth, she was afraid of Maeve's disapproval. She was afraid that Maeve would say all the things to her that Zoe had once said to Maeve about Isaac, and would make her feel that what she was doing was wrong. Which might have been all right if part of Zoe hadn't been thinking exactly the same.

She'd talked about it at great length with Aidan the night before. Everything he'd said had been reasonable. Persuasive. Reassuring. He'd talked about the coldness that had arisen between him and his wife, but he'd also kept up his defense of her. He'd said it was just a very sad thing, and not her fault. And he'd looked at her with eyes that were clear and open and honest. She felt as though she could see right into him as she held his gaze.

Perhaps if he'd painted Greta as some kind of awful person, Zoe would have broken it off. She wasn't young and naïve enough to fall for that, and she wasn't going to let herself become one of those women who blamed her rival. Not when her rival had all the rights. However much their marriage might be a sham, Greta was being wronged with every touch or kiss between them. She had a right to know.

Aidan had told her, though, that he was sure Greta had cheated on him in the past, and that had helped her feel better, too.

"There were seven months where she barely seemed to notice me," he said with a slightly bitter smile. "She only seemed to have any energy when she was going out to meetings, and she put . . . she put all this effort into how she looked. Which wasn't happening at home."

"Did you confront her about it?" Zoe had asked him.

"I felt . . . torn," he'd answered thoughtfully. "It made me feel wretched, but I almost wanted it to carry on and come to a head, so we could end things in a way that wasn't my fault."

It had been hard not to feel for him. She couldn't imagine no longer loving the person you'd married, but not being hard-hearted enough to just leave them.

"So if he's forty," Maeve said, "has he been married before? Any kids?"

"He's thirty-nine," Zoe said, feeling a horrible nervous twist in her stomach. "And no kids." She picked up a can and turned toward the cupboard before she added, "He has one almost-ex-wife, though."

"Almost-ex?" Maeve's tone was whip-sharp. "What does that mean?"

"That he hasn't managed to divorce her yet," Zoe replied, keeping her back to Maeve. The usually awful prospect of organizing her cupboards was suddenly appealing. She needed to keep her hands busy.

"Is he in the process of it?"

Zoe started pulling tins out and stacking them on the counter. "He will be," she said. "In two months, once his inheritance from his mum is in their account. He doesn't want to do her out of that by starting things now."

There was a pause, punctuated by the solid clunk of each can on the worktop.

"Do you think that's true?" Maeve asked in the end.

Zoe gave a slight outbreath and turned to face her friend. She didn't like the expression in Maeve's pale eyes. The concern and the slight satisfaction she thought she saw.

Zoe could read quite a lot into that expression. That Maeve felt rather exultant at this turning of the tables, and maybe a little superior now that she'd told Isaac she was never going to see him again. Which was spectacularly unfair, Zoe thought. Isaac, unlike Aidan, had been a happily married man before Maeve had come along.

"I think so, yes," she said at last. "I think he's a decent man. He doesn't tell me how awful she is. He says a lot of their unhappiness is his fault, too, and it's desperately sad how they've fallen out of love. He says they both know it."

"So he's talked to her about it?"

There was another pause, this one because Zoe was thinking back for what was probably the fiftieth time over what Aidan had said. She'd certainly had the impression that the two of them had at some point agreed that things weren't working, but when she tried to remember him actually saying it, she came up with nothing.

"I'm not sure how open they've been," she said finally. "As far as I can tell, it's very much out in the open that things are over. But then . . . I can see how you'd get to a point where nobody can bear to bring it up."

Maeve watched her for a little while longer and then sighed and looked away. "I can see that, but . . . I can also see a situation where he's decided it's over, and she still thinks things are OK."

"I'm sure it's not like that," Zoe said firmly. "And she cheated on him a while ago, which he never confronted her about."

"OK," Maeve said, lifting her tea. She was still looking off into the distance somewhere, her expression thoughtful. "So . . . she doesn't know about you, then?"

Zoe felt a momentary drop in her stomach. It was partly having to admit the truth, and partly the knowledge that Maeve was going to give her a lecture. Maeve, who always asked for advice and never took it, and would come back asking the same questions next time, stuck in the same loop, perpetually. Maeve, who always made the wrong decision. Maeve, who had pursued a married man for a year.

"No," Zoe admitted. "No. She doesn't. But she will."

Maeve nodded very slowly, and then fixed her gaze on her. There was less judgment this time, and more sympathy. "Be careful, Zo," she said. "Just be careful."

13

Hanson peered out at the outside world as she made herself porridge. It was gray and dull-looking, but at the moment, dry. She weighed her options and decided on a run. She'd invested in a light running backpack a couple of months before, and it had meant the freedom to run to work a few mornings a week. Having deposited a towel and wash kit at work, she could get away with stuffing her suit and shirt into her backpack and changing at the station.

She was doing her best not to think any further about the night before, and the drink with Ben Lightman that had come to an abrupt end. She'd told herself several times over how glad she was that she didn't have a hangover, and then she'd focused on the coming day instead.

She went to find her running gear and began to pull it on while periodically stirring the porridge. She'd always liked to run. Although she'd never been particularly fast, the sense of getting away from everything and everyone was always appealing. She also liked the way her mind wandered, often coming round to decisions and solutions as she ran. In fact, the only time she'd found running a challenge had been while dating Damian. Letting her mind wander had become a terrible thing. It had allowed her time to give in to all the negativity, and she would find herself stopping before she'd even realized it, her legs too heavy to continue and her brain reeling.

The feeling had followed her even after she'd finally split up with him. He'd made sure she kept thinking about him by harassing her with messages. It was all part of the narcissism that had made him the hideous bully he'd been.

But over the four months since she'd blocked all forms of communication from him, she'd come back to her running and started to love it again. She even loved planning it, making sure she had a route of the right length, and ate and drank the right things before and after.

This morning, she packed most of the porridge into an oblong Tupperware box and shoved it down to the bottom of the bag. The small remainder, which was the most she could eat straight before a run, she ate standing at the stove before shoving the pan into the sink to soak.

She was fully ready and pulling the backpack on when her phone buzzed. She gave a small growl and pulled it out of the little pocket in the top of the rucksack, trying not to tangle the cable of her headphones as she did it.

It was Angeline, telling her that she'd messed up, and could Hanson call her?

Hanson removed the headphones with a sigh and pressed the Call button.

THE PRESS CONFERENCE involved a lot more questions than Jonah would have liked. All he was really there to do, as far as he was concerned, was to appeal for information. He got through his piece all right, asking anyone who had seen Zoe on Thursday or earlier in the week to get in touch.

The problem was that a lot of stories had already started circulating in the media, and so Jonah had to field questions about whether the attack appeared to be racially motivated, about when she had been discovered, about whether anyone was currently in custody.

It was always difficult answering questions in an open manner when there was information they wanted to keep hidden. The time of discovery of the body, for example, and how they had been alerted. So he told them that a friend had been worried after not hearing from Zoe, and that nobody was in custody. As to a racial motivation, he could only say that there were no indications of that at present, but that they would, of course, look into it if it arose. He felt somewhat harassed by the time it was done but had at least made a good go of it.

Hanson was clearly poised, ready and waiting for him back in CID, unintentionally adding to the feeling of pressure. She rose as he entered, wet-haired and ruddy-cheeked, presumably from some sort of fitness, which made Jonah feel bad. He'd only made it out of bed in time for the press conference.

"Morning, Chief," she said as she came to walk alongside him.

"What's going on?" he asked.

"Angeline called," Hanson replied. "She was full of self-recrimination, because last week she lost her keys, including the key to Zoe's flat. Says she didn't want to admit it at first but knows we need to know."

"Lost how?" Jonah asked, letting them both into his office.

"She thinks she left them at a pub, and didn't realize because Maeve let her stay on her sofa. They were handed in three days later to the police, and her letting agents returned them to her. Her room keys have a tag on."

Jonah pulled out a pastry and started in on it, talking around mouthfuls in what he knew must be a fairly unattractive fashion. "Do we know who she was at the pub with?"

"Some of her course mates, apparently, but she messaged Maeve Silver and Zoe to tell them she'd got drunk and was feeling panicky."

"And then Maeve told her to come round?" At Hanson's nod, he said, considering, "And we don't know for sure that she left them at the pub?"

"No," Hanson replied. "It's possible, for example, that she took them home to Maeve's and passed out, and Maeve took advantage of that and went to get a copy made."

Jonah nodded. "Or that someone else went and picked them up from the pub."

"Yup," Hanson said.

"Can you check her story?"

"I've left a message with the letting agents," she said with a slight smile. "I figured it could be fabricated. I mean, it's an easy way to divert attention from Angeline being one of the only people with a key."

"That occurs to me, too," Jonah said, and took a long chug of coffee. "Do you have times for when our interesting people are coming in?"

"I've emailed you," Hanson replied. "Zoe's landlord's first."

"Good. And Ben said he'd be in soon. I might take him into the interview," he said apologetically. "If you wouldn't mind making up a few leaflets requesting info and going to see Zoe's neighbors?"

Hanson sighed, thinking of the rain that had started falling toward the end of her run, and the well-heated car she could have driven to get here. "Do you have any waterproofs I could borrow?"

"FELIX SOLOMON," THE impeccably dressed landlord said, holding out his hand to Jonah. It was a strange move, Jonah thought. Witnesses and suspects alike were usually nervous. They rarely asserted themselves calmly. The impression Felix gave was of a consultant arriving to help with a job, not of a potential suspect.

Jonah took the hand and received a brief, warm handshake. "DCI Sheens. I'm glad you could come in for a chat." He glanced at Lightman, who had brought the landlord to his office. "Which room are we in, Ben?"

"Three," Lightman replied. "And there's coffee on the way."

Jonah let his sergeant lead the way and watched Felix follow him.

There was such assurance to the way he moved. It wasn't that he swaggered, just that he seemed entirely unfazed by everything he saw.

It was difficult to know how to interpret it. Jonah had seen some killers with an air of untouchable self-belief, but they'd usually given themselves away by smugness. He thought briefly of the few bankers he'd interviewed, who had been on the calmer end of the spectrum, and wondered whether Mr. Solomon's working life involved a lot of high-pressure meetings.

Felix maintained a neutral expression as the tape started rolling, and nodded equably when Jonah asked him if he was Zoe's landlord.

"Yes. Zoe moved in five months ago, in June."

"And how did she find the place?"

"She knew me through the coffee shop," Felix said.

"So you were friends?"

"Yes, I'd say so." He nodded. "It happens when you're a regular. Gina and I, the owner, you know, we became quite close a few years back. And quite a few of the staff come and sit and chat on their breaks."

"What do you go there to do?"

"To work, largely," Felix said.

"What's your occupation?"

"Oh, I'm retired in terms of actual work," he said. "I'm trying to write a memoir, which I acknowledge is a silly thing to do when I've never really written anything before. So I take my laptop and a note-book and I spend a few hours in there every day, working my way through more coffee than is healthy."

"Did you move here on retirement?"

"Yes, though I only came from Brighton." He gave a smile. "I originally moved to Woolston in a house that was too big for me but I moved again a little over two years ago. It seemed sensible to be more self-contained and invest in a second property that would generate income."

"So how did renting your flat to her arise?" Jonah asked.

"Zoe was looking for somewhere to live, and she knew I'd had problems with my tenant in the past. It was a good thing she asked. It gave me the motivation to kick the tenant out and move her in."

Jonah gave a slight frown. "You kicked the tenant out for her? Isn't that rather a long way to go for someone you know only casually?"

"Not when the tenant is a huge pain, and when the friend has told you she's being harassed by her ex-boyfriend," Felix said evenly.

"Do you know the identity of the ex-boyfriend?" Lightman interjected.

"Aidan Poole," Felix said. "A lecturer and, unfortunately, one with a wife."

"You learned this from Zoe?" Jonah asked.

"Yes. She'd sometimes let on about the difficult stuff." Felix glanced between Jonah and Lightman. "I'm assuming you're looking into him, so I probably don't need to add all that much. But I would want to look at him quite hard. What she told me about how he behaved . . ."

"Are you talking about his behavior in general, or during the breakup?" Lightman queried. Jonah always appreciated his sergeant's precision, his need for clarity.

"Both, really, but when she broke things off, he essentially stalked her and tried to make her take him back," Felix said. "It was awful for her. Zoe was an easy victim because she was kind, and she wanted to see the best in everyone she knew."

"Did she ever report him for it?" Jonah asked, knowing the answer.

"No," Felix said, and fixed him with a wry grin, "which I'm sure you must know. I suggested that she should, but she felt for him. Which is why people like Aidan Poole end up winning out."

"So she asked for a flat," Jonah went on, "and you helped her. Presumably she wanted to keep the address from Aidan."

"Absolutely," Felix said. "She told me she'd had to speak very firmly to her friends about it. Her former housemate, Maeve, was a bit of a pushover when it came to Aidan. After Zoe broke up with him the first time, Maeve let him into the house, and it meant he was able to talk Zoe round. And then the second time, she told him what time Zoe's coffee-shop shifts had moved to, so he found her again."

Jonah glanced at his notes. "This is Maeve Silver."

"Yes, that's it."

"Did she give a reason for this behavior?" Jonah asked.

"She said she wanted it to work out. She thought they belonged together and just needed to find a way." Felix gave an exasperated sigh. "Romantic bullshit. She'd be an abuser's dream, that one."

"You think Aidan was manipulating her?" Jonah asked slowly.

"To an extent, yes," Felix said with a nod. "And to an extent, I think Maeve did it all herself. She liked him, and liked the dynamic of them all together."

Jonah gave him a thoughtful look. The response, and the analysis of Zoe's friendship, was both considered and convincing.

"But Maeve didn't have access to the new flat? She didn't have a key?"

"No, I'm sure she didn't," Felix said. "It was one of the things Zoe was looking forward to. There was no way she could come home and find Aidan in her sitting room. I'm not entirely sure Maeve knew where the flat was."

Jonah made a point of noting this down in his book, and then changed tone deliberately as he looked up again. "You did have a key, however."

"Yes," Felix agreed. "I had a landlord's set."

"And were you in the habit of using them?"

"Only when a plumber had to get in or when Zoe had locked herself out," Felix said with a disappointing lack of willingness to rise to Jonah's words.

"Can you describe your movements on Thursday evening?" he

asked, hoping that the change of tack might unsettle Felix Solomon instead.

Felix nodded, a very slight smile on his face. "I'm happy to, though they're not that easy to corroborate. I was predominantly in the flat, tidying and then watching documentaries."

"Which documentaries were those?" Lightman asked.

"Oh . . . I'm watching *Africa* at the moment," Felix said. "And then there was one about the Kray twins. After that I . . ." He laughed. "I watched an awful traffic officer real-life thing. *The Real Road Police* or something. Those things are terrible, but it's addictive TV."

"So that was until late?" the sergeant went on.

Jonah was mentally adding all of that up, and wondering whether this viewing would have taken him up to 11 P.M., when Aidan had seen someone enter Zoe's flat and assault her. Even if they had, they were no alibi, and Felix only had to climb a single flight of stairs to get to Zoe's flat.

"Yes, I watched them until . . . probably after midnight."

"From what time?" Lightman asked in his usual flat tone.

"I'd say I tidied up from around seven. The TV would have been on by nine."

"A thorough tidy, then," Jonah commented.

Felix gave a small smile. "I know. I'm a bit obsessive about cleanliness. There was laundry and mopping and vacuuming in there, too."

Jonah wasn't certain, but he thought he might sense a hint of bullshit. It was strangely hard to tell with the self-assured Mr. Solomon. He didn't press for now. Better, he felt, to catch him out later by bringing it up again.

"What about before seven?" he asked, aware that, if they discounted Aidan Poole's statement, they could only pin down Zoe's death to some point after late afternoon.

"Ah, now that I can prove," he said. "I had my friend Esther over for tea from four. She left at about five. I have her number on my phone if you need it."

Lightman nodded, and wrote down the number Felix read out. Jonah watched for a moment, thinking of Felix's friendships with coffee-shop staff and the implication of loneliness. He asked, "Is she an old friend? Another one from the coffee shop?"

"She has a flat in the block as well, which she Airbnbs," Felix said. "I've known her off and on for a few months. She's a very kind soul and I think she picked up on the fact that I can get lonely at times."

"You don't have family?" Jonah asked.

"No. Unfortunately not." It was said affably enough, but Jonah felt that Felix was closing the question down somehow. He decided to make a show of respecting the man's boundaries for now.

"You mentioned to my constable that you'd seen Zoe arriving home. Can I clarify what time that was?"

"It was while I was getting the house straight," Felix replied. "I wish I could be more specific about the time, but my impression is that it was eight, eight-thirty or so. Certainly before I started watching things at nine." He gave a small shrug, and then his eyes cut across to Lightman and back and his tone changed. "I'd like to tell you about something that may or may not be relevant, but which I'd certainly want to take a look at if I were you."

"By all means," Jonah said.

"Zoe's next-door neighbor," Felix said, fixing Jonah with a very set gaze, "is a convicted pedophile."

There was a brief silence, and then Jonah said, "Can I ask for more details?"

"Piers Lough, in Number Fifteen," Felix said. "He moved in a year ago and he seems to work from home a lot."

"How did you come by this information?" Jonah asked. "As far as I know, requests to view the sex offenders register are limited to people with young children."

"There are other people with kids in the block of flats," Felix said quietly. "And word gets around. I'm not saying that pedophilia is any proof of the desire to murder a young woman, but it's certainly a sign that he has problems. And someone who can hear Zoe coming and going and is right next door is in a pretty good position to take her keys at some point."

"Well, we'll certainly be looking into it," Jonah said. "That's everything covered so far, except for the key to Zoe's flat. Could I have it?"

"Oh," Felix said, his hand going toward his trouser pocket and then stopping. "I haven't brought it. I'm so sorry; I just wasn't thinking . . . Can I go and get it for you?"

"That would be helpful," Jonah said. "We need the crime scene to be secure."

"Naturally," Felix said, and rose with a nod.

HANSON HAD MADE four house calls by midday, and found out nothing of any interest whatsoever. She'd taken advantage of a brief lull in the rain to do the houses around the block of flats. At three of them she'd had no reply. She'd stuffed a flyer through the letter box in each case and moved on. The other four explained that they had variously been out on Thursday or at home with the curtains drawn. None of them had seen anything. Which was the trouble with investigating a crime that had occurred in late November. Nobody had been hanging around on balconies or in gardens, drinking or smoking or chatting.

As the rain started to increase again, she headed to the front door of Zoe's block and let herself in using Angeline's sequestered key fob. She headed up to the second floor and knocked at Number 17, right next to the murdered girl's flat on its left-hand side. She was pleased to hear footsteps approaching, and she smiled at the woman inside when she answered. But to Hanson's disappointment it turned out that the resident had been away all week and only returned late on Friday night.

With a sigh, Hanson moved on to Flat 15, which was at the end on the far side of Zoe's. She glanced at Zoe's shiny number 16 on the way past, thinking momentarily of the scene in the bathroom.

Flat 15 turned out to be occupied by a young man with a slightly harassed expression. He sighed when she asked for his help, but he let her into his sitting room—a carbon copy of Zoe's—and even offered Hanson a cup of tea.

"That's OK, thanks," she told him with a smile as he drifted toward the kitchen area. It was best not to accept hospitality. It made it harder to leave in a hurry. "I'm just here to ask whether you saw or heard anything strange on Thursday night."

"Thursday?" he asked, looking around with a distracted expression as if wondering what he'd come to the kitchen for. "Umm . . . What sort of things? Has there been a burglary?"

Hanson felt a rush of surprise. Most of the other neighbors had known what she was asking about as soon as she'd explained she was from the police. Was he really unaware that his neighbor had been murdered?

"No, I'm afraid there's been a murder."

He stopped looking around and focused on her. "What?"

"The young woman living in the flat next door, I'm afraid."

"Oh my God," he said, and leaned back against the counter, his eyes strobing left to right, left to right. Trying to remember something, she thought. "Zoe. The artist."

"Yes, I'm afraid so." Hanson looked away from him, scanning the flat. There was a desk by the window, with an open laptop and a huge pair of headphones. It looked like he'd been working. And then her phone buzzed, and she pulled it out to look at a message from the DCI.

Tip-off from Felix Solomon about man in Flat 15. Piers Lough. Apparently a sex offender. We're checking it out, but suggest waiting to interview him.

"What happened?" the young man asked, and Hanson did her best to smile up at him as if her pulse rate hadn't just doubled.

"Sorry? Oh. We're investigating," she said, aware that her voice sounded strained. "But we'd class it as a suspicious death, so we really need to know if you saw or heard anything."

She wondered if she should message the DCI back, or pretend that she needed to leave. But it seemed ridiculous. He might be a sex offender of some kind, but that didn't mean she had to be afraid to be in the same room as him.

"Right," he was saying. "God, that's really horrible. I was . . . I was here. On Thursday night."

Hanson gave him an attempt at a smile and pulled out her notebook.

"That's useful to know," she said, telling herself that she was going to do this interview right and stop being pathetic. "Could I ask if you saw or heard Zoe coming or going from the flat that evening?"

"No, I wasn't . . . I've been working flat-out. I'm supposed to be audiotyping a load of files and they arrived late, and since Wednesday I've barely been outside. Sorry." He waved a hand toward the laptop.

"That's all right," she started to say with a smile.

"Oh, wait." His eyes flicked left to right again, and then he said, "You know I actually think I did hear her. It must have been on Thursday. I was trying to work and someone was talking really loudly, and it kept cutting through the audiotapes to the point where I was having to stop and rewind. It was driving me mad, and I was thinking of going and finding out who it was and having a go. But then it quieted down."

"That's really useful," Hanson said, scribbling in her notebook but wondering whether this might be a way of diverting attention from his criminal record. "Do you know what time that was?"

"Ahh . . ." He was thoughtful again, and then offered, "It would have been nineish. Maybe a bit later. Not really late because I remember thinking it wasn't the kind of time where you could call the police and complain . . ." He gave a sudden short laugh. "And I know that sounds totally over the top, but that's how stressed out I've been about it all."

Hanson gave him what she hoped was a sympathetic smile as she watched him carefully. She wondered about the slight sheen of sweat on his face. About the nervous fiddling with his hair. "Can you give any more details? Was it an argument?"

"Yes, I think so," he said. "Though I was mostly hearing only one voice. I couldn't hear any words," he added. "It was just this booming right over the top of the voices on the tape."

"A male voice?" she asked.

"Yes, definitely."

"And you say it suddenly ended? What time would that be?"

"Well, not much later . . ." He broke off, and then said with a triumphant smile, "Nine twenty-seven! It was at nine twenty-seven. I'd told myself if he didn't shut the hell up by nine-thirty, I'd go and bang on the door."

"And you think it came from next door?" she asked.

"Oh, well, I'm not certain." He gave her a worried look. "Sorry, I didn't mean to pretend I thought . . . It could have been from above or below, to be honest. I was getting it through the headphones. It must have been from one of those three flats, though, as you don't get noise from any others. It's unusual to hear anything at all. They're reasonably well insulated."

Hanson nodded, a little more convinced by his uncertainty than she had been by his certainty. Perhaps he really had heard something. Though it might have nothing to do with Zoe's death.

It occurred to her then that an argument might tie in with the bruising on Zoe's hand. What if the argument had become violent, and Zoe had ended up hitting her attacker? Might she have some of the killer's DNA on her knuckles?

She decided that she could both check his story and narrow down where any noise had come from. She just needed to check the flats above and below.

"That's been really, really useful, Mr. . . ." She tailed off, realizing that she hadn't asked his name, and only knew it from the message from the DCI. She smiled politely. "Could I take your name?"

"Oh, sorry," he said. "Piers. Piers Lough."

She wrote it down despite already knowing it and took his phone number and email as well. And then she thanked him and left, profoundly relieved once she was out in the hall with the door shut behind her.

LIGHTMAN SETTLED HIMSELF at his desk, immediately comforted at having a task list that played to his strengths. Things had been up in the air since yesterday, and although working on a Saturday wasn't exactly routine, it still gave him a sense of normality.

He decided to tackle the alibis before the sex offender. Alphabetical approaches to lists were his go-to whenever there wasn't a clear order of priority.

It wasn't the easiest task to call the Swardadines and ask them if they could confirm their own movements on the night of their daughter's death, but Siku seemed to approve of his thoroughness at least.

"Just as long as you're being equally rigorous elsewhere," she said. And then, after a pause, "You haven't found out any more about what Aidan was doing?"

"We're checking his story using a digital trail," Lightman said immediately, glad that he'd read the DCI's notes on his interview of the night before. He didn't add that the digital trail seemed to support Aidan's innocence. That, as far as Lightman was concerned, was up to the chief to reveal. "We're taking it very seriously, given his relationship to Zoe."

"Good," Siku said. She then went on to explain that she'd been doing locum work at Highfield Surgery in West Hampstead, one of several urgent clinics to which she gave locum hours during evenings and weekends.

"Thank you. And your husband?"

"Martin was at a dinner, I think." There were muffled movements, and then Siku called to her husband. "Martin. Martin! Was it a client dinner you were at on Thursday?"

"Fuller and Michael," came the audible response.

"Got it, thanks," Lightman said. It would be easy enough to check that with Martin's own firm, though he doubted he'd get an answer on a Saturday.

He finished the call with more thanks, and found an admin number for Highfield's clinic. In contrast to most surgeries, it turned out to be useful calling on a Saturday. The out-of-hours service was running and he eventually managed to talk to the clinic manager, who confirmed that Siku Swardadine had been on with them from 6 P.M. until 3 A.M.

So that was the mother ruled out, then, Lightman thought, putting the phone down. There was predictably no reply at Martin Swardadine's office, so he made a note to call again later and then again on Monday if he'd had no joy.

Greta Poole's press dinner proved easy to google, and the event organizer's mobile phone number was listed on the website under the name Penny Dawson. Penny answered after a few rings.

"This is DS Ben Lightman from Hampshire Constabulary," he said. "I've got a boring bit of pro forma to do. I just need to establish that Greta Poole was an award presenter at Thursday's dinner."

"Right," Penny said, clearly thrown. "I . . . Who did you say?"

"DS Lightman," he repeated. "From Hampshire Constabulary. If you'd like to check the website and call me back, that's fine. I'm listed on there."

"That's OK," Penny said. "I just wasn't expecting a call. Yeah, Greta was presenting the award for science writing that she won last year."

"Was this an after-dinner presentation?"

"Yeah. The guests all sat down at seven forty-five, and then we did the awards at nine. Greta did hers . . . fifth, I think? Sorry . . ." Her tone suddenly changed. "What exactly is this for?"

"Just establishing timings before an altercation a little later in the evening," Lightman said. "It's highly likely that Mrs. Poole wasn't involved, but we have to check."

"Oh, right," Penny said. "Well, I don't think she can have been in an altercation later on. She was at the dinner until really late. She helped put one of the other delegates to bed."

"Ah, that's useful," Lightman said warmly. "Thank you. Do you know what time?"

"That must have been . . . a little before one?" Penny replied. "I wasn't drinking, by the way. In case that helps."

"That's great, thank you," Lightman said.

So Greta Poole was unsurprisingly also placed in London on that night. The third alibi he had on his list was Felix Solomon's, though it was for a time earlier in the evening than Zoe had almost certainly been killed. While it was technically a box-ticking exercise, it represented a good opportunity to talk to a suspect's friend.

He put a call through to Felix's friend Esther, who answered with initial trepidation but warmed up swiftly when she learned they wanted to ask about Felix.

"Oh, you don't think Felix has done anything? He's such a gentle soul." She had a warm, lively voice and an accent that Lightman thought might be of Czech origin. "I did have tea with him, and then I went to drive home. I think I headed off at about five, maybe?" she said. "I started thinking I'd better get moving to be back to make food. I live in Winchester now."

"And how did he seem?"

Esther gave a sigh. "He was like he sometimes is. A little in need of comfort."

"Comfort?" Lightman thought back to the man they had just seen, who had seemed to need no help of any kind.

"He has PTSD," she said. "Sometimes it gets really bad, and he needs company. He often calls when it's awful, just to hear some-one's voice. I answer when I can, but I have a family, you know?"

"I'm sorry to hear that," Lightman said. "Do you know what it dates back to? The PTSD?"

"He never told me, and I wasn't going to pry," Esther replied.

"Well, that's helpful. Thank you."

Lightman ended the call and started to type his notes up carefully, thinking that the chief would want to know this unexpected side to Zoe's landlord. Though perhaps it was a surprise only to Lightman.

JONAH FOUND HIMSELF considering everything that Felix Solomon had said for some time after he'd left. He still couldn't quite put a finger on what it was about the man that unsettled him. It was some-where between his calm and the way he spoke. It was as if he knew everything Jonah was going to ask before he asked it.

He realized that Hanson would probably still be near to the crime scene when Felix arrived home. He called her mobile.

"How's it going?"

"Good," Hanson said. "Though unfortunately I was already in Flat Fifteen when you messaged."

"Ah," Jonah said. "Sorry about that. All OK?"

"I think so," she said. "He seems nervous, as I suppose you would be with a criminal record. He also said he heard a man yelling in what he thought was Zoe's flat, and the upstairs neighbor's just confirmed it. So it wasn't fabricated, and while it could still have been him doing the shouting, it'd be weird to draw attention to it if so."

"What time?" Jonah asked, sitting up.

"Nineish. Done before half past. So a while before the probable time of death, but it's interesting."

"That it is," Jonah agreed, thinking of the two wineglasses that had been on Zoe's worktop. If Zoe had argued with someone, it was possible that it had been the killer. And if she'd drunk with them, they might well have the killer's DNA on a wineglass. "Are you still at the flats?"

"Just leaving now," Hanson replied.

"Could you hang around for a bit?" Jonah asked. "Until Felix Solomon gets back? I'd like eyes on him, particularly as he still has Zoe's key. He claimed he hadn't brought it with him, but I have a strong suspicion that wasn't true."

"Sure," Hanson said with what he sensed was false enthusiasm. "What did he have to say, apart from the sex offender stuff?"

"Not much of an alibi," Jonah said. "He's also strangely self-confident, and he's clearly a smart guy, both of which are ramping him up in the suspicion stakes."

"OK. I'll be here."

HANSON OCCUPIED HERSELF with strolling up and down Latterworth Road on the out-of-town side of the block of flats, keeping the door in sight and glancing over at it frequently. It was a wide, quiet road, and it should be reasonably easy to spot Felix approaching. At that point, she would have to follow him inside as quietly as she could. There was nowhere within the building she could get away with waiting.

She found herself thinking about Piers Lough again, wondering what he'd done to end up on the sex offenders register. She wondered whether Zoe had known about him, or had trusted him as a friendly next-door neighbor. The thought was skin-crawling. Though it had been Felix Solomon who had had a key to the flat, she thought. Not Piers Lough.

She turned again at the top of the road, and saw Felix making his way on foot toward the front door. She immediately pulled her phone out and pretended to be making a call, but Felix didn't seem to notice her.

She waited until he'd let himself into the building, and then began to walk as quickly as she could toward it. The door had just closed by the time she got there, and she checked that he was no longer in the hallway before using the fob.

There was the swish and bang of a fire door closing somewhere above. She hurried to the stairs and then went up them as silently as she could, taking them two at a time but planting her feet carefully. She peered through the glass panel in the fire door toward the first floor, but there was no sign of Felix. His door was shut, too.

She hesitated, and then climbed up to the second floor, taking care again to be quiet. The fire door was shut here, too, and there was no sign of anyone outside Number 17. But by flattening herself against the door and peering at an angle, she could see farther, all the way to Zoe's door and a little past.

And there was Felix Solomon, standing frozen in front of the door with a key held out in the palm of his hand. Hanson reached for her phone, thinking of photographing him, but then he looked up suddenly and met her gaze.

She reacted quickly, despite the thumping of her heart. She opened the door and stepped into the hallway with a smile.

"Oh, hi," she said as he swiftly and unsmilingly returned the key to his right-hand trouser pocket and turned away from the door.

"Good afternoon," Felix said, and his slight smile was back once again, easy and confident. "You're not looking for me, are you?"

"No, no," Hanson said, for some reason feeling like she was the one who had to explain herself. "I'm just . . . trying to find Zoe's cat." She gave him a nod.

"Oh," Felix said, his expression showing sudden concern. "Is he missing?"

"We haven't seen him yet," Hanson replied. "But hopefully he's just hiding somewhere in the flat."

"I hope so," Felix said. "He's a beautiful thing. Snow white and a total charmer. He's probably missing her a lot."

Hanson was closer now, and the corridor was well lit enough for her to see that Felix Solomon's eyes were damp.

"You must miss her, too," she said quietly.

"Yes." Felix nodded. "Yes, I do. And I want you to catch whoever did it."

"What were you doing up here?" she asked gently.

Felix glanced toward Zoe's door. "I was trying to summon up the courage to have a look inside. And before you say anything, I know it's a crime scene. I wasn't going to touch anything, and you'll have done all your prints already. I just wanted to see the empty flat and know . . . well. Know that it's true."

Hanson watched him steadily, and then said, "I'd better take the key, if you don't mind?"

Felix fixed her with a very steely gaze, despite the hint of tears. "It is . . . my flat, you know."

Hanson simply held her hand out and waited. Felix continued to hold her gaze for a few seconds and then looked away. He made a frustrated sound and pulled the key out of his pocket. He pressed it into her hand.

"Do a good job, Constable. And make sure your chief does, too." As Hanson nodded, he said, "I mean, the best job you've ever done. Zoe deserves it."

14

"Will you do my eyes for me, too?" Angeline asked from the bedroom doorway. "If you have time?"

Zoe smiled at her in the mirror, wetting the tiny paintbrush she was using to apply gleaming gold to her lids. "Of course I have time. Give me five minutes." She leaned forward to paint a tiny flower on the outside of her left eye, and then picked up a freshly glued rhinestone with a pair of tweezers and placed it in the very center of the petals.

She loved the gleam of it all. The way it took attention away from everything else, including the slight crookedness of her teeth, her round face, and what she had always thought an ugly nose. It made people look at her eyes instead. The important part of her.

She glanced at Angeline. "Your dress is gorgeous," she said.

Angeline beamed at her and stretched the pale-gray velvet to one side. There wasn't a lot of spare material, even on Angeline's tiny frame. "It was one of the ones from the Clothes Show last year. Fifteen quid."

"Oh my God," Zoe said, adding a gleam of bronze just at the base of her eyelid. "How do you do that? I spent two days there and only came back with overpriced skin products that some horribly beautiful woman intimidated me into buying."

"I'll take you this year, if you like," Angeline said.

"Definitely," Zoe said, and then she rose. "Right. Your turn."

Angeline took her place on the padded seat in front of the vanity table, and Zoe opened up one of the drawers. "What would you like? I think maybe silver colors to match the dress." She cast her eyes over Angeline's face and figure. "With some blue in, I think?"

"Whatever you think!" Angeline said with a shrug.

Zoe smiled, glad that things between them seemed to be back to normal. Angeline hadn't wanted to see her for most of the last month. She'd been hurt when Zoe had lectured her on her drinking and putting herself at the mercy of strangers. She'd told her that Zoe wasn't her bloody mother, and she'd left Zoe's flat in tears.

Zoe had felt a strange terror that she'd driven Angeline to be stupid again. She imagined her calling Richie, or some other strange man with nasty things on his mind. She'd tried calling her, but Angeline had rejected her calls repeatedly and hadn't even read her messages.

Zoe had had to rely on Maeve and Victor to watch out for her, and it had been an anxious few weeks. But in the end, Angeline had capitulated and called to ask, in a small voice, if she could come and meet Aidan, too.

Zoe cast her eyes over her friend again, taking in the darkness of the smudges under Angeline's eyes. She wondered how much sleep she'd had during this past month, and how much she'd drunk. Well, however much it was, Zoe could at least help her cover up some of the effects.

She drew out her full set of metallics, all of which had been ordered from a specialist online store. It generally catered to burlesque dancers and circus performers. Just looking at the shimmering silvers, golds, bold pinks, blues, and greens made Zoe smile.

"These ones," she said, pulling out a silver, an ice blue, and a blue the color of the evening sky. "We'll do the eyeliner first, though."

Her eye pencil and liquid liner were already out. Zoe never

did a look without them. The dark liner turned her eyes from ordinary to stunning, and the few times she'd met her friends without
applying it, they'd asked her if she was feeling unwell. She had
sighed, and then gone home and put some on, not wanting to destroy the illusion that the huge eyes everyone commented on were
natural.

Angeline, on the other hand, had enormous eyes as a result of
barely eating. Her delicate face was dominated by them, making her
look like a china doll, or—as she'd told Aidan—like Bambi, depending on whether she was wearing makeup.

"Look up at me," Zoe said, and leaned in to add eyeliner.

Angeline closed her eyes and smiled. "It's so nice having someone
put makeup on for you," she said. "It feels like being looked after. It's
like when my mum used to look for head lice in my hair."

Zoe gave a slight laugh. "Do you need me to do that, too?"

"Hope not," Angeline said.

"Are you going to stay here tonight?" she asked as she worked.
"You can sleep in my bed if you like."

"Oh . . . No, I don't think so." Zoe could see the way Angeline's
brow drew into a frown. "I'll go home." There was a pause, and she
added, "I'd probably better do some laundry and then . . . work."

"Sure." Zoe was unable to fight off the anxiety that arose in her
stomach. It wasn't hard to tell that Angeline was lying. And she had a
suspicion that she'd been hiding another liaison that would make
Zoe's skin crawl.

ZOE DIDN'T LIKE the way Maeve was looking at Aidan. It was a cold
look, appraising and analytical. She found herself squeezing his hand
under the table repeatedly, and ordering drink after drink.

She wasn't sure how Aidan could seem so unfazed. Zoe felt like
she'd done everything wrong. She shouldn't have had both girls
there, so he was left having to compliment Angeline and debate with
Maeve all at once. She shouldn't have booked a popular restaurant,

either. It was overrun with people and the staff had the constant air of wishing they'd hurry up and leave.

They needed quiet. They needed the chance for Maeve to talk to Aidan and understand what he was like, and for Angeline to relax and stop flinching. Perhaps even to eat something. And for Zoe to stop feeling like her attention was being torn in multiple directions.

But Aidan just went with it all, seeming not to notice any difficulties. He smoothly mopped up Angeline's drink when she spilled it, and didn't seem to mind that some of the red wine had spattered his expensive blue sleeve. He smiled in appreciation as Maeve argued with almost everything he said, treating her as a valued opponent instead of getting angry with her.

To Zoe, he was wonderful. His arm slid round her from time to time, and he drew her gently into the conversation frequently, referring everything to her without pressure. She felt at the center of everything, even through the haze of worry.

Zoe felt immeasurably proud of him. Proud of owning him, in a sense. The thought was tinged with its own worry, because Aidan wasn't really hers. Not yet. He belonged to Greta still, and the two of them were enjoying a stolen season. There would be divorce paperwork and house sales all too soon.

"Bloody good food," Aidan said after the main courses had been finished. Angeline, of course, had pushed most of hers onto Maeve's plate, and then Aidan's, but she'd managed a few mouthfuls. "Drink, anyone? I'll go to the bar. Zoe's not allowed. She'll only end up ordering Jäger Bombs."

Zoe looked at him gratefully. Her glass of Rioja had been emptied for the fourth time some time ago, and the longer she'd sat waiting for another refill, the edgier she'd become. She didn't want to be overthinking the complex dynamics. She wanted a warm glow that made everyone seem like firm friends.

"Another gin and tonic, Maeve?" Aidan asked as he made his way round the table.

"Thank you," Maeve replied, and actually smiled a little this time. "I tell you what, I'll come and help you carry them."

Aidan agreed with a grin, and Zoe felt wrong-footed, as though Maeve had taken her place somehow.

Angeline seemed glad that Aidan had shifted, though. She came to scrunch in next to Zoe, tucking an arm round her waist and leaning her head on Zoe's shoulder.

"He's good fun," she said quietly. "I like him. And you're happy with him, aren't you?"

Zoe kissed her on the top of the head, feeling a flood of gratitude toward tiny, porcelain-fragile Angeline.

"Yes, I am," she said, not even feeling much of a pang when she went on to think about Greta. "I just hope he can sort out the divorce soon."

"He will," Angeline answered confidently. "You're wonderful. He'll want to spend all of his days with you."

Zoe laughed, her eyes drifting over to the light-strewn bar. "I think you might be biased, my darling. But I hope so." And she gave Angeline a squeeze. "You doing OK?"

She felt Angeline nod against her shoulder. It was a sleepy nod, closely followed by a huff of air. It reminded Zoe of her parents' King Charles spaniel cuddling up to her, and she grinned. A little of the worry was seeping away, though she wished she knew what Maeve was talking to Aidan about. She could see her mouse-brown curls almost touching his dark waves as she leaned over to talk to him. Two lots of hair looking like they might merge.

And then Aidan turned, his eyes searching for her. The moment he saw her, his expression lit up, and she wasn't so worried about what Maeve had to say. This was right. The two of them were right.

SHE DIDN'T END up talking to Maeve alone until later on, when Aidan had gone out to hail a cab, which he insisted was better than calling one.

Maeve took a large gulp of her gin and then leaned over to rub Zoe's forearm.

"All right. He's not a horrible cheating slime bag," she said, and her mouth twisted into a smile. "He's a good person who's found himself in a difficult situation. And you two are gorgeous together."

Zoe had a sudden strange urge to cry. It was probably two parts relief to two parts alcohol, but it made her feel a surge of huge affection for her infuriating housemate.

It would all be easier now. Maeve liked Aidan. She approved of Aidan. Who gave a shit if she never listened to a word Zoe said?

"I'm so glad you think so, too," she said, and momentarily knotted her fingers through Maeve's.

"Ah, steady on," Maeve said, pulling her hand away with a laugh. And then she leaned over and gave her a proper hug. "Could you just . . . make sure you tell Victor, too?" she said.

Zoe's pleasure dimmed a little, and she withdrew from the hug. "Yes, of course I will," she said, although the idea made her feel a heavy weight of dread.

"Otherwise, he's the only one who doesn't know, isn't he?" Maeve persisted.

"I know."

"But it's all OK," Maeve added, as if understanding how she felt. "Aidan's such a charmer, Victor'll be won round."

Zoe heard a call from the door and turned to see Aidan triumphantly beckoning her over from where he'd summoned a taxi the old-fashioned way.

"Even if he is a bit of a Luddite," Maeve added.

Zoe grabbed her coat and bag, and said a hasty goodbye. "See you tomorrow," she said to Angeline, who was now sitting with her feet tucked up on her chair. In this more optimistic mood, it seemed ridiculous to worry about some stupid guy Angeline had met on Tinder and was probably bored with by now.

She knew the two girls were watching as she went over and kissed

Aidan lingeringly on the lips, but she didn't feel it mattered. He gave her a very young-looking smile, and put his arms around her for just a moment. "Let's get you home," he said, and let his hands drift onto her backside.

As he turned and ushered her out, his arm still around her, she felt suddenly like everything was going to be all right now.

15

"Sir?" Lightman said, tapping on Jonah's door with a pen.

"Yup." Jonah drew his gaze away from the middle distance and gave Lightman a nod. "What have you got?"

"Alibis check out for Siku Swardadine and Greta Poole, and for Felix Solomon's early-evening tea. His friend Esther mentioned that he suffers from some form of PTSD, which I thought was interesting. Apparently he can have bad bouts, and tends to call her in a panic."

"Hmm. Maybe he's not quite as together as he seems," Jonah said. "I wonder if he was in the habit of calling Zoe at the worst moments, too. In Juliette's initial chat with him, he mentioned calling her, and apparently they chatted quite a bit in general."

"So he might have become reliant on her," Lightman said.

"Exactly. I'll see what her other friends have to say about that when they get here."

"I looked up Piers Lough, too," the sergeant went on, "and Felix Solomon has it wrong. There *is* a Piers Lough in the database, but it's not that Piers Lough. The convicted pedophile is twenty-one years older. He changed address without notifying the authorities a few months ago, and they've listed this address as potentially his. But the Piers who lives next door to Zoe has been there a year and a half and was involved in a local pantomime last Christmas. I've checked the pictures, and they look nothing like each other."

"OK," Jonah said, and then he laughed. "A groundless smear, then."

"Yes," Lightman replied. "Though I wondered about how Felix Solomon found out. I don't see how many rumors can have come about when the police weren't sure if he was the right man. They can't have notified any young families in the area based on that."

Jonah absorbed this and then said, "Absolutely right. So how the hell did Felix Solomon latch onto it?"

"If I had to guess," Lightman said evenly, "I'd say he's the sort of man who googles all of his neighbors. There are articles online mentioning this other Piers Lough. And assuming all he'd seen was his neighbor's name on letters or something, he could easily have jumped to conclusions."

Jonah brooded on this for a moment. "The nosy retired neighbor," he said. "Or, just possibly, someone desperate to send us in the wrong direction."

"Yeah. That's another possible explanation," Lightman replied.

Jonah's phone buzzed. Hanson, presumably with an update. He nodded to Lightman to let him go as he answered.

"I have news for you, before anything else," Jonah told her. "The Piers Lough in Zoe's building is not the sex offender. Wrong age, wrong body type."

"Oh, right. Thanks," she said, and he wasn't sure if she was relieved or disappointed.

"Did you see Felix?"

"I did. Felix got back and went straight up to Zoe's flat. When I got up there, he was standing outside the door with the key in his hand. He hadn't gone into his own flat, so he must have had it with him. Exactly as you thought."

"What did he have to say for himself?"

"He claimed he wanted to go in there to fully understand that it was all real," she said.

"But you're not convinced," Jonah said.

"No, I'm not. And I'm not positive on this, but I wondered if he was trying to solve the crime himself."

Jonah gave a half laugh. "I guess he isn't the first would-be Poirot."

"No, but I've been wondering if there's a reason for him being particularly interested," she said hesitantly.

"Interested in Zoe?"

"No, in policing," she said. "Because I know this sounds odd, but several times when he's spoken, he's reminded me quite strongly of you. Are you positive he's not an ex-copper?"

O'MALLEY ROLLED INTO the office at 1:45, and Lightman raised his eyebrows at him.

"You do realize it's Saturday? If you're going to stay on the blackmail case, you also have the privilege of keeping hold of your weekend."

"This is all true," O'Malley said, nodding, "but if I kept my nose out of the murder inquiry, I wouldn't be able to tell you how to do your job. Where's the fun in that?" He sat himself down and swung his chair around to face Lightman. "So, go on. A rundown."

Lightman gave him a swift summary of where they were as far as he knew.

"So we've realistically got three friends, one of whom has a key, plus a landlord, as likely suspects," O'Malley summarized once he was done. "And a father who may or may not be exonerated due to being in London, and a boyfriend who was almost definitely back at home in Alton and on Skype to her."

"That's about it," Lightman agreed. "And the CCTV footage from the back of the building and farther up the road has arrived. So if you feel like scrolling through endless hours of that . . ."

"Sling it over," O'Malley replied. "And any photos of the friends and family while you're at it. I've only met two of them."

JONAH HAD TO laugh at himself. It had taken him a mere minute to find Felix Solomon's police record. Hanson's feeling that Felix had reminded her of Jonah was a little uncomfortable, but proved to be absolutely on the money. He had been a DCI, too, but based in Brighton. He'd therefore been part of East Sussex Constabulary rather than Hampshire. He'd almost definitely been on some of the same training courses as Jonah without him ever remembering.

Felix had retired early, at the age of fifty-three. Jonah had, sadly, no immediate access to psych reports, but his friend Esther's comments about PTSD were right. Felix had quit policing after three months of erratic behavior and therapy, both triggered by a particularly awful incident involving a family.

The fact that he'd been a DCI once made perfect sense of several things, including why he had been so comfortable in the interview room and why he'd had a constant aura of knowing what Jonah was about to do. Other things, it shed less light on. It was still unclear whether Felix had been involved in Zoe's death.

The attempt to get into her flat could indeed have been a desire to investigate for himself. Jonah found it depressingly easy to imagine himself in Felix's shoes, retired and out of the loop but determined to find out who had killed his friend. But equally, if Felix had for some reason decided to kill Zoe, he could well have wanted to check up on the crime scene. He might even have wanted to alter something to frame someone else.

And then there was the tip-off about Piers Lough. It was suddenly a great deal more likely that Felix had learned of this through sources he shouldn't have been using. A former colleague was one option, if Felix knew someone on the force who was willing to run a risk for him. The other option was that Felix still had access to the Brighton database. And this idea made Jonah feel distinctly uneasy.

While mulling this over, he pinged an email over to DCS Wilkinson asking for the psych reports and the case files for the event that tipped Felix Solomon over the edge. He was unlikely to get a response until Monday, but it was another thing crossed off the list. And then he rose and went to talk to O'Malley.

He didn't get particularly far. Lightman glanced up and said, "Have you got a minute, sir?"

As Jonah approached, Lightman angled his screen so that they could both see it.

"This is the camera at the bottom of Latterworth Road. It's the junction you'd pass if you were heading from the direction of town to Zoe's flat."

"OK," Jonah said.

"This is ten forty-nine P.M. onward. So a few minutes before the probable time of the murder."

The frozen black-and-white image of a T-junction jumped to life as Lightman pressed the Play button. There was a jogger halfway across the screen. Male and powerful-looking. Jonah watched the build and the face, trying to set it alongside the suspects they'd seen so far, but it didn't match any of them. He was too big for either Aidan Poole or Victor Varos.

"Keep watching," Lightman said as the junction grew quiet again.

At just after ten-fifty, a man appeared on-screen wearing a tracksuit and cap, his walk made off-kilter by a large sports kit on his back. None of his face was visible, and for some reason, watching him, Jonah felt like he knew that. A few steps later, he put his hand up to the cap, as if checking that the brim was covering him, and Lightman paused the video.

Jonah felt a sensation of cold make its way up his spine. Everything about the figure shouted wrongness. The covered face, the apparent awareness of the camera, the hurrying walk. And he'd been walking toward Zoe's flat just over ten minutes before someone may have let themselves in and killed her.

"Does he appear again?" Jonah asked.

"Not on this camera," Lightman said, fast-forwarding. The sped-up footage captured a couple walking comically quickly away from town at eleven. Lightman slowed it down to normal speed as they left the frame. The only figures to come back toward town were a frumpy-looking woman in a fur coat and a man walking his dog.

"There's nobody from eleven-thirteen until eleven-thirty," Lightman said, "and then a girl on a bike and another elderly man. I've scanned through up until midnight and there's no sign of him coming back."

"Check the other video feed, the one from the car park," Jonah said. "See if he makes it as far as the block of flats."

"Will do."

"If it looks like he went as far as the flats, we'll need to look at tracing him back to wherever he came from. Which will mean more CCTV." *And,* he thought in frustration, *more time spent waiting for it to come through.*

"You think it's definitely a he?" Lightman asked.

Jonah hesitated. "It's pretty hard to tell under the cap. It's a fairly male walk, but I think they know they're being observed, so that could be faked. I'm not positive on height, but definitely taller than Angeline Judd. Do we know how tall Maeve Silver is?"

"Not hugely tall," O'Malley called over. "Maybe an inch or so shorter than I am."

"So she might be big enough," Jonah said.

Lightman rewound the video, his expression thoughtful. "If it turns out they went toward Zoe's flat, I'll look into getting a height estimate."

Jonah left him to it, and went to start off another line of inquiry.

"So, Domnall," he began, "you know how you're supposed to be on the blackmail case . . ."

"Ah, I was, so," O'Malley said, lifting his hands off his keyboard. "I'm only helping out Ben here for a few."

Jonah laughed. "I wasn't about to tell you to get back on it. It was more whether you fancied extending your investigations to a related incident."

O'Malley gave him a shrewd gaze. "This wouldn't by any chance be a related incident that has a direct bearing on your murder case, would it?"

"It could be," Jonah agreed. He leaned on the empty desk across the aisle from O'Malley. "Zoe's landlord turns out to be a former DCI from Brighton, which Juliette worked out and I totally failed to clock."

"Felix Solomon?" Lightman asked from beyond O'Malley. "Oh. Well, I suppose that makes sense."

"It does and it doesn't," Jonah said. "If he's a former copper, then I'm concerned about where he's getting his information."

"Ah, and now I see the blackmail link," O'Malley said with a grin. "You want me to work out whether he's finding information out that he shouldn't be able to through a clever bit of hacking."

"Yes, I do," Jonah said. "And you'd need to be looking at the Brighton database . . ."

O'Malley gave a low laugh. "Jesus. You didn't say you wanted *me* to do hacking . . ."

"I'm hoping that's not necessary," Jonah said, offering a small smile of his own. "And if it is, of course I wouldn't suggest it . . ."

"Leave it with me," O'Malley replied, and then he added, "I think I'm going to need someone more technical." He held up a hand. "You can leave that with me, too."

By the time Maeve Silver arrived at the station, Lightman had confirmed that their figure in the cap had passed the other camera in the car park for the flats. He or she had been on the right side of the road to reach the door to Zoe's flat, so it was quite possible that they had gone inside.

Lightman had also spent some time getting reference points for the individual's height, a difficult thing to do, but it was helped by having a range of other individuals on the camera to compare it to.

"I'd put the bottom range at five-eight," Lightman told him. "Could be anything up to six-two."

"That doesn't rule out anyone except Angeline, by the sounds of it," Jonah muttered. "I'll see if we get anything out of Maeve Silver on the subject."

Maeve arrived at reception shortly afterward, and Jonah went to show her up. She had, he thought, the look of someone who was barely holding it together. Her eyes were overly bright, and every time Jonah spoke to her, she would nod with excessive enthusiasm and say, "Sure. Sure," then tuck a curl behind her ear, only for it to fall forward again.

He noticed that she was also wearing a crucifix on a chain beneath her light-blue shirt. Which probably meant she was a fairly committed Christian, given that she was only in her twenties.

Jonah let her into the interview room, and saw her brighten as Lightman sat opposite her. It was the standard reaction from most women, and quite a number of men.

With the tape rolling, Jonah began gently. "A death like this can be a huge shock," he started. "We understand that it'll be difficult to talk about. But could you tell us when you last saw Zoe?"

Maeve nodded, and folded her hands in her lap before she started. "We were all together on Wednesday night. We met for food at La Mejican. You know it? It was me and Angeline, and Victor and Zoe. So we were together. I haven't . . . didn't see her after that."

"So you had no contact from her on the Thursday?"

"No." Maeve shook her head. "That's not unusual. We'll often talk every few days if we're both busy."

"And no knowledge of her movements?" Jonah added.

"No, I'm afraid not. I know Angeline was going to see her, but. . . ." She shrugged, and then sniffed and rubbed the back of her hand to each eye briefly. "I thought about dropping in, yesterday, while I was cycling past, but there were police everywhere. I thought it was probably someone else's flat. I wanted to believe it was, you know? But then when I tried to call her, there was nothing." She gave a short, teary laugh. "I was there trying to tell myself, you know . . .

that it was just a coincidence. But then I went to see Victor and he said she'd not shown up for work, and I knew. I knew something awful had happened."

Maeve was shaking as she pulled a handkerchief out and blew her nose. She looked as cut up as Angeline Judd had, but seemed unwilling to give in to the feeling.

"Sorry. I'm sorry." She gave Jonah a watery smile. "You need to ask questions."

"That's all right," he said as kindly as he could. "It's not an easy time. We can give you a minute if you like."

"No, you're OK. Go on."

Lightman rose silently and went to fetch a cup of water from the dispenser in the corner. He filled it and handed it to her in silence.

"Thank you," Maeve said, smiling again.

"Were you anywhere near Zoe's flat on the Thursday evening?" Jonah asked, watching for any change in expression. Maeve's eyes followed Lightman as he sat down once again, but there was no other visible reaction. No sign of stress.

"Ah, no. I had a ladies' supper." As Jonah gave her a querying look, she explained, "It's a church thing. Where the girls all get together and eat. We alternate. Girls one week, boys the next. You know."

"And what time was that?"

"Ahhh . . . sevenish? I was a bit late, if I'm honest." She gave Lightman a brief, self-deprecating smile, and then looked back at Jonah. "I guess I was there until, like . . . nine-thirty? Something like that. And then I went home."

"How did Zoe seem the night before?" Jonah asked. "The Wednesday?"

"She seemed fine," Maeve said. "I mean, she'd not really been herself since she and Aidan broke up the last time. She was pretty messed up about it all."

"Do you think her mental health had suffered?" Jonah asked.

"Yeah," Maeve said. "No question. I think it was a bit fragile before. She'd suddenly lost all this weight, and the eye-makeup thing went from an occasional going-out to all the time."

"Sorry," Jonah said. "Eye makeup?"

"Oh, I guess . . . She loved to do this elaborate stuff. Incredible colors and designs, like swirls of black or gold, and rhinestones stuck on. It was more like a painting. Kind of using her face as art, like."

Jonah nodded slowly. "And you think the increase in that was due to . . . insecurity? About Aidan?"

"Well, I don't know. It was just a theory." Maeve looked a little uncomfortable. "It was just that the eye paint always seemed to me like a way of . . . I guess of diverting attention. It was noticeable and people always commented on it. I figure it's easy to hide behind that stuff, right? And then when it looked like Aidan might still be closer to his wife than she'd thought, she got a bit obsessive. She had to look perfect all the time, and not just when she saw him."

"Did she have other worries about Aidan?" Jonah asked. "About his fidelity to her?"

"I don't think so," Maeve said. She went momentarily pink, which Jonah found interesting. "Having a wife was plenty."

"He never . . . tried to flirt with you?"

"Ah, no, of course not," she replied. And she really blushed this time, and looked at her hands instead of at Jonah or Lightman. "He wanted me to be on his side, was all." And then she said quickly, "Angeline says Zoe and Aidan had got back together." She lifted her eyes to Jonah's face. "Do you think that was recent? I didn't realize."

"It seems to have been fairly recent, yes," Jonah agreed.

"God," Maeve said. She pulled another tissue out and fiddled with it, her eyes on the crumpled folds. "I felt like she was hiding something. Isn't it awful that she didn't tell any of us? Even me, when I was the one person who didn't tell her to chuck him?"

"So there wasn't anything unhealthy in their relationship, as far as you were concerned?" Jonah asked.

"No," Maeve said with a shake of her head. "I mean, I don't think it's ever great to cheat. But if you take out hiding from her for a long time that he hadn't started divorce proceedings, then he treated her really well. He did all these nice things for her, and made her feel looked after." Maeve glanced at Lightman, almost in appeal. "Zoe was always the one helping everyone else, and it was so nice seeing her getting something back, you know? And they always just seemed to have so much fun. He's so different from all those awful needy dickheads she'd dated in the past."

The insulting term made Jonah smile in spite of himself. Maeve clearly wasn't above judging people harshly, Christian or no. "What about when they broke up?" he went on. "There's some suggestion he started harassing her."

"Ah, I don't think it was harassment," Maeve said, flushing again. "I felt for him, actually. He wanted to explain himself and try and make things right. And then she moved away. I think when she thought it was really over she was devastated, and she didn't want to see anything that reminded her of him. Not the house, not him, and not even us for a little while."

Jonah watched her pick at the tissue again. "Why did they break up?"

"Well, the first time, it was because Aidan had been on holiday with his wife, and Victor found out . . ."

"Victor found out?"

"He saw on Facebook. Aidan had hidden some posts from Zoe but Victor could see them. I think Aidan must have forgotten he'd added him, or not realized it was him. Victor calls himself some weird gamer name on there."

"Do you think he had a vested interest in the breakup of their relationship?" Jonah asked quietly.

"Ah, you mean . . . is he in love with her?" Maeve sighed. "Yes, he is. And I guess he also wants what's best for her. But he's not violent, you know. I mean, he has a temper, but it's . . . a flash in the pan. A brief mood, and then it's gone."

"And Zoe definitely wasn't interested in him? Nothing ever happened between them?"

"No," Maeve said quietly. "And nothing ever will now. Poor Victor."

HANSON DUMPED HER bag on her chair and peeled off Sheens's soaking-wet jacket. It was a good thing it had been long on her. Her thighs were mercifully dry, even if her lower legs were sodden.

"That's it," she told O'Malley. "I'm not going out there again. You or Ben can do anything else while I drink tea and huddle in front of a heater somewhere."

"I'm not even supposed to be working," O'Malley countered.

"So why are you?" Hanson fired back with a grin.

"I'm a victim," O'Malley said with a sigh.

"Are they in with Maeve Silver?" she asked, jerking her head toward the interview suite.

"Yeah, the Christian friend."

"Is she?"

"I'd say very," O'Malley intoned. "She's got a crucifix and an air of constantly trying to be nice in the face of terrible temptation not to be."

"One of those," Hanson said, and sat down as close to the radiator as she could while still being able to reach her desktop. The chief spilled out of the interview suite with Ben Lightman a moment later, accompanied by a curly-haired girl who must have been Maeve. She looked like she'd been emotional recently, Hanson thought, but at the moment she was smiling and laughing at something Ben had said.

Hanson couldn't help rolling her eyes. Why was there always this queue of adoring women just waiting for him to fall for them? A pretty face wasn't everything.

The DCI left them to it and came over to her desk. "You were dead right on Felix Solomon," he said quietly. "He used to be a DCI in Brighton. Early retirement with PTSD. I've requested the details."

"Oh, great!" Hanson said, trying not to seem too pleased.

"I've got O'Malley looking at whether he's been accessing police data he shouldn't be able to see," the chief added.

"So I've got you to blame," O'Malley said, looking up at her.

"I had another thought on Felix Solomon," Hanson said. "If he's in the habit of using his landlord's keys inappropriately, maybe his former tenant might have had the same experience. I could ask for her details."

"That's not a bad thought," the DCI said. He glanced at the wall clock. "Victor Varos is in next."

"Might you want a charming young constable in the interview with you?" Hanson asked.

Sheens grinned at her. "You're on."

"Thanks, Chief," Hanson said, opening up the database to grab Felix Solomon's number.

She tried not to feel too pleased at being chosen once again. She knew it wasn't about talent. The DCI chose his fellow interviewer purely on the basis of who would help him the most. It didn't matter how well you'd done in the last interview or whether it felt like it was your turn. If you didn't get picked, you didn't get picked. But she supposed, as her English teacher had liked to say, he wasn't running a bloody democracy.

"Am I a suspect?" Victor asked, the moment Jonah reached for the tape recorder.

"We're not treating anyone as a suspect at this time," Jonah said soothingly. "We try to record interviews with people connected to the victim in case we miss something at the time that is crucial. Having tapes and then a transcript means we can review and get it right. Nothing more."

Victor gave him a prickly look. The young Brazilian did prickly pretty well. He had an intense, piercing gaze, and the kind of chiseled bone structure and dark beard that went well with his brooding expression. He looked strong, too. His lack of excess flesh made the veins and muscles stand out on his arms.

Eventually, in the face of Jonah's bland expression, he nodded. Jonah rolled the tape.

"I'd like to ask you about the last time you saw Zoe," he said. "When was that?"

"Wednesday," he said. "Wednesday night."

"Can you explain the circumstances?"

Victor shrugged. "We went for dinner at La Mejican. The four of us. Angeline, Maeve, Zoe, me."

"Did you often go out together?" Hanson asked.

"Yes," Victor said shortly. "We were friends."

"And how did Zoe seem?" This question was Jonah's.

"Same as always."

"She wasn't unhappy?" he persisted. "Didn't seem like she might have been hiding something?"

There was a pause. Victor looked as though he were being forced to say something he disliked. "She rushed off at the end," he said eventually. "She said she was tired, but I saw her read a message and then go. I thought maybe it was a man. I didn't know she was back with Aidan Poole. It makes sense now."

"You think she went to meet him?"

"Yes," Victor said. "And I think that bastard killed her."

"But this was the previous night," Jonah said.

"I don't mean then," Victor said dismissively. "I mean that he was clearly back in her life and manipulating her, and I think he killed her."

"It was Aidan Poole who raised the alarm."

"So he killed her and then regretted it," Victor said, his eyes full of anger. "He would regret it. She was the best thing in his life, and he never deserved her."

Jonah considered his next words for a few moments. "You seem very keen to believe Aidan was responsible. How did you feel about Zoe yourself?"

"She was my friend," Victor said tightly.

"And how did you react when you found out they were together?"

Victor's head moved quickly, like a cat's, as his gaze flew to Hanson and back again. "Someone told you I vandalized his computer, didn't they? I didn't do it on purpose. I knocked his coffee cup over because I was angry."

"Angry because he was dating the woman you wanted?" Hanson asked, leaning forward.

"No," Victor said aggressively. "He was . . . he was rude to me."

Hanson gave a small smile. "Come on, Victor. I've worked barista jobs. Customers are rude to you on a daily basis. You deal with it. There was more going on, wasn't there?"

Victor gave her a look of loathing that surprised Jonah. It was unusual for potential suspects to be so obviously antagonistic toward an officer.

Hanson, he was happy to note, kept on prodding. "You'd always liked Zoe, hadn't you?" she said. "You hated Aidan because he was in your way. At what point did that hatred transfer itself onto Zoe?"

Victor shook his head. "I didn't hate Zoe. Not ever. Not for a minute." He fixed Hanson with a hard, angry stare. "She was only the victim of a manipulative man." He suddenly glanced toward Jonah. "Who said that? About the coffee? It was Maeve, wasn't it? Of course it fucking was." He jabbed a finger into the table. "Maeve would say anything to make Aidan look better, even if it screwed over every other person on this planet. She's obsessed with him."

"What makes you say that?" Jonah asked evenly, more than interested that this was the conclusion Victor had jumped to when Maeve had in fact defended him.

Victor snorted. "Most of her behavior for the last year. She kept having little private chats with Aidan, apparently about Zoe. And she kept pressuring Zoe to stay with him, or get back together. All the time." He looked disgusted.

"What would her motivation be for keeping them together?" Hanson asked.

"It meant she got to keep seeing him," Victor said, as if it should have been obvious. The curled lip he directed at Hanson looked personal. "And she's got issues, too. She won't have sex before marriage, but she sure as hell liked to watch those two kissing. It's like she got off on it."

Jonah spent a few seconds both thinking this through and writing it down in short form. It was hard to know how to respond. He wondered whether he could believe this of Maeve Silver. "Do you think she could have wanted to hurt Zoe herself?"

"I don't know," Victor said, suddenly looking away with a shrug. The anger seemed to step down dramatically now that he was no longer under direct pressure. "I guess not. But if she knew Aidan had done it, I think she'd do anything she could to cover it up."

JONAH SPENT SEVERAL minutes sitting in his office after Victor had gone, trying to decide what he thought of the Brazilian's accusations. On one level it seemed like childish mudslinging in the face of a few harsh comments. On another it chimed with Maeve's embarrassment when he'd asked if Aidan had hit on her.

He wasn't too worried by the suggestion that Maeve might be covering up for Aidan. There was too much pointing toward Aidan Poole being at home. They had more CCTV footage to scroll through, but he doubted that Aidan was going to appear on it, and he doubted still further that their man in a cap was him. It would have made no sense at all to call emergency services to a crime and bring attention to it if he had been anywhere near Zoe's flat at the time.

It still remained possible, Jonah thought, that Maeve had been wound up by Aidan to do something while he remained at a safe distance. It was also possible that she had acted on her own. When Zoe and Aidan had broken up, she might have believed it was her turn. It was even possible that Aidan had encouraged that. And if so, finding out later that Zoe had taken Aidan back might have driven her to violence.

And then there was Victor's own obsession with Zoe to think about. He wasn't sure how well Victor's volatile personality sat with a carefully plotted crime, but it was possible that long-term, burning anger could create cold planning instead of hot rage.

The other thing he'd gotten no further with was mapping Zoe's movements on the Thursday. Aside from Angeline seeing her in the morning and Felix's call, they had nothing definite. Nothing until Felix apparently saw her return home around eight-thirty, which, if true, meant that she'd left her flat at some point.

Meanwhile, Victor had suggested that Zoe was meeting up with someone Wednesday night, but that she'd kept hidden who it was. A fact that hadn't come to light in anyone else's statements. If she'd left the flat Thursday, it might have been in order to meet up with the same person.

Lightman tapped on Jonah's door a few minutes into his reverie. "I've got some more movements on CCTV that I think might be interesting."

Jonah followed him and drew up one of the many vacant chairs. Lightman clicked to expand one of several snapshots he'd saved. The frozen image showed a view through an arch, and Jonah knew it must be from the camera positioned in the car park behind the flats. "This is five-twenty on Thursday," Lightman said. "The camera is farther down Hill Lane, so that's close to the center of town."

He hit the Play button, and Jonah watched as a car appeared and disappeared along the road, heading toward town, followed by a punky-looking woman in a leather jacket and glasses. And then another figure did the same. They were hurrying, hands shoved in jacket pockets and legs moving quickly as they passed across the archway.

Lightman paused the film just before the figure left the screen. It was clear from this frozen frame that the figure was Zoe, her hair pulled up into a bun as it had been when she'd died.

Jonah felt a shiver run up his back. It was always unsettling to watch the dead on camera. "And we've picked her up returning home, too," Lightman said.

He loaded up another clip, taken from the camera near the block of flats. The time read 8:31. More than three hours after Zoe had left her flat, and almost exactly when Felix had said he'd seen her return.

After a moment or two, Zoe appeared in the frame. She was walking more slowly this time, her right hand going for her pocket, where presumably her key was. But she slowed down and then stopped before she got to the door, and by her movements it was obvious that she was talking to someone out of the shot. Someone who was presumably standing right next to the front door, and had been waiting for her.

"Do we get to see them?" he asked.

"Unfortunately not," Lightman said.

The conversation went on for a few minutes, and then Zoe half moved forward, hesitated, and then went off-screen toward the front door. She didn't reemerge.

"Felix Solomon's flat," Jonah said thoughtfully. "Which side is it?"

"Juliette has it marked down as this end of the building," Lightman said, gesturing to the right-hand side. "Looking out onto the road."

"So he probably wouldn't have seen someone waiting by the door," Jonah said. "He claims only to have seen Zoe. The time is right, too. Though there's a chance, I suppose, that he was actually the one waiting there."

He watched it again, taking in Zoe's attitude. The faltering steps. The distance between her and whoever had been waiting for her. The way she stood back on her heels. The way she fidgeted right and left.

"Is it just me," he asked, "or does she look frightened?"

16

September—fourteen months before

A quarter of an hour before the Michaelmas exhibition opened, Zoe realized that she was actually quite drunk. The pre-drinks had not been a good idea, not when they had started at five and she'd had almost nothing to eat for lunch. She needed water, but there was only Prosecco on offer on the table near the hall. It was meant for the guests anyway.

She made her slightly unsteady way to the bathroom, trying to smile at her tutor on her way past. Thankfully Annette was clearly preoccupied with an issue over some fabric on a display and gave her only a vague smile in return.

Zoe let herself into the loos and leaned heavily against the sink, hands flat on the wet marble counter. She took a few breaths and then ran the tap and scooped up mouthful after mouthful of water. She was drenching her clingy white dress and its single draping sleeve, but she couldn't summon enough energy to worry about it right now.

It was several minutes before she felt like she'd watered down the alcohol enough, even if the effects were going to take a while to kick in. She straightened up and had to try hard to focus on her reflection, which showed an imperfect version of herself. Her dress was blotched with grayish wet patches, and some of the white-and-purple makeup around her left eye had dribbled down her cheek and then dried there. It must have been like that for ages.

She pulled some of the paper towel out of its holder hastily, and wet it a little. She rubbed off the makeup as much as possible and then pulled her dark-brown eyeliner and glittering purple paint out of her bag. She could at least cover it up.

You shouldn't have got drunk, she told herself. *Why did you get drunk?*

But she knew why. She was so much thinner than she used to be; and she hadn't had the food in her system to help her.

Being thinner was a good thing, of course. A conscious choice. It wasn't the same as Angeline and her obsessive control over food. Zoe had just decided she needed to feel better about herself, a month after she'd found out that Aidan was still technically married.

It had happened after Aidan had casually mentioned how he'd been bowled over by Greta's beauty when he first met her. Zoe, halfway through another expensive dinner, had felt absolutely sick.

She'd taken Aidan back to her house as usual afterward, but had found herself unable to sleep. At one-fifteen she'd crept downstairs with her phone, taking care not to step on any of the noisy floorboards on the first-floor landing. Maeve wasn't the heaviest sleeper.

She'd looked up Greta Poole for the first time, half hating herself for doing it. The series of professional photographs she'd immediately uncovered on Google Images had horrified her. She shouldn't have been surprised that Aidan's wife—ex-wife, nearly—was beautiful. He was an attractive man, and it made sense for him to be with someone gorgeous. It had been wishful thinking on Zoe's part to imagine Greta as a frumpy creature. That he no longer loved her because he'd realized he could do better. But it had been such a comforting illusion.

The worst part of staring at photo after photo was probably not the inadequacy. It was the mean-spiritedness of the feeling. She'd never been the sort of person who resented other women. But then she'd never been in a relationship with a man who was still extricating himself from a marriage.

She'd also never been particularly into dieting, but some strange switch had been flicked in her head as she sat there in the darkened sitting room, the phone screen the only bright point. From then on, it had been easy to say no. To take food out of the fridge, and then put it back, uneaten. It had almost become satisfying.

Now, four months later, she was almost two stone lighter. Her once-round face was all angles and planes, and she'd had to replace most of her clothes with smaller ones. Tighter ones. Like tonight's asymmetrical white dress, which clung to her.

Despite her new, thinner figure, and the admiration it seemed to inspire in everyone else, the inadequacy was still there. Her glamorous reflection didn't make her feel any better. She wondered how much thinner she'd need to get. How much weight loss would it take to stop feeling threatened by the gorgeous woman Aidan had lived with for most of his life? The woman he still cohabited with, even if he slept in a separate room.

She wished Aidan would move out now. That he'd stop waiting for the divorce papers. In truth, she wished he'd move in with her. It was what he wanted. He'd said so. But he'd made no firm plans.

Alone in that bathroom, with damp palms and makeup that just wouldn't go right, Zoe had a sick worry that he didn't really care. Tonight meant so much, and he wasn't here. When she really, really wanted him to be here for her, he'd put his work first.

She had almost asked him, when he'd told her that he couldn't get out of this conference, whether she really was the woman of his dreams or was, in fact, just an ego boost to get him through his divorce. But then he'd told her he was going to take her away for her birthday, to somewhere hot and secluded and wonderful, and she'd felt guilty for even having the thought. He did so much for her. Of course he loved her.

But it had still been hard, watching her prize-winning painting go up and knowing that he wouldn't be there to see it with her or to hear her talk about it. All the others would be here. Angeline and Victor and Maeve. Even her lovely boss, Gina.

Zoe stopped trying to correct her makeup and rinsed her hands. She told herself to be grateful for her friends, and then she walked back outside with a very determined smile.

ZOE WAS ALMOST sober by the time she arrived back at the house with Maeve. With the sobering up came a feeling of profound tiredness, and she'd persuaded Maeve to leave early with her.

She checked her phone every few minutes in the taxi home, and wondered if she could get away with calling Aidan. But it was only nine, and he was likely to be at the dinner. She couldn't stand the idea of being the needy girlfriend who interrupted his work time, so she eventually put her phone away in her bag.

She felt strangely flat after what should have been a wonderful evening. After what *had* been wonderful, even if Victor had predictably gone off in a strop at one point, and even if Felix had looked ill. She'd been startled to see him pale and shaking; startled partly by the aging effect it had had on him.

The rest of the night had been a series of congratulatory conversations where she'd blushed and smiled and accepted the compliments. She'd enjoyed it. Of course she'd enjoyed it. But she was profoundly glad to step out of the taxi onto the pavement outside the house.

She let them both in while Maeve hunted furiously in her oversized bag for her keys. She was checking her phone yet again as she walked into the sitting room and was therefore slow to see the incredible creation on the kitchen table.

There were flowers, dozens of them. They were clutched in a box with extravagant ruffles of plastic and ribbon and tissue paper. All of them were white or pink, like some hugely oversized wedding bouquet. Lilies so large they looked like triffids, and great heavy peonies and spiky irises between them, with sprays of leaves and gold twigs.

"Ah," Maeve said, behind her, and sneezed twice. "Sorry. They came after you left. I figured I should leave it as a surprise. You might have to keep them in your room. My nose hates them."

Zoe approached the table with none of her earlier doubts. She couldn't help grinning as she plucked a gold envelope from amid the sprays and opened it. The card inside said "Congratulations" in gold, and inside, stuck in on a printed label, she read:

To the most talented woman I've ever met. I'm so proud that you are mine, and I can't wait to celebrate in person. Your Aidan xxx

She handed the card to Maeve, who read it with a raised eyebrow. "He's all right, that man of yours, isn't he?"

"Yes," Zoe said, smiling stupidly. "He's not bad."

17

It was now a wet Saturday afternoon in an empty station, but the whole team was still working away. Hanson had viewed the CCTV footage of their suspicious character in a cap and Zoe's conversation with an unseen person. She had then announced firmly that she wanted to check the other camera for whomever Zoe had been talking to.

"She spoke to someone she was afraid of," she'd said to Jonah, "shortly before neighbors heard shouting in her flat, right? There's every chance this is the same person, and that he reappeared with a cap on and a dodgy walk. They argue, and he comes back later to kill her. If we can catch them on the other camera heading up to Zoe's the first time, we should be able to see who it is."

"It's a good theory," Jonah said, and didn't add that their suspect might have approached from the other direction. There was only a fifty percent chance that they had come from town, and past the camera they had footage from.

He also found himself wondering about the desflurane. Was it really possible that someone had gotten their hands on some after the argument and before she was killed at eleven? It was a ninety-minute window, which seemed a bizarrely short time to get hold of an unusual drug. Though it was still possible that the argument had simply been a trigger for a long-considered plan. The final straw that drove the killer to it.

O'Malley had taken a break from trying to hack a police database, and was now going through footage from the same camera much earlier in the evening, when Zoe had left her flat. His remit was to work out her destination and whether she looked like she'd spoken to anyone. It was frustrating that they had no access to other cameras today, and no likelihood of any until Monday, when the Intelligence staff would be back.

That mystery trip of Zoe's was bothering Jonah. They should have pinned down her movements by now. She'd been gone for more than three hours, and she had come back at eight-thirty looking frightened. The journey seemed significant. He'd checked through the interview transcripts they had so far, and nobody except Felix had admitted to seeing her that evening. Nobody had mentioned her having plans, either.

So what they currently had was a trio of mysteries: three hours of unaccounted-for time, an unknown person waiting at the door of the flat, and an unknown (quite possibly the same) person involved in an argument with Zoe some two hours before her murder.

With all that in mind, he sent Lightman out with two aims. The first was to try to talk to Angeline Judd again. Angeline might either have been too distressed to remember seeing Zoe later, or have lied about it.

The second aim was to find the position of any CCTV cameras farther into town and see if he could arm-twist the owners directly into giving him access. If it turned out that nobody was willing or able to reveal Zoe's last movements, they would have to use other methods.

ANGELINE'S FLAT LOOKED to Lightman much more like student accommodation than Zoe's had. It was in a large 1970s-style building that had presumably been built to house the undergraduates, and it was accessible by a very long diagonal staircase that ran all the way up the side, punctuated by small square landings that led to each floor.

Despite having called ahead to check she was there, Lightman had to wait for a full minute before Angeline came to the door. She was wearing pajamas, little lace-edged shorts, and a strappy top, and looked dopey, as though she'd taken too much Prozac. He supposed that wouldn't be unreasonable in the circumstances.

"Who is it?" she asked, a strange question to put to someone's face.

"I'm DS Lightman," he said. "I called earlier?"

"Oh. Yes. OK."

She backed up, and he followed her inside, trying to keep some distance. Her underdressed state made him feel that it was inappropriate to step inside.

The place was tidier than he'd expected, though there was a glass, a mug, and a plate next to the bed and what looked like a newly opened bottle of vodka in a plastic bag on the table. It was also slightly larger than he would have guessed from the corridor, and included its own kitchenette and sitting-room area as well as the bed. One of the kitchen drawers stood open, as if Angeline hadn't quite gotten round to closing it. There was an en suite bathroom, too, though the door was almost shut.

Angeline slid her arm behind the door and grabbed an off-white bathrobe off a hook. She shrugged it on and tried to pull it round herself, but when her hands reached for the belt they came up empty, and she let it fall open.

"I just have a few things to ask," Lightman told her quietly. Angeline moved slowly to the bed and sat on the edge, so he perched himself on the sofa. "We've tried to check up about your missing keys, but nobody can recall who handed them in, unfortunately."

"I don't know, either," Angeline said, her voice aimless and flat. "Lost them."

Lightman looked at her more carefully, wondering if she was drunk or maybe badly hungover.

"Perhaps you might be able to help with information about the night Zoe was killed," he said. "You saw her that morning, didn't you?"

"Yes," Angeline said, and then looked quickly from side to side, as if there might be other people there. "I told you."

"Did she mention any plans for that day?" he asked, determined to plow on. "Something she was doing later on?"

"No," Angeline said. "She sometimes went to Argentinian tango classes on Thursdays, though," she added.

"What time would that have been?"

"Eight something." Angeline shrugged. "It normally went on quite late."

Lightman reflected that this was definitely not the right timing for Zoe being out from five until eight-thirty. It was unlikely she could have made it to the tango class that night, given the argument that had gone on until nine-thirty.

"Did anything strike you as strange this week?" he tried. "Any arguments between Zoe and her friends?"

Angeline looked suddenly hurt and angry, and began to shake her head. "Why do you have to keep making me feel bad? I already said I was sorry for . . . for getting upset. When she told me she only liked to paint me because I was broken. How would that make you feel?"

"I think you must have told a colleague of mine rather than me," Lightman said gently, "but I'm sorry to bring it up again."

He decided that this was not likely to go anywhere. They would be much better off bringing her in when she was sober. He stood, and it was as he was levering himself up that he saw, tucked down beside the arm of the chair, a pair of men's navy trainers.

"Do you have a boyfriend?" he asked.

"No," Angeline said, and this time it was quick and dismissive instead of melodramatic.

Lightman glanced at the shoes, which had the tongues pulled up and, bizarrely, no laces in them. "So whose are these?"

Angeline moved unsteadily to stand up and then leaned over to look. "No idea," she said with a shake of her head.

As he turned away, he heard her mutter again to herself. He was positive she said "no laces" amid several indistinct sounds.

He moved toward the door, and then, with a sudden thought, over to the kitchen drawer. Glancing inside, he saw a cutlery tray with forks, dessert spoons, and teaspoons in their places. To each side there were cooking and serving utensils. And in all of that, not a knife to be seen.

He excused himself and started to call the chief on the stairs. He wasn't sure if it was relevant to their inquiries, but someone had been in that room and had cleared out anything Angeline might hurt herself—or anyone else—with.

HANSON AND O'MALLEY gave him an update on the CCTV footage. They'd made little headway with their suspects but had successfully picked up Zoe walking farther toward town, down Hill Lane, on a single supermarket camera they'd managed to talk the owners into giving them the feed from. It gave them little indication of where she was ultimately headed, but she was still hurrying.

He wondered if he ought to call Wilkinson to speed up the CCTV harvesting. During serious investigations it was accepted that rank might be pulled. But it was the sort of card you couldn't play too often, and the DCS might query whether this was sufficiently vital information to justify stepping in. That usually entailed potential threat to life, and there was no particular reason to suspect that the killer might strike again.

"Did you make any progress on Felix Solomon hacking our systems?" Jonah asked O'Malley, shelving those thoughts for the time being.

"Actually I made a surprising amount," O'Malley said, minimizing the video app and bringing up a very outdated-looking database instead, on a sickly green background and full of buttons with console script on them. The overall impression was that it hadn't been updated since the '90s, and he could have guessed without being told that this was a police database. "I've had some live tutoring from a particular young man named Ziggy, who got thrown out of a computer science course, and I'm now seeing logins for the entirety of East Sussex. Which, needless to say, is not something I should be seeing."

"Jesus," Jonah said quietly. "So what's that telling you?"

"That there are literally hundreds of group logins for particular cases that were never closed down after they were opened up," he said, scrolling up and down a list to the right of the screen, "and I'm going to bet that ones like 'Executive Team Internal Corruption Inquiry' have quite extensive access." He shook his head. "My next move is to narrow down all the ones that were open before Felix Solomon retired. But if you're asking if he's probably been nosying where he shouldn't, it's a definite possibility. All of this is remotely accessible and it wouldn't take a genius to try a few old logins and see if they worked."

"Thank you," Jonah said, not sure whether he was worried about Zoe's landlord or inclined to think he'd be doing exactly the same in his shoes. "And see if you can recruit that young man to work for us. The alternative is too awful for words."

LIGHTMAN HAD SENT over details of three cameras farther into town by five. One was owned by Barclays, one by a betting shop, and one by the council. There was a bit of a void on the western side of the Latterworth Road junction, but the cameras they had looked likely to cover wherever their mysterious figure in a cap had come from.

Jonah decided it was time to get in touch with Wilkinson. Weighing his options, he decided on a message rather than a phone call. It might create a delay, but it was unlikely that they'd get any footage until later that evening as it was. Sunday was distinctly more likely. He included details of the three cameras, apologized for disrupting, and held his breath as he sent.

It took ten minutes to get a response. Wilkinson said he was out with poor signal but would be home before six, and would get on it.

Jonah let out a sigh. That meant they were still looking at Sunday, but it also meant they were likely to get the footage. The detective chief superintendent generally got what he wanted, not least because he was well known around Southampton.

That also meant Jonah had nothing else to do at the moment. With CCTV the next day and forensics on Monday, they were essentially on hold unless they chose to weigh in on more interviews. Jonah felt strongly that these would go better if they had more information, however frustrating the delay was.

So it was time to let work lie and get some exercise. He glanced out of the window at the driving rain with a slightly rebellious feeling. He wasn't going to miss the chance to get out on his bike, no matter what the weather threw at him.

He picked up his phone prior to leaving and saw that he had a few new personal emails. Opening them, he realized that he'd entirely forgotten Roy Upson's stag do that night.

He felt strongly tempted to claim he was working. But he saw they'd been booked into some whiskey tasting and had all been allocated a pair. He should have canceled a lot earlier.

And he should go. He knew that. He'd seen very little of his cycling group recently, thanks to a few bits of work spilling over and a temporarily broken bike. He also hadn't seen a lot of Stephen and Andrew, his two remaining school friends. It was sad to admit that Roy, a forty-year-old big kid whom he cycled with every couple of weeks, was probably one of his closest friends these days.

He'd go. He didn't need to stay out late, or drink as much as the rest of them. He could easily sit and sink tonics and then excuse himself once they were too battered to notice. Though whether sitting at home for the rest of the evening and brooding over the case would actually be any better than staying out and creating a hangover was anybody's guess.

. . .

It was strange how the day had just kept on going. Aidan had felt repeatedly that something would have to happen; something that would stop everything. Some kind of accident that would strike down him or Greta. A heart attack (him) or some kind of devastating moment of understanding when she saw Zoe's death on the news (her). He hadn't expected to go on existing in a state of constant fear.

But somehow an abortive morning jog had rolled on into early Christmas shopping with Greta, which she luckily always took charge of. He'd done little more than follow her around and hold things. Later, he'd drunk tea and listened to her tell him about her repainting of the downstairs bathroom the previous day, which was still wet and couldn't be used. And he'd smiled stiffly when she'd reminded him about the god-awful dinner party they were supposed to go to.

He had asked to shower before her, more because he wanted to step away from her cheerful conversation than because he was relishing getting ready. At least once he was dressed he could pour himself a drink.

He also had messages from Maeve to deal with. They had begun arriving late the night before, hours after Zoe had been found, and had continued relentlessly. Maeve was devastated. She needed to see him. How was he coping? The police were asking about everything. On and on they went, no matter how gently he tried to tell her that he needed space to grieve.

He was almost as afraid of Greta seeing those messages as he was of her seeing what he'd sent to Zoe. It would look like something had been going on between him and Maeve, too.

Standing in front of the drinks cabinet, he pulled out his phone again and, with a feeling of resignation, told her he'd meet her the next day. He just hoped that would keep her quiet.

His hand was shaking as he returned the phone to his pocket and picked up a glass. It wasn't all fear. He was searingly angry, too. So angry that he couldn't sit or stand still.

The first whiskey, which was definitely at least a double, went down quickly and fierily and made him want another. He told himself he'd slow down with this one, but he was on his fourth and feeling decidedly dizzy by the time Greta emerged twenty-five minutes later.

He had the glass halfway to his mouth when she walked into the room, and he ended up stuck like that for a moment. Everything about her was dazzling, from her tight red halter-neck to the new necklace that divided it down the front in a line of gold. From her sleek legs to her perfectly applied lipstick. She'd done whatever it was she did to her hair that made her face look elfin and otherworldly.

Aidan felt desire and immense sadness rise in him at once. He put his glass on the table clumsily and stood up.

"You look totally hot, Greta," he said. "How did I end up with someone so bloody beautiful?"

She beamed at him. "I have no idea," she said, shaking her head and then laughing. As he came over to her, she tugged at the Ted Baker shirt he was wearing. "You know, you're pretty handsome, too."

He slid his arms around her backside, and pulled her in for a very long, very sexy kiss. When he broke it off, he asked her, "How long do we have?"

"About five minutes," Greta said, but she put her arms around his neck, and he could see the same desire in her, too. "Maybe we should get going? Michael hates it when we're late . . ."

"Bollocks to Michael," Aidan said, and then suddenly remembered that Michael had flirted with Greta last time they went out together. He felt suddenly angry. "What's more important? Us, or that bastard?"

"Well, he is an awfully successful man," she said, her voice teasing.

Aidan slid his hand around to the front of her thigh, and then upward. "But can he do this?" he asked.

"No," Greta murmured, leaning her head against his and taking a shaky breath. "No, he can't."

Jonah's plans to be sober at the stag do turned out to be hopelessly over-optimistic. It wasn't simply that it was hard to avoid drinking at a whiskey tasting and dinner. It turned out that he was also his own worst enemy.

He remembered, once he'd rolled in a little late and greeted everyone, that he liked these guys. They were fun without being excessively laddish, and he felt like he owed them just for asking him along. It made him feel generous, and that meant buying them all an extra glass of whiskey at the tasting. It meant a bottle of Champagne at the dinner, and then a couple of bottles of red.

By the time they arrived at Jean-Pierre Wine Bar, he was rolling, and in a mood to find everything humorous. He felt glib and witty, a louder, more confident version of himself. It didn't surprise him when they told him there was a woman at the bar who kept looking at him. He was worth looking at now. He didn't need to go and flirt with her to check.

He got unsteadily to his feet to buy the next round, thinking that he might as well see what this woman was like. He guessed it must be the brunette. She was standing with two men who looked, to Jonah, to be a couple. Her head was turned toward them at the moment, and away from him. But as he approached, she glanced his way.

Jonah came to a total stop.

"Michelle," he said.

He should have looked earlier. He could have been prepared, and had something to say. Instead when his ex-fiancée smiled at him and said, "I thought it was you," he had nothing. Nothing at all.

Michelle dipped her head, looking as embarrassed as he felt. But pleased, too. As if him being there meant as much to her as it did to him.

"Is it a stag party?"

Jonah glanced back at his table and found some kind of a voice. "Yeah," he said. "Do you remember Roy?"

"Oh, I . . . Yes!" She leaned her head to look. "He had a Dutch girlfriend, didn't he?"

"Yup! Wedding's on the fifteenth."

"Tell him congrats from me," she said.

Jonah nodded at her. At the woman he'd spent six months unable to get over, until Jojo had reentered his life. He'd been so happy to feel hardened against her.

"What about you?" he asked. "What are you up to?"

"Engagement party," she said. "They ran out of bubbles, so we made a break for it."

She nodded to her friends. He realized he'd been rude to them, and held out a hand to each in turn. He had an impression of wariness and guessed Michelle had told them who Jonah was. They went back to their conversation immediately afterward, and he was relieved.

"How are you?" he asked then, in a lower voice.

"I'm OK." Michelle gave a funny little smile. "I gave up teaching."

"You did?" Jonah asked.

"Annoyingly, you were right," she said with a little laugh. "I was starting to hate them all."

"I wasn't right," Jonah replied with a rush of shame. "Everything I said to you was wrong. I was an arsehole."

"Well, sometimes arseholes get it right," she said with a shrug. "It's been a massive relief having grown-up conversations at work."

"I have those," Jonah said. "But I think they're sort of overrated." Michelle laughed, and it was without any conscious thought that he said, "I miss you."

"I thought you'd be happy I was gone," she said, her eyes searching his face. "All I was doing was making you unhappy."

"No," Jonah said. "I was making me unhappy." And then, after a pause, he said, "See? I need you. I can't even do grammar anymore."

Michelle laughed again, a louder, freer sound. She tucked her hair behind her ear, and said, "Do you want to get out of here?"

"Yeah," Jonah said, trying not to grin too widely. "I do."

HANSON HADN'T MEANT to work so late. At five, as everyone else was heading off, she had decided to have a brief look at the figure in the cap. A quick check. That was all.

The brief look had led her to think she might be able to tell who it was if she tidied it all up enough, and she'd spent a good two hours using the image-enhancement tool that their Intelligence team could probably use a lot better. The results hadn't been great, but she ended up with one snippet where the lower half of the face was visible. After that, she'd gone online and searched images of all their suspects and tried to put them alongside, to see if their face shapes matched.

She'd eventually had to admit to herself that you couldn't tell anything for sure from the image she had, and she'd shut her machine down with a feeling of exasperation. It was only then that she realized she would be catching the bus back, which meant a wait in the day's constant rain.

Groaning inwardly, she decided it would be better to run to the bus stop and at least build up a little warmth on the way. She pulled her running kit back on, which was mercifully dry if crispy after many hours on the station's bathroom radiator.

She eventually left the deserted station in a lucky dry spell. Putting her '80s playlist on and slotting her iPhone into the sleeve of her running jacket, she started to jog across the small visitor car park.

She was halfway across when one of the few remaining cars suddenly started up, its headlights cutting across the air in front of her. She jumped, then laughed at herself. She nodded to the invisible driver as she ran across in front of them, out toward the entrance to the main road.

Once she had passed, the car eased its way out of the parking space and started to follow her. She could tell by the direction of its lights that it was now behind her. Turning her head, she diverted to run across the empty parking spaces to her left, giving it extra room to pass.

But as she ran on the car maintained its slow crawl behind her. There was another car parked ahead, so she had to dodge back into the lane the following vehicle was in. Despite there still being plenty of room, the driver made no effort to go past.

She began to feel a creeping sense of unease. Thoughts of Zoe's body made their way through her mind, and she cut abruptly across a gap between two cars, running over the grass toward Southern Road. There were cars moving in both lanes, but Hanson chose a small gap and went straight across, and then sprinted round the corner of the Novotel and into the retail park car park. There, she slowed down, knowing that you couldn't drive into the car park without going all the way around onto Harbor Parade. By the time anyone had a chance to follow her, she would be through it and at the bus stop by TGI Fridays.

There was a bus pulling in as she drew up to the stop, and by the time she was on it she'd started to feel ridiculous. Nobody was following her. She was just freaking out.

SHE GOT OFF the bus two miles from home, with two housing estates to run through before she arrived. She'd chilled off on the bus and was glad of the movement.

The darkness of the run was punctuated by visions of early Christmas lights. It was one of the oddly moving things about living in one of the less expensive areas of Southampton. Everyone seemed to want to light their houses up more brightly, for longer.

She liked to sprint the last section to her house, and she picked it up with a quarter of a mile to go. She started to count down as she got closer, knowing she could start from roughly sixty at this point. She pushed through the countdown.

Forty seconds. Come on.

The music playing from her iPhone was unhelpful. It was more a steady keep-it-going track than a sprint one. She was blowing hard, and her legs felt like they were being used by someone else. But she pushed onward to thirty seconds. To twenty.

And then, at eighteen seconds to go, she stopped. Not because of the pain in her body, but because there was someone standing next to the door of her house, just within the radius cast by the overhead porch light.

She thought of the car back at the station car park, and then for some reason she thought about Zoe, stopping to talk to someone as she arrived home. About the fear in the way she had stood and shifted, and how the figure had been waiting for her.

Hanson pulled her earphones out and backed up a few steps, then moved sideways into the driveway of the nearest house so that she was screened by the conifers on their front boundary. She hoped her neighbors weren't watching.

She couldn't see her own driveway now, but she could see the whole way down the road. She'd know if the person waiting for her left.

It might be the chief, she thought suddenly. *Or Ben.*

She slid her phone out of the pocket on her sleeve and brought it to life, silencing her music entirely. Lightman or the chief would have messaged, at least, before turning up. But there was nothing on her home screen, and nothing when she checked her messages, either.

She lifted her head and saw a figure emerging from her driveway. They glanced up the road toward her, and she moved farther into the shade, her view obscured by branches. But when she took another look a moment later they'd turned the other way, walking steadily off toward town.

Hanson watched them furiously, trying to work out if this was someone she knew. She was confident they were male. The short hair and the shape of the back in a dark jacket. The gait.

She found herself certain, as she watched them, that this was no friend. And she suspected this was someone who shouldn't know where she lived, someone connected with the case.

She pulled out her front door key, thankful to find that she had remembered to lock the door when leaving for her run that morning. She paused inside with the door closed, and then, quickly and with arms that shook slightly, went to pack her overnight bag.

18

September—fourteen months before

September wasn't supposed to be like this. The heavy blue skies and clammy warmth made Zoe imagine that Aidan had decided to take her with him to Kyoto. She daydreamed as she walked through Winchester with sultry music playing through her headphones, about the two of them leaving the conference behind and climbing a mountain to escape the heat. And then she would think about a wet, heated kiss. About his hands on her. And then she snapped suddenly awake at a pedestrian crossing, flushed and wondering whether anyone had been able to tell what she was thinking.

She tried to get her mind back on her work, which had been going so well that she didn't want to lose momentum. She was keen to finish her new piece today, regardless of how long it took her. After that, she was going to take a photo and send it to Aidan so he could see it, this new work in which she'd captured him along with herself.

Walking from the muggy heat outside into the cool of the School of Art was like gliding into water. Zoe pulled her hair up to expose the back of her neck and shivered as a blast of cold from one of the air-conditioning units hit her damp skin.

She climbed the stairs to the first floor and pulled her earphones out of her pocket in readiness to retreat from the world. She wound the cable around the fingers of her right hand, enjoying the squeezed feeling in her fingertips.

There was a slightly strange atmosphere as she walked in. Mitz and Sinead were standing together near the door and by the way they grew silent immediately, she thought they had probably been talking about her.

Caz, one of the quieter girls who sometimes brought her coffee, stood and came over to her with a smile that was almost defiant. "I like the piece," she said.

"Oh . . ." Zoe wasn't sure quite how to respond. "Thank you."

Caz trailed along beside her as she made her way to her corner.

"There's something pretty great in destruction," Caz said. "Isn't there?"

And then Zoe was confronted with the reality of what she was talking about. Her current, almost-finished piece, *Descent,* had been cut through with vivid red. The angelic male shape in the background, which stood in its own different light, remained untouched. But across the pale figure in the center had been scrawled the painted word "Whore."

THERE WAS STILL an awful feeling in her stomach as she arrived home and lowered herself onto the sofa. Annette had, of course, been wonderful as soon as Zoe had alerted her to the vandalism. Her art tutor had kicked security into action, and set about trying to find the culprit. She had also subjected all of her students to a threatening lecture about the integrity of art and told them they needed to come forward if they knew anything, before the campus security cameras made it obvious.

Nobody had confessed or revealed anything, however, and for all Annette's reassurances that it was easily fixed Zoe felt like the piece had been ruined. She wasn't sure she would ever feel able to work on it again, or spend time in that art department without being afraid of who was watching her.

She wished Maeve could have been home. She would have been so upbeat and direct about it all that Zoe would have been forced to cheer up, and the good feeling might have stayed with her until bedtime. But with Maeve out at her Alpha meeting and Aidan half a world away, she felt alone and vulnerable.

She was still sitting there when someone knocked on the door, and she felt a rush of affection for Maeve, who must have come home early and forgotten her keys. But as she opened the door, she saw Victor instead, with a fierce look on his face.

In spite of an immediate desire to close the door again, she asked him in. He clearly had something on his mind, and it might even help her to think about someone else's worries.

"I'm sorry," Victor said as soon as he'd sat on the sofa. He often apologized when he needed to talk about something, and Zoe smiled at him and shook her head.

"You don't need to be sorry. Everyone needs a chat sometimes. Shall I put the kettle on?"

"It's OK," he said. "I . . . I'm not upset. Well, I mean, it's hard. But not really for me so much as . . ." He gave a funny little sigh. "There's something you need to see."

He pulled his phone out of his pocket, then left her waiting in a state of gradually increasing nervousness while he loaded something up.

"Here," he said after a minute, and held the phone out to her.

Zoe took it, unsure of what she was going to see but feeling a dull sense of certainty that it was going to be about Aidan.

It was a photograph on a Facebook page, she vaguely realized. But it was hard to register other details when what she was seeing was a photograph of Aidan and his wife with a panorama behind them. It was clearly a selfie taken by Greta, who looked outdoorsy and happy and utterly beautiful. Their arms were slung around each other, and they were smiling.

"It was taken this afternoon," Victor said quietly.

Zoe saw that he was right. It was from today, and the location was tagged as Kyoto. Which was where the conference was supposed to be. And she realized that the view was familiar. He'd sent her a photo of it that afternoon, only there had been no Greta in it. No Aidan. Just the view and the words "Missing you."

The adrenaline running through her made everything feel unreal. She started scrolling pointlessly down the newsfeed, and realized that it was Aidan's. He'd been tagged in the photo. Greta was tagged, too.

"He must not have realized she'd tagged him," Victor said.

"But . . . why didn't it show up on my Facebook?" she asked blankly. "He's my friend, and all his stuff should show up straightaway."

"I'm guessing he's got settings that block a lot of things from you, just in case," Victor said. "But he forgot to block me."

Zoe had to walk away from Victor. She couldn't stand seeing the sympathy and triumph all mixed up in his eyes. She thought she might be sick, but couldn't stop looking at that photo, scrolling up and down to see if the date changed. Checking to see if it was a memory from a previous year, but knowing that it wasn't.

She picked up her own phone, and opened WhatsApp. Opening their last conversation brought up Aidan's photo of that empty view, and it felt as though it were burning her. When she'd asked where it was, he'd written a cheery "Saga Valley viewed from above!"

Below her original reply that it was beautiful and she missed him too, Zoe started typing another message.

I'm breaking up with you. I'm doing it over WhatsApp, because you don't deserve anything else. You fucking liar. You made me believe it was all legitimate now. But you're on holiday with your wife. You never broke things off with her, and I know that now. I'm done with you.

She sent the message, and then used Victor's phone to save the image of Aidan and Greta. She sent it to herself over Messenger.

"What are you doing?"

"Breaking up with him, and making sure I have proof so I can't be talked round," she said. She handed his phone back. "Thank you."

Victor took it and nodded. And then he said, "I'm so sorry. Do you want me to make you a cup of tea?"

Zoe tried to smile at him. "That's supposed to be my line. Don't. Look, I . . . I need to be on my own for a while. OK? I'll let you know when I feel up to having visitors."

Victor nodded, but his expression was somewhere between disappointed and rebellious. "I always think it's better to have company . . ."

"Not just yet," she said firmly. "But thank you."

Before he left, he gave her a hug. She couldn't relax into it. She was too angry and hurt and tensed up against everyone, including Victor.

"See you soon," she said.

She couldn't sit down after that. Not until, twenty minutes later, Aidan had called back to ask what the hell was going on.

"What's wrong with you?" he asked, and the anger in his voice was awful. Not just hurtful, but a little frightening.

Zoe hung up without speaking, and then sent him the photo of him and Greta, and then she silenced his messages so she wouldn't have to listen to any more lies.

19

Jonah woke at six with a piercing headache and felt the weight of anxiety descend upon him. He was often like this when a hangover struck. He would feel a huge sense of regret and fear of everything he'd done, a seamless linking of the choice to drink too much with every other decision he'd made.

Being in a strange hotel room didn't help. As he levered himself upright and glanced over at Michelle, who was still in a deep sleep with her hair spread over her face, he felt like he was in some strange parallel universe where they hadn't broken up. Where the last year hadn't happened.

He needed water, and Tylenol, and his own bed. Until he'd slept this off, he wouldn't be able to think about all of it rationally. He could decide then whether he'd messed everything up or recovered something he'd considered lost.

Michelle didn't stir as he gathered his clothes and dressed. There was no reaction as he pulled out the sheet of Tylenol tabs he had in his jacket pocket and popped four of them out, two of which he put next to her on the bedside table before he went to fill a glass with water from the bottle in the mini bar and placed it alongside. She only gave a vague murmur as he leaned down to tell her he'd better get going. He hesitated before leaving, worried that she'd think he'd used her somehow.

But it wouldn't help them if they ended up talking while he felt like this. He'd say stupid things, and he'd hurt both of them. He let himself out quietly, wincing at the sound of the door closing behind him.

HANSON WOKE AT seven when someone in a neighboring room turned some kind of early-morning chat program on at levels loud enough to be heard across the street. She spent a few minutes staring up at the plain white ceiling, depressed to find herself staying in a cheap hotel room all over again. Having left this behind once Damian was well and truly out of her life, it gave her a heavy, glum feeling to find herself back here.

It didn't help that the whole episode seemed a lot less threatening now that it was morning and she was surrounded by Travelodge noises. It made her wonder whether she'd overreacted and wasted sixty-one pounds she could have usefully spent elsewhere.

She'd been planning on calling the chief this morning to tell him all about it, but it now seemed too embarrassing. What had she really seen, after all? Someone waiting at her house and trying the doorbell, and then leaving when there was no answer. Those were the facts of it, when you removed the feeling of threat.

Perhaps she could mention it when the chief updated them, she thought as she rose sluggishly, feeling stiff muscles tighten. But by the time she'd showered and dressed, the chief had messaged them all to let them know they had no CCTV as of yet, and no forensics until Monday. He suggested they get on with their weekends until they had more to do.

She tried to see it as a good thing. It meant she could go and see her mum and off-load all her work worries. It would be nice. Comforting, even. Even if she wouldn't feel able to mention the figure outside her door.

Lightman messaged her a short while later, making sure she'd gotten the chief's message and asking how she was doing. She felt sorely tempted to be honest with him and mention what had happened. She could get his thoughts on it, and he'd probably be able to reassure her that it had been nothing.

But Ben had shown that he didn't want to share personal things with her, and it felt awkward to tell him her own, particularly when they amounted to a feeling of fear. And so she just told him she was fine and glad of a day off, and then started getting ready for a trip to her mother's back in Birmingham.

MAEVE LET HERSELF out of the house a good ten minutes later than she should have. It didn't seem to help that she'd cut everything that wasn't essential over the last couple of days. Instead of being perpetually behind in a frantic, too-tightly-packed schedule, she instead seemed to lose time staring into space, so very deep in awful thoughts that she surfaced with a feeling of disorientation. And she still felt like a failure about her lateness, and was convinced that people were judging her. Even now, when she'd just lost her best friend.

Her bike was locked up out front, where she had fallen into the habit of leaving it. The house had a side passage to a courtyard where her bike would be a lot safer, but she never seemed to have time to take it down there.

She pulled out her keys and saw that there was some kind of flyer attached to the bike. It was sodden with rain and clinging to the frame, and she growled to herself as she tore it off. Even then, there was still a lot of wet paper attached to the bike.

She pulled it open and saw that it was a handwritten note rather than a flyer. The thick marker pen had stayed where it was, and she could read the words easily.

Keep your slutty little mouth shut.

She stared at it, her heart feeling diseased in her chest. Broken.

She looked compulsively up the road toward the town center, and was turned in that direction when she felt a powerful blow to her right shoulder.

She grabbed at the bike as she fell, but the gesture did nothing but bruise her hand. She still went down, hard, onto her knee and elbow. The terror of her sudden defenselessness was awful, and she flailed as she tried to get up, feeling like she was in some kind of a dream where she couldn't move properly.

She scrabbled her way to her hands and knees, wincing as they touched the wet pavement, and looked up to see a tracksuit-clad figure jogging round the corner and out of sight.

HAVING CHECKED IN on the case and told his team to stand down for now, Jonah slept for most of the morning. He then woke up feeling guilty that he'd spent so much time out of it. He expected to see a message from Michelle waiting for him, but there was nothing.

He decided he'd better be the one to make contact, given that he had left her sleeping. He wrote a brief note saying how nice it had been to see her and apologizing for being in a state. He asked if she'd like to meet up later, or in London.

Her reply had arrived by the time he was out of the shower, and it was painfully brief.

Already home. Drop you a line in the week maybe?

And that was it. No expression of pleasure at what had happened, but no regrets, either. Nothing to tell him that she felt anything at all, or acknowledging that it had opened everything up all over again for him.

Jonah shoved his phone away, sank a coffee, and then pulled on the cycling kit that still had damp patches from the day before. The headache hadn't entirely gone and it looked like it had been raining again, but anything was better than sitting around thinking about Michelle, and Jojo, and what might or might not be wrong with him.

• • •

THE BIKE RIDE did a lot to clear Jonah's head, putting Michelle into the background and letting him think more clearly about Zoe Swardadine and the people who might have killed her. He sprinted along the Godshill road, turning everything around in his head: The missing three hours. The figure in the cap. Zoe's tense, frightened movements as she'd spoken to someone at the door to her flat, who could have been any of their suspects except Aidan Poole, who hadn't known where she lived.

He found himself thinking about Zoe herself after that, and how much she seemed to have changed over the last months of her life. He thought back to what Maeve had said about her weight loss and her eye makeup. There had been no trace of makeup when she'd been found in the bath, though that wasn't necessarily surprising. Then he recalled her face on the CCTV camera, and was pretty certain she'd had no elaborate eye makeup. It would have shown up even in black-and-white footage.

Did that mean she hadn't been going out to meet anyone when she left the flat? She hadn't received any messages triggering the sudden departure. They knew that from her phone records. Perhaps she really had been trying to follow someone. Maybe they should distribute some images of the woman with glasses, in case she had been trying to hurry after her.

The other thing her lack of makeup might signal, he thought, was a total breakdown in Zoe's mental state. A point reached at which even her excessive grooming had stopped.

The strangest thing in looking at that last day was that Zoe's actions seemed markedly out of character. Everyone had described a long-suffering, supportive friend. Even Maeve's description of depression hadn't included a disregard for either other people's feelings or her own appearance. Yet she had told her friend she was broken, and argued with someone that evening.

He wondered if the clue to all this was Wednesday night. Perhaps one of her friendships had reached a breaking point, tipping Zoe into anger at everyone around her. Perhaps that point had hit the friend in question just as hard, and made them decide to kill her. Or perhaps Zoe's sudden, harsh mood the next day had made her do something that had triggered her murder.

There was a message waiting for him from Michelle when he pulled his phone out at the farthest point of his ride.

> Sorry for being a bit short earlier. Just hungover as hell and feeling like an idiot. Happy to talk later this week. Xx

Jonah sighed as he read it. It still didn't exactly exude positivity, but it did make him feel less like he'd just lost her all over again.

He couldn't blame Michelle for being uncertain. Even in his fitful sleep this morning, he'd found himself wheeling between a desperate longing to make things work, sudden irritation at himself, and a pining for Jojo to be in touch. It was anything but simple, and if he were honest, he wasn't sure what he would have said if they had met up again.

JONAH WAS ON his way into the station on Monday morning when he received a call from an unknown number.

"Hi." The voice was female. Hesitant. "It's . . . it's Maeve Silver. I just wanted to let you know about something that happened yesterday."

He listened while Maeve described the note on her bike and the violent shove that had sent her sprawling onto the pavement.

"You didn't get any idea of who it was?" Jonah asked. "No impression of age? Gender?"

"No," Maeve said miserably. "It was . . . They had a tracksuit on. They were jogging. I think they were pretending to be a jogger."

"What color clothing?"

"Just . . . dark. Maybe black."

Jonah thought back to their figure in a cap from the CCTV footage. It was just possible that the same person had pushed her. Though it was also possible that the note had nothing to do with the runner, and she'd been shoved out of the way by someone in a bad mood.

This was assuming, too, that the incident had actually happened.

"Do you still have the note?"

"Yes," Maeve said. "It's kind of beaten up, but . . ."

"Can you bring it into the station?" Jonah asked. "We'll get you to do an official statement, if you don't mind. I'm hopeful that whoever killed Zoe will be picked up soon, anyway. We should have a lot of forensic information back soon."

"Good," Maeve said. "That's a relief."

He wondered whether she really meant it as he hung up.

Jonah's optimism took a slight dip on opening up his emails. There was nothing from forensics yet, but there was something from Wilkinson. The DCS had put through CCTV requests, but he also wanted an update on the blackmail case the next day. He gently reminded Jonah that he had agreed to commit half of his resources to it. As a high-profile case, Wilkinson's email continued, it was important they didn't let it slide, however important a murder investigation was.

Jonah called O'Malley and asked him to head in as soon as he could.

"I want you to be full-time on the blackmail case today," he told him.

O'Malley agreed without argument. He arrived within fifteen minutes, looking only slightly thrown together, and buried himself in the blackmail files.

Ten minutes after that, Linda McCullough called Jonah.

"We've got your fingerprint comparisons in," she said. "Do you want a rundown?"

"Sure," he said, refreshing his email and seeing a forward from her.

"Male one, who was on the glasses, door, and light switch, is Victor Varos."

So Victor could well have been there that night, Jonah thought with satisfaction. *Either arguing with Zoe or killing her, and possibly both.*

"Recent prints, you thought?" he asked.

"Yes, not overlaid much," she agreed. "Male two, who features over more of the flat but is quite overlaid, is Felix Solomon, her landlord."

"OK. Not unexpected."

"Male three, who only appears on the bathroom-door lock, is Aidan Poole. The boyfriend, I think?"

Jonah took a breath. "Aidan Poole?"

"Yes."

"There's no doubt about that?"

"None," McCullough said. "The prints are clear and recent."

Jonah thanked her, and said he'd read the rest later. He hung up and felt totally outraged. Outraged that Aidan had sat in the interview room and lied so consummately about not knowing where she lived. That from the very first, he'd done everything to suggest he had no idea of the address.

Jonah gave a sigh of disgust, opened the door to CID, and called to Lightman and Hanson.

"You two get yourselves ready. We're about to go and arrest Aidan Poole."

20

October—thirteen months before

Zoe was screwing everything up at work. She'd had to remake two drinks already thanks to putting milk into one instead of soy, and making normal coffee instead of decaf for the other. Mieke had been so supportive when Zoe had told her about the breakup, but that had been two shifts ago and she could tell that her colleague was starting to get impatient underneath it all.

It wasn't actually the breakup that was affecting her today. The background pain was still there and it still made her feel like crying every time she thought of it, but she was managing better now. She'd started being able to think about other things. About dating other men.

The problem today was that Angeline had come in, and she wasn't alone. She had given Zoe a defiant, possibly even triumphant smile as she'd arrived with Richie. Zoe couldn't look at him without remembering the way Angeline had been draped over him at that dockside bar.

What was she doing with him? Zoe couldn't understand it. He was just so, so *awful*. From the way he almost bellowed everything he said and glanced around the coffee shop, she could tell he was convinced he was some kind of a tough guy. And she hated the way he looked at Angeline like she was a possession.

She realized that her next customer was waiting for a drink, and she turned to smile apologetically before seeing that it was Felix.

"Oh, hi," she said, feeling herself brighten in spite of everything. "How's it going? I haven't seen you in too long."

"It's fine," he said, smiling back at her. "Better for seeing you, obviously. I just had a bug and decided I wouldn't spread it around."

"Very thoughtful of you. I just hope you missed me."

"Every second."

She grinned as she cleaned the milk-foaming wand and set about making his flat white.

"How are things with you?" Felix asked. "Is Aidan well?"

Zoe flinched and tried to keep smiling. "Oh, we're not together anymore."

Felix looked genuinely taken aback. "Oh, I'm so sorry. Foot right in mouth. Are you OK?"

"Fine," she said. And then, over the noise of the milk steamer, she added, "It turned out he wasn't so very separated from his wife."

"Ah," Felix said. "That's . . . crap."

Zoe nodded, then shrugged. She stopped the steamer and started to pour the foamed milk into Felix's coffee. "Yeah, well. People can be crap."

"I never liked him, anyway," Felix said with a wink. "You deserve someone much less sulky."

Zoe laughed, even though she didn't really feel like it. "Well, he's definitely sulking now. He keeps trying to pass on messages through my friends, and he turns up everywhere I go. I had to change my shift to avoid him."

"At your house, too?" Felix asked.

"Sometimes," Zoe said.

There was a pause, and then Felix said, "That's not right, you know. If that behavior goes on, you need to go to the police. It's harassment."

"It's not really . . ."

"Zoe, I used to be a bloody copper. Trust me on this."

Zoe gave a shrug, then nodded.

"Secondly, if you want to move somewhere else, then I can help. I've got to end my tenant's stay because she's no longer paying her rent. If you want to move in, you'd be doing me a favor."

Zoe looked up at his kind expression, and smiled. "Thank you. That's really lovely of you. I think . . . I think moving right now would be too much. But, you know, if it's empty in a few weeks and I can't deal with it . . ."

"You just tell me," Felix said firmly. "I'm not in a rush to fill it." He gave her a significant look. "Nobody should have to feel like they aren't safe in their own home."

ZOE FINISHED HER shift at six, helped Mieke close up, and then cycled back down Hill Lane toward home. She scanned the street outside, looking out for Aidan. He didn't seem to be waiting for her. She wasn't entirely sure whether she felt relieved or not. It was so hard not to miss him while trying her best to shut him out.

Zoe thought again about Angeline and Richie and wondered whether he'd harassed her friend into giving in. But then, why hadn't Angeline said anything? Presumably because she was ashamed of him.

Well, Zoe thought, shoving her bike behind the side gate, it was up to Angeline who she wanted to hang out with. Zoe wasn't her keeper.

Stop worrying about everyone. They're all adults and they can manage without you.

It was something Aidan had said to her on numerous occasions, and she hated that it was his voice she heard now.

She let herself in, hoping that Maeve would be in her room. She was in the mood for some peace and quiet.

The hall looked normal, with no extra coat hanging up. Even Monkfish gave her no heads-up. He just twined himself around her legs as usual and then scampered toward the kitchen. So there was nothing until Zoe walked in on Aidan sitting in her own armchair, with Maeve curled up on the sofa opposite him.

He saw her and he jumped up, a look of awful happiness on his face, which then turned into uncertainty.

She shook her head at him. "What are you doing here?" she asked as coldly as she could.

"Sorry, Zo," Maeve said, uncoiling herself slowly. Her face was hot pink, and Zoe wondered what exactly she'd walked in on.

Maeve hurried out, and Zoe knew she should turn and leave, too.

And then Aidan said, "Please." He looked at her with such a soft, sad expression that she found her resolve crumbling. She wanted to hear what he had to say in spite of herself.

But she wasn't going to sit down. Not yet. She stood in front of him and shrugged. "What is it that you want to say?"

"I know exactly why you did what you did," he said, fixing her with a calm, steady gaze. She couldn't help noticing the shadows around his eyes. She wondered if he'd been sleeping as little as she had. And she couldn't help seeing all over again how handsome he was.

She tried to look away, but it was hard. Particularly when he started speaking again.

"I know exactly why. Because it all seemed like a pack of lies. I *had* lied about some of it. Or at least hidden some of it. But I need to tell you the full story, because it isn't as simple as it looked. Will you please just let me?"

"If you tell me, first of all, what you were doing in here with Maeve," she said. She folded her arms across herself.

"With Maeve?" he asked, mystified. "I was waiting for you. She let me in. I think she took pity on me and . . . Look, don't blame her. I explained everything and she realized we needed to talk. Which we do." He watched her with what looked like momentary anxiety, and then he said, "Let me make you a cup of tea."

He went to the kitchenette and flicked the kettle on, and then opened and shut the cupboard before going to the sink and lifting her blue polka-dot mug out of it. He started to wash it, and it seemed stupid to stay standing while he did it, so Zoe sat in her armchair and tried to rally all her defenses. She brought to mind that picture of him and Greta. She held on to the sick sense of discovery.

She tried as hard as she could to force back the part of her that badly wanted there to be a reasonable explanation for it all. She shook her head, quickly and hard. There was no reasonable explanation. She knew what she'd seen.

Aidan brought the tea over, one hand on the handle and the other steadying the edge of the mug. She was pleased to see that his hands were shaking as he put it on the coffee table in front of her. But it was such a strange thing, seeing him again after three weeks, and here, where they'd spent so much time together. She felt like it couldn't be real.

"Let me start with what I didn't tell you," Aidan said. "I didn't tell you that Greta doesn't want her parents to know anything about the breakup. I know it sounds like she's making an excuse to keep it quiet, but I don't think it is. There's never been anything but acceptance from her. She knows that we're done."

"You aren't done," she said icily.

She left the tea where it was, steaming very slightly. She'd been looking forward to a drink once she got home, but it was as if he'd made her a cup full of deliberate forgetting. She would happily go thirsty rather than take it.

"Greta and I are finished," he said firmly, "but I understand entirely why you think we aren't. The photo looked like a couple on holiday. And I hadn't told you she was going to tag along still. She'd bought the ticket months ago, and we tried to get a refund. We didn't manage it, but we did get separate rooms and both of us thought that it would be OK."

"Well, it wasn't fucking OK," Zoe said. "It wasn't OK at all. You went. On holiday. With your wife. No part of it is OK. And whatever you two decided in your cozy little chat at home means actually nothing."

"I know," he said with a sort of despair. "I know it wasn't. It wasn't OK and I knew that, and that's why I didn't tell you. I knew you'd be upset about it, but I felt like it was the one thing I could do to be kind to her when I was breaking everything apart."

"Why did you need to be kind," Zoe asked, "if she agreed? It was a relief, wasn't it?"

"For God's sake," Aidan said, a loud and harsh explosion, and suddenly he felt uncomfortably close. Frighteningly so. Zoe flinched backward as he slammed the other mug down onto the counter. "Are you really that naïve?"

She found herself staring at him, her heart pumping wildly. What was he doing here? Why had Maeve let him in? He shouldn't be here, never mind looking at her with this cold, hard fury.

And then the fury seemed to dissolve, and he said, "I'm sorry. I'm such a bloody twat. I'm . . . I'm so sorry." He rubbed his hand over his face. "Of course you don't know how it feels to divorce someone. It's still heartbreaking, even when you want it. It's still hard to say goodbye to eighteen years spent with someone. You're an empathetic person. You must understand that. We both cried our hearts out, and she probably had plenty of moments of doubt, wondering if breaking things off was the right thing. I was there for a few of them, and I had to be firm. It made me feel like shit, but I needed to do it for you and me. And now . . ." He was suddenly half crying, his voice hoarse and angry and choked up. "Now I've done it, and I've messed it up, and I've lost you. Every hard thing I'd done to finally be with you was for nothing, because of one stupid fucking photo."

Zoe found herself looking at her hands, moving one finger at a time as she hung absolutely torn between sympathy and a refusal to give in. It was awful to see him dissolve into tears. He was never emotional if he could avoid it. He would so often retreat behind sarcasm.

But he'd told her she was the one person he could be vulnerable in front of. And it was more than she could stand to hold back from him as he sobbed. The memory of his anger and her fear fell away in a moment.

She put her arms around him and tucked her head into his neck, close to his ear.

"Don't," she said. "It's all right. It's not . . . I'm not lost. I'm not. If you can just be honest with me, we'll make it work. We can make it work. I promise."

It felt so good when he turned and pulled her into a wet, salty kiss that it didn't even feel like stupidity. Even when she opened her eyes and saw Maeve standing in the doorway, watching them with a weird, intent expression.

21

Without needing to be told, Aidan knew it was the police calling. He should have gotten there first and picked up the phone. The reality of it hit him the moment Greta had lifted the handset.

She had only just come in from the garden after a good hour spent hacking away at the Buddleia. They were both "working from home" today, and Greta tended to use his presence as an excuse to do house things instead of actual work. Aidan usually joined in or frittered his time reading newspapers. Today, though, he'd sat and watched her through the kitchen window, barely glancing at the newspaper he'd laid out on the table.

"Jesus, it's cold out there," she'd said as she closed the door behind her. "I'm not doing any more today."

Aidan smiled at her. "You've done plenty. Would you like a coffee?"

And then the phone cut through their conversation, and she placed the gloves on the worktop before picking it up. Aidan found himself fixated on her reactions, frozen and staring like a cornered animal.

"Hello?"

He loved how she answered the phone. The cheery lilt to her voice that had more of her Hungarian accent than any of her other speech. It felt like his heart was breaking as he heard her say it. He knew what was about to happen. He knew what the sounds on the other end of the line meant.

Greta glanced over at him. "Yes, he's here. Why do you need him?" There was another pause, and Aidan watched her face grow very still. "OK. We'll be here," she said.

She hung up and turned to him with an expression of confusion. It was almost childlike, and so very unlike the anger he'd braced himself for.

"Who was it?" he asked.

"The police," she said. "They're on their way." There was a pause. "Why are they on their way?"

He could see that she was afraid of what he was going to say. They were united in that for a moment at least.

Even now, faced with the inevitability of being exposed, he felt his whole body resisting him. There was still a small part of his mind that wondered whether he could cover this up. Whether he could meet the police outside and pretend to Greta that he was needed as a witness.

But he knew, in reality. He knew it was all going to come out. The only weapon he had left was being the one to tell her, so he could at least try to explain some of it from his point of view. If that was even possible.

"Come and take a seat," he said. "I'll explain."

He waited until she was sitting opposite him, and then said, "I need to tell you something." It was easier if he didn't look at her.

"OK . . ." There was a false lightness to her reply that only made him feel worse.

"You will have every right to hate me. And I need you to know that I accept that. I . . . I've done something so stupid . . ." His voice was shaking, and he was humiliatingly close to crying. He couldn't cry. It wasn't fair to cry when she was the one about to hear this. "I had an affair. With a student at the university."

There was a pause where he could hear her breathing, and then she said, "What the fuck, Aidan?"

He couldn't help looking at her. Her eyes were bright, but her skin was pale, as if he'd drained the life out of her.

"I know," he said. "There's no . . . there's nothing I can say that will justify it. It was a terrible thing to do and I tried not to so many times. I knew it was wrong. But it wasn't here, and somehow I convinced myself that it wasn't connected with us, and it didn't affect us. . . ."

"It didn't affect us? You were putting your cock into someone else, and it *didn't affect us*?"

It was more hurtful than he could have believed. He felt a rush of defensiveness. "Please don't say it like that," he said. "It's not . . . it's not necessary. It's done."

"It's done? The affair?" She gave him a piercing look. "Because she dumped you? Because guilt finally crept in?"

"Because she's dead," he said, and he choked on the words. "Because someone killed her. And it should have been over before, anyway. We broke up over and over. . . ."

"Oh my God." Greta rose and walked away from him. She turned on her heel and then back again, her hand up to her mouth. "Someone killed her," she said, as if trying to make herself believe it. "What? How is that even real? Is this more bullshit?"

"No. I wish I . . . It's been on the news," he said. "It's real and it's horrible. It's such a fucking mess. I'm so sorry. I'm so sorry, Greta. I've ruined everything."

She turned toward him. "Do they think you killed her?"

"I don't know," Aidan said. He almost felt like laughing for a moment. A little bubble of hysteria that rose and burst and was gone again.

She stood absolutely still, watching him, and then said in a whisper, "Did you kill her?"

He was genuinely stunned. Of all the questions he'd been waiting for, this had never even crossed his mind.

"Greta, for God's sake," he said. "Of course I didn't. You know I didn't! I'm not even capable—"

"How do I know?" she fired back. "How am I supposed to know that? I thought you'd never hurt me. I would have . . . have bet everything that you would never do that to me. Not you. I used to tell people . . ." She turned away, a catch in her voice. "I used to say, 'I don't ever need to worry about that. Not with Aidan. He's the most loyal person I know.'"

"I'm so sorry," he said again. And, God, it was awful. It was worse than he'd thought it could be. She was hurting and he couldn't do anything to make it better. "I didn't think I could, either." He half rose to move toward her, but she wouldn't look at him.

"How old was she?"

"Twenty-seven," he said.

"For fuck's sake." Greta turned and kicked the bottom of the fridge, and then kicked it again. "You fucking pathetic cliché."

"I know," he said desperately, standing up fully. "I know."

"Why?" she said, swinging on him. "Why did you do it? What was so wrong that you needed that?"

Aidan opened his mouth but found himself at a loss. "It . . . I don't even know. I don't know, Greta."

"Oh, come on," she said. "You must have been pretty unhappy to go and screw some student. What is it? Do I have too many grays? Too much cellulite?"

"No," he said, and he took a step toward her. "Greta, I love you. And I've never thought you were anything but beautiful. Never. You're the most amazing person . . ." The end of the sentence was choked off by emotion, and he tried again. "I've tried to . . . to work it out. To work out what's wrong with me. The only thing . . ." He swallowed. "The only thing I've ever felt is that maybe you don't care about me that much. When things are going wrong. When I'm suffering or hurt or just . . . failing. And I know it's pathetic. I know it is. And the only thing I can think of is that I got sympathy from Zoe in a way that maybe we've forgotten how to give each other."

Greta stopped pacing and stared at him. "So I don't care about you? When I've been here, year after year? When I've been with you as your mum got sick, and been with her, too. And of course I cared about her, but I was doing that for *you*, Aidan. I'm your wife, and I was . . . This is bullshit."

She turned away from him and stalked into the hall.

"Where are you going?" he asked, and he came after her with real panic running through him.

"To get you a suitcase," she said. "I want you out of my house. I hope the fucking cops take you."

"Please don't." He rushed and grabbed at her arm as she turned the corner onto the staircase.

"Don't touch me!" she said, and it was so close to a scream that it made him flinch.

"Please, Greta. Please don't kick me out. I'll go. If I have to go with them and convince them that I didn't do it, then I will, and then I'll find somewhere else. I'll give you space. I know I deserve it. But please don't throw everything away."

She gave a half laugh, and leaned over the banister to spit at him, "*You* threw everything away, Aidan. I'm just the one dealing with the fallout."

Aidan put a hand out to the wall and tried to find some steadiness in it. It felt like there was a great gaping hole somewhere nearby. It was going to swallow him. He couldn't breathe properly with the fear. She didn't even know the worst of what he'd done. She could never know. She could never, ever know.

THE HOUSE LOOKED serene as they arrived. It was a large, square, expensive-looking place, even on a road full of expensive houses.

Chilworth Drive was not somewhere Jonah had ever been. It was the sort of place that gave the impression it didn't *do* crime. The reality, of course, was different. Jonah may never have been there, but he'd been called to crimes that were both violent and petty on streets like this.

He climbed out of the car ahead of Hanson and Lightman. The squad car pulled up on the road beside the house, disgorging the two uniforms they'd brought as backup. Jonah knew the sergeant and constable vaguely, but wasn't entirely sure of their names. They only ended up working together at times like these.

He nodded to the sergeant and then made his way to the front door. There was a pause before it was opened, and, when it was, it was flung back with startling force.

Aidan's wife, a tall, slim figure, stood there with eyes that blazed.

"He's here," she said. "You can have him. I've packed his suitcase, and if you want to ask me any questions, you're welcome."

She stalked away from the door, and Jonah felt undeniably awkward as he stepped inside. Aidan Poole was at the foot of the stairs, his face a picture of misery. Jonah wondered how much of it was feigned.

He shifted to allow the other officers inside. "Aidan Poole, I'm arresting you on suspicion of the murder of Zoe Swardadine."

THERE WAS ALREADY a trio of onlookers on the other side of the road as Aidan was loaded into the back of the squad car. A middle-aged dog walker, a power walker, and a woman in slippers, who looked like she'd come out just to gawk. Jonah didn't envy either of the Pooles this public spectacle.

Jonah himself hung back to speak with Greta, though he began to suspect that his quiet explanations of the process weren't getting through to her. She was standing just outside the door, watching the scene and shifting constantly on her feet. She seemed not to know what to do with her arms, which she folded and unfolded repeatedly.

In the end, Lightman suggested that she should come inside and have a cup of tea. Although Jonah was eager to begin questioning Aidan, he felt they owed her some support. She'd just been told two pretty awful things about her husband, after all.

So Jonah let his sergeant guide her into the sitting room, while he and Hanson hung back in the hall. Something in Lightman's manner seemed to soothe her. She was able to sit down, and to ask him what would happen and what she should do.

Lightman explained that there was counseling available to her, and that she might want to call someone.

"Could you stay awhile?" Greta asked, her eyes steady on him.

Jonah met Hanson's gaze. She rolled her eyes and he tried not to laugh. "Ben's magic touch," he murmured.

The sergeant extracted himself a minute later, having promised that he'd be on hand if Greta needed anything.

"Tenner says she calls within twenty-four hours with some kind of crisis," Hanson said as they got back into the car.

"I'm not taking that bet," Jonah said, and Lightman just shook his head, smiling very slightly.

"MR. POOLE," JONAH began, "I'm now interviewing you as a suspect in the murder of Zoe Swardadine, which I want to know you understand in full. It's important, given you've decided not to bring a solicitor."

Aidan Poole's face was pale but set. "Yes," he said. "I understand that. I don't need a solicitor because I had absolutely fuck-all to do with Zoe's death."

"Then why did you lie to us?" Jonah asked.

"About what?" There was something in Aidan's expression that told Jonah he knew that he'd lied. He knew damn well.

"About not knowing where her flat was," Jonah said.

Aidan glanced at Hanson, and then back at Jonah. "What? I didn't know where her flat was! What the hell?"

"It was a pretty complex bit of deception," Hanson chimed in.

"Deliberately not providing an address either time you spoke to the police, and then waiting for it to be brought up."

Aidan's expression was dumbstruck. "I didn't know it," he said, after a moment. "I really didn't."

"It was always a bit of a stretch," Jonah said. "The idea that you didn't know where your own girlfriend lived."

"I told you," he said, a shake in his voice. "She kept her distance after the last breakup. Maybe that's because I'd acted like an idiot before, or maybe she just wasn't sure she'd made the right decision taking me back. I don't know. But she didn't tell me, and she'd told everyone not to let on."

"So how did your fingerprints come to be found in the bathroom?" Jonah asked.

There was a total silence, and Aidan's face had the expression of someone who'd just been shot.

"What? They couldn't have been."

"Because you thought you'd been too careful?" Jonah asked.

"Or because you wore gloves that day?" Hanson said. "Was there another time you'd forgotten about, when you went to see her and stayed awhile?"

Aidan shook his head slowly and then with a gradually increasing tempo. "I didn't," he said. "I've never been there. Not once. I still don't know where it is."

"Perhaps you forgot that you'd locked the bathroom door when you killed her?" Jonah said. "Was it one of those instinctive actions that you didn't even think about? Because you didn't want to get caught murdering your girlfriend?"

"I didn't murder her," Aidan said, and there was an awful, pleading note in his voice. "I didn't touch her. I called you because someone else killed her and I *heard*." He looked between them. "I showed you the Skype call, didn't I? Look, I would have said on the call if I'd had the address."

"Maybe you had other reasons for not giving the address," Hanson said. "Maybe you wanted some time to go by, so it was less clear when she died. So the window included the time when you called her instead of the time when you killed her."

"No," he said, a little more aggressively. "This is total crap. I didn't know where her flat was."

"And yet you'd been there," Jonah said, not shifting an inch. "You'd not only been there, but been in the bathroom where she died."

"Oh my God, please stop saying that," Aidan said, and he shoved the heels of each hand into his eyes, the fingers curled into fists. "I hadn't. I hadn't been there. And I don't understand."

"What happened?" Jonah asked. "An argument? Did she break up with you? Did it sound like it was for good this time?" He paused. "Or did she threaten to tell your wife? To tell the university? Was she going after your job?"

"Shut up!" Aidan said suddenly. It was whip-sharp. For a moment he looked at Jonah with a hatred as intense as any he could remember. And then he took a big breath. "It doesn't matter how many times you say that crap. It didn't happen. None of it happened."

There was a pause, then Hanson said softly, "Maybe we're being unfair. Maybe you've convinced yourself, too. If it all went wrong and you were desperate, maybe afterward you talked yourself around. Started to believe that you saw what you claimed you did."

"Jesus," Aidan said. "What's wrong with you? I was never there. I never hurt her. I'm not fucking insane." And then he suddenly straightened up, his face becoming set and hard. "All right. I want that solicitor now."

HANSON CAME TO find Jonah a short while after Aidan Poole had been escorted out to make his phone call. Jonah had balled up a piece of Blu-Tack and was throwing and catching it, then rolling it a little more perfectly into a sphere before throwing it again.

"What do you think?"

"I think he's lying," Jonah said. "I think he's been lying from the beginning. But what's interesting is that he thought we were going to ask about something else."

"I thought that, too," Hanson agreed. "What else are we missing?"

"And are we right in thinking he's lying about the flat?" Jonah said quietly.

Hanson rubbed the back of her neck for a moment, and then said, "So what if he's lying in one sense but not another? What if he really didn't know the address?"

Jonah gave her a considering gaze. "You think he followed her home, but then never worked out what the actual address was? Or didn't write it down?"

"Could be," Hanson said slowly, "or someone else could have taken him there and let him in. Maybe he was nervous because he thought that person had talked to us."

Jonah nodded, but wondered if they were being too convoluted about this. Both of those theories felt off to him somehow.

"It's possible," he said in the end, "but I feel like he was worried about something else." He saw Hanson's expression and gave a small smile. "I know. Verging on an assumption. And you don't have to agree. But a few things occur to me. The first is that Zoe was away from her flat from five-twenty until eight-thirty that evening. If she came home at eight-thirty, why did Aidan Poole have to wait until eleven to Skype her?"

He could see Hanson thinking this over. "You think she'd arranged for someone else to visit once she was home. The person who was waiting for her."

"Possibly. She then argued with someone," Jonah said.

"But that's several hours before the Skype call, so there's still a lot of unaccounted-for time. We know the Skype call was at eleven," Hanson replied. "Though . . . we don't know for sure whether that call showed anything at all, do we? If he'd killed her, he could have been in the flat and just made a call from his mobile to her Skype and accepted the call himself." She paused. "Can we get a location from his mobile?"

"Yes and no," Jonah said. "We can only get the nearest mast, but that should at least tell us if he was near the flat or at home."

"Which would help a lot," Hanson said. "Shall I go and request it?"

"Yes," Jonah said. "It'd be good to rule him out." At Hanson's sigh, he added, "Sorry. I'm not saying you're wrong, it's just . . . if I had to put my finger on the one bit of truth we've had from Aidan Poole, it was his account of the murder."

Hanson gave a slightly frustrated shrug. "Well, we've got to start somewhere." She turned away and then faltered in the doorway, and turned back. "Sir, in Aidan Poole's account, he never saw her, did he? He never actually saw Zoe on the screen."

"No," Jonah said, going back over Aidan's account in his mind. "No, he didn't."

"So what if you were Zoe's killer, and you knew Aidan was going to talk to Zoe. Say you'd killed her earlier in the evening," Hanson said, "and you wanted to give yourself an alibi."

"You could fake a scene in the bathroom," Jonah agreed slowly.

"You could even record audio of the real scene and play it back when he called," Hanson said.

"But how would you know Aidan was calling at that point?" Jonah asked. "And, more significantly, how would you pick up the Skype call unless you were waiting there? If you sat and waited and picked up, you'd be setting up an incredibly complex alibi for a time you were actually in the flat, which makes no sense."

"No, true," she said. "Unless there were two of you . . ."

HANSON RETURNED TO her desk wondering whether they'd been looking at everything all wrong. Of course it would be possible to fake the time of the murder, if your only witness was watching through a screen that had a limited viewing range. The forensics had only placed her death between late afternoon and the early hours of the morning. Zoe could have been dead hours before.

She knew the DCI hadn't been sold on the theory. She'd seen it in his expression and in his cautious responses. But that was his job, she thought. He was meant to keep an open mind. It was up to his team to work with every unlikely theory, in case one of them turned out to be right.

Wondering how much precedence there was for a pair of murderers, she pulled her keyboard closer and opened Google, then searched for "murdering couples." She'd just pressed the Enter key when DI Walker emerged from the kitchen. In response to her glance in his direction, he gave her a smile and ambled over, carrying his coffee cup.

"Are you any less soaked today?"

"Yes, thank God," she said, grinning. "Hey, can you think of any famous couples who've murdered people? As a pair, you know?"

"Sure," Walker said. "Bonnie and Clyde, Homolka and Bernardo, Faye and Ray Copeland . . . the Birnies . . ."

"Whoa," Hanson said, grabbing a pen. "That's loads. Which is helpful but also . . . concerning."

The DI laughed. "I did a criminal psychology paper on group killers. A lot of couples featured."

"You did criminal psychology?" Hanson asked, pausing to look at him. "Where was that?"

"Winchester."

"Ooh, local boy."

"What about you?" he asked.

"Oh, I did straight psychology," Hanson said. "Which was great, and I've used it a lot since. But I sometimes wonder about going back and specializing in the criminal side. I keep thinking it might help."

"Well, I've definitely found it useful," Walker said, lifting his mug thoughtfully. "I mean, I only have to be in a room with a killer to know they did it."

"Really?" Hanson said, and then realized that he was joking. "All right, yeah. Maybe it's not vital."

"Sorry," Walker said, laughing. "You should definitely think about it. I think it all helps, and if your style is to get inside the heads of your suspects, then it's even better."

Hanson gave him a grin, and went back to her work with that in mind. She supposed that probably was her style. Whenever she wasn't involved with simple fact-finding, she generally thought about why people might have acted in a certain way.

And maybe that was what she should be thinking about with Zoe's case. What would the motivation be for a couple killing her together? And why would you want to fake the time of the death, if her thoughts were right? One of them had to have an alibi for 11 P.M., otherwise what was the point? But it also had to be someone who had been free to commit murder earlier on, working with someone else who was free at eleven to create an elaborate cover-up for their accomplice.

Maeve, she remembered, had been busy up until a little before ten, and then free. Maeve also had a track record of letting Aidan into Zoe's house, and Hanson decided to start looking at her more intently. She loaded up the transcript of Maeve's interview and began to read. She was just getting into her stride when the phone on her desk rang.

She sighed as she realized it was the crime desk transferring a member of the public with information about Zoe's death. She'd hoped that anyone who was going to provide information on Zoe would have called in over the weekend.

The call handler told her that they had someone who seemed credible.

"I think you should talk to him," he said.

"OK. Put him through."

There was a click, and then a young man's voice said, "I think I saw the girl, the one on the news this morning. It's hard to be sure, but she looked very like her."

"OK, thanks. Can you tell me when and where this was?"

"So this was on Thursday night," he said. "At my local."

"Where's that?" Hanson asked, wondering whether he was just about to overthrow all of her theories. If he'd seen Zoe later on the night she'd died, she couldn't have been murdered by the person shouting at nine. She moved the handset so she could take notes.

"It's the Bridge. It's on North Road, near the uni campus."

Hanson scribbled this down, and then said, "Great. So when did you see her?"

"This would be lateish. Ten maybe. She came to meet a guy who was already there and look after him."

Hanson felt one of the strange drops in her spirits that always came when a pet theory was overturned. If this was true, then Zoe really had died at eleven or later.

"Was he drunk?" she asked.

"Pretty paralytic," he said. "She came in, and then he pretty much fell off his seat at the bar, so she took him outside."

The little Hanson knew of Zoe tied in with someone who would go and look after a drunk friend. Or one who was pretending to be drunk. "Could you describe him?"

"Well, ish . . . He was an older guy. A lot older than she was. I don't know. I was thinking it was a shame. She clearly deserved better than some old drunk."

Her pulse began to pick up a little. "So when you say he was old, was he gray-haired?"

He let out a breath. "I think it was gray? I'm not sure."

"Any facial hair?"

"Some, I think," he said. "Beard and mustache, though maybe long stubble."

Hanson scribbled on her pad, and asked, "And how was he dressed?"

"Pretty well," the guy said. "Expensive-looking shirt and trousers."

Which unquestionably sounded like Felix Solomon.

"Did you see them after she took him outside?"

"Oh. Yeah, I did. I wanted a smoke, so I took my beer outside and sat at one of the tables out the front. The guy was upset, and she was hugging him and, you know, comforting him. And then he was sick into a plant pot, and after that she called a cab and they left."

"What time was that?"

There was another huff of air. "I'm not sure. Probably ten forty-five?"

Hanson shivered. Ten minutes before Aidan's assumed Skype conversation, Zoe had left a pub in a taxi with someone who looked like Felix Solomon.

"Do you know what he was upset about?"

Her informant paused. "I don't know. He definitely said something about being useless and a waste of space, and she said he wasn't. But other than that I'm not sure."

"OK, thanks. Can I take your name and contact number?"

She thought again about Aidan's fingerprints on the lock. Maybe there hadn't needed to be two people involved in Zoe's murder. Maybe there had only needed to be one. A man who had run his own cases, and knew exactly how to manipulate a crime scene. A man who used to be a DCI.

22

May—six months before

It was just a regular Tuesday. A Tuesday on which he and Greta had done a verbal download of the day's events to each other, and sympathized and laughed, and then had gone on to talk about the other people in their lives while forking seafood tagliatelle in a white wine sauce into their mouths, and drinking a little more than either of them had meant to. Such an ordinary evening.

But it was also the sort of evening that made him feel that his other life must be a fantasy. He was so used to this life, lived in this house, with this woman. The idea of it all ending—of the two of them going their separate ways and perhaps just meeting up every few months for lunch—seemed unreal.

He and Greta ended up on the topic of their friend Antony and his loss of libido. The conversation continued as they loaded their plates into the dishwasher and rinsed their hands. He kept listening while he checked his phone.

A couple of messages had arrived, and they were almost definitely from Zoe. There was a little red two at the top left of the app, but nothing on the home screen. There were only two contacts he'd muted so their messages didn't flash up. Zoe, he'd muted to keep her messages from Greta. Maeve was the other, and he'd muted her for everyone's benefit, including his own. However strange it felt to think about Zoe right now, it was nothing to the shameful regret he felt when he thought about her housemate.

He had never, ever meant for anything to happen with Maeve. He'd enjoyed winning her over, and he'd liked the way her gaze locked onto him the moment he entered a room. He'd always known that her investment in his relationship with Zoe was as much about her own interest as it was about Zoe's. But there had been strict, strict boundaries.

Unfortunately, when Zoe had broken the relationship off things had ended up off-kilter. He'd become dependent on his conversations with Maeve because they had brought him closer to Zoe somehow. They had given him a potential way in. And last October, it had been Maeve who had let him into the house and allowed him to talk Zoe round.

The trouble had come only when he'd met Maeve at a bar. He'd been drunk and overwhelmed with sadness when the meet-up had started, and he'd ended up confused. Two weeks had passed since Zoe had spoken to him, and he'd been desperate. And maybe his pride had been wounded, too.

He could still remember, with horrible clarity, how he'd begun to focus on Maeve instead. How he'd told her what a wonderful person she was, and worked harder to make her laugh. To make her blush with pleasure.

She'd been so gloriously intoxicated with it all. He'd pushed through her initial resolve, but she hadn't quite given in to him completely. She'd kept the table between them and resisted attempts to hold her hand.

So he'd done an awful, unforgiveable thing. He'd leaned over to her and said that he'd always been crazy about her. Ever since he'd first met her. That he'd seriously wondered if he was with the wrong person.

It had been profoundly stupid. The only saving grace was that Maeve didn't believe in a physical relationship before marriage, and a kiss had been as far as it had gone. Having to backtrack the next day had been excruciating enough as it was.

They'd been OK in the end. After he'd explained to her that he had been projecting what he felt about Zoe, Maeve had admitted that she'd been doing the same. It was Isaac she wanted, another married man. Aidan had just been a stand-in for him, for a moment. That was all.

But from time to time, she would still drop him a few lines. Sometimes they would mention Zoe, and sometimes not. Either way, they all seemed to be fishing for something, and he found himself not quite trusting her apparent nonchalance.

"But he just needs to talk to her about it," Greta was saying. "How hard can it be? She's his wife!"

She'd said this last time they talked about Antony, and Greta had ended up angry with him when he'd demurred. She never had been able to understand how the truth could get snarled up inside you somewhere. He doubted she'd ever in her life felt a huge conflict between the need to speak and a total shutdown. It wasn't a matter of just talking. Not when your whole body was against you.

If you were Greta, of course you just *said it*. Whatever you were thinking. It poured out of you because that was how you were wired.

This evening, he felt a nostalgic fondness for that fierceness. An affection for everything about her.

"I know," he said quietly with a smile, and then he added, "Do you want a whiskey?"

"Sure." She grabbed a cloth and started wiping down the stove. "I'll make a coffee, too."

He went ahead of her into the sitting room and opened the messages with a small squeeze in his chest. It happened every time Zoe sent him something, and was the one thing that seemed to bridge the two separate lives he was living.

There was a picture. When he enlarged it, he realized it was Zoe's room, but changed. It was now dominated by a very large, very modern-looking bed with a velvet headboard.

She'd sent him a message underneath, too.

Look what I got! It's a floor model! No more backache and cold feet for you! Hooray! Xxx

He sighed. She wasn't supposed to spend money on him. That wasn't how it was meant to work. He was supposed to treat her. To spoil her. Having her splash out on a bed all for his benefit made him feel wretched, not least because he often gave her old, small bed as an excuse for not staying over.

He'd brought this on himself. He'd had a furious rant to her about how difficult Greta was to live with, and how much he was itching to get away. Which had been fairly justified at the time. His wife had been trying to dictate to him how he should manage his career. It just didn't feel so justified now, when they were getting along.

He pulled out two glasses and the whiskey, splashing a moderate freehand shot for Greta, and a larger one for himself. He took a good plug, and then almost spat it back out. Greta had pushed the bottles too far back on the sideboard again, and they'd ended up near the radiator. The whiskey was warm and unpleasant.

He felt his good mood sour almost in an instant. He'd told her *so many times*. So many times. It was one of the things that had ended up becoming a wedge between them, this apparent lack of willingness to adjust her behavior when it mattered.

"Is there any ice in the freezer?" he asked her as she appeared with two coffee cups.

"I don't know," she said, and went to settle herself on the sofa.

He felt irritated with her as he went back to the kitchen. Greta had caused this. She should go and get the bloody ice.

He slammed open three of the freezer drawers, and then slammed them shut again with a noise of irritation on finding no ice. He was going to have to go out to the chest freezer in the garage.

"I'll get some from outside," he said, waiting for her to apologize. Or at least sympathize.

"OK" was all she called back.

He was chuntering to himself as he shoved his feet back into his shoes and went out into the back garden. It was a filthy day, and the freezer was all the way out in the garage.

He'd grabbed a bag of ice and locked the garage back up by the time he remembered his phone. It was sitting on the table by the drinks.

Had he left the conversation with Zoe open? The one that made it painfully obvious that he was in love with another woman?

He hurried back to the back door and through the utility room, flung his shoes off, and walked straight to the door, to find Greta sitting peacefully on the sofa exactly as he'd left her, her legs tucked up underneath her, with the remote in her hand.

He felt his muscles droop in relief. She hadn't checked his phone. Of course she hadn't. That wasn't the kind of thing Greta did. She was open and honest, and so she assumed that he was, too.

"Do you want to watch another episode of that one with James thingy in? The Irish guy?" she asked him.

"Sure," Aidan said, feeling a little shaky with the aftereffects of the adrenaline. He sat himself down companionably with her as she fast-forwarded through the adverts, and left his phone right where it was on the sideboard.

IT FRIGHTENED ZOE how angry she seemed to have become. How hard it seemed to be to swallow down her frustration at everything that didn't go right, and how quickly she could descend from joy into a deep, immovable rage.

She'd felt so hopeful as she'd messaged Aidan the photos of her glorious new bed. She'd spent several weeks researching beds and mattresses, and eventually decided that the velvet headboard with a brand-new memory-foam mattress was going to be the ultimate in comfort. Better still, it looked good. Like the kind of furniture that Aidan seemed to appreciate.

But Aidan hadn't even replied. He'd read her message quickly enough and then, instead of sharing in her enthusiasm, he'd said nothing at all, which had produced a swift drop in her mood. It had only gotten worse when, instead of Aidan messaging, Felix had messaged instead.

It was unfair to be disappointed, and still more unfair to feel harassed when Felix mentioned the flat again. He really wanted Zoe to move in, and he brought it up at least once a month. He was trying to be helpful, she knew, but also to help himself. His tenant had remained two months behind with her rent, despite promises to catch up.

She sent him a quick thanks and insisted that she was enjoying living with Maeve at the moment, and then asked how he was, which proved to be a mistake. He sent three huge long messages complaining about an agent who had promised to read a few chapters of his proposed memoir, and then, after months, had suddenly said it wasn't the right kind of thing for him right now.

She was certain Aidan would have messaged by the time she'd replied and then made a cup of tea, but there was nothing. She felt as though she were stuck waiting on him as she tried to focus on a film and then some of her work. They had an eleven o'clock Skype date, as usual. At least she could talk to him then.

Only Aidan didn't log on at eleven. His icon remained unavailable, and there was nothing from him on Messenger, either. She watched as it grew later and later, almost willing him not to contact her at all so she could go ballistic. How hard was it to send her a message? To let her know that he was running late?

None of this was good for her. She knew that. She had changed in so many ways over the last few months. Once upon a time, she had been the independent one. The one who had other things to do, which needed to be worked around. She'd often been late, and smiled to herself at Aidan's enthusiasm.

She wasn't sure when any of this had shifted, either. Months ago, if she were honest with herself. Though there had been a few weeks in October, after the exhibition, when he'd been in constant contact. When he'd made her feel like he couldn't do without her.

Seven months later, she was reduced to helpless, tearful rage. It was the third time he'd been late to talk to her this week. And yet she never gave him a hard time. She had promised herself a long time ago that she would never be one of *those* girlfriends. The ones who hassled and harried their partners until they pulled away. She had always favored breezy nonchalance and a pretense of being busy, too.

But it wasn't good enough, any of this. Tonight, she really saw that. As he finally logged on and began to type her a message, she knew that whatever apology he came up with wasn't enough. She couldn't just accept it and move on with the conversation. Not when she'd spent the last three hours sick with fear that he was talking intently with Greta about their marriage, and deciding to try again.

His message eventually popped up, and it was even more casual than the last one.

So sorry, darling. We started talking about finances and it got complicated. Didn't realize we'd been talking for QUITE so long . . . How are you doing? Xx

She sat looking at that message for several minutes. For long enough that he sent another message.

Really missed you today! That's great about the new bed. Such a thoughtful thing to do. Want me to call now? xx

Of course she did. She wanted to see his face, and to remember how much she loved him. But that was why she shouldn't do it. He would always manage to melt her anger.

I'd rather just message.

She sent that, and then wrote a longer message, which he waited for without trying to argue.

Aidan, none of this is good for me. This waiting and waiting. I understand that there have been issues with the money, but those are issues you can sort out directly with Greta after you've moved out. I can't sit and wait for that any longer. Until you've actually separated, I shouldn't even be thinking of you as single. For the last seven months you've essentially still been married, and I'm the one who's suffered for that. I've had to accept these crumbs of your time, and your constant care for Greta's feelings. Though that second one makes you a wonderful person, it also makes you easily swayed. I'm so afraid all the time that you're going to change your mind, and every delay makes you seem more like you are. It's torture, and it needs to stop. You need to leave her. Not in a month, or in a few weeks. Now. This weekend. Or we can't be together. I can't do this anymore. I'm sorry.

There was a pause in which she felt her heart pounding, and then he began to type a series of short messages.

I'm so sorry. You're totally right.

I didn't realize you were feeling like that, but I should have guessed. That was crap of me.

Have you got time to meet up tomorrow for lunch? Let's meet in
person and sort all this out.

I love you, and I never want to hurt you. Xx

Zoe breathed out slowly. He hadn't run a mile. That was good.
She'd put her foot down and it had worked. It was all OK.

That would be nice. Love you too. Xx

She read his messages again as he typed more, wondering whether
she should ask for clarification. Did he mean he was actually going to
leave Greta now? In a couple of days? She wished he'd just said so.

His last message arrived, and she had tears in her eyes as she
read it.

Don't worry about anything, my darling. I'm going to make everything right. Xx

SHE WAS EARLY for lunch, but Aidan arrived only a few minutes after
she did. She smiled at him as he walked through the door, profoundly
relieved to have him there, but there was something solemn in his
greeting and she began to feel afraid.

He gave her a hug, and it should have been reassuring, but his lips
only went to her forehead and not to her mouth. Zoe felt a trembling
start in her limbs, and she sat down feeling as though none of this
were real.

"Look. I've been . . . selfish," Aidan said as he tucked his chair in.
A momentary crease of what looked like anger crossed his forehead.
"Worse than selfish. I've been an idiot. I've not been able to see what
was in front of me, and I've ended up hurting two people who don't
deserve to be hurt."

"It's all right," Zoe said quickly, trying suddenly to dismiss her concerns. To put everything back how it had been. "I was just upset."

"No, it's not," Aidan said quietly. "None of it is all right. I should never have started a relationship with you. I thought I knew my mind, but I didn't."

Zoe thought she might be sick. What had she done? This wasn't what she'd wanted.

"After what you said, I had to really think about it. To think, in full, what it meant to break up with Greta." He let out a long huff of air. "And it made me realize that I don't want to do that. Somehow, underneath everything, I care enough about her that I want to make our marriage work. I woke her up last night and I told her how I felt, and she admitted that it was how she felt, too."

It was every nightmare she'd had for the last seven months all come true. He was telling her he loved Greta more. He was telling her it was over.

"Don't," Zoe said, hot, humiliated tears starting to flood her eyes. "That's not what you think. We love each other . . ."

"We do," Aidan said, and he reached a hand out to touch her cheek. She let him do it. "And that's the real tragedy of this. That I love two wonderful women, and I have to choose. I have to let you be with someone else, someone who can give you his whole heart instead of half of it."

"So I get no choice in this?" Zoe asked. "I get no say at all? That's it, and you've decided between the two of you that she's in and I'm out?"

"I'm sorry," Aidan said.

Zoe stood, the tears mingling with a vicious fury now.

"Fuck you, Aidan," she said. "Fuck you, and fuck the day I met you. You've ruined everything. You've broken me, all just as some . . . experiment to see if you really preferred your fucking marriage."

"Zoe, don't," he said, and she saw that he was pale. That she had hurt him. "I still love you and I still want you to be happy. Let me help you. Let me look after you, as a friend. You deserve a good friend."

"I don't want anything to do with you," Zoe said, and she knew it was finally, honestly true. She snatched up her coat and shoved her chair under the table, hoping that it had hit his leg. That it had hurt him, too. "I never want to see your face again."

By the time she was yards away from the restaurant she'd pulled out her phone and started to block every form of contact from Aidan. But it wasn't enough. She needed to remove him from her life at last. Irreversibly.

She searched for his name in her emails and deleted every message between them. She removed the conversations they'd had on Skype—thousands of messages. She deleted everything in her messages folder, and then she opened up her photos and began to delete each picture that included him.

And then she messaged Maeve and told her that if Aidan contacted her, she needed to ignore him. That they were done. That he wasn't allowed into the house, and he wasn't allowed to know where she was, either. Which she knew in her heart of hearts that Maeve would not go along with.

So after that, she messaged Felix and said she might be interested in the flat after all.

23

O'Malley had spent the morning feeling like a kid being kept out of a sweet shop. It wasn't that he really minded working on the blackmail case. It was more the obvious picking up of pace on the Zoe Swardadine murder, and the frequent conversations between Hanson, Lightman, and the DCI about developments.

By lunchtime, however, he'd begun to feel as if he'd made some real progress. It had suddenly occurred to him that all the information being used as leverage had come from things that had happened in people's homes. Affairs. Illegal activities conducted from a home office. The question had been how this information was being accessed by the blackmailers.

Remembering the login codes used by Felix Solomon brought a potential answer to mind, and he dropped his new friend Ziggy a message on WhatsApp. The IT student took only a few moments to reply.

O'Malley explained that he thought hacking might well be involved in this blackmail case, but added that not everything was electronic.

So would you be able to spy on people, like? In their homes?

Ziggy's reply was quick and enthusiastic.

Yeah, sure! You'd just have to hijack their webcams.

O'Malley asked whether they were only looking for technical people.

No, you can pay people to do it on the dark web. It only costs a few hundred quid for a specific IP address or account. You can also buy lists for much less. Like a guy who likes looking at young girls might buy access to a whole load of cameras that belong to teenagers.

God, O'Malley thought. That was horrible. He said so to Ziggy, and then asked if you'd need access to their computer.

No, it's just done remotely. That's why I put tape over my webcam. You should consider it too. You never know who might have a thing for middle-aged coppers . . .

O'Malley couldn't help laughing.

I'll bear it in mind. Thanks!

JOJO'S FIRST MESSAGE in several days arrived as Jonah was deep in thought about Aidan Poole. He'd left Lightman to take Maeve Silver's new statement and log the note as evidence. He needed to think.

He felt a rush of guilt as he saw Jojo's name on his phone, and wondered how it was possible to want both her and Michelle to message, to tie himself up into knots about both of them. Perhaps this was how Aidan Poole had ended up, he thought.

It was a cheerful message, and a longer one than usual.

Hey, Copper Sheens! How's the policing? I've been off the grid for the last while, but it's been worth it. Some of the most incredible places out here. I found a nine-meter waterfall that had so little force behind it that it barely disturbed the pool below, and you could see all the way to the stones at the bottom. Today, I got woken up by a gemsbok. You should google it. I can't remember feeling so much in touch with all things wild. Except maybe when I was five and I got lost at the pond-dipping center. I should have signal for a while now. Xx

He read it three times, and had no idea how he should reply. What could he say that wouldn't be duplicitous? But what would be the point in sending her a message about Michelle when she was out there trying to live her life?

He was still looking at it when Hanson tapped on his door.

"Sir," she said. "I've had an interesting call through from a civilian."

Jonah gave a guilty start and put the phone down on his desk. "Fire away!"

"It's a guy who's pretty sure he saw Zoe looking after a considerably older, well-dressed drunk male at a pub on Thursday night between ten and ten forty-five. He thinks the male was gray-haired and had a short beard and mustache."

"That's pretty high on the list of interesting things," he said. "What happened to them then?"

"They took a cab, which she called."

"Did you get the name of the pub?" he asked, already reaching for his keys.

JONAH EXPERIENCED THE usual lift in his spirits when he left the station. It didn't matter that Aidan Poole's solicitor was due at any moment, or that a filthy-looking rain was falling. It also didn't matter that he had loaned his raincoat to Hanson. The feeling of leaving his desk was still energizing.

He only managed to find a parking space a quarter of a mile from the pub, but he timed his dash from the car reasonably well. He was rain-spattered when he walked in, but not drenched. The pub was warm enough, too. It was more a gastropub than a watering hole, with big old-fashioned brass radiators installed as a feature.

There was a girl on behind the bar, round-faced and slightly flushed and wearing a gray vest. He gave her a smile as he approached.

"Are you Amy?" he asked her. "I'm from the police. Tanya said I might have a quick word with you."

"Yeah, she said." Amy glanced around at the three occupied tables, and then nodded. "Can we do it here? Tanya's in the cellar."

"Sure," he said, and pulled up one of the barstools. They were blue velvet and deeply upholstered, which was always a mistake as far as he was concerned. Making barstools comfortable just encouraged the solitary drinker to stay longer and sink lower. Which was good for business and generally bad for policing. "Tanya said you were behind the bar on Thursday?"

"Yeah." Amy picked up a cloth and started wiping the bar down. "Six until closing."

"I wondered if you remembered seeing a young woman in here," Jonah said, opening a file of printouts and sliding a photo of Zoe out of one of the clear plastic wallets inside it. He placed it on the counter facing Amy, and she stopped mopping in order to look down at it.

Her mouth pinched at one side as she considered, and then she said, "I don't recognize her, I don't think. I mean, she might have been here. But I don't remember her ordering or anything."

"She would have come to the bar to help a friend of hers, who was fairly drunk," he said without force. "Perhaps you remember a man here? A chunk older than her? He was drunk enough to slide off his stool."

Amy looked uncertain. "Well, it was pretty busy, so I might not have noticed . . . There were a few guys in here ordering. But . . . did he come on his own?"

"We think so."

Amy shook her head slowly. "I can't remember anyone being that bad. There are some guys who come in just to get lonely drunk, but not that many. It's more groups and people coming for food."

Jonah flicked on to the next plastic wallet, and pulled out Lightman's printed photographs of a range of men, their suspects included. He removed Zoe's picture, and laid them all out like playing cards instead. "Any of these men?"

Amy shoved the cloth away and gave the photos her full attention. He watched her eyes move from photo to photo, and tried not to feel disappointed. It was clear that none of them were jumping out at her. She glanced at Felix's photo and moved on at the same speed.

On the very last photo, that of a dark-haired young man with no beard who was simply an actor they had on file, she hesitated. "Maybe him," she said. "But I'm not really sure."

"That's fine," Jonah said, piling all the photographs up again and sliding them back into the wallet. "It's actually really helpful, so thank you. I've left a message with Tanya asking the other staff member to give me a call when he has the chance. And if you remember anything, just give me a ring."

He left his card, and then stepped outside a little regretfully. The rain was still going, and there was a strong scent of salt in it as if the clouds had picked up part of the sea and were now raining it down on them. He jogged most of the way back to the car.

He was thoughtful as he climbed into the Mondeo and set off again. Although memory was a flawed thing, he would have expected Amy to have remembered Zoe and Felix from only three nights before, and particularly if Felix had been drunk and making a fool out of himself. The bar wasn't large enough for her never to have come near him, and if it had been busy, surely she would have clocked someone occupying a stool for hours.

It made him doubt their witness's account. It wasn't uncommon to find that someone had invented a story. It was odd, though, that

Hanson had been interested in what the caller had to say. He'd generally found her to be a good judge of character.

The cyber team should have finished with Zoe's phone by now. Looking at her call list would be time well spent. And there might be more on the phone, too. Something that ruled Aidan Poole firmly in or out.

O'MALLEY WAS IN the midst of writing up his findings from Ziggy, and putting them forward as a theory about the blackmail case. He'd done a very complete job of shutting out distractions from his team members and their case. So complete, in fact, that only when Hanson called something loudly to Lightman about webcams did a connection occur to him.

He grabbed his phone again and added another message to his chat with Ziggy.

> Could you use Skype to do all the above? The spying?

There was a short delay, and then Ziggy sent him a reply.

> Yes. One of the most common ways as it's easy to hack and already has webcam privileges.

O'Malley was halfway to the DCI's office when he realized that the chief was still out. He told himself to be patient, and went to add a new file to the Zoe Swardadine case.

JONAH CALLED THE cyber team on his way back to the station and was glad he did. The report on Zoe's phone had indeed been completed. It should have been sent with the fingerprints, but was actually sitting in someone's out-box.

He took the stairs two at a time on the way back up to CID, and did little more than nod to his team as he headed for his office. The report was there, he saw.

He loaded up Zoe's list of calls first, and saw that there had been no call to a local number on Thursday evening. In fact, there had been no call to any number of any kind that night. The last phone call on the list had been at just after five, from a number listed as Felix. The timing tied up with what Felix had told them, though Jonah wrote it down with curiosity. There had been three other calls from Felix, each lasting no more than a few seconds. What had been going on there? It surely couldn't have been poor signal in a flat where she routinely received calls.

Scrolling down, he saw a call just after ten on the Wednesday, which had come from Zoe's father. It had lasted a more standard fourteen minutes.

And then, below that, he saw a listing for B-Cab, at 10:45 P.M.

He sighed as he typed the number into Google, and confirmed that it was a local taxi company. It looked a lot like their witness had seen Zoe, but on the wrong day. It was frustrating, but he would at least now be able to call the taxi company to get a further description, and also go and show the identity pictures to the Wednesday-night bar staff at the Bridge instead. There was hope of identifying Felix Solomon if it had been him.

He scrolled on through Zoe's phone. He found numerous sporadic calls to and from Felix. He also found Maeve, Angeline, and Victor, and several to and from her parents.

He paused as he reached three weeks earlier, only now realizing what was missing. There were no calls to Aidan listed. Had she not had his number saved? There were no entries that looked like any name she might give him.

He looked up Aidan's number on the database, keyed it into the file, then hit the search button. There were results under Aidan's name. But none were recent. The last calls and messages were from May.

With a sense of unease, he opened up the files related to her Skype account. Searching, he found Aidan's account pretty quickly. But again, there were no calls to or from him for the last six months. Nothing since the twentieth of May.

He looked at that, and then, feeling a little shaky, stood and walked out to where his team were all buried in computer work.

"Did anyone check whether the Skype ID Aidan had called on his phone was actually Zoe's?" he asked.

"Yup," Hanson said. "I put it in the notes from his interview. It's definitely hers."

"It doesn't appear on the Skype calls on her phone," Jonah said.

Hanson gave him an uncertain expression, and O'Malley drew breath as if to speak just as she continued. "I don't think you can modify that info on Skype, so I'm pretty sure he must have called her," she said. "Did someone delete it? The killer? Realizing they'd been seen?"

"I don't know," Jonah said. "It's . . . strange. There are no calls at all to or from Aidan from Zoe's phone in the last six months, either. If they were back together and Aidan was Skyping her, surely there should have been other communication."

"I've been wanting to talk to you about that," O'Malley said. "I started looking into webcam hacking for the blackmail case, and I found out from Ziggy that you can hack someone's Skype account so their webcam comes on when you want. I've been looking it up, and you can watch whatever they're doing without them knowing or having to answer a call or anything. It doesn't even turn the little webcam light on."

Jonah stared at him for a moment, and then said, "Well, that explains a lot."

It was clear to Jonah from the moment he walked into the interview room that Aidan's solicitor had briefed him. The lecturer was so purse-lipped in his silence that it was almost comical.

As Jonah went over the position of the fingerprints for the benefit of the solicitor, and gave Aidan an opportunity to explain their presence again, he was looking mutinously at the table. It was the solicitor, middle-aged and more academic-looking than Aidan, who spoke for him.

"My client has already explained that he had no knowledge of how this could have happened," he said. "He was not aware of the location of the flat, and has not been there."

"Thank you," Jonah said. "We won't continue with that line of questioning for now. Our main interest is elsewhere."

Jonah saw Aidan's eyes flicker up to his face and then down again. He couldn't help smiling to himself as he lifted a sheet of paper and scanned it, letting a pause develop. He could sense Aidan Poole's anxiety building.

"So," he said at last. "You have claimed several times that you were in a relationship with Zoe Swardadine at the time of her death. We have recently discovered that claim to be false."

Aidan moved his head away and let out a breath. His solicitor gave him a sideways look that was almost funny. Clearly Aidan hadn't been entirely honest with his legal counsel.

"You broke up with Zoe in May," he said. "The reason you were ignorant of her address was that she moved to get away from you. You hadn't spoken in months."

Aidan fidgeted, and his solicitor leaned to whisper to him, though God knew what he was saying when he had clearly been caught on the hop.

"We spoke that night," Aidan said.

"Oh, so was this a new development?" Jonah asked. "She suddenly decided to talk to you?"

There was a pause, and Aidan said, "Yes."

"And yet," Jonah said, looking down at his papers again, "your alleged call to Zoe didn't show up on her Skype account. No communication between the two of you shows up on her phone. Not since May, when you broke up."

There was a very long silence, and then Aidan gave something like a sob.

"I'm sorry," he said. "I'm so sorry."

FORTY MINUTES LATER, Aidan was being released pending further investigation. They had informed him that they were intending to bring charges about the webcam hacking, but needed to look into the likelihood of conviction and whether or not Aidan had distributed any of the material he had recorded. The cyber team had been booked to pick up Aidan's laptop and desktop in the interim.

It was unlikely that they'd bring him in for the spying until the question of whether he had murdered Zoe Swardadine had been fully answered. Though if Jonah were being honest with himself, it had already been answered for him. The breakdown in Aidan's defenses had been complete. He'd spoken unstoppably about how he'd been convinced it was for the best that Zoe and he were apart, and how much he'd wanted to make his marriage work. How he'd thought he and Zoe could be friends, and how her sudden absolute shutdown had driven him mad.

"I didn't mean to . . . you know. To perv on her. That wasn't how it started," he said. "I was genuinely afraid that she was going to hurt herself, and nobody would tell me anything. There was just this wall of silence. Even Maeve shut me out in the end."

Jonah listened in tight-lipped silence, aware that Hanson was doing the same and reacting with just as much incredulous disgust.

"So I found a way of seeing what she was doing. And I knew it was wrong. I did know. I'd just got to this point where nothing else mattered. I thought just checking in on her would make it all go away. I dug until I'd found a site where people would do this for me, and I paid them three hundred quid for access to her camera."

"But it wasn't enough?" Hanson asked. "Checking up on her?"

"It turned into an addiction," he said. "The weirdest addiction. I got a kick out of seeing her at random times, and it would cheer me up. Seeing her face after what became weeks and weeks."

"And on Thursday night?"

Aidan shrugged. "It was just another night. I'd hoped she'd be online earlier. With Greta out, it would have been nice. I was thinking of putting the TV on and kind of . . . watching it with Zoe."

Jonah decided not to think too hard about that as he went over the presence of fingerprints once again, and pushed for an answer to how they had gotten there. And in spite of Aidan's torrent of confession, he shook his head at Jonah and said, "I wasn't there. I've never been there. And the only thing I can think of is that someone's trying to take me down."

As he finished signing for his belongings, and slid phone, keys, and wallet back into his pockets, Jonah couldn't help but agree with him.

JONAH WAS DEEP in thought as he made his way back to his team. Hanson was already at her desk by the time he drifted over and pulled up an empty chair.

"You think he's telling the truth," Hanson said, and Jonah nodded.

"On balance, yes."

"The truth about . . . ?" Lightman asked.

"About never having been in the flat," Jonah replied. "He thinks someone wanted to set him up, and I'm inclined to think the same. It's too specific, those prints in that one significant place and nowhere else."

"So the question," Lightman said, "is who would want to do that."

"Yes," Jonah agreed. "I mean, killers don't generally frame people. It's difficult, and it adds a whole layer of stuff to get away with."

"Could revenge be a motive?" Hanson asked, leaning on one elbow and crossing her legs. "Someone really wanting to take Aidan down as well as killing Zoe?"

"I'd say it's more likely than any other motive," Jonah agreed.

"Victor would probably like to see him locked away," Hanson went on. "And what about the girls? Did Aidan spurn either of them, maybe?"

"Not that we know of," Lightman said. "Something to look into?"

"Definitely," Jonah replied. "I also wonder whether the most likely person to frame anyone is the one person who understands crime scenes fairly well."

"Felix Solomon," Hanson murmured.

"The thing we need to bear in mind," Jonah said, slowly, "is that the fingerprints might actually let off whoever argued with Zoe at nine. An argument could just about have led to a vengeful murder less than two hours later, but it can't possibly have led to those fingerprints being placed. There's simply no way somebody could get out to Alton and engineer taking Aidan Poole's prints in time to get back and kill Zoe by eleven."

"Unless the prints only appeared later," Hanson said thoughtfully. "Felix had a key."

"So unless it was Felix, then it's profoundly unlikely that the killer was the one arguing with her. And even then, it seems a lot more likely that the whole thing was planned a long time in advance. And while whatever Zoe did that evening was clearly important, and perhaps triggered the murder happening that night, it probably wasn't the real reason she was killed."

"More of a last straw," Hanson agreed. "Yeah."

Jonah glanced at Lightman. "Do we have any CCTV from farther into town yet? Anything on the shady character with the hat who was walking along Zoe's road? I'd say, of everything we've caught on camera, that figure is the most likely to be part of a long-planned murder. The awareness of the cameras. The clothing. It all spells planning."

"We've got quite a lot in now," Lightman said. "I've started trying to track the guy in the cap back, but there's a lot to sift through." He paused. "I know what you're saying is that Zoe's movements are less of a priority, but I feel we should still be looking at where she went when she left the flat. And there were also several cars that went by during the probable time of death . . ."

"OK," Jonah said. "Let's split it three ways, then. Juliette, see if you can find out where Zoe went during the gap. And whoever it was who was waiting for her when she got back. Domnall can take the cars."

"So I would, but I'm back on the blackmail case," O'Malley said, glancing up from his screen. "Given what you said this morning . . ."

Jonah grinned, having already made the decision that he would have to own up to Wilkinson in the morning. "This is clearly related. At least one of those cars might have a blackmailer in it."

"I'm sure they might," O'Malley said with a short laugh. "I've forwarded you an email from Ziggy about those logins, by the way. One of those Felix had access to was set up to track grooming networks and was cleared for a veritable host of things, including countrywide sex crimes. So if he's been looking at all that, he could easily have picked up Piers Lough's name."

"Wonderful," Jonah said. "Do you want to see about getting them all closed down while I go and talk to him?"

FELIX DIDN'T ANSWER the door immediately, and Jonah wondered whether he didn't want to talk. But after a second knock and a twenty-second pause, the door opened and Felix's face appeared.

Jonah experienced what was probably his third shock of the day. Although the man looking out at him was undeniably Felix Solomon—he was dressed in one of the sharp, dark-gray suits and was as well kempt as ever—he was almost unrecognizable. Felix's face was pallid and his eyes wide. The usually quizzical expression had been replaced by a slack-mouthed panic.

"I'm sorry," the former policeman said, his voice much quieter than Jonah remembered it. "I've . . . It's not a great time."

He looked as though he might shut the door, and Jonah felt instinctively that he needed to talk to him now, while his defenses were down. "I'm sorry if I've disturbed you," he said, "but I could use a little help."

Felix hesitated, but the appeal worked. He backed away and let Jonah into his flat, where the TV was on in the background with the news showing, the sound off. There was a laptop out on the kitchen table, Jonah noted. He wondered whether Felix had been trying some more hacking.

He followed Felix's gesture and sat on the sofa. Felix was decidedly unrestful company. The retired copper stayed standing, seemingly unable to keep still, and his breath came in uneven, ragged gasps.

"Is it . . . trauma?" Jonah asked gently, though he knew that much already.

"Yes," Felix said. "It just . . . There are triggers." He waved a hand toward the TV screen.

"I suppose the news is a difficult one," Jonah said quietly, burning with curiosity about what had done this to a fellow DCI. And then he added, "There have been a few bad memories for me, too. But I guess I've been lucky so far. Nothing has been terrible enough to . . ."

Felix's breathing continued in disturbing gasps. "Still . . . should have been tougher," he said. Jonah thought about pursuing this, but decided he was better off pushing him about the hacking.

"We need to talk about your information on Piers Lough," Jonah said next, in a firmer tone. "Which, I want to add, proved to be inaccurate. This Piers Lough is entirely the wrong age to be the absconded pedophile."

Felix gave him a surprised look that cut through the visible panic, and then turned and started to pace up and down, his breathing still noisy. "All right," he said. "Could still have been him, though."

"It could," Jonah said, "but the more important thing at this point is that you've been accessing police databases when you are no longer entitled to do so."

Felix paused, and gave him a slightly pathetic look. "I don't . . ."

"I'm not planning on causing trouble," Jonah said, "but I will be shutting them down."

"Don't," Felix said, leaning forward to put his hand on the kitchen table. "I need to be able to help. God knows, I didn't help her when she was alive . . ."

"How so?" Jonah asked.

Felix shook his head, but then spoke anyway. "She gave me a tirade. The afternoon that she died. She lost patience with me and told me I was selfish and, well, that I was wallowing in it."

Jonah remembered the series of phone calls from Felix, and nodded. And then he thought of Angeline, and how Zoe had told her she was broken. It had been on the Thursday, too. On that same day.

Jonah badly wanted to know what could have happened to the kind, comforting, supportive friend to make her turn on all of them. While he knew that her murder had probably been planned, it could still be part of the same story. If Zoe had been suddenly brusque and unsupportive to one of the many people who had clearly leaned on her, it might have made the decision for them. Most killers had some kind of an emotional reason for seeing it through.

"Do you think it was fair of her to say that?" Jonah asked after a moment.

"It . . . was a harsh thing to do, and ignored many things," Felix said. "I was bloody furious with her. So I didn't talk to her that evening. I didn't check up on her, even though I knew she'd said it because she was desperate. I feel like . . . like I drove her to do something." He shook his head. "I think she invited someone round, and I have an awful feeling it was Aidan Poole."

Jonah wondered again whether Felix had some reason for wanting Aidan Poole in the frame. He watched Felix carefully as he said, "Why Aidan?"

"Because she'd never got over him," Felix said, nothing in his manner altering. "He . . . changed her. Maybe not just him. All of it. Maybe it was the rest of us, too."

"There was nothing she said that day that led you to believe she'd invited him over?" Jonah persisted.

"No," Felix said, and shook his head. "She didn't say anything else, really. She hadn't mentioned Aidan for weeks, though I think she often wanted to."

"So you didn't argue with her again?" Jonah asked. "On Thursday evening?"

Felix shook his head. "I didn't want to see her."

"We have witnesses to an argument at nine o'clock," Jonah persisted. "And CCTV has so far picked her up speaking to someone at the front door on her return to the flat. We should have an image of whoever it was soon."

"It won't find me," he said flatly. "I saw her come back while I was upstairs, and I was still too angry with her to want to know. I walked away from the window because I hated the sight of her just then."

Jonah decided it was time to bring up their two newest lines of questioning, starting with Aidan Poole's fingerprints at the scene of the crime.

Felix moved over to the wall where two framed commendations hung, scanning over them without really reading.

"Have you seen Aidan recently?"

"Of course I haven't!" Felix said, sounding momentarily irritated rather than panicky. "I only knew him through Zoe, and I didn't like what I saw."

"But perhaps you had them round while they were still together?" Jonah asked, turning to him with a neutral expression. "Or invited him over for drinks?"

"I've never invited him anywhere." Felix's expression was flat and unhelpful, but there was obvious disgust there. Disgust toward Aidan, Jonah thought. This was something he wanted to pursue further in the station, where it would all be on record.

"What about Wednesday?" Jonah asked, deliberately changing tack. "Did you see Zoe on Wednesday night at all?"

"On Wednesday?" Jonah couldn't tell whether Felix was surprised or not. He was well aware that the apparent panic might all be a sham, but it was one that didn't seem to slip. Felix was either genuine or incredibly practiced at playing the anxiety card.

"Zoe met someone late," Jonah said. "Someone matching your description."

"What?" Felix stared at Jonah. "No, it . . . it wasn't me. I was here on Wednesday. I'd had a bad night."

"Not bad enough to go out drinking?" Jonah asked. "To get so drunk that you needed a taxi home?"

"No," Felix said. He was still moving, and Jonah was beginning to find the constant motion wearing. He wondered how Felix's friends coped with him when he was like this. How Zoe had coped. "No, I went nowhere. Who was she meeting? Was it a new boyfriend?"

"If they matched your description, they were certainly on the old side for a boyfriend," Jonah said with a raised eyebrow. "Wouldn't you say?"

"Some people look older than they are," Felix said, momentarily looking at him with a flicker of control once again. "I've never been one of those."

Jonah would have agreed at any point up till this afternoon. Right then, however, Felix looked his age. More than his age, perhaps. He had been suddenly transformed into a frail old man, and seeing it made Jonah feel uncomfortable.

"I don't think Zoe had any other friends my age," Felix went on. "Did Maeve mention any?"

"We're looking into it," Jonah said.

"For God's sake," Felix said abruptly. "You said you wanted my help! How can I help if you won't tell me anything?"

Jonah nodded. "Well, if you want to help, you can do it properly."

He rose. "Come into the station tomorrow and help us instead of hacking in the background."

Jonah wondered, after he'd said it, whether he'd given Felix the impression that he might be allowed access to their files. He thought of correcting that impression, but he could see the profound effect that this idea had had on Felix. His breathing had become noticeably quieter and his cheeks had color in them again.

Jonah let himself out of the flat and drove back to the station with a strange, repetitive prayer to nobody in particular in his mind, a prayer that he would never find himself shut out and desperate for scraps of detective work, eager to help a DCI with his own agenda.

24

June—five months before

Latterworth Road was so very unlike anywhere Zoe had ever wanted to live that she almost turned and walked back home. The quietness. The suburban semis. The mothers with push-chairs. To live here would be like some kind of exile, and—worse—like accepting that her life was done now. That she would never again be the young, attractive, carefree student.

It was hard not to hate Maeve just then. To be as angry with her as she was with Aidan. If Maeve had been the friend she should have been, Zoe could have stayed.

But what was she supposed to do when Maeve undermined her at every opportunity? When she forwarded messages from Aidan, and told him where Zoe could be found? Three times she'd arrived back at their house to see Aidan's car parked nearby, and every time Maeve had apologized and told her he'd taken her by surprise. That she hadn't meant to let him in. That she'd been worried he might do himself some kind of harm.

She needed out quickly, and that meant saying goodbye to their tatty old house with its view of the river; to the bars and the pubs; to the feeling of living life as she was supposed to. It meant accepting Felix's offer, because there was nowhere else available to move into by the weekend.

Felix looked so pleased to see her as he opened the door that she felt heavy with guilt. She couldn't seem to summon up the energy to be excited. He strode up the stairs ahead of her, telling her how glad he was that she was keen.

"You're going to be a much better tenant than the girl I've had," he said.

"Has she moved out?" Zoe asked. "Is it definitely OK?"

"Yes," Felix said with a smile. "She moved out yesterday, so you just decide what you want to do."

He opened the bland wooden door and let her in, holding it for her and gesturing like someone presenting a show of some kind. Zoe tried her best to see it with unclouded eyes. To see the space and the light, and not the awful blankness of the place.

"The furniture's all new," he said as she gazed around at the pale sofa and the sleek kitchen. "I was thinking of getting a desk in here. Do you think that would be useful?"

"That would be great," Zoe said, smiling at him.

She walked through to the bedroom, which was bright with reflected light from a wall full of mirrored wardrobes. The bed was hospital-bare, with its rolled-up duvet and pillows.

"Those are mine," Felix said, gesturing, "so you may as well have them."

Zoe nodded and drifted toward the wardrobes. For want of something better to do, she opened one of them.

"Oh," she said. And then she gave an embarrassed laugh. "It looks like she left some stuff."

She pulled the door back to let Felix see the shirts and jackets that were still hanging inside.

"Oh," Felix said. He moved forward with a jerk, and instead of taking a closer look, shut the door with a bang. "Don't worry about that. I'll forward them on."

Zoe felt quite suddenly as though he was too close. She stepped backward, and gave an awkward smile. "Great," she said. "Good to have so much hanging space. I've got too many clothes."

For a moment Felix said nothing, and then he smiled again, all warmth and confidence. "You and me both," he said.

He followed her as she moved back into the sitting room and stood in the center of it. She could tell that he was watching her keenly to see if she liked the place. She didn't know how to tell him that she couldn't seem to like anything these days.

"So," he said in the end. "What do you think?"

"It's great," she said. "Thanks so much."

"You want to take it?" He was clearly delighted, and she wanted to feel delighted, too.

"Yes," Zoe said, giving him her best attempt at a smile. "I'd love to."

"Wonderful," he said. "Wonderful. Do you want . . . Why don't you come and have a cuppa and I'll print out a contract?"

Zoe felt as though she'd rather go home, but she nodded anyway and followed him down the stairs and across the first-floor landing. As they reached his door and he was reaching for his keys, his phone buzzed.

She watched him pull it out of his pocket and read something. Just a quick scan over a message. And it was like watching the vitality drain out of someone. He was suddenly, between one moment and the next, a different person. An older one, whose breath sounded unsteady and whose hand faltered as he tried to unlock the door.

"Is everything all right?" she asked him.

"I'm . . . It's all right," Felix said, and drew in an unsteady breath. "I'm fine. Fine. Just . . . a stressful message from an old colleague." He looked up at her, and said in a strange voice, "He's not well. That's all."

She nodded, and suddenly remembered how he'd been at her exhibition last September. She had a sense that there was a lot going on with Felix. A lot that was hidden.

It took him three attempts to get the key into the door and turn it, and although Zoe would have loved an excuse to leave, she felt incapable of leaving him like that.

"Let me make *you* a cuppa," she said. "You can sit and chill."

It took Felix fifteen minutes to actually start talking. He'd barely spoken during that time, but he'd let her chatter at him and it had calmed him to the point where he could talk, and the fact that she was there, helping him, made Zoe feel that everything was all right. That this was what she was here on this Earth to do.

She could help the others, too. She would make amends with Victor and Maeve and go back to helping and supporting them. Caring for all of them and letting her light move into them somehow was enough. She could be happy just watching them bloom.

"I have PTSD," Felix eventually told her. "And it gets triggered by such strange things. Sometimes just . . . an image, or a sound. It's so difficult to predict."

She nodded, and brought her cup of tea to the sofa so she could sit opposite him. "Or a message?" she asked.

"Yes," Felix said, and took a breath. "Yes, sometimes."

"Was it to do with work?" she asked. "The trauma?"

With a sigh, Felix started to tell her. It had been seven years ago, and he'd been a DCI. He'd been on the hunt for a serial rapist who had come close to strangling one of his victims.

"I was on the way back from an interview. Late on, this was. And the operator notified me of a crime that might be related. A small girl saying her mummy was being attacked."

Felix had swallowed a big gulp of tea before carrying on. She'd seen the brightness of his eyes, and understood that he was trying to swallow down a great deal else besides tea.

He'd arrived before the squad cars. It had been one of those things that happened sometimes, because he'd only been two streets away. The house had been quiet, but the front door was slightly ajar and moving every time the wind blew.

"I knew I was too late," he said. "I got my baton ready and headed in, but there should have been sounds of some kind, or the mother and daughter should have been out at the front waiting for the police."

He'd found the daughter clutching at her unresponsive mother. There was a wound in the little girl's abdomen that had bled profusely as she'd crawled over to her mum.

"She was four or five," he said. "A beautiful little blond thing. She was . . . she was still alive, and she was so frightened of her mummy not moving. When I came over and I pressed my hands over her abdomen to try to stop the bleeding, she asked me if she was going to die."

Zoe reached out and took his hand, feeling a lump in her own throat and such sorrow for him.

"I lied to her," Felix said. "I said, 'You'll be fine. The doctors will be here soon. Can you hear the sirens? That's them. They're going to look after you.' And she said she felt wrong, and her eyes were funny. I had to take a hand off the wound so I could stroke her cheek."

There was a long silence, and then he said, "She died a few minutes before the ambulance arrived. That little blond girl who'd tried to help her mummy. And I don't know quite why . . . or maybe I do . . . but it broke me. It broke me in two, and I couldn't do it anymore," he said.

They'd had to remove him by force in the end. He hadn't been able to let go of her hand.

"And you left, after that?" she said, squeezing his hand. "You stopped being on the force?"

Felix gave her a strange look. It was halfway between angry and beseeching.

"No," he said in the end. "I lasted a few more months. And then I lost my cool with a suspect, and I beat the living hell out of him. And then there— Well, they looked through my desk and they found this . . . this little doll of the dead girl's. I'd taken it from her bedroom. For some reason the only thing that made me feel better was to comfort it. To keep comforting it. I think somewhere in my mind I felt like I was comforting her. . . ."

It took Zoe a long while to sleep that night. There was a compulsive horror to thinking of that poor girl, and of Felix. And for some reason the most horrifying thought of all was of him cradling a dead child's doll.

25

Jonah returned to the office and shut the meeting-room door. He sat back in his chair, trying to get everything in his mind in order while his team scrolled through hours of CCTV footage to trace Zoe's movements and discover the origins of the figure in the cap. It was a fact he felt a twinge of guilt about. But as the DCS often liked to remind him, there was no point hiring a cleaner and spending your days scrubbing the bathroom. Which, if nothing else, was a good reminder of the difference between Jonah's life and the DCS's.

Currently he had what was a familiar problem in investigative work. There were big areas with nothing pinned down, and a host of people who seemed to be dodgy. He could only be thankful that they lived in an age when there were so many ways to trace people.

On top of that, certain elements of procedure needed to be adhered to. He was very much aware that it was time to update the Swardadines on the developments since the press conference.

Deciding that it might be helpful to talk through Zoe's drunken Wednesday-night companion with them, he put a call through to the Swardadine home phone.

Siku answered almost immediately, her "Yes?" sharp.

"It's DCI Sheens here," he said. "I wanted to let you know where we are, and also ask a few questions."

She listened in silence while he told her about Zoe being out on

Thursday during the early evening. He wasn't surprised to learn that she knew nothing about it. He went on to the sighting on the Wednesday night.

"An older man?" Siku asked.

"Yes," Jonah confirmed. "Silver-haired and expensively dressed, by the description."

"Her landlord," Siku said immediately. "Felix."

"We're looking into that. At the moment he denies any such meeting." Jonah left a small silence, and then asked, "You don't think she'd been in touch with anyone else? No . . . dates? After she broke up with Aidan? I know this man was older, but perhaps, after that relationship . . ."

There was a pause, and Siku said, "I don't think so. She might not have said if she'd gone on a few dates, but . . . I was trying to encourage her to find someone else, and she was quite resistant to the idea. It was so frustrating. She'd never managed to detach herself from Aidan properly."

Jonah agreed, and then, after another pause, said, "There is some news concerning Aidan Poole that I think you need to know. It doesn't implicate him in the murder in any direct way, but it's significant."

"Has he done something else?" Siku asked swiftly.

"Well, yes and no. He lied when he said that he and Zoe were back together. They broke up finally in May, and she cut off all contact. He has admitted that he saw her because he was spying on her through her webcam."

There was a silence, and then Siku said, "That sneaking bastard!"

Her voice was painfully raw with emotion, and Jonah had little to offer to console her. There was nothing he could do to alter the facts, and it was only right that they knew first, before it got out in some other way.

"I'm so sorry," he said. "But at least it's caught up with him. He'll almost certainly be prosecuted."

"It must have been him," Siku said in a low, fierce voice. "He spied on her and he killed her. He was obsessed, wasn't he?"

"It's a possibility," Jonah said, "among a lot of others. And I'll let you know as soon as we know anything else."

Hanson had clearly been waiting for him to finish the call, as she appeared in his doorway straight afterward.

"Bit of a CCTV breakthrough, sir," she said. "We've got Victor Varos getting into a cab at eight in the city center and heading out in the rough direction of Zoe's. I'm going to check other points along the route, but it's quite possible he was the one waiting at her flat for her."

"Good work," Jonah said with feeling. "Can you send me the footage?"

He sat at his desk to watch it, wanting to feed it into his thinking rather than have the team's opinions at present. There wasn't long to wait before Victor appeared on the screen. He was a dark-clad figure who rolled up to the taxi rank by Holyrood Church. He had a light jacket on, where other figures walking past were muffled up, and his walk was meandering.

He leaned in to speak to the first taxi driver, and then climbed in. It took him a while to open the door.

Jonah ended the reel after the cab had driven off northward. Victor had boarded a cab at eight, drunk and headed in the direction of Zoe's house. He could well have arrived, had no response to buzzing, and waited for her.

Jonah was working this through in his mind when his phone rang. He didn't recognize Martin Swardadine's voice at first. Since the first call he'd had with him, Martin had lost the urbane self-satisfaction. The perfect enunciation and projection. In their place was something flat and cracked and rough.

"I'm so sorry, Officer," he said. "I've unintentionally wasted your time. There wasn't another man. The drunk idiot she came to help on Wednesday night was me."

. . .

LISTENING TO MARTIN was not easy. The shame that pervaded his account was uncomfortable to hear, and Jonah instinctively wanted to make Zoe's father feel better about it all.

Martin told him he had an alcohol problem. It was something he'd been trying to keep from his wife for years. He'd eventually unburdened himself to Zoe.

"She was so easy to talk to," he'd said, emotion running through his voice. "I felt terrible leaning on her, but she was so good at making me feel better. She had this faith that I could sort it out, but she never judged me when I didn't. When I put off going to get help, or when I screwed up and went on a bender, she was always there."

"And you were here in Southampton that night," Jonah said.

"Yes. I was." There was an awkward pause before Martin carried on. "I'd stayed the full day, and the meetings hadn't gone well. I could just tell that they saw through me. Some people do. They . . . they ask these questions and the way they look at you when you try to give them the usual bullshit . . ." He cleared his throat loudly down the phone. "I told Siku I'd better take them out for dinner, and instead I went and found the nearest bar. I shouldn't have called Zoe. She didn't need that. She had enough of her own to deal with."

"She came to meet you?"

"Yes," he said. "She always would. No matter what she was doing. She's come to rescue me before in . . . in London, sometimes. This was worse, I think. I remember being really sick, and I wasn't in a fit state for much. So she took me to the station in a cab and she bought me water and crisps and chocolate while we waited for the last train, and then she made me eat and drink until it wasn't so bad. She even asked if I wanted her to come along, but by that point I'd started feeling a bit more together and I told her to go home. And then . . . and then I fell on my bloody face getting onto the train, and she had to help me up. I wasn't even hurt, just . . . pathetic. I felt like such a failure just then. Such a bloody useless failure."

Jonah finished making notes, and then said, "It would have been useful to have had this information earlier, Mr. Swardadine."

"I know," he said roughly. "I know. I'm so sorry. When you asked about her, and Siku was there . . . I was just ashamed. I've told Siku now. I've told her. Even though it's the last thing she wants to hear right now."

"Well, I appreciate you coming forward," Jonah finished. "We'll be in touch soon with any updates."

He hung up the call and went out to his team once again.

"I'm going to ask Victor Varos and our witness from the pub to come in, but, in the meantime, can someone hassle Martin Swardadine's work until we know for sure about his alibi?"

VICTOR PROVED ELUSIVE. By six, while the CCTV hunt was still ongoing, Jonah had tried his mobile and the coffee shop, and called Maeve and Angeline to ask if they'd seen him. Neither had.

Their phone-in witness had arrived at five-fifteen, looking fairly uncomfortable about the mix-up between days.

"I was there both nights," he said by way of apology. "And I guess I just assumed it was the Thursday because that was the night she'd gone missing."

Faced with a range of photographs, he immediately identified Martin Swardadine, despite the photo being a very polished, professional one.

"That's him," he said. "He had a bit more stubble, but it was him."

He was on his way out when Lightman received a call back from Martin Swardadine's work. Jonah saw Lightman's eyes flit over to him, and waited for him to take the details.

"He was definitely in London," the sergeant said, once he'd hung up. "There were two of them at the client dinner, Martin and the CEO. They all got pretty drunk but it was Martin who called a cab for them at eleven-forty. He was there."

"Well, that's one thing cleared up," Jonah said with a nod. "He couldn't have reached Zoe within the pathologist's time of death, and he definitely wasn't there at our probable time of eleven P.M." He turned to Hanson. "Did you get anywhere with Felix Solomon's tenant?"

Hanson shook her head with a meaningful expression. "He claims he can't find her details. Having seen how religiously tidy he is, I'd say that's deliberate obstruction."

Jonah nodded, and then said, "I'd be interested to hear what she has to say about him in general. I wonder if the neighbor can help?"

"The non-pedophile neighbor?" Hanson asked.

Jonah gave her a grin. "The non-pedophile as far as we know."

THE HOUSE SEEMED to be shifting and creaking more than it usually did, the sounds cutting through the rain at random intervals. Greta had thought she was past noticing them anymore, but with Aidan gone it was as if the house had gained an unsettled personality and was determined to remind her that she was alone in the early darkness. How much worse would it be later, when she had to sleep alone?

She had her laptop out, a sign of her determination to get on with work, despite her miserable husband. But predictably she hadn't written a thing. Instead she had gone over and over the conversation with Aidan. She'd felt the hurt of what he'd done each and every time, and wanted to shout at him all over again.

She knew she'd been cruel. In some ways, she had probably given him reason to believe he'd done the right thing. She'd been harsh and cold and bloody furious. But at the same time she couldn't bring herself to regret it. Her one consolation for all the deceit was that she had laid into him. She'd made him feel it.

And now, several hours later, she desperately wanted to talk about it with someone. It was impossible to keep it all in. But the urge to pour it all out fought with a feeling of total humiliation. He'd slept with a student, and all the passion and strength and love she'd poured into her marriage had meant nothing. Neither had every care to keep herself thin and fit and beautiful.

"Fuck you, Aidan," she said to herself, for what must have been at least the fiftieth time. "Fuck you for making me feel this."

And the thing that was worse than that, that she didn't want to admit to herself as she blocked and then unblocked him from her contacts, was that part of her wasn't strong or cold or angry. Part of her just wanted him to walk back in and tell her it had been a huge mistake that he would never, ever repeat. Part of her ached to believe that he hadn't loved someone else, and that she really did mean everything to him.

She needed a bloody drink. It didn't matter how many times she'd told herself that she was strong enough to cope without it; it was still the only thing she wanted to do.

There was a trembling in her legs as she headed for the kitchen and took out one of the big half-bottle wineglasses they'd been given for their anniversary. She filled it and put the bottle away. And then she took it back out again and carried it back into the sitting room. She waited for the first few gulps to start to make her feel better, and when they didn't, she downed the rest of the glass steadily, then filled it again.

God, she hated him. She hated him more than she'd ever hated anyone in her life.

The first buzz of disconnected warmth had arrived by the time she looked up and saw a face staring in at her from outside the window. For a moment she thought it might be Aidan. But she knew his face too well. Knew the shape of him in silhouette. This was another man, someone she'd never seen before, and he was standing a few meters from the window.

The jolt of it did something horrible to her chest. Her eyes locked with his as she stared back, and then he was turning away, flitting out of sight.

Greta's heart was hammering. She felt sick with fear. Where had he gone? What had he wanted?

She ran to the front door and put the chain on with shaking hands, and then she thought of the back door and the French windows. She skittered over to each of them in turn and clicked the locks. And then she picked up her phone and ran to the bathroom. She locked herself in and sat on the edge of the bath in darkness, every part of her shaking.

She thought of the police, and then she thought of the sergeant who had made her tea earlier. About how strong and capable and calming he had been.

She'd already saved his number into her phone, which was a good thing, as her hands were vibrating so much with fear that it was hard to press the buttons.

HANSON'S HEAD WAS pounding, a wave of pain radiating out from her eyes. The pain had kicked in forty minutes after she'd started scrolling through the CCTV footage, and it had only gotten worse, despite a couple of Tylenol washed down with cold tea.

The initial elation of having found Victor Varos had been followed swiftly by disappointment. She couldn't seem to find him closer to Zoe's flat at the right time, or, in fact, anywhere that she was expecting him to appear.

Fifteen more minutes, she told herself. *And in those fifteen minutes, you'll find him.*

She was glad of the interruption when Lightman's phone rang. It gave her an excuse to look away from her screen, blink a few times, and rub at her head again.

She watched him as he said, "DS Lightman." And then, "Does he seem to be there now? Yes, OK. I'm going to send some uniformed police round and I'll be there as soon as I can."

He hung up just as the DCI emerged once again, and Hanson gave him a quizzical look.

"Greta Poole just called," he said. "She says someone was staring at her through the window, and she's not sure if they're still there."

Hanson punched her hand in the air triumphantly. "Told you! Lightman's fangirls never disappoint."

JONAH LEFT FOR home at half seven. Lightman had confirmed that he was at Greta Poole's, and the situation seemed to be non-threatening.

There was still no sign of Victor Varos, and although his absence was beginning to concern Jonah, there was little he could do by staying on at the station. It was possible he was simply ignoring their calls, or turning up to bother Greta Poole, but it was also possible that he had absconded. And that he had done so because he had something to hide.

The CCTV footage was inconclusive. Victor could have been at Zoe's at nine and argued with her. He could also have returned later with the intention of killing her. They just couldn't prove either.

Jonah had asked O'Malley to stop by Victor's flat on his way home, to see if he got an answer. For now, that was all he could do.

He took a route that led him past the top of Furzley Lane, where Jojo's cottage was probably repaired by now. He tried to catch sight of the chimneys, thinking as he did so of the night when he'd glanced this way and seen the evening sky scalded an angry red.

There was nothing to see tonight, though. The chimneys were out of sight, even through the almost-bare trees, and he felt an ache at the distance between them, an ache that lasted even as his thoughts moved seamlessly to Michelle.

Lightman called him a little farther into the journey with another update on Greta Poole's intruder.

"It looks legitimate," he said. "One of her neighbors saw a man running from her driveway down the road at about the right time. Greta Poole herself seems quite with it, if slightly intoxicated."

"Interesting," Jonah said. "Did either of them provide a description?"

"Nothing except 'a probably male figure' from the neighbor,"

Lightman said. "Greta's not entirely clear. She realized it wasn't Aidan from the shape of the hair and the stature. She didn't see the face that clearly, and it was all very quick. She had the impression of a beard or a scarf over his lower face, but that was about it."

"No coloring?"

"No."

"That's a shame," Jonah said thoughtfully. "I'd be interested to know if it was our missing young Brazilian suspect."

"I've asked her to call if she remembers any more details."

Jonah rang off, and had made it home by the time O'Malley called. "No Victor here, but I've asked his flat mate to let us know when he's back."

"Great. Thanks, Domnall."

It was dinnertime, and he had nothing particularly easy to eat. On inspection, he found he had the ingredients for some kind of coconut curry, so he started to cut onions. He made himself a cup of tea once they were braising, his thoughts returning to Jojo's house and the fire, and at that point he realized that he'd never replied to her message.

For some reason, having missed the window to reply to her made him feel worse than the fact that he'd slept with his ex on Saturday night. He wrote a long, apologetic reply in stints between chopping and stirring. He included a brief explanation of how the shit had hit the fan at work, and asked how much longer she was going to insist on staying out in the arse end of nowhere. He said nothing about Michelle, or how confused he felt, and he didn't feel much better by the time he'd sent it.

He had a plate of food in front of him when O'Malley called again.

"Your man Victor is back home," the sergeant said. "The housemate sent me a message."

"Is that just now?"

"It was, so."

Jonah glanced at the clock on the microwave. Nine-forty. Two and a half hours since someone had gone to Greta Poole's house to spy on her.

"Thanks, O'Malley. Would you do me a favor and look up train times from Alton to Southampton?"

"Sure, Chief," he said. "Just as long as I don't have to head back out there."

"No," Jonah said decisively. "We'll leave him for tonight. But first thing tomorrow, he's having a visit in person if he hasn't called back."

He managed to get midway through his curry before the next phone call. With a sigh, he decided that he'd just have to accept that his night wasn't his own.

"Sorry, Chief," Hanson said. "I've had a call from Angeline on my mobile asking to talk to you. I did explain that I was at home, but she was quite insistent. She sounds drunk, if anything."

"She has something to say?" he asked.

"Apparently so."

"All right. I'll call her. She might end up saying more when drunk than she otherwise would. Can you message me her number?"

He ate a few more mouthfuls while waiting for the number, and then called as soon as he had it.

"This is DCI Sheens, Miss Judd," he said. "Can I help you?"

"Yes," Angeline said. "You can. I know who killed her."

Angeline's words were labored but she sounded triumphant anyway. Jonah felt instinctively skeptical, but he'd learned a long time ago that the most unlikely people could prove to know their stuff.

"Who killed Zoe?"

"Obviously," she said with teenagerish rudeness, "it was Victor. He lied, and he said he hadn't seen her, but he did see her."

Jonah tried not to sigh. He bit his tongue to keep from asking Angeline why she hadn't mentioned this earlier.

"When did he see her?" he asked instead, pushing his plate aside and scrabbling around for a pen and paper. He failed to find any paper with his searching hand and ended up grabbing the envelope from a gas bill, which would have to do.

"On Thursday," Angeline said with apparent satisfaction. "He lied about it, and I caught him. He knew about what we argued about in the morning, but he was supposed to have not seen her since Wednesday. And when I saw him on Thursday night, he was arguing with someone."

"I'm sorry?" Jonah said. "You saw him when?"

"On Thursday night," she said. "When I was going to buy some wine."

Jonah paused with his pen. "You haven't mentioned this before."

"Didn't I? I suppose I must have forgotten. It's been . . ." Her voice caught, and in spite of the apparent drunkenness, Jonah suddenly had an unnerving feeling that Angeline knew exactly what she was doing. That this apparently fragile woman had a sharp, cunning side to her that none of them had yet seen.

"You said he was arguing," he said.

"Yes. On his phone."

"Can you describe exactly what happened?" Jonah said calmly, part of his mind on what Angeline was trying to do. Had she decided to throw Victor to them out of some kind of revenge? "From when you left your flat? Your flat's on what road?"

"It's on Hill Lane," she said.

He scribbled that down, and then asked her to clarify which part. Hill Lane ran north to south through the city and past the common. It was briefly in parallel with the much shorter and smaller Latterworth Road, and was only a couple of streets away from it. Jonah had driven up it on the way to Zoe's flat.

He asked Angeline for more detail, which revealed that her own flat was half a mile south of Zoe's.

"And where were you going?"

"I told you. The off-license. For wine."

There was a low buzz of noise in the background, and Angeline was silent for a moment.

"Is there someone there with you?" he asked.

There was a fractional pause before Angeline said "No" belligerently, and then asked, "Why would I need someone with me? I'm not a child."

"Of course not," Jonah agreed. "So you went along the road to the off-license."

"And I saw Victor shouting at someone on the phone. Well, I heard him and then I saw him."

"And what time was this?"

"I don't know exactly," Angeline said, "but it must have been before the off-license shut, and that's midnight."

"But it might have been much earlier?" he asked. "At eight or nine?"

"No, it was later," Angeline said. "I saw the ten o'clock news. I'd fallen asleep and then I woke up and it was on, and it was horrible."

Jonah tried to put this into his mental picture of that evening. And then he asked, "And were you drunk when you saw him?"

There was a momentary pause. "It was before I went to buy wine," she said coldly.

Which wasn't actually a no, Jonah thought.

He asked Angeline to come into the station the next day to give a statement, wondering exactly how much this account could be relied on. There was the sudden apparent memory, and the fact she had probably been drunk, and was almost certainly drunk now. There was another sound in the background just before he hung up, and Jonah felt certain that someone else was there with her. He would very much like to have known who it was.

It was hard not to think about Felix Solomon, who had had access to police data. Might he be able to see their own files somehow, and be aware that attention had just fallen on Victor Varos? And might he have been the one there with Angeline? How well did the two of them know each other?

So far, his current thinking hadn't gotten beyond a few basics. The mainstay was that Aidan Poole had been framed. Which meant access to his fingerprints.

Zoe had argued with someone at nine, but he had never been entirely comfortable with the idea of a murder planned and executed within ninety minutes, as the direct result of a row. Too much stood against it. The care taken to make it look like a suicide. The desflurane. The fingerprints.

Angeline was now claiming that Victor had seen Zoe, and Jonah was already beginning to think that the most likely time was at 9 P.M. Victor could easily have argued with her. He had proven himself to have a temper, and it was quite possible that they had fallen out if Zoe had suddenly become unsympathetic and angry, as seemed to have happened. But he couldn't see Victor then returning to carry out a cold-blooded murder a mere hour and a half later.

Perhaps the killer *had* argued with Zoe, but much earlier on. Both Angeline and Felix had fallen out with Zoe much earlier that day. He only had their account of how serious it had been, and exactly what they had argued about.

Victor might be able to tell them a lot more about what had gone on with Angeline. If he could be persuaded to talk to them.

For a moment Hanson's theory that there had been two people involved came swimming to the top of his thoughts. He had instinctively doubted it, but now, with that strange phone call behind him, and the realization that Angeline and Felix had both been on bad terms with Zoe when she died, he wasn't quite so sure.

26

November 21, 4:45 P.M.—six hours before

Zoe had been wandering for hours, at times overwhelmed by feelings of self-loathing and at times so angry with every single person in her life that it made the inside of her head feel like some kind of an inferno, full of an awful, searing heat that threatened to lash out at the people around her.

She was just so tired of their bullshit, and of her own. She'd tried so hard to believe that other people's joy could be enough, but last night some kind of a switch had tripped in her. She had realized profoundly that her whole way of thinking had been based on a fabrication.

She had finally understood that other people's happiness meant nothing. It meant nothing at all. Maybe that was because none of them seemed to get any happier. It didn't matter how often she propped them up. It didn't matter how often she patiently talked to them about the cause of their unhappiness. None of them ever changed. Not Maeve. Victor. Felix. Angeline. Not her father.

The only one who changed was her. She sank with them, drowning in all their crap.

And maybe it was also because other people's happiness could lacerate you. It could cut through you and make you want to howl.

It had been Greta Poole's happiness that finally broke her. She'd spent so long telling herself that Aidan's wife was welcome to him. That he was a cheating bastard who would hurt her again.

And then, last night, she'd seen them. She'd left her friends in order to help her father, and seen Greta and Aidan in a restaurant a mere two doors down, illuminated at a window table. And they had looked radiant and beautiful together, and Zoe had had to lean over the gutter and empty her guts out into it like some stupid drunk.

As she'd straightened up, she felt strangely weightless. She imagined that some kind of terrible burden had suddenly broken away from her and left her without anchor or direction.

Not knowing where else to go, she went to rescue her father. It was a habit, nothing more. The same habit that had guided her through the process of helping him, even while she'd known it was hollow and false. Even while she'd hated him.

That habit had carried her as far as the train and then it had abandoned her, leaving behind unrestrained rage. As her father had made to step onto the train she had shoved him, hard enough that he'd banged the side of his head on one of the vertical rails of the train before he fell. She hoped, viciously, that it would still show in the morning, so everyone he worked with would realize what he was.

As he sprawled on the ground and groaned, she'd felt no shame. None of the horror she should have felt. She felt only a strange freedom, and she was smiling as she helped him up and pretended to fuss over him, telling him that he'd tripped and she'd tried to save him.

He'd messaged her in the morning to apologize, and she'd felt nothing but disgust. And so she hadn't replied. Not today. Today, she no longer cared. She no longer cared about her father's feelings, or about Angeline's. It was almost satisfying to tell her friend that she was worthless. Broken. And to really mean it.

And then she'd left the flat at the right time for her classes, her face gloriously bare of makeup, and she'd walked in the opposite direction, hating herself and everyone else in equal measure, and only after a very long time feeling a numb nothingness that was almost bearable.

Half a mile from the flat, her phone rang. It had sunk to the bottom of her bag and she couldn't lay her hands on it immediately. God, she hated that cheerful ringtone. Why in the hell had she chosen it? It was pure torture.

"Shut up!" she shouted at it, scrabbling to pull it out of her bag so she could end the call. "Shut up, shut up, shut up!"

It stopped for a blessed moment, and then it began again. Whatever selfish bastard was ringing wasn't going to give up that easily.

She finally managed to find it with her hand and pull it out. She saw Felix's name, and thought about ending the call. But she was too angry to simply silence him.

She answered it, and heard his rapid, distressed breathing. It had always, always made her feel for him. She had always soothed him. Always. But today it meant nothing to her. Nothing except a hideous weight of responsibility that she didn't want.

"I can't talk now," she said. "I'm sorry. I'm not well."

She hung up. And three seconds later, he rang again. She picked up, feeling like he was attaching a physical weight to her stomach. Her chest. Her head. It was impossible to bear.

"I'm so sorry," he said. "But I don't have anyone else. I tried to . . . talk to Esther, but—"

"You need to find someone else," Zoe said. "I'm sorry, Felix. I can't do it right now. Find someone to call."

She hung up, but the phone rang again and she felt the helpless fury overwhelm her. She answered it with a vicious, "What?"

"Can you please just come and see me? Just for a minute?" Felix said.

"Do you not care about anyone other than yourself?" she asked.

"Of course I do." There was surprise in his voice. Shock. And it was so good to hear.

"Then why aren't you listening?"

"Because I'm not . . . good. I need . . . I need help."

"When do you ever need anything else?" Zoe asked loudly. "But you won't help yourself, will you? You claim it's all the NHS's fault, or the force's fault, but you won't bloody listen! You won't go to therapy, you won't take the bloody drugs, and somehow it's everyone else who's to blame. And then it's me who has to deal with this shit, isn't it? It's me."

"How can you say that?" he was half crying, half-angry, and almost hyperventilating. "I don't mean to be like this!"

"Yes, you do," she said. "You do, or you'd actually try to change. I'm not going to carry on pouring my happiness down the drain of your unwillingness to lift a bloody finger. I'm not going to do it, Felix."

She hung up, and this time she turned her phone off. She was shaking, a tremble caused by anger and exhilaration. It felt just as good as when she had attacked Angeline that morning, telling her she was broken and disposable.

Part of her wanted to find someone else to call up so she could lash out at them, too. Or tell them what a fucking useless twat Felix was. She wanted to use words so awful that they burned the air.

She let herself into her flat, her face drawn so tightly into a scowl that it began to hurt within minutes. She couldn't keep still. She had to move.

She realized that Monkfish's food bowl was empty and his water bowl low. She filled it with no less anger, resenting this other form of care. But Monkfish didn't even come when she put it down or when she called. Perhaps he could sense her mood, and knew to keep away. It was so like a bloody cat. They were never there when you needed comfort. It was all about them.

I hate them, she said to herself. *I hate all of them. Why can't everyone just leave me alone?*

For minute after minute, she did nothing but hate, until a trickle of something else hit her. Remorse. Horror. Something.

Oh God. What was she doing? What was she doing?

There was a more rational, kinder part of her still there somewhere. It told her that her friends were good to her, too, when they could be. It told her that they cared about her as much as she cared about them. Why couldn't she believe that anymore? Why couldn't she feel anything beyond this red-hot rage?

She went to the window by the desk and threw it open. She'd taken the catches off the windows the day she'd moved in, and it opened all the way out onto the street, leaving the cold November air to flood in unhindered. She leaned out farther than she should have to try to catch it. She needed it all around her and in her lungs to stop the heat of her anger. Otherwise she might just burn up.

She imagined herself depicted in paint, her form wreathed in flame. Around her, in this oil-painted version, there was nothing but dust. The collected, floating fragments of the people who had once orbited around her.

As she leaned out farther, she found herself listening to a voice from below. Someone was on the phone, standing near the front door and talking cheerfully to someone who must have been her boyfriend.

"No, I won't be long," she was saying. "I've just got a necklace to find and then I'll head home . . . Yes." And a quiet laugh. "It's definitely revealing. I'll show you. OK. Bye."

She leaned a little farther out until she could see the door and the woman who was now crossing the road.

The jolt of recognition nearly tipped her out of the window. What was she doing here? She wasn't supposed to be here. This was Zoe's place. She'd already taken everything from her. Was she going to come and take her peace, too?

She found herself moving. She barely remembered to take her

keys out of the door on her way out. She could only think about the smile on the woman's lips in profile. The chirpiness of her voice.

Zoe made it onto the street while she was still in sight, and it never occurred to her to wonder what she was doing. She was going to chase her down. She was going to hurt her, and it was going to serve the stupid bitch right.

27

Jonah arrived at his desk at a little after seven and found Felix Solomon's psych report and the summary of the trigger for his breakdown sitting in his in-box. He opened the summary up first, and read with a feeling of inevitability the series of events that had tipped Felix over. The mother. The girl. Her bleeding to death in his arms.

The language of the report was factual and emotionless, and yet Jonah still had to stop and take a few deep breaths after he was done. His own experiences made it all too easy to imagine. And to imagine how it might have made anyone fall to pieces. In the end, no matter how many years of this stuff any officer had seen, each and every one of them was still a human being.

He went on to the psych report after that, which was a bit more human. The police psychologist who had seen Felix four times over the next three months had been clear: He had been traumatized by what he saw. He had admitted he was having trouble sleeping and focusing, and had been found on more than one occasion sitting at his desk in the morning still dressed in the clothes of the day before with no apparent awareness of the hours passing.

From there, it had gotten worse. The psychologist was asked to see him for a fifth time when Felix had pursued an unwilling witness into their house and harangued him, before getting into a fistfight with him and breaking the man's nose. The psychologist's strong recommendation had been compassionate leave for a month, rather than suspension, but Felix had insisted on suspension. It had meant getting back to work after two weeks instead of a month.

The final interview made Jonah's pulse pick up. The background to the interview was given in full. During the suspension, DCI Solomon had smashed his car into the side of a clothes shop on Brighton High Street. It had been full daylight. When blood tests were taken later, he was found to have consumed four of the diazepam tablets he'd been prescribed, along with two tramadol tablets he'd gotten from somewhere. There was no question that he'd fallen asleep at the wheel.

After the DCS had requested that Felix's desk be checked for illegally procured medication, a child's toy was discovered. It became clear that this had been taken from the crime scene that had triggered his trauma. He claimed that he had no memory of taking it.

After that, he had been given a choice of retirement or losing his job. He'd also been handed a driving ban and a suspended sentence. It had been too public an event for it to go any other way. The police had to treat their own more harshly than they did others. That much was understood.

Jonah leaned back in his chair to think about all this. That child's toy was a disturbing note. Why had he taken it? As some sort of strange trophy? Because the little girl had gotten under his skin and he wanted to hold on to some part of her?

He found himself trying to balance sympathy for the man with the knowledge that he was an intelligent, savvy ex-copper who, at the very least, had probably abused his access to privileged information.

HANSON HAD WOKEN early, her mind already working and her headache gone. She was immediately mulling over Victor Varos and Felix Solomon; Angeline Judd and Maeve Silver.

O'Malley had messaged her the night before to update her about

Victor Varos being the probable intruder at Greta Poole's house. The knowledge had been something of a relief, even though they hadn't actually pinned it on him yet. It made it extremely likely that it had been Victor outside her house. It was the same kind of behavior, and it could well have been triggered by her aggressive questioning in the interview room.

Giving the figure a name and face made her feel a great deal less anxious about it. Acknowledging that she still needed to be careful when heading to and from work, she still felt as though the reality was better than her worst imaginings.

With that tied up, she found herself abruptly transported back to the suspicions that had gripped her before Felix Solomon had possibly been seen with Zoe, and before Victor Varos had appeared on CCTV.

"There might still be two of them," she muttered to herself. But more than that, it might still be one of the girls. Even Angeline, with her slight build, could have killed Zoe. A drugged woman would be easy enough to finish off.

She ate a piece of toast as quickly as she could and got dressed. It was still dark as she got into the car, but she was wide-awake. Today was the day they were going to crack this, she decided. That *she* was going to crack this.

Along with the DCI shut away in his office, DI Walker was already at his desk when she arrived at seven-ten, and she gave him a wry grin, feeling only slightly disappointed at not having the floor of CID to herself. Total quiet was a rare treat that she tended to savor.

"Can't sleep either, hey?" she asked him.

"No," he said. "Too much going on in my head."

"Same," Hanson said with a sigh. "I'll be a wreck by midafternoon, which'll be just when the chief wants me to be intelligent."

Walker smiled, and she had to admit that there was something companionable about having someone else there. And she could hardly complain about the noise. Walker went back to his work and sat with quiet focus. He wasn't close enough to her desk for her to hear his fingers on the keyboard.

She made coffee, then loaded up her desktop. She figured she could justify leaving the CCTV footage for now. She was in early, after all, and the extra time was her own.

She returned to the transcript of Maeve's interview and read it again from the start. She wished she'd been there to see Maeve's expressions. Trying to understand a person fully from her words alone was tough.

But even so, what stood out to Hanson was that Maeve wanted to protect Aidan. She was the one person who seemed to think well of him, and said so. There was lots of justification of her positive attitude toward him. That he was fun. That he had treated her well. That he just didn't want to hurt his wife. But then, when faced with the obvious fact that he'd stalked Zoe, she still tried to defend him. And there was an obstinacy there that Hanson found interesting.

She felt that they ought to talk to Maeve again, and she'd like to be the one doing it. She checked her watch. It was only ten past eight. Too early to call her, really. She could probably ring in twenty minutes or so.

Ben arrived as she was making this decision. She gave a vague, embarrassed smile, still undecided about how to interact with him. Mercifully, the phone rang on her desk at that point and she grabbed it. "DC Hanson," she said. "How can I help?"

"Sorry, I'm not sure if I'm talking to the right person." It was a woman's voice. Well spoken and the accent more southeast of England than Southampton. "I was Zoe . . . Zoe Swardadine's tutor."

"Oh, you're on the right line," Hanson said. "I'm on DCI Sheens's team, and we're looking into what happened."

"Good," she said. "I wasn't sure, though . . . Essentially I'm reporting a theft. The theft of one of Zoe's paintings."

Hanson straightened up. "This is from the art school?"

"Yes," the woman on the other end of the line said. "It's the Winchester School of Art. I realized it had happened this morning, though I'm actually not sure when it was taken."

"Can I take your name and the address?" Hanson asked.

The DCI emerged from his office a few minutes after she'd ended the call. "Morning, Chief," she said. "We've got an interesting occurrence at Zoe's art department."

Sheens gave her a vague look, and then something seemed to click. "One of her paintings?"

"Yes," Hanson said, and narrowed her eyes at him. "Good guess. It's been stolen."

"Right," he said. "I'll come and take a look with you. Lightman, can you make sure Victor Varos is here by the time we get back?"

Hanson also left Lightman with a request to go see Maeve Silver again, frustrated that she was having to delegate a potentially important conversation.

"There's something bothering me about her attitude toward Aidan Poole," she explained, "and we've barely looked at her so far."

The DCI had agreed with that. "I'd also like to know more of her thoughts on Victor Varos," he said.

That meant it was just the recently arrived O'Malley left to plow through CCTV work.

"Youse all go and enjoy yourselves," he said airily as Hanson picked up her coat. "I'll be fine here with my elderly eyes becoming steadily more myopic."

"Ah, it's too late for you, anyway," Hanson said with a grin. "And at least this way we save your poor knees."

Sheens updated her about Angeline Judd's phone call of the night before, telling her his instinctive suspicion at its coming so soon after they had caught Victor out in a lie.

"What do you think her intention was?" Hanson asked.

"I'm not sure, which concerns me a little," Jonah said. "The fact that she pretended nobody else was there is also concerning."

"Could have been Aidan Poole," Hanson commented.

"Yes," Jonah agreed. "Or one of a number of people. Either way, I'd be very interested to know whether Victor Varos really did walk down her road and rant at someone on the phone."

Hanson let out a huff of air. "They're a pretty complex bunch, aren't they?"

"I'd say so," Sheens agreed.

There was a pause, and then Hanson said, "This person you thought you heard in the background of the call. It makes me think . . . You know how people with eating disorders often set themselves up with two people who are key to them? Generally it's one who enables them and one who stops them. A good cop, bad cop kind of deal."

"Really?" the DCI asked. "That's not something I'd heard."

"I had an anorexic friend at school," Hanson said. "And for a while I was the bad cop." The DCI laughed, and she grinned. "Yeah, all right. It's quite ironic. Generally speaking, you tear them apart and I put them back together."

"I'm sure you could do bad cop if you wanted," he said, though she wasn't sure if he was quite serious.

"Anyway," she went on, "I wonder if this unknown person is the other figure. The good cop. Ben said when he visited her, someone had taken away anything she could hurt herself with."

"Wait," the DCI said. "I'm confused. Which one is the good cop?"

"The enabler," Hanson said. "They would look after her, but also enable the eating disorder and the other stuff that goes with it. The drinking."

"But not suicide?"

"Who'd do that?" Hanson asked with a slightly shocked laugh.

"You'd be surprised," the DCI said darkly, and Hanson decided not to ask.

"So anyway, I think we ought to ask Aidan Poole whether he's been hanging out with her. I mean, he did get kicked out of his house. And if she was in love with him . . ."

"It's crossed my mind," the DCI agreed. "I've also wondered about Felix Solomon. And there's no reason it couldn't be Maeve Silver, either. She's clearly a lot more together than Angeline."

"True," Hanson said. "Though there are quite a lot of people who fit that description."

A BRIEF CALL to Maeve had elicited the information that she was at a church meeting, but didn't mind seeing Lightman afterward. She had another hour before classes, she told him. So he offered to come and meet her there, curious to see her in this setting.

He found St. Agnes of Rome Church easily, though it wasn't quite what he'd expected. He supposed it was the name, implying an old-fashioned building. Possibly a Catholic one.

But this place was all modern. It was a large circular building with one flattened end full of angular, contemporary stained glass. It was also clearly Church of England or similar. He'd guess it hadn't been up for more than a couple of years, and it was interesting to see such a big, clearly well-moneyed place in contrast with his own failing village church. This place spoke of a vibrant, growing congregation. Back in Newcombe, they could barely fill the place at Christmas and Easter, and it wasn't a large building.

A board up at the front announced "STAR timetable," and a quick glance showed him that there was a service, prayer meeting, or men's or women's group every day of the week. On Sunday, there were six different events, including a lunch and a supper. It was clearly thriving.

Through the glass doors was a large reception that reminded him of crematoriums, except that there was a tea-and-coffee area with brightly colored mugs.

There were voices coming from an open door to his right, and he moved toward them until he could see in through the gap. There was a small group sitting in a circle, and as he came into hearing range, he caught a male voice saying, ". . . for the rest of the week. As long as you're still happy to host at number four, Johannes?"

"Yes, definitely," came the reply. "We'd love to see everyone."

Lightman moved around until he could see both the first speaker and Maeve, who were next to each other at the head of the room. The leader was a tall, extremely thin young man with dark hair and a perpetual smile. He grinned round at them all, while Maeve looked less engaged. More preoccupied.

"Great. Thanks, Johannes. Anything else . . . ? OK. That looks like we're done, then."

There was movement as the group began to rise, shifting chairs and turning to talk to one another. Maeve was slow to stand, and then, at a question from the group leader, she turned to Lightman. As she saw him, she switched on a smile with some effort, and came over to him.

"Hi," she said. "I think we met at the station?"

"That's right," he said, giving her a smile as he watched the chairs disappearing into piles around the room. When he looked back at her, her expression had drooped and he thought she seemed strained. Drained, even. "Long day?" he asked.

"Ah, not really. Just, you know . . ." She shrugged. "There's another room through there with comfy chairs if you need to ask some things."

"Sure," he said. "I'll try and keep it quick."

"No bother," she said, and then her eyes drifted to the clock on the end wall of the room, and she suddenly looked harried. "Ah, is that the time? OK, we might have to keep it quick. We're supposed to finish by ten."

"Quick is fine," he reassured her, and she led him through to a smaller room that had some deep leather armchairs in it. Another sign of the affluence of this place.

Maeve shut the door behind them and then said, "Oh, did you want tea? Coffee?"

"No, that's OK," Lightman answered. "I won't keep you long enough."

"Grand," Maeve said. "So, what do you need from me?"

"A few things," he said. "You raised some concerns over Victor Varos in your original statement."

"Ah, not concerns," she said quickly. "Not really. I was just explaining how he felt. I don't think he killed her."

"But he might have argued with her?" he asked.

Maeve gave him a wary look. "Did someone else say so?"

"There's quite a lot of evidence pointing to a row with her earlier on Thursday evening," Lightman said, knowing that he was stretching the truth a little.

Maeve gave an awkward shrug. "I don't know about that."

"You didn't see him on Thursday?"

"No," she said, shaking her head. "I was at the ladies' supper, and after that I headed home. But even if they did argue, I don't believe he hurt her. He loved her."

"What about Aidan Poole?" he asked. "Would Victor have been willing to hurt him?"

Maeve gave a laugh that clearly said it was an absurd idea, but he noticed that the laugh cut off all too quickly. "He didn't like him, but that's all."

"Victor never threatened Aidan or got into a fight?"

Maeve paused for a telling second, and then said, "No, I'm sure not. Just that time at the coffee shop."

"What exactly did he say to Aidan?" Lightman persisted.

Maeve shook her head with a roll of her eyes. "Look, you can't take stuff literally."

"That's understood," Lightman said gently. "But it would be useful to know."

"He said he'd kill him if he came back," she said. "But you know he didn't mean *kill* him."

"You don't think so?"

"It wasn't Aidan who ended up dead, was it?" Maeve asked, her eyebrows raised but with a glimmer in her eyes. "It was Zoe."

"It's possible," Lightman said, as evenly as he could, "that Victor could have seen him as the one standing in his way until she was single, and then realized that actually it was her."

Maeve shook her head, and then looked up toward the ceiling.

"Someone killed her," Lightman said. "I know you don't want to believe it of your friends, but someone did."

"So you tell me," Maeve said with sudden energy, "but I keep wondering if you're wrong. Siku told me they weren't back together at all and maybe she'd never really got over it. Maybe she was in real despair and none of us realized." She looked at Lightman with eyes that were filling rapidly with tears. "She was so hurt when he broke things off with her that last time. In May."

"What happened to Zoe later on Thursday?" Lightman asked, shifting the topic. "We've got her leaving the flat at five and not returning till eight-thirty, and I'd like to know what happened during that time."

Maeve shook her head. "I don't know what she would have done. Maybe she crumbled and begged Aidan to take her back." She gave him a fierce, bright-eyed look. "And then she decided she'd had enough."

"I understand you think she might have been in despair," Lightman said quietly. "But Aidan Poole witnessed an attack."

"Maybe he wanted to believe that," she said with that same fierceness. "Maybe what he saw and heard was her deciding she'd had enough. But maybe he couldn't deal with that. Maybe he knew it was his fault. But what if he never really saw the door move?"

Lightman nodded as though he was taking this in, while he watched her earnest expression very carefully. The two questions that immediately occurred to him were how she'd known about the door moving, and why she seemed so keen to paint Zoe's death as a suicide.

THE SCHOOL OF ART hadn't looked that promising from the outside, but once he was in its curving hallways, surrounded by color and texture, Jonah began to feel like he never wanted to leave. His eyes were on every piece and every detail as he and Hanson followed Zoe's tutor, Annette Lock, a willowy blond woman in a wrap-around cardigan.

"So we have no CCTV of the inside of this place, it turns out," Annette had told them. "But we do have some out at the front. The office says they can send that to you. It wasn't maintenance, in case you wondered. I checked with them first in case there had been a mix-up."

She stopped midway along one of the ground-floor corridors and gestured at the wall. There wasn't much to see. Just a picture hook, a big expanse of wall, and one small handwritten card pinned in space. It had Zoe Swardadine's name, and then *Her Painted Eyes* as the title, and beneath that it said "Willart Long prize–winning piece."

"Is that quite a gong, the prize it won?" Jonah asked.

"Yes," Annette said with a funny, taut smile. "It's a beautiful piece of work. Really wonderful."

"She was talented?"

"Yes," Annette said, nodding. "Though she started out only good. The single-figure paintings she did for some months were perfectly fine, but not . . . not stunning. Not like the later stuff, when she added a second figure in and began to experiment with the interplay between them."

Hanson gave her a curious glance. "Was it a man? The figure she added?"

Annette tilted her head. "It was a shadow, but it was essentially masculine."

Jonah wondered whether that particular man represented Aidan Poole. He would be interested, he thought, to see some of Zoe's art.

He scanned up and down the corridor, thinking that the curve of it made it easier to take something without observation. The thief would only be visible for a short distance in either direction.

"When did the painting go up here?" Hanson asked.

"At the end of last year," Annette told him.

"Do you think it would be valuable?" the constable asked.

"I don't . . . That's hard to say." Annette put her hands together in front of her abdomen, the motion pushing her elbows out awkwardly. "It's not usual for a graduate to sell much art, however good it is. Nobody knows who they are. But maybe there would be interest in her because of her murder. But then . . . what's the point in thinking about stealing it if you couldn't publicly say that it was hers?"

Hanson gave a slow, thoughtful nod.

"Well," Jonah said, "I've generally found, in the world, that there will be someone, somewhere who's into any single weird thing you can think of. It wouldn't surprise me to learn that there was someone who liked to collect art by murder victims."

"God," Annette said. "That's hideous."

"It is," Jonah agreed. "How many people would have known this was here?"

"Anyone who came here, I suppose," she said uncertainly. "I mean, it's not exactly private and you don't need a key card or anything to access it unless it's after hours . . ." She stopped short suddenly, and then said, "You know, I should have thought about it before. It's not the first time someone's interfered with her work."

"It isn't?"

"No." Annette pulled her arms up and folded them across herself. "One of her paintings was vandalized last year." She gave an awkward non-smile. "It wasn't very nice. Someone wrote 'whore' across it in red paint. They'd used her oils and she ended up abandoning the piece because it was upsetting as well as difficult."

"Does that kind of thing happen often?" he asked.

"No," Annette said with a trace of offense. "Of course not. Look, they're all art students in here. They know how much personal connection there is with a piece. Zoe was shattered by it, and we didn't manage to identify the perpetrator. We started locking all the workshops at night after that until the end of term, even though there were students trying to get final pieces ready and wanting to stay on and pull all-nighters."

"But you didn't continue that practice this term?"

"No. Because nothing else happened. And we thought . . . to be honest, we just thought she must have dumped someone and paid a high price. She didn't offer any information, but I got the impression she knew who it was."

Jonah nodded again, thinking about that word. *Whore.* It was quite particular. Quite old-fashioned. And it implied someone who had known that she was having an affair.

He left feeling that this was a weird addition to an already weird investigation. It was profoundly unlikely that anyone but the killer would have taken it. But they'd run a huge risk, if so. It seemed to point to some kind of obsession with Zoe, which went against the current trend of his thinking. He'd been inclined to believe that the killer had felt coldly resentful toward her by the time of her death. So why do so much to have something of hers?

"WHAT ARE YOU thinking?" Hanson asked a few minutes into the drive. Jonah was still lost in thought, and was startled by the question.

Hanson, he had discovered, wasn't as willing as O'Malley and Lightman to leave him to his musings, but he didn't find it quite as annoying as he might have expected. At times, like today, he felt that he needed to talk it all through.

"Quite a few things," he said. "Mainly that this doesn't fit with what I'd begun to put together. The planning, the apparent suicide, the constant awareness of observation . . . that seemed like someone who felt cold toward Zoe. Someone she'd argued with. So why steal a painting? Why decide to keep something of hers, at a huge risk?"

There was a pause from Hanson, and then she asked, "That might depend what was in the painting. I mean, it may well have had Angeline posing in it. Which might have meant it was about her. Or maybe Zoe had put something in it that pointed to the killer somehow, and they wanted to hide it from everyone."

Jonah nodded slowly, and saw a text message notification pop up on the display. The beginning of it read Hi, this is Piers Lough. . . .

"Could you tell me what he says?" Jonah asked, nodding at the phone.

Hanson picked it up, opened the message, and said, "Oh, he's got in touch with Felix Solomon's former tenant, someone called Shannon? She didn't pass on forwarding details because there was an argument over rent and apparently Felix got a bit unpleasant and she doesn't really want to get involved in anything."

He could feel Hanson watching him, as he debated with himself how to reply.

"OK. Can you tell him thank you, and to see if Shannon wouldn't mind just talking to us briefly to reassure us all is well with her. Hopefully we can gently encourage her to say a little more."

Hanson was still typing her message when Lightman called to give them the lowdown on Maeve Silver. Her attempted suggestion that it might, in fact, have been suicide was one that Jonah found immediately interesting. As Lightman had noted, she seemed to know the specifics of what Aidan had seen. That wasn't information that had been released by the police.

"So she's either been talking to Aidan, or she knows what he saw because she was there," Jonah said.

"That's what I was thinking."

"Did you get the impression she was keen for us to believe it was suicide?" Jonah asked.

"Hard to say," Lightman said. "It's possible *she* wanted to believe it."

"If she saw Aidan," Hanson said, "she could have tricked him into touching something so she had his prints."

Jonah nodded. "Agreed. That might be the most interesting side to it. There aren't all that many people who would have had a chance to get hold of Aidan's fingerprints, and it sounds just possible that Maeve was one of them."

VICTOR VAROS WAS not, it turned out, at the station by the time they got back. He had fobbed them off for an hour and a half as he apparently "had to work his shift and had no choice."

"Did he sound to you like a man who had something to hide?" Jonah asked with a raised brow.

"He did," O'Malley said, "but everyone sounds like that to me. I'd lay good odds on him being the one who threatened Maeve Silver."

"I'd say he's the favorite," Jonah agreed.

"CCTV-wise, there's one thing in his favor, and one that's against him," O'Malley added. "I've picked up the cab he took at eight on the night of Zoe's murder turning off down West Bargate. Which is toward his house and not Zoe's. But I also took the liberty of checking the camera feed that's near the station for last night, when Greta Poole saw someone outside her house. Victor cycled past like a man possessed at five-eighteen. That would have put him in good time to catch the five forty-two to Alton."

"That's great work, Domnall," Jonah said.

"Ah, sir," Hanson, who was still hovering with her bag slung over her shoulder, said at that point. "I was meaning to mention before. I think he may also have been loitering outside my house on Saturday evening."

Jonah watched her for a moment, feeling caught off balance. "Outside *your* house?"

"There was someone hanging around as I was running home," she said, a slight flush to her cheeks betraying the apparent calm of her voice. "I saw him and waited until he'd gone before I went in. I thought at the time it might be him, but it was hard to see. He went off the other way down the street and my priority was getting inside and warm." She gave a small shrug. "But I guess it would be logical. I gave him a hard time when we saw him."

"I'm a little concerned at the idea he would know where you live," Jonah said in a low voice. "Do you have a landline listed in the phone book?"

"I don't think so."

"OK. I'm going to the coffee shop now. And Victor can brace himself for a bloody grilling."

"There's a lot stacking up against him," O'Malley commented. "You don't want to take a uniform and bring him in?"

Jonah felt a stab of surprise, and then realized that there was nothing to be surprised about. A lot of his recent theorizing had gone on entirely within his own head.

"Yes. Well . . . Victor's facing two potential charges of harassment," he said, making himself stand still for a moment and share his thinking, "but I have a strong suspicion he had nothing to do with Zoe's death."

"Because the cab went the wrong way?" O'Malley asked.

"Not quite," Jonah said. "I'd say the cab going the wrong way just tells us that he wasn't the one waiting outside for her when she arrived." He picked up O'Malley's iPad where it lay half-covered by a wad of paper, and loaded up a map of Southampton. "He picked the cab up at eight, in the city center. It would be no more than fifteen minutes to get to Zoe's, but he didn't go that way. He went toward his house, which is a twenty-minute walk from the flat."

"So . . ." Hanson said, following the finger he was tracing over the route, "you think he changed his mind, and went to see her after he got home?"

"Exactly," Jonah said. "I think he went home and then, because he was drunk and dwelling on it all, set off on foot across the park. He would have arrived in plenty of time to head in, have a drink, and then argue with her at nine."

"Why do you think that was him?" O'Malley asked.

"He knew that Angeline had argued with Zoe, which he shouldn't have known," Hanson answered, before Jonah had a chance to. "And he's been avoiding us, and nobody else has let on that they saw Zoe at that point. It's also exactly the kind of thing that someone with a clearly high level of angst would do."

"The interesting question," Jonah said, "is whether Victor saw who was waiting for Zoe when she got home."

HANSON WENT TO dump her bag at her own desk once the DCI had left, and found a Post-it note stuck to her computer screen, asking her to call back someone called Luke on a mobile number. She pulled it off with a tut and rubbed the mark off her screen, and then waved it at O'Malley.

"What's this?"

"Oh, some guy with information for you," O'Malley said. "He seemed to have been told to speak to you and you only, so I said to leave a number."

Hanson nodded, fairly used to being the first one to take calls for the team. That was what came with being the only detective constable.

"Oh, thanks for calling back," Luke said in a voice so enthusiastic it was jarring. "I'm so keen to speak to you. I've got to dash to make the post, but could you come and meet me afterward?"

"What's this about?" she asked him.

"Maeve Silver," Luke said. "I'm a faith leader at her church. I saw one of your colleagues talking to her, and I think there are a few things you need to know."

"Sure," Hanson said. "I can be in town in twenty minutes . . . ?"

"How about that vegan coffee shop on Queensway? Half an hour?"

"Sure," Hanson agreed. "See you there."

Her phone rang again before she could leave the building, and she picked it up with a slight sigh.

"DC Hanson. How can I help?"

There was a pause, and then a woman's voice said, "Is DS Lightman there? I just had something I wanted to talk to him about."

Hanson went through several thoughts, the first being that this was Greta Poole once again. But the voice was wrong. A different accent, and a lighter tone.

"I'm afraid he's not in the office at the moment," she said, "but if you want to discuss anything, maybe I can help?"

"Ah, no, you're all right," she said, and Hanson realized that this was Maeve Silver. The suspect Ben had just been to see. "I'll give him a call back in a few."

Hanson shook her head as she put the phone down. The whole team could do without the estrogen brigade.

"I'll be back in an hour or so," she told O'Malley. "I'm handing over the baton of being Ben's PA. Use it wisely."

JONAH SAW VICTOR'S expression as he walked into the coffee shop, and he recognized it as a man who had been caught. He finished serving a customer at the till, and then turned to talk to the young man who was working next to him. And then he lifted his apron off and came to stand in front of Jonah.

"I said I was working," he said.

"And I said it was urgent," Jonah replied quietly. "Or do you not want to find your friend's killer?"

Victor gave him a look that was somewhere between angry and defeated, and led him to a table in the corner.

"All right," he said. "What do you want to know?"

"Let's start with last night," he said. "You went to Aidan and Greta Poole's house. Why?"

"I didn't—" Victor started to say.

"You aren't as good at covering your tracks as you think you are," Jonah said firmly. "You were caught on camera."

There was a moment of silence, in which he could see the muscles in Victor's jaw working, and then the young Brazilian said, "All right. I was . . . I just wanted to talk to him. Well, no. I wanted to punch him."

"Why?"

"Because he killed her," Victor said, lifting his chin. "You may be too trapped in procedure to see it, but he did."

"Procedure is what ensures we don't arrest the wrong person," Jonah replied. "And you need to think about that and listen to me. There is someone out there who wants to make us think it was Aidan Poole. But there are some very, very persuasive reasons to believe that it wasn't him, and you need to help us find out who actually killed her." He fixed Victor with his hardest stare. "Have you been to the Pooles' house before?"

Victor shook his head. "No." It was sulky. Unwilling.

"How did you know where Aidan lived?"

"I googled him," Victor said with a slightly defiant air. "I did it months ago. When he first started dating her. I wanted to go and tell him to leave her alone."

"And you didn't?" Jonah insisted. "You didn't, oh, I don't know, take something of Aidan's that you thought might come in useful later?"

Victor looked at him in what seemed to be genuine confusion. "No. I told you. I hadn't been before. I never went because . . . Maeve told me Zoe would never forgive me."

Jonah almost laughed. "She might have been right about that."

He looked at the rigid tendons standing up on Victor's arms, and he said, "I think you've been angry for a long time, and I also think that some of that anger spilled over toward Zoe on Thursday evening."

Victor's head snapped up. "I didn't do it!"

"But you did go and see her," Jonah pressed. "You took a cab back from town."

"But I didn't take the cab there . . ." Victor stopped, and Jonah smiled at him.

"You didn't take the cab there? No. You went home, but then you started thinking about Zoe, and that she might have started dating someone else. She'd rushed off the night before, and it felt unfair. You'd been waiting for her to get over Aidan."

Victor said nothing. His gaze was on his fingers. He was bending and straightening them rhythmically.

"Did you cycle there?" Jonah asked. "Or did you walk?"

There was a long pause, and then Victor said, "I walked. I couldn't find my bike keys."

"And did you pass anyone along the way?" Jonah asked. "Anyone you recognized?"

Victor gave him a strange look. "No. Why, should I have?"

Jonah watched him for a moment before saying quietly, "But you got all the way over there, and then Zoe said no, didn't she? She told you she wasn't interested." There was a pause, and Jonah went on. "Did it surprise you, the mood you found her in? Was she suddenly not the kind, supportive girl that you loved?"

"There was something wrong with her," Victor said. "Something . . . that he did to her. It wasn't her. She was . . ." He paused, and then muttered, "*Como um diabo.*"

"She told you, as harshly as she could, that she'd put up with your attempts to control her for long enough," Jonah said. "And you ended up blazingly angry."

There was a silence, and then Victor said, "Yes."

"But you decided to go and see her again later."

Victor looked at him with the expression of a cornered animal. "No. No, I didn't kill her."

"Tell me what happened," Jonah said quietly. "You were seen. You were seen on Hill Lane. We know you went back there."

There was a long pause while Victor looked toward the counter, moving his jaw as if grinding his teeth. And then he said, "I don't know what I was thinking. I felt like I couldn't go anywhere else when I was that angry. It was impossible to sit at home, so I left."

"When?"

"I don't know. Eleven. Eleven-thirty. I'm not sure."

"You went to Zoe's."

"Most of the way," Victor agreed quietly. "But I was walking and thinking and for some reason I got fixated on it being because of Maeve. It wasn't . . . it wasn't fair. But I just decided that it was all her fault. She'd always been so keen on Aidan and I . . . I called her."

"You called Maeve?"

"Yes. I shouted at her. I told her she'd ruined everything."

Jonah watched Victor's expression. "Did you wake her up?"

"No," Victor said, shaking his head a little defensively. "She was still out."

"Still out?" Jonah asked.

"Yes. She was cycling somewhere. She was out of breath when she answered."

Jonah nodded, trying not to let his expression tell Victor what he was thinking: that Maeve had claimed to have gone straight home after her ladies' supper and to have stayed there.

For the first time in days it had turned sunny. A breeze seemed to have come in and carried all the clouds off with it, leaving a suddenly blue, brilliant sky. Hanson grinned up at it, thinking that she'd timed this interview well.

The wind was still coming in off the sea, however, and it came straight up the road and cut through her suit jacket as she hurried along the road from her car. She shut the door to the coffee shop behind her as quickly as she could, and made her way to the counter as she looked for her interviewee. She doubted that a faith leader would have a dog collar or anything, and wondered how she'd recognize him. But a lanky man occupying an armchair in the window looked up at her and waved, removing the need for guessing.

The guy already had a drink, but she decided it was worth keeping him waiting to order something hot. She asked for an Americano and left it black, grateful for the heat in the mug as she carried it over. She dropped into the free armchair, which was a lot more comfortable than its shabby appearance had led her to believe.

"This is good. Thanks for suggesting it," she said.

"No problem," he said. "Luke Searle."

"Juliette," she said, and shook his proffered hand. It was large, and a lot warmer than hers. "Thanks so much for calling."

"I'm just keen to help. There are a few things you should know," he said. And then he gave a slight, thoughtful sigh. "It's difficult with Maeve. She's a good person, she really is. She does a huge amount for everyone around her, and there's nobody I would trust more when it came to aiding someone."

She waited for him to start in on the "buts," feeling a thrill of anticipation. It didn't take all that long.

"But I think . . . I think it's fair to say that she gets a bit carried away with people."

"How so?"

"Well, there was . . . there was a pastor at the church who ended up leaving, in part because of her." He pulled a doubtful face. "I don't think it was her fault. It was just a misreading. She thought he was interested in her. And I mean, by that, interested in her as a woman and not spiritually. She got a little obsessed with him. . . ."

"She did what?" she asked. "Harassed him?"

"Basically, yes." Luke gave a sigh. "But she didn't think she was. She wasn't trying to. It was just a misunderstanding. He was kind to her, and she got the wrong end of the stick. Maybe she was going through a fragile time. I don't know. Anyway, it was a particular problem because he has a wife and kids. And then when he stopped communicating with her entirely, she poured her heart out to me and another leader at the church, telling us she couldn't be at the church anymore."

"So . . . how did he end up being the one to leave?" Hanson asked.

"Well, we gradually started realizing that it was all in her head," Luke said. "And we talked to him quietly, too. He was desperate to sort it out, and also really unwilling to hurt her. He actually decided to go in the end. He'd been offered another ministry in Cardiff, close to his parents' home. And just to say, Maeve felt awful about it. She said that wasn't what she'd wanted. She hadn't meant to force him out. And I'm positive she didn't. It was all just a bit of a mess."

Hanson didn't find it hard to imagine Maeve Silver as an obsessive other woman. She gave off intense vibes, and her determined support of everyone only made Hanson suspect that she was stamping down on her emotions. Or perhaps that she was playing the part of the good Christian girl without ever really feeling it.

"Could you give me more detail on the harassment?" she asked Luke. "What did that consist of?"

"She called him and messaged him constantly," the faith leader said. "At first it was about scripture and her faith, and then later it was about how much she loved him and needed him." He sighed, and then added, "I think he was a little guilty of not telling her bluntly enough to stop. Because he's a kind person and was thinking of her as a poor soul. A bit of pragmatism might have helped."

"Was there any stalking?"

"Well . . ." He made a frustrated noise. "I don't think it should be labeled stalking. I think she wanted to see what he was like with his family at one point, and she followed them to a park. After a while he realized she was sitting on a bench, watching them, and he took his wife and kids back home. She never tried to approach or say anything. She just watched them."

Hanson thought, with a slight chill, about the transcript of Victor Varos's interview. Of how Maeve had watched Aidan and Zoe, and how he'd thought it was because she wasn't getting any.

She was now wondering whether the truth was a little different. Perhaps she'd been watching them because she hated anyone who stood between her and Aidan, just as she'd hated the woman who stood between her and her pastor. Perhaps she'd been thinking about what it would feel like to kill Zoe Swardadine.

28

Aidan woke to find himself fully dressed and lying in a room he didn't recognize. The Premier Inn, he realized. He'd made his way there as soon as the police had let him go. He didn't remember deciding to lie down.

He sat up, and felt as though he was waking from a dream that had lasted for days. A dream in which he'd only had to think about his own pain and loss. Why hadn't he been thinking about Zoe's killer? Why hadn't the fact of her murder mattered most of all?

He looked back at everything he'd done since Thursday and didn't recognize himself in any of his actions. He supposed it was the effect of grief, but it was also stupid. If the police had been less sharp, he'd have been charged with her murder by now.

Well, it was time to wake up. Not just to wake up but to *do something*. Not just for himself but for Zoe.

THE CALL LIGHTMAN had been half waiting for and half dreading all morning came as his cab was approaching the station once again. He breathed out and then answered.

"Hi, Mum," he said. "How's it going?"

"Oh, Ben," she said. And he didn't need to ask her anything more.

"It's OK, Mum," he said. "It's OK."

He could hear her near-silent crying down the line, and wondered what he could possibly say to comfort her.

. . .

"Chief," O'Malley said, leaning in at his door. "I've found Zoe Swardadine on camera during the time she was missing. I've picked her up at five twenty-eight, heading down toward town."

Jonah glanced up at him, lost somewhere in thoughts about Maeve Silver's lie about being at home on Thursday night and about Felix Solomon's key. He nodded slowly.

"Just toward town? Can you trace her farther?" Jonah asked.

"Probably," O'Malley replied, "but what's interesting is that the woman in glasses is still in front of her."

Jonah frowned and levered himself out of his chair to take a look. O'Malley loaded a video and played it, and Jonah had a side view of the woman this time as she strode toward town. Her spiky hair was easily recognizable, as were the grungy jacket, boots, and jeans. It was definitely, as O'Malley said, the same woman. And there, shortly after her, came Zoe, still hurrying.

"What do you think?" O'Malley asked. "That looks like pursuit to me."

"It does," Jonah agreed. "But why? Why would she pursue an un-identified woman? Unless she's another art student? She'd had work vandalized, but that seems a bit tenuous."

"I'll keep looking, so," O'Malley said. "Now we've got her farther on, it should be easier to track her through the city-center cameras."

"Thank you," Jonah said. He gave a short sigh. "You haven't seen Maeve Silver at any point, have you? On a bike, maybe?"

"Not yet, no," O'Malley said, and then asked, "Why so?"

"Victor Varos tells me that he called her late, at what must be a while after eleven, and caught her cycling." He shook his head. "Which, if true, tells us that Maeve wasn't at home on Thursday night as she claimed."

"Want me to bring her in?" O'Malley asked.

"Yes," Jonah replied with a slow nod. "But do it casually. Say there's something Lightman forgot to ask her."

He returned to his desk and heard the quiet ping of an email. Annette Lock had been as good as her word. The photograph of Zoe's missing painting had arrived in his in-box.

He loaded it up and absorbed the pale, fragile figure wrapped in shadow. The arched back as if in pain or ecstasy. The way the shadowy form coiled round her. But the real focus of the painting was the figure at the back, its head thrown back to the sky, and its eyes missing or . . . or sealed up somehow. A lurid flash of red in its abdomen interrupted the stormy blues and grays and whites of the rest of it, and it was hard to look away from the livid gash.

"O'Malley," he called. "Do you know much about art?"

"Next to nothing," his sergeant called back. "But I'm willing to venture an opinion. No answer from Maeve Silver's phone," he added.

The sergeant came in and stood at his shoulder, and the two of them looked at the image for a few seconds. Then O'Malley let out a huff of air. "It's good, isn't it?"

There was a tap on the door again. Hanson stood there, ruddy-cheeked and bright-eyed. "Sir, useful info on Maeve Silver."

"What's that?" Jonah said without looking up. He knew he wasn't giving her his full attention, but the painting was talking to him somehow.

"She hounded her former pastor out of the church," Hanson said from the doorway. "She stalked him, and his family, to the point where he had to move cities."

Jonah looked up at her slowly. "When was this?"

"Eight months ago," Hanson said.

"So she might conceivably have moved on to Aidan Poole," he said.

"That was my thinking."

He found his eyes returning to the painting.

"What are you two looking at?" Hanson asked.

"Sorry. It's Zoe's missing painting," he said. "We've got the photo. Actually, I'd quite like your thoughts."

He turned the screen toward her, and watched her as she scrutinized it.

"Oh," she said. "Well, that's sort of conclusive."

Jonah looked at her in genuine confusion. "Conclusive how?"

"About why they took it. Well, it probably is." Hanson turned the screen back round toward him and O'Malley. "You felt it strange that someone would take something from someone they hated, and I said it might show something about the killer. But actually what it really does is justify the killing."

Jonah looked again at the painting. "Talk me through that," he said.

"The two figures in the front are Zoe and Aidan," Hanson said.

"But that one's Angeline Judd," O'Malley argued.

"Yes, Angeline is the model," Hanson explained, "but it's actually a self-portrait. She's painting Angeline, who looks damaged, to represent herself." At O'Malley's doubtful expression, she grinned. "Look. Annette Lock said she'd only started putting that shadowy figure in recently—since she started dating Aidan, yes? Before that, the central figure was always alone."

"So, Zoe and Aidan are engaged in their lovemaking," Jonah said, "and now there's this third figure, and she and Aidan are hurting her."

"Exactly," Hanson said, standing back with a brilliant smile. "She's acknowledging that their relationship is harming someone else."

"Right . . ." Jonah said, looking again at that blinded face, and the bright, gory wound in her stomach.

"So I think they took it to prove Zoe knew exactly what she was doing with Aidan Poole." Hanson's gaze was piercing as she turned back to Jonah. "She knew they were hurting someone, and that means killing her was justified. That's what it looks like to me, anyway. And if you ask me, it's ninety percent likely to be a woman who did it, too, given that the figure in the painting is female."

Jonah's eyes found the blinded woman again, and he began to see what Hanson meant.

. . .

LIGHTMAN LOWERED HIS phone with a long breath out, and saw that there was a message waiting for him. It must have come in while he'd been on the phone.

> Can you come and meet me at my house? I've got a few things I really need to say.

He frowned at his phone, and sent a quick message back asking who it was. And then he realized, before he'd even had a reply. He sighed, supposing this was one of the downsides of being approachable.

"Sorry," he said to the cabdriver. "Can you take me somewhere else?"

JONAH WAS AWARE that O'Malley was waiting for him to talk, but he couldn't spare any thought for speech. A great many things had suddenly started to make sense.

Of course it was a woman. It was a woman who had made it her business to procure a key for Zoe's flat. It was a woman who had the best possible opportunity of getting Aidan Poole's prints all over that door lock. And it was a woman who had planned all of this coldly, out of revenge . . . and just possibly out of a warped desire to win the affections of the man she loved.

HANSON FOUND HERSELF thinking about the conversation with Luke Searle on repeat, interrupted only by occasional thoughts of Victor's statement. The fact that Victor and the faith leader had described Maeve in the same terms worried her. The fact that Maeve had so clearly wanted Aidan Poole to stick around worried her further, and the revelation that Maeve had probably lied about her movements was worse.

Maeve had never seemed to have a strong motive for killing Zoe.

But what if she'd had a motive after all? What if she'd met up with Aidan, thinking he'd fall for her now that he and Zoe were no longer together? And what if he'd rejected her?

They needed to talk to Aidan Poole. Straightaway.

She'd already gotten to her feet when she saw Felix Solomon entering CID with a strangely determined glint in his eye. The uniformed constable he was with knocked on the DCI's door, and she sat back at her desk with a frustrated sigh.

It took her a few minutes to stop thinking about Maeve and wonder why Felix had turned up at the station.

JONAH'S MOBILE RANG as he was at the point of getting up from his desk, and he smiled slightly as he read Angeline Judd's name on the screen. His mind was already racing a long way ahead of what she was going to say, but he took the call anyway.

"DCI Sheens," he said.

"One of your officers was having coffee with Luke Searle," she said, her voice clear and absolutely lacking the dopey quality it had had before. "I want to know why."

"I'm afraid I can't give you information on a case," Jonah said.

There was a tap on his door, and he turned to see a uniform out there with Felix Solomon. He held up a finger to gesture that he wouldn't be long.

"Don't be stupid!" Angeline was saying. "I'm not asking for information about the case. I want to know what bullshit Luke has been spreading about Maeve."

"Again . . ."

"He's a snake," she said. "What did he have to say? That Maeve was a stalker, or some shit like that?"

Jonah made a noncommittal noise. In part because he was happy to let her speak, and in part because he was thinking of the questions he was about to ask Felix Solomon.

"She never stalked Isaac. He seduced her," she said. "She held out for a bloody year, and he kept on at her and on at her. I saw them together, and I saw his messages. And when it all came out, he lied, and Luke Searle sided with him, the sexist prick."

Even with half his mind elsewhere, Jonah couldn't help feeling surprised that Angeline was speaking up for her friend. Everything he'd seen of her had pointed to someone needy and manipulative. To find her a loyal friend in a pinch was both surprising and a little heart-warming.

"So you can prove this?"

Angeline gave a laugh. "Yes, I can prove it. And if you want a quick note of proof, if Isaac was so bloody innocent, why did he invite Maeve to stay at a hotel with him on Thursday night?"

"We weren't aware of that," Jonah said, and he pulled a piece of paper across the table. Not to make notes, but to write a list of names. "Maeve told us she'd headed home after a dinner."

"Probably because she didn't think the timings were relevant, and she really didn't want to talk about it," Angeline said. "He told her on Tuesday that he'd left his wife for her. And on Thursday, she finally, finally gave in and slept with him, thinking it was true love. And then guess what? Having got his way, he naffed off back to Cardiff and hasn't contacted her since. She's heartbroken about it, and now Luke is busy undermining her when he should be having that guy thrown out of the church."

"That's all very useful."

"You don't believe me, do you?" Angeline asked bitterly. "You think she killed Zoe."

"No," Jonah said quietly, "I don't. I know she didn't kill her."

There was a sudden, long silence. And then Angeline said hastily, "I've got to go. I'll . . . bye."

And then she was gone.

Jonah slid the phone back into place on his desk and stood up with an increasing sense of urgency. He beckoned for the uniform to show Felix in.

"You couldn't have timed your arrival better," Jonah said as Felix settled himself into one of the chairs. He waved Hanson over to him and gave her the piece of paper he'd scribbled on.

"Can you print off photos of all these people for me, and then cut them up?"

HANSON'S FRUSTRATION WAS gradually giving in to a sense of curiosity as she stood at the printer. Was he asking Felix to identify someone? It was an odd thing to do. Felix knew so many of the people associated with the case by name.

However, she thought, frowning down at the photographs emerging from the machine, *not all of them.*

FELIX WAS FEELING in control again, Jonah saw. There was nothing to show the shell of a man he'd been the day before. He'd accepted coffee and was now sitting back comfortably in the chair opposite Jonah's. He was fairly sure Felix would have preferred to sit on the other side of the desk, where Jonah was.

As they waited for Hanson to use a rotary cutter to slice the photos up, Jonah said, "Can you quickly take us over what happened on Thursday afternoon?"

"In the afternoon?" Felix asked, raising his eyebrows.

"Yes," Jonah said. "When you met your friend Esther for tea."

Felix frowned. This clearly wasn't the question he'd wanted or expected. "Well, I told you. She came over at four."

"By arrangement?" Jonah asked. "Or was it a spontaneous thing?"

"Spontaneous," Felix said. "Not some prearranged alibi . . ."

"Did you bump into her?"

Felix glanced over at O'Malley and then back. "Yes," he said. "I did. She'd been up checking on her flat and I bumped into her on the stairs, so I invited her in for a cuppa."

"Exactly which flat is that?" Jonah asked.

"I don't know," Felix said with a shrug. "I've never asked."

"And she never volunteered that information?"

"No."

"Was she coming down from the second floor?"

There was a pause, and Felix said, "Yes, but I'd really like to know what all these questions are pointing to. I came to help."

"And you are helping," Jonah said, standing and opening the door to Hanson. She handed him the sheaf of photos and he gave her a grin of thanks before returning to the desk. "Is Esther one of these women?"

Jonah laid the photos out on the table, and Felix's hand went straight to one of them.

"That's her," he said. "Different hairstyle, and she wears glasses these days, but her."

Jonah gave him a small smile that did little to show the satisfaction he felt.

"So can you tell me why you're asking this?" Felix asked.

"Because Esther isn't who you think she is," Jonah said. "The woman you identified is Greta Poole."

29

The door lock. That was what Aidan needed to think about. There couldn't be many people who could have planted his prints. Whoever had killed Zoe must have had access to prints of his.

He was now sitting at the desk of the hotel room, his laptop open in front of him. He didn't know the first thing about how to plant prints, but that was what Google was for.

He started typing "How to . . ." but the first search term that was suggested made him stall.

How to tell if your partner's having an affair.

God. Was that really humanity's most frequent query? Or was it a search result that had been triggered because Greta had searched for it at some point on one of the machines he used?

He felt a wave of profound sadness at the thought of her typing that in. Had she suspected something? Had she pushed the truth aside because it was too painful to think about?

He suddenly found himself desperate to know. To know whether she had been aware on some level, and what she was thinking now. Whether she was done with him, or whether there was some hope of reconciliation.

The familiar urge was too strong to ignore, though in the past it had almost always been Zoe he had been snooping on. It had started with checking her messages while she'd been in the shower, and realizing exactly how much Victor messaged her. That had made him wonder what Victor sent her on email, and it hadn't taken him long to find out her password.

The snooping had become a habit, and it had been impossible to break it even after he'd ended things. Particularly after he'd ended things. It had been his way of feeling part of her life still. And then, finally, he'd graduated to spying through her webcam, which had let him at least watch her when he couldn't have her.

He'd hardly ever thought of checking up on Greta. He remembered having an idle browse of her emails once or twice over the years, looking for some nice mention of himself, or for clues to what to get her for Christmas. There had never been a great deal to see. She told him everything about herself.

But now he wanted to know. He wanted to know, with a terrible intensity, what she was saying to people about him. About them. He was desperate to know what she was going to do.

He pulled out his phone, and opened up Safari. He still remembered the Gmail password she'd had a few years ago, and he doubted she'd ever changed it. She'd never been big on security.

To his grim satisfaction, her account opened for him easily. And there were her emails, all arranged neatly into folders.

The first page didn't seem to show him anything particularly interesting, but she was a demon for filing things away. He wouldn't really know unless he searched.

He searched for his own first name first. But that brought up, as he should have predicted, every email he'd ever sent her or she'd ever sent him, thousands upon thousands of results that would take forever to wade through. He didn't have time for that.

He thought about searching for Zoe's name, but realized that he'd never told her what it was. He'd kept that little piece of information back. He couldn't bear to search for himself under "cheat," so he searched instead for "Southampton."

That brought up just forty results, which was much better. A bunch of Trainline confirmations, and further down, what looked like a promising email to her mother, until he realized it was from a few months ago.

He was slow to look properly at those Trainline confirmations. Slow to wonder why there were so many of them. Slower still to start wondering why they'd all come up more recently than that email to her mum from July.

He opened the first one, which congratulated her on her ticket purchase to Southampton. It was from yesterday afternoon, he saw. And it gave him a strange feeling to imagine that Greta had been there, too. Where he had been.

And then he opened the second one and saw that it was from Thursday night. It was for the nine fifty-one from London Bridge to Southampton, and the truth of what that meant hit him like a wave.

"JUST OVER HERE," Lightman told the cabdriver. The large, beautifully built house was lit by a cold sun from a temporarily cloudless sky, and it seemed a little sad somehow. It was too large to be occupied by one woman. Or even by a couple, really. It needed kids. Life. Noise.

He'd booked the cab through an app, using his card, which meant no messing around with cash. He stepped straight out onto the pavement. The door opened. She'd clearly been waiting for him.

"It's so kind of you to come," Greta said once he was at the door.

"No problem," he said. "I hope you're doing OK since last night."

"Yes," she said, nodding and leaning her cheek against the edge of the door. "It's been a hard twenty-four hours, but in a weird way I think realizing how much I'd missed and quite how bad it was has been good for me. I don't think I'll ever be that blind again." He gave her a small smile, and she suddenly laughed. "Sorry," she said. "Come on in."

She moved aside, and he stepped into the house.

. . .

"I WAS THINKING that Aidan must have met up with someone recently, and they'd tricked him into picking up a lock before it had been installed on the door. Maybe they'd even taken the lock off their own bathroom after he'd visited. But obviously the person who was spectacularly easily placed to plant it was the woman who shared his home."

"But we weren't thinking about her," Hanson said, her gaze following the signs to the motorway as they made their way north out of Southampton toward the Poole house. She couldn't help feeling a sense of chagrin that she hadn't been the one to figure it out. She'd made all the right connections when it came to Maeve, and had still been wrong. "She had an alibi all evening, and we thought she didn't know about the affair."

"And her alibi placed her in London," Jonah added.

"But she knew all about it, didn't she?" Hanson said quietly. "And Aidan and Zoe never realized."

"Yes," Jonah replied. "She's far from stupid, and Aidan doesn't have as much of a poker face as he'd like to think. I'm guessing she became suspicious and checked up on him. She might even have looked at his phone or computer for an innocent reason and seen messages he hadn't deleted quickly enough."

"But then she didn't confront him," Hanson said. "Which I suppose must have been either pride or a hope that he was going to leave Zoe."

"Yes," Jonah said. "I was assuming the latter, but maybe she plain hated the idea of it going public."

Hanson suddenly thought of Lightman, who was probably back at the station by now. "I'd better let Ben know."

We're on our way to make an arrest. Are you back at base? You could probably catch us if you hurry.

. . .

"It's on his desktop computer," Greta said as she showed Lightman into Aidan's study. "I'd never thought of looking before. Which makes me sound seriously stupid."

"Or like you have very few trust issues," Lightman demurred.

"Well, maybe I should have had some," she said, her eyes gleaming in the increasingly orange sun that was illuminating the room. "I think . . . I think he killed her."

Lightman nodded slowly and then looked at the screen. There was a folder open on the computer's navigation. It was named "Lecture Notes." And it was full of images, which Lightman did his best not to look too hard at. They were all images of violence, and almost all of them featured women.

"He's a psycho, isn't he?" she asked in a surprisingly steady voice. "He's got hundreds of them. All in this folder, which was hidden from the navigation. I thought there was nothing to find until I asked it to search for files that weren't indexed. And then . . ."

Lightman gave a long breath. His first thought was that someone had tried to get into the house the night before. Maybe they'd come to plant this evidence. Or maybe it really had been Aidan, trying to get in and delete it before it was found.

"I'm sorry you had to see that," he said.

"I don't know why I didn't think to check before."

He felt a buzz, and he reached into his pocket for his phone. There was a message from Hanson about an arrest. Were they going to pick up Aidan? Or had something pointed them elsewhere? He itched to ask, but Greta was leaning over him to maximize Chrome.

"I looked at his browser history, too," she was saying. "Look."

Scattered amid ordinary searches, there were phrases like "How long does it take to bleed to death from a wrist injury?" and "Where are the arteries in the arm?"

He frowned as he scrolled down. These weren't all recent. Aidan clearly only used the desktop sporadically. Some of the searches were from months ago.

Was it really possible that someone else had had access to this over that long a time frame? Or had it really been Aidan?

He heard Greta's breathing change into a sob, and he minimized the screen quickly. She had her face hidden behind her arm and was crying into the sleeve of her cardigan.

"I'm so sorry," he said. "Is there anything I can get you?"

"No, it's OK," she said, wiping at her eyes. "It's fine. I'll make a cup of tea. Would you like one?"

"Sure," he said, even though he didn't really want tea. He wanted to message Hanson back, but he needed privacy if she was going to tell him who they were arresting. It wouldn't be in the least bit appropriate to let Greta see that. As she moved toward the kitchen, he called, "Is there a bathroom I can use, too?"

"Out in the hall," Greta said.

He picked up his phone and, while walking, sent Hanson a brief message back to tell her he was at Greta Poole's and that she had a hard drive full of evidence. He was hopeful that he'd get a reply while he was still in the privacy of the bathroom. The kettle clicked on in the kitchen, and he heard Greta pulling cups out of the cupboard.

"SHIT," HANSON SAID.

"What's up?"

"Lightman's at Greta Poole's house." Jonah could feel the way her gaze came to settle on his face, appealing to him. All while his own insides jolted and seemed to get left behind somewhere down the motorway. "What should I do? Should I call him?"

"Just send another message," Jonah said, as evenly as he could. "Say we've got a bit of a situation with a suspect and you need him to head back as soon as he can. Best not to alert her if she can see his phone screen."

"OK." Jonah could see her hands were shaking as she typed, and he remembered driving through infuriating rush-hour traffic a few months ago to try to protect Hanson herself. "It'll be OK," he said. "She doesn't know anything, and Ben's got a calm head on him."

LIGHTMAN ALMOST WALKED into a rack full of drying clothes, and heard Greta shout, "Sorry. I should have sent you to the other one. Aidan's always on at me about it."

He edged inside and turned to shut the door. It clicked in place, but there was no lock on it. Just an unpainted wooden space where a lock had once been.

He was absolutely still for a few moments, his hand on the handle. His phone, back in his pocket, buzzed, but he didn't pull it out.

I should have sent you to the other one . . .

He took a breath and then very quietly he opened the door again.

She was waiting for him, a look of mingled grief and anger on her face. Resting against her leg in a tight grip was a long, pointed kitchen knife.

"HE'S NOT READ it," Hanson said after a minute.

"Give him time," Jonah replied. "And he might have seen it on his home screen, anyway."

"What if he doesn't read it?"

"Then he'll probably just call up with his evidence and leave, and then we can move in," Jonah soothed. Though he had to admit that there was a trickle of worry running through him, too. Greta had fooled him for days, and her husband for months. She was bloody smart. And she was also strong and unpredictable. Jonah didn't like any of those things in a killer.

"FUCK," GRETA SAID. And then she gave a tearful laugh. "What an idiot. I'm . . . I'm sorry. I've done this to you. It wasn't your fault. I just had a moment . . ." She gave a sniff. "I guess I was just too much into the tearful-wife act and got sloppy. Though . . . you know, it isn't all an act. It's a year's worth of pain, too. All built up and waiting to come out."

"It's all right," he said, and gave her a smile that was as calm and reassuring as he could make it. He knew that Greta meant to kill him. She was a strong woman with a knife. She had a good chance of injuring him. Yet he didn't feel particularly scared. Not after the sterile hospital he'd left his father in, and the thought of a slow, painful dwindling.

"It isn't all right, though, really," Greta said. "I'm going to have to do what I did to her, only you don't deserve it." Her brow creased with worry. "I don't feel like I have a choice."

"Of course you do," Lightman said, and he gave a short laugh. "Knowing what you've done isn't the same as successfully convicting you of it. A whole lot happens during a court case, and it's hard to really prove what someone's done. Particularly when they've been careful."

Greta seemed to consider this for a moment, and Lightman thought about his phone, still tucked away in his pocket.

"It's a lot harder to get away with two murders than one," he added quietly. "And my DCI knows where I am."

She nodded. "So you'd have to have obviously left here. I'd have to use your car, and make sure I drove past enough cameras."

Lightman felt a cold sort of admiration for her. She was so quick to understand and to plan. It wasn't just about taking care, he thought. It was about having the sort of mind that could take a problem apart and find a solution in moments.

"A camera might well pick up that it was you driving," he said.

"I'd need your clothes," she said, looking him over.

"Or we could go and look at the proof of what Aidan did," he said with a meaningful look. "You've got plenty enough there to convict him, or at least to cast significant doubt."

"And spend months in court trying to win the sympathy vote in order to get out of jail? You think I want to be crying in front of them all about how he was a terrible person, and admitting to the world that I was weak enough to let him do it? I'd have to play the wronged wife, and I did everything I could—*everything* not to be her." Greta shook her head and raised her chin. "I'd rather go down fighting."

"Maybe you should fight the right person," a quiet voice said from behind Lightman's left shoulder.

It was such a shock that he actually turned away from Greta and the knife. And it was very lucky that Greta was just as startled by her husband's arrival as he was.

"Twenty-two minutes," Hanson said, reading the time off Jonah's GPS.

He glanced at her. "Nothing from Ben yet?"

"No."

"I'm sure he's fine," he said reassuringly, but he still squeezed his foot down harder on the accelerator.

"What are you doing here?" Greta asked, and as she spoke to her husband, her voice lost all of its warmth. It was cold now. Furious. Disgusted.

"I came to talk to you," Aidan said. "Because I realized what had happened. And after that, after initially being angry, I realized that I'd done it to you."

"Why do you have to be here?" she asked. "Just go to hell and burn!"

"I need to tell you how sorry I am." He stepped forward, and she was immediately on alert. She lifted the kitchen knife and held it out in front of her with a noise like a wildcat.

"I'm not going to listen to anything you say!" she said. "I'm done with listening. You have lied and lied to me. You couldn't even love me enough when she'd dumped you. You wanted her so much that you had to . . . to . . . to *perv* on her. I've never felt so humiliated in my life."

Lightman was more caught up by their conversation than he should have been. He needed to move. He needed to get Aidan and himself out of there or find a way of disabling Greta. But it was hard to move when he couldn't look away from the two of them, hanging there in a moment of hurt and hatred and almost violence.

"I know," Aidan said. "I know how much that must have hurt. I've done awful things. Because I'm a loser. You were right." He took another step, but Greta didn't move, and he was now only inches from the knife. "I wanted to be with you because you're strong and you're beautiful, and then I couldn't cope with it. I was looking for your approval when I could never get a word of it from my mum, and that wasn't your fault."

Lightman forced himself to take stock of the situation properly. Greta was blocking the kitchen doorway, and he didn't think he could make it to the stairs. Aidan was unfortunately blocking his access to the front door. But if he would just step a few feet farther into the room, Lightman would be able to run for the open front door behind him.

The only obstacle was Greta, who was holding the knife out toward Aidan and doing everything to discourage him from walking forward.

"I gave you approval," Greta spat. "I gave you constant pride in yourself. Even though you could never be proud of me in case it somehow emasculated you. I gave you bloody everything a person could and instead you chose that . . . that . . . that *whore*. And you told her that I was cold to you."

Lightman took a step farther away from Greta, and closer to the front door.

He might, he thought, be able to get past Aidan, just. Ideally, he needed to shove Aidan out of the door with him. He thought it through as he took another slight step to the left. Lunge. Grab. Drag. All before Greta had a chance to do any damage with that knife.

The question was whether he'd be putting Aidan Poole in too much danger.

"I told myself over and over that you were cold and unappreciative and uninterested," Aidan said quietly. Tears started tracking down his face. "It was my one defense for being a . . . a shit to you. And I know it was unfair. But it was the only thing I had to level at you. That sometimes you didn't pander to my ego as much as I wanted. But I had you all wrong, didn't I? Just unbelievably wrong. You were thinking of me all the time. And you weren't this straightforward open book, either. You were hiding so much hurt and carrying on anyway."

"Stop doing that!" she said.

"Stop what?"

"You're saying what I want to hear! You're just . . . you're just *lying* all over again."

Aidan shook his head. "I'm not saying it because I hope you'll take me back, even though I don't think I'm ever going to stop wanting that. I'm saying it because it's what you deserve to hear and I should have said it a bloody year ago and grown up enough to save the two of us." He raised a hand to rub at his cheeks. "I've never not been obsessed with you. With the way other men look at you, and with the way everyone is drawn to you. I only managed to stop thinking about you by pretending you were someone else."

Lightman was almost in position. Aidan was doing a good job of holding her interest.

He was going to have to act and risk getting it wrong. He could see that. Greta wasn't backing down.

"Stop moving!" Greta said suddenly. She was speaking to Lightman this time. She'd seen the danger.

"Greta," Aidan said, his hand up, "you don't need to hurt him. You don't need to hurt anyone. I love you. I love you so much. And I don't want anything bad to happen to you."

"If you love me," she said, a shake to her voice that hadn't been there before, "then you'll get the hell out of here and let me deal with this. You'll leave, and then maybe you'll help me to cover it up if I need you to."

Aidan gave her a funny little smile. "Darling, neither of us is getting out of here. That's not how this ends, is it?" And with that smile still on his face, he stepped forward.

Lightman totally failed to take advantage and get out. He was convinced he'd just seen Aidan walk into the point of a knife.

But somehow the knife was by Greta's side again, and then behind Aidan's back as she clung to her husband. They were lost to him in a fierce embrace that made him want to edge out of the room.

Instead he gently removed the knife from Greta's hand and walked outside.

30

Jonah saw the first of the flashing lights at the same moment Hanson drew in a gasp of air next to him. It was hard not to floor the accelerator for the last hundred yards, but he drew up carefully behind the squad car at the curb. There was no ambulance, he saw. No ambulance, at least yet.

Hanson had her door open before the car had stopped and was moving at almost a run up to the house.

"Ma'am!" one of the two police officers who were standing near the driveway called.

"Where's Ben? Where's Sergeant Lightman?" Jonah heard her ask as he opened his door to follow her.

"Juliette." It was Lightman's voice, speaking from somewhere out of sight. Jonah hotfooted it around until he could see Ben. He was just inside the front door, with a paper cup of tea in his hand. He also, by that time, had Juliette Hanson folded into a hug.

Jonah gave him a brief grin and then raised his eyebrows at the nearest uniform. "Any chance of a sitrep?"

Greta had been driven away from the scene a few minutes before, and Aidan had begged to go with her. Unsure whether they ought to be arresting him as well, the uniforms ended up agreeing.

They had wound up in two different interview rooms, and Aidan had already told the arresting sergeant twice that it was all his fault and he should be the one going to jail.

"It's pretty fucked up, isn't it?" Hanson had muttered from her position in the corridor as they watched Aidan being brought a cup of coffee. The four of them—including O'Malley, who had refused to be left out—were preparing themselves to start the process of charging Greta Poole. "Does he really still love her after she killed his mistress?"

"I think he might," Lightman said. "When he started in on all that apologetic stuff, I thought he was bullshitting to give me time to get out. I thought he was being clever. And then he went and invited her to stab him . . . and I can't see any reason why he'd do that, or sit and defend her, if he didn't love her in some weird way."

"It's funny," Jonah muttered. "Every move of his has been characterized by weakness. Even his strongest one. Theirs is a pretty screwed-up story."

Hanson turned to look at him and frowned. "I don't agree. It's not their story. It's Zoe's story. However weirdly romantic this end-of-it-all stuff is, Greta murdered her. It was Zoe who was the bloody victim, not Greta Poole."

"Amen to that," Jonah said, and then he sighed. "Shall we get started?"

"I COULD TELL the day after he first slept with her," Greta said, her voice as strong and as measured as it had been before all this. She sat with her arms out in a triangle on the table in front of her, the tips of her fingers together and her thumbs moving ever so slightly to brush past each other. "He was jumping every time his phone buzzed and trying to look at messages without me seeing. It was painfully clear."

"But you didn't confront him about it?" Lightman asked her.

"I didn't know how to begin addressing it until I had proof," she said. "Which turned out to be easy to get. I got up early on the Saturday morning and took his phone downstairs instead of mine. I looked at his messages, and then on WhatsApp, and I found out everything I needed to know."

There was a shake in her voice, and it was clear to Jonah that this was still an awful memory for her. A single point of trauma from which everything else had spread. And it hadn't been necessary for it to go like this, he thought. She could have done a very different thing and just left him.

"What stopped you walking out on him then?"

Greta hesitated. "A few things. I don't know exactly which was the strongest. It was humiliation partly. My initial reaction was to scream at him, but I realized that meant I'd have to throw him out. And if I threw him out, then everyone would know. They would know what he'd done, and they'd judge me."

"Don't you think they would have judged him?" Jonah asked gently.

Greta fixed him with a withering gaze. "Have you ever seen what happens when a marriage breaks down like that? Like it did for my mother? Have you seen how it's never, *ever* the man's fault? No, it must be because she'd let herself go, or was too boring, or wasn't pleasing him in the bedroom . . ." She put her hands flat on the table and curled her fingers up until the knuckles went white. "I learned pretty young how that one goes. And I wasn't going to let that shit happen to me. I'd put too much into being this perfect wife. Did you know that I've never gone a day of this marriage without putting makeup on?"

Jonah nodded, and it seemed to take a little of the anger out of her.

"So you hoped that he would stop the affair?"

"Yes," Greta said. "I hoped he would see reason. How could he not, when I was just perfect? I spent more time on cooking, and I ate less myself. I pumped poison into my face to get rid of the lines, and I gave him more fucking head than any man has ever had and survived."

It was awful, and it was funny, and Jonah tried not to give in to laughter. That kind of thing never sounded good on a recording. Though he thought Greta might have appreciated it. He let out a breath instead, and said, "But he kept on with the affair."

"Yes," Greta said, and her voice was suddenly thick. "He did. And I knew, because he's no good at deception, for all he thinks he is. He had his phone synched to his other computers, and sometimes when I was at home, the messages would flash up on the desktop. I didn't even need to log on to see them."

He thought about how she had seen many of Zoe's messages and only some of Aidan's. Had that setup been part of what had driven her to kill? Because all she could see was the other woman flirting or sexting, and not his replies that had played an equal part in their dialogue?

"When did you make the decision to kill Zoe?" he asked quietly.

"It wasn't an instant decision," Greta told them hesitantly. "It was a culmination of a lot of things. After I tagged him in a photo on Facebook to make sure she knew about me, she dumped him. I could tell from Aidan's face after he read her message. I thought it was done."

"But it wasn't?" Jonah asked.

"No, it wasn't." Greta's voice was hard. "She took him back in under a month. There's no way she could claim ignorance after that. She knew about me, and she chose to keep on doing it. It got harder and harder to forgive her."

"But they were no longer together when you killed her," Jonah said. "Aidan had ended it. Wasn't that enough?"

Greta shook her head. "She'd done too good a job on him. He was still . . . fixated. I went through his machine, and I found images of her that he'd screen-shotted. Images taken long after they broke up, when she didn't even know he was watching. And God, that felt worse than anything has ever felt." She took a sudden breath. It was part inhalation and part sob.

"Tell us about that night," Lightman said. "Thursday night. It was meticulously planned, wasn't it?"

"Of course it was," Greta said. "I had to be free of her. I wanted Aidan not . . . not to be . . ." She shook her head again and breathed in, and was suddenly the strong woman again. The woman who had acted. "I went to her flat twice that day. The first time, I took clothes with me, which I left in a locker at the DW gym near the station. I needed to check that she had an art knife I could use, one that was unquestionably hers, and I decided to avoid later hassle by taking it with me."

"I'm curious about that," Jonah said. "I don't understand why you made it look like a suicide but then also framed Aidan."

Greta laughed. "I hadn't really decided to frame him, even then. There was a weak side to me that just wanted Zoe out of the way. I thought that might be enough. But I had backups. All the images I'd spent weeks adding to his computer, and the painting, and the fingerprints." She shook her head. "I still had the option of reporting the theft of that bathroom lock. It would do enough to cast doubt on the prints. I could have let him walk. It was that awful fake Christian, Maeve, who decided it for me. The moment Zoe was dead, she was messaging Aidan again."

"Again?" Jonah asked.

"Oh, they had history," Greta said bitterly. "I thought it was just a one-off. A kiss when Aidan was drunk and upset at being dumped. He seemed to be keeping her at arm's length. But he agreed to meet her and I could see it all happening again. She was going on and on at him. Messages about who might have killed Zoe. Saying they should try to find the killer together, and that she didn't believe it was him. I did my best to warn her off. Some of the things she said . . . she was getting a little too close for comfort."

Jonah nodded, glad that they could definitively lay the attack on Maeve at Greta's door, and said, "Thank you. I'd like you to tell me how you became Esther."

Greta gave a slow, brilliant smile. "That was a lot of fun. I knew where Zoe worked, and it wasn't hard to find out where she lived. I'd been watching her for months without her ever noticing. When I decided I needed to punish her, I parked my car outside Café Gina, and I followed her home. I did a better job of that than Aidan." She gave a little throaty laugh. "I'd already seen her talking to Felix in the coffee shop, so I got him to let me into the flats. I said I was checking on my tenant and they weren't answering the bell. It was enough to get him talking, and from there, it was so easy to work my way in with him."

"And you took the spare keys to Zoe's flat, and copied them," Jonah said.

"Weeks ago," she agreed. "I actually bumped into him on the day, did he tell you? I went to check on the knife so I was prepared. I was letting myself out when I saw him. He even asked me in for tea again, and never stopped to think." She leaned forward. "He was pretty slow for a police officer, you know. He never stopped to ask which flat Esther owned, or why she was only there occasionally. He spent too long talking about himself and his problems."

"So you had the knife," Lightman said, "and the keys."

"Yes," Greta said. "I went home to change for the dinner, and on the way the little whore gave me all the proof I needed that she deserved to die. She must have recognized me, because she started following me."

"We caught some of it on camera," Jonah said. "Can you explain what happened?"

"She attacked me," Greta said flatly. "Poor little heartbroken Zoe went for me. The first I knew was that someone had shoved me over, and I was suddenly facedown on the pavement, and the little bitch was kicking and punching me. And do you know what she was saying? That sweet little thing?" she asked. "She was telling me I'd taken everything from her and she wished I would die. *She* said that to *me*."

There was such anger in Greta's expression. Such a sense of righteous fury. It made Jonah feel cold.

"What happened?" Lightman asked. "Did you manage to fight her off?"

"It didn't last all that long," Greta said. "A stranger, a fairly strong man, got hold of her and pulled her away. She ran off, and I told him not to worry. I said she's a family member and troubled, and he left it. It's a good thing people don't take assault by females that seriously, you know. It might have ruined everything if I'd been connected to her."

Jonah let out a sigh. He wondered increasingly whether Greta were in some kind of denial about the prison sentence she was facing and the severity of what she had done. It was in no way a "good thing" that the police hadn't been involved. If they had, she might never have killed a young woman.

"So you went back home after the attack," Lightman said, after a pause, "and then you went to the awards dinner?"

"I did," she said. "An event can be one of the best places to leave unnoticed, you know. I chose a tight, clingy dress that was short enough that it wouldn't show under other clothes. I sat through dinner, and gave my award, and then pretended to take a phone call. In fact, I picked up my coat and went out through the garden entrance and got into the taxi I'd booked. I made it onto the nine fifty-one from London Bridge. I'd covered up my dress with my coat, and with my boots on I looked reasonably casual."

"And then you changed," Jonah said, "into a tracksuit and a cap."

"Yes," Greta said. "I changed at the gym and left with my hold-all. And then I walked to Zoe's flat, and I let myself in."

Jonah didn't want to hear the rest, but Greta told them anyway. About the desflurane and how Zoe being in the bath already had felt like a gift from the gods.

"Didn't you worry that Aidan might see you?" Lightman asked her at one point.

"Don't be stupid," she said irritably. "I wouldn't go all that way if

I hadn't checked. I knew he couldn't see beyond the hinge of the door. I'd loaded up his little spying program and tried it."

"Did you know he'd be watching then?" Jonah asked curiously.

"I didn't know," she said with a strange smile, "but I hoped that he might."

She finished with an account of how she'd changed clothes again, to resemble a frumpy older woman, and left the flat. Jonah remembered that there had been a woman in a huge coat on the CCTV footage. He hadn't had any reason to look at her twice.

And then he thought about how much of all of this came down to observation. Aidan, observing Zoe without consent, and Greta watching him do it. Maeve and Victor both watching the affair and taking their own kicks and hurts from it. The CCTV that Greta had known about and avoided.

He remembered someone, perhaps a scientist, saying that nothing really happened unless it was observed, and he felt as though there were a bizarre truth to that.

"What happened to the hold-all?" he asked.

"I filled it with some of Zoe's clothes and shoved it in the wardrobe," Greta said with a shrug. "Nobody was going to check there, at least not immediately. I went back and picked it up again Sunday. Oh, you might need to go and feed her cat. The stupid thing was sitting outside the front door when I was letting myself in."

Jonah shook his head slightly, in part at her intelligence, in part at her arrogance, and in part at the bizarre note of care for an animal when she had just murdered a young woman.

And then she suddenly lifted her head and said, "Oh, did you find the painting?"

"The one you stole?" Lightman asked.

"I did not steal it," Greta said, her voice suddenly harsh. "That painting was mine from the moment she put me in it. It was *mine*. It showed me that she deserved what happened. She put me in it and she painted out my eyes and showed the two of them hurting me, and that meant she knew what she was doing. She knew that she was hurting me with every moment she spent with Aidan. She just thought I was blind. But I wasn't blind." Her voice had returned to normal now. "I was never blind."

And she'd told them, after that, where the painting was: in the spare room at the house, hanging apparently innocently on the wall.

"It didn't worry me if anyone saw it, because they'd assume Aidan took it," she said with a smile. "It was just another piece of evidence against him."

"Which was before you threw Aidan out," Lightman said, frowning. "Weren't you worried about him seeing it?"

Greta laughed and shook her head. "I could absolutely rely on Aidan not to break from his routine and look in there. And, you know, even if he had gone in, I don't think he would have recognized it. In all the time he and Zoe were together, they barely spoke about her work. I don't think he cared whether she painted cartoon kittens, as long as she kept giving out."

Lightman went through a few more details, clarifying and tidying up, but that was pretty much all of it. The whole, grubby truth.

"You know," Greta added, after they were done, "when I went back home, after the dinner, I was so happy to see his face. I could tell he'd seen something while trying to perve on her, and was tearing himself to pieces over what to do. It was so good to make him feel like that."

HANSON HAD LISTENED to Greta's testimony from the viewing gallery. O'Malley had come and gone, interested but not fascinated like she was. Perhaps, to him, it all seemed too easy now.

She only left after Greta explained about the painting, partly because it looked like the interview was finishing, and partly because she was feeling such a burning sense of anger on Zoe's behalf.

She could hear her phone ringing on her desk as she left the interview suite. She recognized Siku Swardadine's voice as she answered, and was glad she'd picked up.

"I'm calling because DCI Sheens left a message," Zoe's mother said, her voice raw with emotion. "You're sure? You're sure you have them?"

"Yes," Hanson said firmly. "We are. I'll have to get the DCI to give you the details, but we're sure."

There was a silence from the other end of the line, and Hanson was about to check that Siku was still there. But then there was a ragged breath, and she said, "Thank you. Thank you."

"I hope it helps," she said quietly, and hung up with eyes that felt embarrassingly damp. She gave a sniff and tried to swallow the tears down. When she looked up, she found DI Walker looking at her, clearly on his way back from the kitchen. She could feel the heat that rose into her cheeks.

"Was that the family?" he asked.

"Yeah," Hanson said. "Hard not to feel for them."

"It's crap," Walker agreed with a nod. "But at least with the case wrapped up you can drown your sorrows in drink."

"I guess so," Hanson said, trying to smile. "How are things with you?"

"Promising," he said. "One of my vandalism cases should go to court. So it looks like that's the pub for both of us later."

Hanson nodded and gave him an uncertain smile. She wasn't quite sure what he was suggesting. Maybe he just meant a group pub trip. A social occasion.

She gave a nod when Lightman appeared at the door to the interview suite, and then buried her head in work. But by seven, it felt like she needed to do something. Lightman hadn't said a word to her in hours, and she was sick of second-guessing why that might be. Whether she'd made him feel awkward by hugging him. Whether she'd spoiled things.

As Lightman headed to the kitchen for a coffee, she stood and followed with a ridiculous sense of trepidation.

"Hey," she said, coming to a stop next to him. "Walker was suggesting the pub. Are you keen?"

Lightman's expression was as friendly and inscrutable as always. "I'd probably better not," he said, and smiled. "I've just spent two days getting over the last hangover."

"You don't need to get drunk," she said, trying to make it sound like banter. "I'm only going for a couple."

His gaze moved past her toward Walker, and then briefly off into the distance. When he looked back, it was with something that looked like a screensaver on his face. Like Ben had checked out somehow. "I'll be good. But thanks."

Hanson felt every step of the walk back to her desk. She felt like she was fourteen again, and walking back across the lunch hall from asking the popular boy for a date. At least this time nobody was laughing.

She bypassed her desk and drifted over to where DI Walker was still at work. She gave him a brilliant smile when he looked up. "Are you ready for that drink yet?"

JONAH'S FIRST STEPS toward getting paperwork together were interrupted by a visitor. A man called Richard Hoskins was asking to talk to him, and he agreed to have him shown up with no real idea of who he was or what he had to say.

He checked his phone while he waited, and saw that there was a message from Michelle. He glanced up, making sure he had time to read it, and then opened it.

He read that she'd been thinking about it all and was positive that it had been a mistake for both of them. That nothing had really changed to make their relationship work, and that she'd been on a few dates with someone at work.

It felt almost like the breakup all over again. The self-recrimination. The desolation. The desire to beg her to reconsider.

It didn't help that he knew she was right, or that this probably made his life easier.

As he put the phone down again, he did his best to pack everything away with it. He needed to focus on wrapping up this case. On giving Zoe Swardadine justice.

Richard Hoskins arrived at his door and proved to be a thirty-something male with gelled hair and a leather jacket that was too small for him. It gaped open over his patterned shirt.

"Mr. Hoskins," Jonah said, shaking his hand and showing him to a seat at the far side of his desk.

"Richie," he said. "Just Richie."

"What can I do for you?"

"Well," Richie said, tugging at his ear, "it's not so much for me. It's for my girlfriend. She's called Angeline Judd."

Jonah looked at him anew, surprised that Angeline was in a relationship with a slightly overweight, unprepossessing man at least ten years older, who sounded like he came from working-class Portsmouth. One with cheap clothes and a pervasive scent of aftershave.

"She's been assisting us in our murder investigation," Jonah said, nodding.

"I know, and I'm glad she wants to help," Richie said, holding a hand up. "But it's hurting her, all of it. I'm hoping she can be left alone for a while."

Jonah nodded slowly. "I think she probably can."

"I did wonder if I should say," he added. "I saw her the evening she died. Zoe."

Jonah thought back to their CCTV footage, and said, "You were waiting for her when she got home, weren't you?"

"Yeah," Richie said. "I think I scared her a bit. I didn't mean to. I just asked her to call Angeline, because she was so upset about their argument. I mean, she never liked me, anyway. I think she didn't trust me. But anyway, I didn't want some stupid row coming between them. She was so dependent on Zoe." He tutted and lowered his head. "She's not got her anymore, though."

"I'm sorry," Jonah said.

"I know, it's all right. She'll be all right somehow." Richie nodded. "I'll do my best to look after her. And she's got Maeve and some of the girls from her course." He gave a sigh. "It's an awful thing to say, but maybe in a funny way it'll be good for her. That dependency on Zoe wasn't good, I don't think."

"Maybe not," Jonah said. And then he rose. "You don't need to worry about us bothering her, anyway, Mr. Hoskins. Zoe's killer is already in custody."

"Oh," Richie said, and then hurried to stand as well. "That's good. That's really good, that is. I'll tell Angeline." He paused on his way out, and turned to ask, "It wasn't a friend of Angie's, was it?"

"No," Jonah said with a smile. "It wasn't."

"Good." Richie gave him a small salute. "Good luck with it."

HANSON AND WALKER had thrown a few pub ideas around before landing on the wine bar on Bedford Place, which Hanson had suggested because it had parking. If she ended up having more than one drink, she wanted somewhere she could leave her car overnight without getting ticketed.

The DI was ready before she was, and Hanson, pulling on her coat, told him she'd meet him there. She went to knock briefly on the door of the DCI's office while Walker headed out. Sheens was staring at his screen with a distant expression.

"See you in the morning," she said.

The DCI looked up at her vacantly and then gave a sudden, firm nod. "Great. I won't be here much longer. Just want to finish my notes on today."

"Congratulations on all of it," Hanson said.

"You, too," Sheens said. And then, as she was leaving, he added, "Great work on all of this, by the way. And particularly on the painting. You had it on the nail."

"Only I thought it was Maeve," she said wryly.

The DCI gave a shrug. "I thought it was probably Felix earlier on, and maybe Angeline. That's the way it goes. It doesn't mean you didn't do a really good job."

"Thanks," she said with a reluctant smile. "I appreciate it."

He nodded. And then said, "Oh. I wanted to follow up on that guy at your house on Saturday. To see if it was Victor Varos. And it doesn't look like it can have been. I put it to him, after everything else, and he seemed genuinely confused. He said he'd been at the cinema, and I've sent a quick message to check. It looks like he really was."

"Oh," Hanson said. And with everything feeling like it was tying up and becoming clearer, this almost felt unimportant for a moment.

"I just wanted to make you aware," Sheens said quietly, "so you can think about whether it was someone else. And, you know . . . whether it might be a problem."

The DCI's gaze was steady, and for some reason she felt herself becoming embarrassed.

"Well, I'll think." She gave a slight smile. "Probably nothing."

And it was only after she'd let herself out that she started thinking of that figure again, and remembered a message from Damian, months before.

I'm at your house . . .

31

Maeve was early. Genuinely, properly early. The tables of Prosecco stood untouched on the grass, their white cloths flapping almost despondently in the breeze, and a waitress in black bow tie and waistcoat was crouched beside the table, shifting bottles around in an ice bucket.

She felt proud of herself for her punctuality. She'd done what Zoe would have done.

She unlooped her handbag from her shoulder and rooted her phone out, looking for a message from Angeline. She'd told Maeve a little earlier that she and Richie would be twenty-five minutes. She just needed to feed Monkfish and then leave, she'd said.

Zoe's cat had been found at last by her next-door neighbor, and offered to Zoe's parents. They had suggested asking one of the girls instead, and Maeve had been relieved when Angeline had accepted enthusiastically. She didn't want that tie. With the year winding down, it seemed to Maeve that she needed to travel. Not to find herself, but to lose herself. To bury all of this in some unknown place and not dig it up again.

Angeline, it turned out, was still ten minutes away. Maeve was alone for a while.

She drifted to the table and picked up a glass, smiling gratefully before the waitress could complain that she shouldn't take one yet, and then she turned to look over the new wing, wondering exactly how she should feel. It was certainly a lovely building, a white-stone glass-and-reflections creation that both matched and outshone the rest of the School of Art. Even the circular moated library, Maeve thought.

She was fiercely glad that it would bear Zoe's name, but felt a burning sense of wrong that her friend had only ever seen it as a building site. She hadn't lived long enough to see this finished creation, with its glinting glass and brilliant white stone; with its freshly laid turf and its deep-brown flower beds planted with peonies and roses that had yet to become tatty or overgrown. Nor the way her parents had stepped in to make up the shortfall after building costs ran too high.

Zoe could have been here in person instead of in memory, just one of the students come to watch the opening and to neck free Prosecco. It was the sort of event that would have suited her so well, with her warmth and her constant, infectious air of fun.

Maeve tried to swallow down the sense of unfairness with some of the Prosecco. As she lowered her glass, she saw that there were a few scattered others starting to arrive. A couple in what looked like wedding-guest outfits. A slouching shape in a dark jacket and shirt with no tie.

And then Maeve's heart squeezed as she realized that the slouching figure was Victor. Victor, who hadn't said a word to her in almost eight months. Victor, who had turned her away when she'd come to the café with Angeline in the strange days before the case had gone to trial.

The words were burned into her, as clear in her memory today as they had been then.

"Why are you here?" Victor had asked her. "There's nothing for us to talk about. Without Zoe, there's no reason for us to talk again."

She remembered the awful, pulsing hurt that she'd felt. The humiliation. The stinging sense of unfairness. And instead of talking back to him like the Maeve of old, she'd been frozen there in total silence.

It had been Angeline who had stepped forward instead. Timid Angeline who had put an arm round Maeve, and told Victor that he was being an arsehole.

"I don't care if you're grieving," Angeline had said. "You have no right to hurt her like that. She's had enough shit to deal with. And personally I couldn't care less whether you cut yourself off from everyone and drive yourself mad. You're the only one that's going to end up hurt."

She'd led Maeve outside gently but determinedly, and rubbed her back when Maeve had started to sob. The first but by no means last time that Angeline had shown a strength Maeve had never even suspected that she had.

She looked at her phone again, and then flicked a glance across the grass, hoping to see Angeline and Richie. It was shameful, but Maeve didn't want to have to face Victor alone.

She turned away from him and walked back toward the Prosecco table, draining her glass as she went so she could take another one.

She was still there, and halfway through another glass, when she heard his voice.

"Maeve," he said from somewhere over her left shoulder. "I'm so sorry. What I said . . . it was bullshit. I was a—a horrible human being."

She had to look at him then, and his expression was almost unrecognizable. There was a softness to it. An openness. As if the fury had somehow been washed out of him to leave someone else there.

She nodded. She knew she should say something. She wanted to tell him that she understood. She also wanted to tell him that she'd been through awful, awful things, too, and that it hadn't been fair.

In the end, she gave a slightly crooked smile and said, "Yeah. You were. But why break the habit of a lifetime?"

. . .

SOME TWENTY MINUTES later, once Angeline and Richie had turned up and Angeline had scolded Victor and then forgiven him, and Maeve had tried not to cry as she'd hugged each of Zoe's parents in turn, they were all called to watch as the Zoe Swardadine Building was officially opened. Siku had been asked to say a few words, and unlike every other speechmaker Maeve had ever known, she really did limit herself to a few.

"I've been so angry that Zoe won't be here to see this," she said, "and that she has missed out on so many things that should have been part of her life. But seeing you all here today, it's . . . I realize that her life was a wonderful thing. So many of you were a part of it, and I want to thank you for every happy moment you all gave her. I'm proud to be here today."

She joined her husband and together they cut through the large white ribbon that had been hitched across the door. Maeve clapped and watched the ribbon where it fell. She couldn't help thinking that it looked like a bright, gleaming flow of paint.

Acknowledgments

The list of people a writer ends up indebted to is always larger than the writer had ever thought possible. I hope nobody who helped with all the twists and challenges of this book ends up slipping through the cracks.

First, thanks to all the wonderful reps at Penguin Random House who have worked tirelessly in support of my books. To say that *She Lies in Wait* would never have got anywhere without you is an understatement. You have made the dream of seeing my books on shelves come true, and it's the best.

To Catherine Wood, Lucy Beresford-Knox, and the other amazing members of the international rights team at Penguin, who have brought my words to a frankly staggering number of different countries and into wonderful languages.

To the unbelievably patient Emma Caruso and her team of wonderful editors and proofreaders, who with their incredible eagle eyes have saved me from terrible things being in print forever by accident.

To Chris H., for being not only willing to answer but wonderfully supportive over my policing questions. (For any errors still in here, I apologize profusely. They're definitely mine.)

To Katie Tull, Allyson Lord, and the wonderful publicity and marketing teams at Random House, who have not only shouted about my books but have made the most incredible reviews, exposure, and opportunities happen.

To the visionary, incisive, and incredibly supportive Andrea Walker. You've been just incredible throughout this whole process, and helped a lot of dreams to come true.

And to the adored Felicity Blunt, agent extraordinaire, official fairy godmother of my life, and absolute hoot. You're at the root of every good decision, and every great step in this incredible process.

Finally, to Rufus, for all the fun, the distractions, the pick-me-up talks (mostly about Minecraft, but hey), and for being so enthusiastic about me reading to you. I'll see about including more child-appropriate material in the next one.

Glossary of British Policing Terms

CID: Criminal Investigation Department. CID sits within police headquarters, and is the home of most of the plainclothes detectives within a regional police force.

DC: Detective constable. A DC is the lowest rank of detective, but one who has already previously trained as a regular officer and been promoted to the rank of sergeant. They therefore have some experience of policing prior to working with CID, but in a detective team might expect to do most of the lower-level work, such as knocking on doors, flyering, and conducting initial interviews.

DS: Detective sergeant. A DS is the rank above a DC, and has authority over DCs. They take on more of an organizational role in most teams, and might deputize for a detective inspector if they work with one.

DI: Detective inspector. A DI is the next rank up from DS. Detective inspectors generally have the freedom to undertake investigations the way they see fit, and might oversee other members of a team, such as detective sergeants or detective constables.

DCI: Detective chief inspector. DCIs are senior officers who will generally lead high-profile investigations and will run a department or team. Their duties include liaising with other parts of the force.

DCS: Detective chief superintendent. A DCS is a very senior officer, and will lead multiple teams and areas of command. They also carry responsibility for strategy and/or policy, meaning that their junior officers will seek their advice when it comes to difficult decisions. A DCS can also do a great deal to smooth the way for other officers, and will be actively involved in high-profile investigations or critical incidents.

Station: The police headquarters as a whole. This can also refer to any individual, smaller base from which the police operate.

Murder on Zoom

How witnessing a killing during
a video call suddenly became starkly relevant

GYTHA LODGE

The idea of invisibly witnessing something terrible has always held a certain power. It is what lies behind our love of books like *The Girl on the Train* and *The Woman in the Window*. These are stories of ordinary (and, in many cases, flawed) people witnessing something hugely significant and their lives being changed forever as a result.

The idea certainly has power for me. When planning a second crime novel, I looked around for a concept that fascinated me, something that made a "whodunnit" into something spine-tingling. In our technology-driven age, perhaps it was inevitable that I happened on the ultimate invisible witness: one who wasn't even there in person, but saw it all through a webcam.

A year ago, while I was writing the book, the story already seemed relevant. These calls were a frequent feature of both my working life and my social life, and technology has led to far more observation than we ever had in the past.

What I hadn't expected was for the world to change drastically in 2020, and for video calling to become one of the few connections between us all.

Watching from the dark

In my novel, Aidan Poole is logging on to his laptop late at night to Skype with his girlfriend, Zoe. She lives in another town, and he is kept apart from her by more than distance. This is a relationship that shouldn't be happening, for a variety of reasons. But Aidan is unable to keep away.

On this particular night, instead of the standard sight of Zoe's face at eleven o'clock, Aidan witnesses an unseen intruder entering her flat. He hears the unmistakable sounds of a struggle off-camera and is certain that something terrible has happened to her. He is proved horribly right when DCI Jonah Sheens's team finds Zoe's body the next morning.

The killer never even saw Aidan, but every part of Aidan's life is about to be upended by what he witnessed. Terrible actions can have terrible consequences, even if the things Aidan saw eventually lead to the killer being caught.

This is *Watching from the Dark*, which came out just as the coronavirus crisis was beginning to reach the United States.

The helpless witness

The strange thing is how much we have all ended up in Aidan's situation. COVID-19 has separated us from our friends, colleagues, and often families. It has cut our access to those important people in our lives to what we witness through a camera lens. And it has drastically reduced our power to help them.

In my personal experience so far, I've had three Zoom calls with friends who are really struggling with isolation. I've listened to them, talked to them, soothed them while they cried, and felt profoundly powerless to actually do anything useful. What I want to offer them is a hug, when all I have is words transmitted—sometimes with poor sound quality—over an Internet connection. It is frustrating and heartbreaking at once, and I know for certain that this is nothing like the heartbreak families have suffered when their loved ones have died alone in the hospital, with only an iPad held up to let them see their final moments, if they are lucky.

Seeing the hidden

But there is another side to COVID, too. Isolation has given us strange insights into the hidden parts of people's lives. Colleagues who look perfectly presented at work are suddenly thrown into a new light when you see their messy house in the background of a call. People you would never have associated with wealth are suddenly revealed to have massive piles. And there is a huge amount of information to be gleaned from everyone's choice of décor. Whether they have a study. Whether they are harassed by their kids or left alone.

I've had many conversations with people who have admitted to being fascinated by these snippets of life. We have been turned into unintentional voyeurs—or perhaps just revealed as the voyeurs we have always been.

And things have been accidentally witnessed, too. I have three friends whose partners have appeared in a state of undress in the background of a work call, because the partners had no idea there was a webcam on. I've seen people snapping at their children in the background, or clearly playing games on their mobiles when they were supposed to be concentrating. And most of us will probably have seen the poor woman who used the bathroom in the background to a work Zoom—and hopefully have been horrified that it's been shared around.

Through all of it, I have found myself waiting, with fascination and horror, to see if *Watching from the Dark* really will come true. I'm braced for the first murder caught on Zoom, and I hope, if it happens, that there is a Jonah Sheens on hand to bring the culprit to in. At least where there are witnesses, there might be justice.

PHOTO © TOM ADAMS

GYTHA LODGE is the author of *She Lies in Wait*. She studied English at Cambridge University and received an MA in creative writing from the University of East Anglia.

imperfectsingleparent.blog
Facebook.com/gythalodge
Twitter: @thegyth
Instagram: @gythalodge